FALLING YELLOW

NEESHANT SRIVASTAVA

Made with ♥ on the Notion Press Platform
www.notionpress.com

This novel is dedicated to my father Late Wg. Cdr. Arun. Bihari Srivastava.

I wouldn't have begun to write without his initial words of encouragement.

"Dad! *You'd love this*"

Contents

Prologue   *vii*

  1. WHERE'S SANTA   1

  2. SCHOOL DIARY   3

  3. EARTHLY CHILD   11

  4. 'R' PERSONA   51

  5. ALONE AGAIN   95

  6. YELLOW OLEANDER   158

  7. MENDING DREAMS   196

  8. THE FINAL LEAP   218

  9. THE FINAL DUNGEON   261

ABOUT THE AUTHOR   265

Prologue

Robin sat listless in the corner of his room with hands around his knees. Cold dust in vagrant flakes made a thick coating on his spectacles that hung perilously on the nose bridge. He could remember red of Santa Clause and his smoky truck. Seasons changed in a constant gaze of the dark and bright. Robin lost appetite, hygiene on the road to annihilation. For him 'normal being' was a higher plane where angels dwell. He could not make eye contact with such angels and was content with a glimpse of purposeful limbs.

"Now an electric spark could make him crackle" was the dictum of an irate psychiatrist on the state he was in. Reuben, his elder brother didn't buy that and uttered in disgust "By the heaven Angel, my dear God I shall not let the devil dance".

There was turmoil in his inner while his outer was at peace.

CHAPTER ONE

WHERE'S SANTA

It was his first of a lifetime. Robin carefully slipped greeting cards large and small with 'Merry Christmas' and 'I love you' crowned on the insides into the red letter box. Too young for the pen, in shaky cursive, he concluded in invisible red ink of a dry sketch pen. In his imagination the letter that parted the fingers into the red letter box invariably fell into Santa Clause's red bag. Hence Robin wasted no time in writing the address on the envelopes. In a quiet room, all by himself, he hugged a dumb inflated toy of Santa and repeatedly toppled over cold ground. The big bubble could easily fit Santa Clause's round asset as Robin rehearsed the unthinkable. His skin turned cold and lifeless, yet he desired to stand like one with Santa Clause. Far away among the crowd he would be lucky enough to catch a glimpse. With his head buried deep into the ground with a half nod, he grinned unto himself before strangers. He frantically looked for a place to hide from the eyes of strangers for reasons only known to him. Santa Clause drove in that evening atop his burning engine with warm hands sitting on a pounding bell. His cheeks spoke of wild cherries glistening in the sun and the snow beard falling on the world famous bulge. Santa Clause leaped out of the red truck that was drenched with smoke. Synthetic to the core, he sang gibberish with a perkiness no one could match that evening. Churning teeth with cold fingers, releasing air from his mouth in patterns new and unknown filled the air with unusual yet cheerful sounds to attract even the indifferent grownups. Robin moved on a square piece of marble at some distance from the one man parade and never crossed its boundaries. His letters of devotion may have reached the Gospel preacher but who was to ask. His gifts lay unopened and untouched. Santa Clause surrounded with children, had raised his eye brows for this lone child but swayed in the tempest. Soon Robin drifted apart without a handshake and a question no one can answer,

"*Where is Santa Clause off to in shards of December, post Christmas?*"

CHAPTER TWO

SCHOOL DIARY

Robin walked an introspective mile with friend Monty after his last day at school. Looking back he saw a group of lads with a relentless wild fire within, gazing at the new world through bar gates of preferred awnings.

"Gentlemen seize the moment, you shall miss it when it's done and gone, turning into night time tales. Cherish now that touched your heart and hold it there" the English teacher was eloquent with young men.

Robin, dressed in full with thick glasses bore the look of a seasoned traveller, perhaps missing the warmth of a topee. He turned his shoes a quarter of an inch into the safety zone when life threw a new question. There was an imminent disaster written all over the insane possibilities. He invariably found him stoned at the crossroads. It was the beginning of adulthood. Adulthood brought its own vices in tobacco and hard liquor which made him shudder in thought, the whole semester. He couldn't match Monty's class when it came to reading classy novels and literature. He was a man of few words and books. He once took to Father Crompton's personal library during lunch to add to his repertoire of flagging beam balances and rubber stoppers. The effort didn't last long and he was back to his old ways of stacking unread books in his study. His father, a well read person, was the last word in such situations,

"Read on Sunny, even if you don't know what's in there and I know you do read, Cheerio!

Come; take a book from my desk"

He was halfway through the Old Testament when ignorance spurred him to flip the remainder.

"Feel the rhythm Sunny, the words will fit in themselves" father encouraged Robin to read. He was the shoe shine boy of the house running small chores and writing letters in colloquial English.

"Very good Sunny, now that's my boy" father egged on Robin.

Robin could feel the soothing sound of thrash of cool waves on the banks of the Ganges running on the other side of the boundary wall of his school campus. He longed for a sight of the river washed by the morning sun in pearls and shimmers. The poor ones worked their way to school on rickety bicycles and a Gandhi bag around shoulders. The rich ones drove the latest line of motorbikes and comfy scooters. Robin was the proud owner of his very own bicycle. He hitched the local transport leaving behind his supple beauty of a dozen years in his shack. It had a silvery blue body, supple body in a cacophony of steel, giving in to a short ride. Robin's first, its body could not bear with the wind and but for him would have seen the junkyard long ago.

Growing up to fit in father's dresses, Robin wore his sleeves with pride. As a child of six Robin put on his father's oversized military cap now and again. After ages, on the border of his teens the time was ripe to walk the parade and fulfil his dreams. With a feverish squint he had tortured his books in negligent light to spoil his eyes. In a sigh, he bid goodbye to stars and stripes for good. He could hardly sail through the medical examination for candidates and would be ruled of challenging positions, high and noble in the Indian Army or Air Force. He sometimes felt a sharp pain in his clenched fist while manoeuvring the soft ball in a game of volleyball. He willingly stepped out of the arena when pros walked in and for a bout of some serious tussle. It was his persistence on the dangling worsted flannel of his grandfather for too long, heavy and obsolete with entangled flakes of wool on its surface that got him into trouble with the Reverend. The coat didn't match school's dress code. Crashing fingers groped for the right grip on Robin's neck pulling the rogue of the heated moment inclined on refusing the violation. The spiteful Reverend swore with dirty words gathered over a lifetime. Robin stood in protest on honest legs following the decorum of the classroom and was the last one to be picked on or mercilessly dragged out of his seat. He believed that his jacket had the right blend of blue, albeit a trifle faded. Yet time had pressed upon this act of misdemeanour which was a profound act of misunderstanding by his standards. Robin was an angel of the street as he raced home in discreet footsteps.

"Sunny, this is a small matter, I'm sure the principal and the staff have made a grievous error, come with me" father consoled an anxious Robin.

Robin's eyes were poised on the table of classy penholders and colourful marbles of paper weights, washed by white light of a buzzing tube. The principal caught the gaze of Robin's hiding eyes,

"Carry on son, it's all settled now" and

"Sir, you don't need to bother about your son", to a proud father.

Days evolved into rich admiration of school leaders, captains, impressive all round. Robin's eyes had made Ruskin, the red house captain, his favourite hero. A skinny young lad, who never missed a smile, dressed up neatly like a gentleman. Robin had the good fortune of locking horns with this erudite genius to the proximity of a burgeoning friendship. He walked up to Ruskin one day as a prelude to future companionship, skipped a few words fitting a captain and directly asked for class notes.

Ruskin's notes had travelled far and wide within four walls of the classroom on grounds of punctuality and graphic assimilation. Accomplishment of the wealthy of thought in the book of greats spurred Ruskin to think big.

"If there's anything else I can help you with, please don't hesitate to ask" Ruskin smiled. His cursive had a calligraphic finish and had offerings from all the days of work. His proud sophistication cast an impression of affluence in Robin's mind. Yet Ruskin was one among the troopers with the Gandhi influence, on a rickety bicycle. On further delving into the matter Robin happened to take a long ride

to his house as a diversion from an errand. Cooped up in a single room with younger sister, Ruskin's bare possessions included a local stereo playing 'Climb every mountain'. A migratory bird he fled his village of the south of kindred folks for an education in the city with the far and unknown.

"Maybe it's this bizarre sense of anticipation that gives me an air of polish but not the sublime. I really don't come from an affluent background. I am in constant search, like everyone out here including you for a higher state of being." Robin was far from convinced but let out a sigh of acceptance.

"My father just passed away. I dedicate this life to his ideals of honesty and simplicity that mingled with an air above the ordinary. Why is a soul, its vision and totality lost after it escapes? What is the worth of a human after all? Isn't he all alone in the scheme of things? We can only live by the light shown by those who left us and fulfil their dreams with our effort. Time for some errands, Rob, I'll catch you later."

Ruskin was the only guy in a camp of forty who could throw his hands freely while swimming. Come summer and he would be ready with his breast strokes and fine dive while others were caught gawking. Robin never bared his chest to outsiders beyond his own room and the thought of swimming was far flung and unbecoming. He did learn a few steps, prostrate on bed from 'Beginners Swim Guide', convinced of taking on the waters one day with swift kick of his strokes. His father's desk was an ocean of knowledge and art and this book lay in its damp corner eaten away by moth. It's puffed up pictures were nondescript yet its major instructions somehow survived the onslaught from those grizzly creatures. With a swivelling nose to catch depleted air on the mat lying on his chest and swallowing fabric to the point of suffocation, he swam like an octopus. He had felt a similar suffocation in childhood when he sat at the back seat of a scooter clinging on to his father's chest with both hands. The machine rode forward and his tight nose intermittently drifted on either side for a pinch of air on father's firm back.

Robin considered himself just about worthy enough for a place in the class photograph which sang a potpourri of distant voices, each one in his own. Where could one find such talent under one roof in a group wasting away in frivolous pursuits or no pursuit at all? If one could raise a perfect crest and swallow a trough in vocals with six strings, the other was an excellent speaker with leadership written all over him. It was the in the glitzy annual day celebrations with song and dance that Robin wished he shared the podium with singers and dancers. He almost walked up to the stage that evening when the wind blew against him in a plea to let it be. Robin was happy in a box of space made by standing books in the four corners of a firm table in his secluded room with lilting air and a surreal audience. He sang in a soft voice that was amplified twofold. He swore to himself of bagging the highest when it came to a demonstration of intrinsic capability before a high audience. It had to be that way one day. He could outshine plenty on that glorious day of reckoning, whenever that might be, so he believed. A boy's school, it laid north side to 'girls only' school and ancient tales rent the air of how girls caught up with boys and vice versa. The customary 'socials' was the platform where boys and girls mingled with rapturous hearts. The thought of girls made the young boys drive on bikes and scooters recklessly, negotiating tight lanes and unduly terrain with pumped up adrenalin. One shade less down a dangerous curve would have stolen the song on lush lips and spelled disaster. How could one miss the age old tale of two lovers Fagi and Pompi, young, true and fatalists? Robin was too entangled within himself to carefully consider a girl. Fagi was the grey eyed beauty, voluptuous and dazzler in school uniform. Her tall, ravishing lover, Pompi across her school boundary with silken tresses, was true as the morning hymn. They held their hands like lovers do and all watched them agape at the wondrous sight. It was their first eye contact at socials and Fagi simply smiled and bent her head while the hero looked on, unflustered. Each one felt a pang of desire, yet walked the other way and disappeared into the crowd. A question that loomed large on their minds was if the other felt the same longing. So Pompi made it a point to pass through the girl's school on his way back home after class on his motorbike. Being rich was a reason for scores of girls and women vying for him. In addition being a debonair with a physique that was admired by plenty, there was more to be seen than met the eye.

"I am a simple man, I don't believe in casual encounters and long for lasting love, hey bud , I am all for one woman ready to be taken away". Pompi was clear in his perception of love and life. His motorbike trudged along in front of girl's school gate while he gazed with intent for his flame. As soon as the machine reached the zenith of the gate entry it was fired with full force and it raced forward. It was on the sixth occasion of his detour with no outcome when he saw Fagi ambling across school premises. He kept the engine warm and watched her pass at arm length. No words exchanged, he swiftly turned the wheels of his motorbike in a circle and raced along, the way back. Pompi felt a sudden gush of warm blood in his veins at the mere gaze of his new found love. Fagi watched in awe, convinced that that both hearts were on fire. It was on a half day, precious Saturday that Pompi decided to alight from his motorbike and take a walk inside the girl's school gate, hoping to find his lover. Bravely carrying Valentine Day's love card he entered the hallway and bounced off to the library. Sister Mary happened to walk that way and he was caught unawares,

"Here you mister, what are you doing in a girl's school."

"Sister, I have been called on special duty as a representative of my school to assist the librarian" he boldly put up a fake one.

"OK, carry on, but make sure you leave as soon as your work is over and please do a good job" Sister left Pompi alone.

Pompi stuck to the library for hours, until finally deciding to leave. During that period he came across many girls, some even giving a hint of infatuation but Fagi was nowhere to be seen. He had walked all the way to his motorbike and fired the engine when his sweet little sugar happened to come out of the gate and walk towards him. Pompi wasted no time,

"*Happy Valentine's Day*" he handed over the card, an expression of his love.

"*Oh, thank you*" she was glad all over. He raced away in a circular motion. There ensued a tale coming from fairy tale book of two people in love and a constant craving for a piece of the other. There were those reckless bike rides with Fagi on the pillion, arms around Pompi's rock shoulders, humming away a song of coaxing lovers. Nights were a revelation of a storm in the eyes of lovers as each one dreamt of times to come. The news spread like fire in both schools as both walked hand in hand oblivious to the crowd on busy streets, even among their own peers. It was time for the annual cultural show. Girls and boys from both schools joined hands for a grand evening with invitees including the honourable Governor among other dignitaries. The two lovers broke a sweat in the rehearsal room for their own duet performance. One was an excellent dancer to help the other who came close to dancing. Far away from books they were on plenty of free time with no one around to hold one another's hand and express their deepest yearning for each other. Sometimes in the middle of their practice when darkness fell behind stage curtains and they found themselves alone, kisses which started as pecks soon spread all over their faces and necks. They felt the thrust of the ocean towards each other and love grew deeper with each step of their dance. It was an uncommon blend of lovers sharing a dance before an exalted audience. The crowd descended into the night of reckoning of sprightly and young blood with a space for those lovers. The young lovers stole the show with their passion and perfect synchronicity of tapping feet to a catchy musical number. All were convinced that the couple indeed had a special relationship with each other. The truth of matter was that the partners in flight were on the ground of breaking ice and telling each other a story. The attraction was infectious and drew the two closer to each other to a point of no return. The show ended on a happy note as the couple bowed down before a high audience. A standing ovation was in order by the esteemed gathering, on an opening note by the Governor himself. The two held each other's hands, waved and parted the gathering to falling curtains followed by the host's final words. The two were getting acquainted with every nook and cranny of each other's persona. Even after spending so much of time with each other they were still strangers. Yet love brought them together and coloured them so deep that every soul yearned for that degree of longing. Post cultural event put an end to regular meetings for indefinite periods and the time the time was apt for recollection and reflection. The two however did meet and Pompi carried his lover home on his two-wheeler, not before the two stopped by for some coffee and the like on the way. Their performance on stage was a declaration of their mutual admiration and it was spelled out clear before both schools. And so the tale thus progressed through time. It is well known that the two got married immediately after school when people just enter a different kind of world. Their love was ripe but not their minds and their colleagues sighed in wonder at the early decision. There were many unspoken tales written with a flicker of hope and dissolved in the sands of nothing. Robin for one fell in love with every girl he saw but was not sure if anything transpired on the other end. He'd rather stay secure in his shell and every time the cold wind blew, he shuddered like always.

"You are willy-nilly there old Sunny, just one more step until graduation and then the world will be your oyster and you shall be the captain of your ship. But please graduate first, my son. You sure have something going, just hang on and you shall be through" father often quipped. Robin grew grumpy at times when father's words hit him and found him pushing through dull chores.

"Life is a process son, look how those two got married fresh out of school. At this age I am in the same process, I'd rather you had fun and enjoyed the process rather than waiting for something to happen."

Hopefuls always spread all over the desired terrain to catch a glimpse of catchy contour and evoke a sense of caring and love in a smitten heart.

CHAPTER THREE

EARTHLY CHILD

Robin was amused with multifarious pods of poison growing in the wild. Fondling with prickly fingers, shorts smeared with latex there was more to the permeating wild ooze than silver spoons. On that amusing terrain he felt the rich gravity around him. Hooked on rich aroma of gasoline, nose roaming its vapours in an air tight tank, he'd rather sink in it eternally. Intoxication was a by product in the way he experienced life. One could find lithesome hands, churning out tunnels and air castles in sand, with the right blend of wet and dry. His mate Bourd with naughty intentions raised a stiff posterior off soggy sand for an evening of amusement. The sound of sand with hands fell on keen ears and they were not giving in until the creation of miniature art. The lofty firing range was a call of the wild with cumbersome slopes and thriving little creatures hiding in its corners, a challenge for young ones to conquer. It was a huge triangle, home to wild life on its slopes. On a bright day the tall monumental gizmo was a mix of light and darkness in its wide chest. Each tender mind made treasure troves in its dark burrows or felt blessed to play a game of hide and seek with plenty to hide. Its top soil rich in alluvium, host to those dead poisons had heard many sanguine tales from little nothing young ones, who willingly learnt the ropes of wild adventure in wisps of raw nature. Ceramic plates were shot in the air in an elliptical trajectory high for young cadets of the military to shoot at as targets. It took pains for Robin to realize that the firing range was there to give meaning to those lofty rings of ceramic plates, acting as a dark shield to make those plates visible, invariably blinded by harsh bright light. Night time no soul wandered in its proximity as it emerged as a dark menacing shadow that all wished to avoid. Moonlight sang lullabies to obscure wildlife swaying gently in a night breeze in its swarthy chest. Parents never kept their young ones on a tight leash even at night knowing full well that those tender legs couldn't spare a few steps on a dark haunted night. Taking a long walk to the range was most farfetched and unbecoming. So on a bright evening Robin dared to conquer its summit turning a blind eye to excuses and pleadings asking him to stay put. He didn't stay for long at the top as he didn't want to wake up the fat ones out of their holes. It was a feverish glimpse from the top of waving hands at the foot of the range, shrunken with time, urging him for a manipulative retreat. The range worked as a boundary line in an evening of cricket for the boys. It was another morning parade to school when he felt warm on the insides. The tripod supported the black platters that were then swung high in the air smashed by diligent gun shots from heated barrels. They stood their ground stubbornly as the soft platters completed semi circular motion with a routine precision. That morning was blessed and what ensued was nearly a figment of imagination of witnessing the old range put to work. This was the only opportunity for Robin in a lifetime to witness the tireless plates kissing the heavens and the chivalrous army men shattering the masonry to dust. In people's eyes the range had died a sudden death inebriated by barrage of the wild. Its slackened walls were overwhelmed by time and ubiquitous children with the last laugh. After all the poor old range was just a screen to make ceramic platters visible in thin air; smashing targets only made it weaker and crumble. It braved the weather, the heinous wild, little children wallowing in its sand. It was a testament to the proficient army; its wall shook with gun shots in short bursts. Riding on the morning train that crossed the range on the other side of a separating fence Robin had to bend down low for a complete view of the rising tower from the inhibited view of barred window. The old engine ejecting rhythmic steam from its top whistled each morning to Robin's sleepy ears. The steel tracks dazzled in the morning light to distract him out of sleep. Robin had dared to the lay down his palm on a cold evening track or flip a coin from his piggybank to watch it squash to a disfigured sheet as the busy train crossed over. Did he raise the bar one day to debauchery when he was involved in a wild escapade with friends? They left a stone goblet on a bare track and let the train rush past in total surrender to speed. The train would probably screech to a perfect wobble, running off the whimsical track for a strangulated moment and assuredly stay that way. The load of the train would push it into red clay, true to a chosen course with linear perfection. The members of the group would be eye witnesses to the tragic turn of events and disperse in total disarray. Innocence seeped into their eyes and blood rushed through their veins. Their sordid expression turned to whimpers like little birds, newly born, crying for pickings from a doting mother in their straw nest. The lads screamed for help while the heavy engine pushed its way to shiny steel disregarding the blocker plaything planted on its way. The pangs of hunger gave way to euphoria; they heard the engine pass through straight on the tracks. Henceforth they would rather be gutless than to try such a thing ever only to see the big engine with appendages burn to pieces.

It was a sweet tryst with here and now. Robin learnt how to stand on roller skates and push that thing to eternity. There were miles of concrete around the officer's mess area and scanty evenings when the sun threw a soft dusk light. His friends on skates formed a huge chain to which Robin reluctantly gave the elbow. Robin learned the ropes at home with Reuben.

Robin created family history with diligent stroke of his pen earning him top rank in National Competitive Exam for engineering colleges. Some college down south offered him a seat and four years of pleasure. Some private college etched out in the mountains away from the city offered him a road to cutting edge technology. College at home was not far away in ringing a bell with its offers. His eyes wandered at the branch/trade allocation table as they bounced down the dais to his old man for an answer. A soft beckon and Robin was convinced about home. Thus began a journey in his own backyard which turned into an ordeal of his own making.

He was a hesitant addition to a family of engineers. Before him, plethora of uncles and granduncles transpired, holding the gargantuan T-square with pride. Did father sneak up to Robin's brown diary and pick up a few lines with mellifluous strain and imagery that didn't fit his shoes? Father was refulgent with pride, with a resolve to stoke the monster in his lad.

"Poets are peanuts in these parts, so don't dilly dally, get a degree, and then you can have your cake and eat it too. In the interim please drop me a line out of the sack you hold."

College was far away from home with the passage covered with dirt tracks. One invariably reached swollen with mud with fresh silica on parched lips. Yet Robin was among the toppers, the best among best and all agreed.

The fading sun cast oblong patches on the veranda in the simmering month of May. The tiles on the marble floor had a quizzical pattern embedded on it that amused young Robin. He could stare at an abstract protrusion for hours and propound a catchy figment; man disembarking his concurring horse or a lady balancing her earthen pail on round shoulders. On closer observation he found objects out of their frames jutting out in surreal motion. It was a continuous world with no ebbs or corners and Robin was at it almost anywhere, anytime. The crying cuckoo pecked its way forward on the broken ledge. These were warning signs of an effulgent traveller in dead heat. Beaks of steel, its shining armour. The messenger prodded constantly in the hard sun regardless for the heedless and ignorant. Like midnight sentry telling in wooden taps, enough for those carefree slumbers. Sky was ablaze with white fire with the blue lost in its eternal depths. Somewhere in the distance a sodden hand, striated with time, angled over liquid eye brows directing sunken eyes into the distance at another draught. Bodies trembled softly to dying breath in a state of exhaustion. Gates of 'R' household stood still disturbed on occasion by evening with pungent chirrupy squirrel chasing the hard nut that was spotted in the morning, hidden securely in dry bush across the entrance. It was a done deal for the striped critter with a deep passion for the nut. The marigolds with thick veins colluded with a soft whiff of dry breeze and shook its whole. Burnt grass lawn had patches of green under shades of Bougainvillea tree and on parts excessively manured and watered. True to habit, the Bougainvillea tree swamped itself with its red and white flowers with an eye for street urchins. Fresh flowers dropped face down, not wanting to be noticed or caressed. Adamant and fixated they did not heed soft lullabies sung by warm winds. There was a deadly unity to the stillness, like the moment conspired and evolution suspended. Thin and lifeless street dogs with tongues hanging down an abyss scampered for some shade. Far from breaking the oppressive tranquillity, their symmetric gait added to the haunting silence. The events reached a dramatic cliff. It was as if the sun would shut off its light the next moment. Or a storm would push through the gates of 'R' and carry the sad tale of its destruction and of what's left in the rubble. The tree branches hung in total surrender, like the final word was out. There was not a ripple to be seen in the roadside puddles with burgeoning wild grass holding giant pug marks, treaded on ruthlessly by cattle, earlier. Even the sprightly crows hung perilously on electric wires with an uncanny visage, undoing the nagging demeanour and a voluble temper. Doting family crowded over silver lines dipping their pointed curvy beaks in tandem with a juggler's precision. Sheets of dust drifted ever so softly on baked roads with fresh tar on its surface, carrying with them twigs and paper that was emaciated and discoloured, not fit to be recycled. Nature with a manifestation of incessant change plummeted to dormancy with a soft beckon to a moment of its own creation. It was indeed a bleak moment, like seconds before a calamity. Like an encore dissipated in the sands of time. The stillness of the lips of every leaf was a harbinger of misfortune with the effulgent nature crying for a release of pent up energy. A crying wolf somewhere in the deep woods could bet on a snare closing in to spell eternal stillness and game.

A silhouette in the distance, brown curly locks glowing in rings of fire was the obvious one meant for 'R'. Elbows dangling with hands buried deep in the pockets of worsted slacks. The stranger walked with aplomb, chest out connoting crisp movements of head in exuberance of youth and perfect crease to the full shirt gripping tight wrists. He was courteously flanked by the upholder of sanity within confines of 'R'. 'R' man was the bread winner in a family of four. The blond fluffy hair of the favoured guest barely crossed the tall shoulders of quick witted and graceful host. Augutus Flavious, the new guest had arrived. The haunting rhythm had subsided and the busy breeze broken the silence. The way side puddle was more voluble, trudged aimlessly by passing cattle. Their plump noses kissed the spiked grass with a smell that rattled their senses but they would not be allowed to hold ground and settle on their haunches. Game to little children perched on their backs driving the caravan recklessly with no heed to the music within. The flippant bougainvillea coiled in the stronger wind letting go of ripe flowers that danced to a new tune. Their ubiquitous flowers chased each other on a particular note of the wind in circles upholding their vicinity in red, white and yellow. They crowded the gates of 'R' preaching an auspicious welcome to its new found guest. The subdued environs portending doom in an ominous build up of numbing silence as a prelude to annihilation was suffused with the din on the street. The ambience as the curtain rose created an illusion like the crest of confusion never existed. The painstaking bubble finally gave way culling out a name in its aftermath, Augustus with strokes of Napoleon, in spectacles. His perpetual slack around his nose bridge with a large frame of spectacles was more than he could hold. His white skin exuded a warm glow of fragrance speaking of the latest line of toiletries tailor made for youthful indulgence. He had an air of aspiring grace, yet someone who had seen glimpses of life through stunning marble eyes caged in thick lenses. Talk of our host, 'R' man, 'R' world moved around him. He had seen life, its varied colours and his barometer had assimilated every twitch in a rampant cosmos. The telling of beads, watching yellow oleanders, atop sparse trees, so tender, drop in submission to the wild summer breeze was enough to fathom the bizarre stakes clouding this world. It all made sense to the seasoned trooper, soldier, learned scholar until his guests like this one were awe struck by his enormous persona. The guest took to the 'R' man like a bumble bee takes to the morning nectar. They walked, feet together, as each held their ground firmly. It was like an egotistical follower talking gibberish before the august presence of the exalted who is nudged on the side by many for his grasp on eternity. Packed in thick army boots, little too garish for his built, the little man walked on. There were rumblings of round and oblong tatters of gravels under stern feet that gave rhythm and music to a delightful culmination.

'R' man had a congenital burden and a choking thirst for glimpses of 'English'. His conscience brimmed with a keen desire to conquer and don English colours from the beginning. The very sound of English was music to the ears, in a land of disparate voices where English was mocked and generally forbidden. Yet the penchant cut its way across to doting ears through BBC and VOA. His English feathers were clipped in stormy skies when the raging society declared him an outcaste, walking enemy lines. The English brethren had sighed in discontent on trying to get across country folks. Their repertoire was a nonsensical effort at catching a smattering of the swarthy lingua with lines like '*There was a brown crow* (Please close the door behind you)'. It sounded like baloney, yet was effective. 'R' man broke the ominous silence before one and all and swore that he dreamt in English. His downtrodden helpers and people were given a taste of the English burp. His more affluent and 'western' acquaintances, he claimed, were phony without an English orgasm. His persona was like that of a man out of Hampshire into the milieu of an Indian village far away from the sounds of English. English etiquette cut across 'R' with knives and forks caressing warm fingers and murmuring glasses atop wavering trays. Sometimes the kids raised their hands in dissent yet conditioned their senses to Victorian delight. 'R' man took vengeance in his early years when he was undone by a lack of 'English' colour. He was declared an outcaste by those chirrupy fathers who were total strangers to people who couldn't speak like them. His determination saw him learn the language and speak in a flow. His love grew and took him loud and clear to the conclave of reverend Fathers and Sisters. They would have him rather than the hoi polloi for a tête-à-tête or matters beyond. It was uplifting and relieving to ramble along with the subtleties of everyday life in the presence of 'R' man. He was their wavelength and beyond, a passing nightmare for folks of the country. 'R' man was most at home when pompous fingers flipped pages of the varied books he had. His piggybank had room for his constant companions – 'Nesfield' grammar with dwindling shadows in fine ink of a 'Scorpio' cursive only he could decipher. A callous bulge of Newbie's English dictionary sang songs of the man crippled inside. Yet toss of its loosely tethered pages with unforeseen curiosity had the innocence of a toddler. Could such a man safe in a canopy of an English summer settle for country lass? Indeed, he sure took off for those divine eyes high among heavens for an English lady enshrined in a poet's heart, yet his roots were deeper than sensibility humans can ever strive for. He may have transcended the barriers of religion and such, his vision seen the bigger picture yet his faith clung like air around beads of eternal Hindu belief. His inclination soon saw him steal pearls out of thin air in his poems of imagery. His love was pure and his poems never saw the printing press or beyond.

Reuben sat listless on the bed. The heat wave cut right across his fair complexion leaving dark patches for keeps. His fixed gaze spoke of sadness and futility. This was his last summer home before leaving for distant lands in search of a higher degree.

He had heard the nightingales and peacocks, impudent with a flourish in the fading evenings following light beams and join in rhythm of scientific proclamation. Depth of thought was a catapult in time for some that ran faster than the eye. This was a college pushed by a nation with an unprecedented adoration for marvel minds. Rare quotients propounded a laid back solitary indulgence for few. Others were in and out of bouts of salvaged respect in a sea of books rubbing the fatigue off faltering eyes. Far off into cold nights when staying upright didn't seem right and each flip of stubborn pages could awaken a neighbourhood, the solitary warriors, pensive at heart, tried to dig into the talk of the town. For enchanted few, a sniff of the whiff was enough to drive the point home and trivialize human acuity of the mind and its conquests. They never felt the pain of burying themselves in books. They watched the geeks late in mellow sunsets swarm the canteens and open fields. Some had to hammer a postulation to a thin cliché before it seeped into their minds. Their mind was a constant factory, overworked and underfed. Reuben joined hands to be a part of one of the best in the country. The best brains from the entire country came here for education, touted as the best college in science and technology.

Stacks of paper that crackled under miniscule cursive of bland mathematical symbols lay on Reuben's desk. Three seasons passed by his window in wools of silence, all ears to constant prodding by birdies on the ragged window sill, in a dearth of human companionship. The feather beak mocking devil nearly popped onto the still mantle of the estranged guest. Reuben's eyes turned black from fatigue and his nothing frame wobbled, falling off constantly as that of a long distance runner after a marathon. His finger nails were long and pale barely gripping the pen with a long line of dirt in its crevices. Father was taken aback with tears of delight to see Reuben churn tomes of scribbled paper. There was a blue ray of hope in father's eyes as Reuben freed his arms. Pleasantries had taken a back seat and Rueben burned in silence. Yellow rays of dying sunlight stretched its arms through Reuben's window, puffs of fan air bounced under his wavy hair and he very nearly authored an epic. His muted survival was a constant gaze at the unthinkable, indefatigable presumptions, farfetched and saddening. A step into his dream college was sometimes just a dream. Yet those starry eyes had seen a way out of the jumbled code. This was Reuben's own line of action, preparing his manuscript of success. His tenacity was folklore in the family and it all looked picture perfect on the outside. He could buy the intelligence of his laid back, frequent friend, on the same road, yet on a rainy day he had to outlive his own mind and storm with his essence. A detour with his friend however did come as a relief for Rueben with moments of laughter and nonsense before matters got serious and out of hand. The evening snack did settle in nicely and father was overjoyed to see his son cast shadows of mirth before sinking into oblivion. A place in the definitive institute where preachers draw the line and intelligence is a rare peak, Reuben had only begun to dream. Alas some magic wand could leave some clue for every riddle and cliff hanger in his mind. Guillotine of aspirations was knocking at Reuben's door and he was far from conquering it all, a little out of breath and balance. He could not feel the earth and all his thoughts were centred on those two days of final judgement. Sometimes he knocked off to sleep on the study table as a testament to his whole hearted effort at wringing the bizarre. He was in and out of wet ink like nitty-gritty ants that seldom stop or a sculptor racing at erecting a bust, enormous and raw. Recalling the missing link by flipping through notes or pages of a thick book in frenzy was like a top CEO of a million dollar company at work in the eyes of the seeker. He had easily achieved the unthinkable with his constant infusion of the convoluted code. Yet coming from the horse's mouth, his effort was just enough to buy him a seat in the lower ranks or no rank if it rained. He had heard ripe mangoes sway, tethered to thin twigs, or ripe litchis burst out through coats or young peacocks rehearse their spring dance in a blazing ordeal, yet his senses did not budge from his moment of silence. Lost in an unnerving and never ending hypothesis, cold on a running nose, frame depleted, swaying in rushes of fan air, Reuben had missed the last word, 'faith'. In a sad 'kurta' (traditional Indian dress) he never took stock of the ground he had covered. But his evening buddy did, reminding Reuben that relaxation is the key to success. The cup of hot tea on the table lost its puffs of steam long before they touched parched lips. His succulent lips had dark streaks and cracking in the dry summer air with no tongue to push a fresh stream of moisture over it. They were as insignificant as the summer flower blooming in the garden. The sea of opportunities was wide and trying to catch the highest wave could lead to a lower and lesser known paradise. Reuben could ride on the philosophy of his snack friend and crack a few difficult ones under his tutelage but on the day of reckoning he was to be the lone one to fire his will and expertise. He sat at the exam for the prestigious college the previous year just to gauge the level of his preparation as an object of amusement. To his consternation there was a lot of work left to be done. He knew the basics right but its anomalous application was a fleeting contortion in the creators mind and aptly posted before aspirants. For some, he marvelled at the subtle deviations from a normal course after the point drove itself home, while at others he was a helpless duck too timid to take on the waters. This was no school exam where tiring examiners posted the same questions each year, though in a fresh new language and print. It was as if some demigod picked new and unknown flowers from the heavens and let them out to puzzled brains. Reuben was at work taking a full day to crack a twister; his part time friend could hand over the pen a little faster, still for some it was a minute game with a nip in the bud in exam time. Yet this was a college with a big heart and an aspirant was not expected and required to crack it all. There was room at the top and bottom. Reuben knew this fact and a small part of him, undisclosed and hidden was gleeful. The stars were out of reach yet he could feel the warmth of the sun and hold a piece of ground all to himself. He detested questions of his whereabouts and cast a negative vibe when fiddled with and would rather people observed him from the outside. Yet his core never thought of giving up, bending over the pen in a reflex action with sniffles filling up the void around him. Summer went, winter arrived. Thin and pale, his sunken body could hardly fill in sweaters and those artistic patterns fell from the roof as ugly aberrations from some fledgling. Seasons changed in a hurry. Countdown began as summer winds gripped the city with pulses rising high, hard to bear the oppressive heat. The antiquated ceiling fan still did its astronomical laps in a thrash of 'loo' air ever so slowly making discordant noises that could make a sleeping baby cry. It sent pulses of warm air in its light brush strokes holding its petty might against the wall to curve loaded paper and coil locks. Sometimes the grunt completely dismantled a line of thought or came in the way of blossoming friendship, deftly put away by stoned senses. The day began with its forced swish, slowly getting into gear. The esteemed guests took the assault ever so nonchalantly as failing background score to their sanguine effort. Reuben's grandfather got the latest line of ceiling fans fitted in this room which had been a lucky charm for his now successful uncles and aunts. Since then no one had dared to replace the arduous blade fanning its children constantly over decades. In the process its nuts and bolts got rusty lending a rhythm and synchronous burr catching up with age and protracted neglect. When the voltage dropped, it sounded like a grinding engine hard to manoeuvre and put away. At high speeds it sounded more like a fan and work negotiated at optimum speed. Nobody cared to oil it or replace it just like rickety doors and windows of the roomy yet antiquated house. It was like a ghost that spread its vapours haunting sleeps and honest tête-à-tête in deep evenings with gentle folk. It cut deep into the conscience and Reuben could hear its grunt even in the exam hall.

The stiff green cactus laden with wild sap wobbled in the heartless warm wind. Yellow oleanders plonked intermittently on seething ground with raven delight. The dusty old ceiling fan was done with its rounds and lay cold and still. It was a normal day for people with personal vendetta against the soil of 'R'. The morning paper was swamped with numbers deciding the fate of aspiring students. In a tight corner a number with broken print brought smiles to Reuben and upholders of 'R'. The number lay secure at the fag end of the exhaustive list and changed the fortunes of a struggling Reuben. It was foggy the least, smatter of bold ink with totally delinked letters. His swinging lips soon turned into streaks of crumpled skin and mist of doubt rose to his uppermost. He thought he had it covered when tragedy seemed to eke its way through his warm and caressing fingers. There was the dismal note that followed that clutched his windpipe. Was it over? Or was there hope brewing on the insides. A soft touch on his collar bone was the last thing he conjured. It was no blessing of a holy day as a sudden thrust of anger wanted to spoon out of the oesophagus. It wanted to blow away the wind and its whereabouts in heated discontent. He swung his true arms and threw the paper away in the impudent waft of breeze. He sunk to his soft bed and looked forlorn. His eyes were still and gazed at emptiness. Life seemed like a hot simmer of the most ghastly summer breeze. However at the corner of his eyes danced a figure, ignorant yet buoyant. He decided to shut himself in a tight corner when the dancing colours pulled him to do away with pent up anger and discontent. His friend stretched the newspaper in his hand and his whole and strict fingers pointed out those magical numbers bolder that ever before. The numbers were bold and tidy enough to be read out as a whole. Suddenly Reuben's heart jumped. He had indeed made it along with his friend. The two friends that had toiled for years had made it and it won't be long before they joined the very best to seek excellence. Reuben wanted to see bold black again lest the heaven call be spurious. He bent over crumpled paper to hear the fair call. He slipped his wavering hands under the canopy and let the pages fly without a doubt on their lips. His eyes were wide open and his breath listless. He had never been so far wide awake in all so many years. The skin on the multifarious money plant had never seen its white so up and jaunty in all so many years. The creaking monster up on the ceiling didn't utter a word or shower petals to cheer homecoming. Yet all joined the victory parade. Reuben was overjoyed at his victory. Robin was amazed at how little hands had worked tirelessly to create a meadow of dreams.

Robin could hear the canister make strange noises by night. He was a man, alas that abstract aberration, timid at times, and who floated high. He tried to escape foams of white light that he saw in dreams as a small boy when it pounded on his tender ears. The disturbance had withered long ago only to be replaced by hallucinations just like those abstract sketches emerging out of those tiles he imagined. How can a dream persist when it dissolves in the rhythms of darkness and emerges repetitiously, uninhibited the next night? He was a sombre six when he saw those scary dreams pretentiously getting closer to suffocate. He was numbed to silence and his visage was of someone in acute pain. It was hard for him to forget those nightmares like someone calling out to him. Like the helpless and the needy he tried to divulge the dream to others but somehow kept quiet on being occupied by other things that mattered. It won't budge an inch entrenched deep in his psyche. He was helpless and clueless by night. He tread softly with bare cold feet in wee hours of the morning with a parched throat when the dream was too hard to handle. Did the dream egg on to complete? Did he start from where he left off for the remainder of the sleep? He wished he could and breathed freely for the remainder of the sleep. The angels warned the harbingers that the journey was going to be long and arduous for little Robin. However when the usual question was put to him as to what he would like to become once he grew up. He simply made a fist by drawing his fingers tightly together and answered softly with a tinge of nervousness,

"I never like to grow up. God keep me this way forever"

As a grownup he still murmured those times unto himself. Vivid and heartfelt he let memories speak to him. One bad dream and it had made the young lad jitter in his senses. Wasn't it a fiend feeding on raw and uncouth mind? It had all transpired yesterday and there was no chance to regress. It is hard to decipher those dreams with nobody to guide him out of the hidden torment. Not even God intervened. The pain of everyday life pinned him to his sullen existence and was real. Greatness, he felt was earned by hardships and in complete isolation.

Thanks to Augustus Flavious, the man who was shaping the world especially the young ones.

Augustus Flavious was born in the city. He was a rebel of the other kind. He believed in freedom far away tucked in a tomato sandwich in a life created by artist's delectable brush of hands in oblivion. The moon had walked past its rose lane and quietly faded to an orange sun. The Flavious household resumed with clanging noises in the kitchen. Mama pressed her grey hair to a worn out blue band and caressed her remaining tresses. Papa had some leftovers from the previous night in that romping party. His head of stone, his natural movements simmering in harsh light and those thoughts beating irresolutely on his insides made it worse. He opened his eyes in disgust and sunk in a fresh glass of water. The little birds were busy picking shiny beads of grain strewn on the ground. They grouped together for the sumptuous meal. Melissa was fast asleep grasping on fleeting moments of time before Mama would storm in her room. Sky was grey and the gold mellow sun produced a faint shadow. The yellow moon was a trifling spectacle like poetry and music to Flavious ears. It haunted the illusionary erudite Flavious succumbing to a bloated ego. There were plenty of books for the so called literary minds. There were the handsome, the percussional besides the holy erotica to summon a tinge of goose flesh. Playing the fool was the potent drug to carry the unwieldy. Broken lines were prey to famished senses. The gathering rarely knew what the ensemble meant. Yet luscious lips were a smatter of the keenly audible. The gullible were enthralled by the mystery lap. There were others who circled out the Flavious household as the relinquished shadow.

It called for isolated beautiful nights accompanying known few with clinkering glasses as an oath to give it all and rest in peace. The new morning bemoaned with sparse lag in headaches and sore throats. They faintly touched the age old sounds of literature and poetry when no one spoke their language with haphazard throbbing of a weak heart. Early that hot afternoon caught in a melee at the local market they had plunged their tight fingers into books of the native language, Hindi. Cosmopolitan and suave they had plenty of conquests and skirmishes in the kitty to state their stolid stand. They were champions of the English which was driving a growing nation insane. A fist of white only fathers with dentures had survived in sparse schools and colleges. They were adored for their intellectual aptitude, balance and the rich white flavour they lent to the school or college. The Flavious also held that promise and colour but were swindling their so called repertoire. They could dine with Robert Frost or Keats and swore they had kissed the road thus. Honest Sundays were spent at the Church with debris of confessions. Blighted and torn they eked out loads of squabbles with every newly tied relationship. How in the Friday party they had demeaned themselves and squashed the family name in a drunken stupor. Life dawned on Flavious household in women and fine wine. They could drift in pristine verses etched out in holy books and written by prized writers of our time. That's what kept them alive and mesmerized plenty. They could keep the audience agape with their spunky English and manners.

Papa had a premonition that something had gone wrong. He popped the cork of champagne bottle. This had fast become a signature sign to all life's problems for the Flavious household. This was a curative to all minor ailments like a splitting headache or an upset stomach. Mama was jostling about the courtyard hard pressed for some tonic to open her eyes completely. Mingled with some chocolates could lend the right favour to her tongue to make a great start for a busy day ahead. She pushed herself to the kitchen and yelled out for Augustus. Melissa fumbled for some earth with her hands dangling to reach out for the alarm. With tight shut eyes she grabbed the baby with both hands and fired the snooze button. Another moment of tight winged sleep was all she wanted before Mama could reach her. Mama's yelling turned into nervous ranting for Augustus if only he could hear her. She checked his bed and found a small note under his pillow.

This bird had flown from the Flavious nest as her little Augi had become a man. There was no point in calling up the police for help as the fleeting dot would never come back. The family huddled together to conjure up a possible rectification to what had presumably gone amiss. Was it her words last night that had made him flee? Maybe not. Was it love or the lack of it that had made the young man look for a different kind of dwelling? No one knew as sadness descended on the Flavious household. Augustus knew how to fend for himself. He was a grown up man. His boots were thick and round and had tasted freedom far away from a tethered existence. He had been baptised lately as someone from the desert and all those years away from home had lend him a shining locket round his plump neck. Uncouth and unrelenting he had been dragged out of desert environs. Freedom meant eking out a living far from familial awnings.

Now he was closer to home before a dwindling Robin. 'R' man had brought home a white angel who spurred in immaculate English. Augustus had groaned when he was thrown out of the desert. Beaten up and barred from exclusive terrain he felt he always had home to look up to. For the upholder of 'R' English was his weakness and strength for a perfect icing. The thought never occurred to him if it would be safe to let the rogue into the premises. He was just glued to English whenever he heard some. He opened the doors of 'R' for the famished and the forlorn. He used his wherewithal to make the young lad feel at home. Augustus was enamoured by the subtle grace and grasp of the English language carried by the upholder of 'R'. How can the purveyor hold such captivating diction of the English language? Augustus' eyes were sombre and his style eloquent hiding a tinge of jealousy. Their voice blended as one in an enthralling conversation. That was when little Robin popped up with a glass of water to meet his sudden saviour. He opened his eyes to the angel and quietly ran away for shelter. The quiet meeting egged on and upholder of 'R' laid down his secret to the sumptuous repertoire. He toiled his way to match the calibre of English brew of fathers. For Augustus it was his posterity and the kind of English family he was raised in. English was his blood and he didn't have to suffer too much in grasping the basics. There were meetings arranged and the angel brought home a taste of English music to rev up the proceedings. 'R' man had contacts at the daily newspaper and that was when Augustus butted in. He extolled the daily and how they now could do well with cutting edge creations, courtesy the hands of Augustus and the flow of his pen. 'R' man was remembered by some fondly while others threw him aside as pompous rubbish. He promoted promise and desire whenever he saw one, if at all he could. He called up his friend, editor of the daily and vouched for Augustus. He clung on to hope for the young lad and made sure he got a little opening. Augustus hung on to the editor like paper weights to paper. He vehemently extolled the daily and how each day it got richer in its submissions. Editor was impressed with his repertoire and fine blend of English on Augustus' lips. He was rampant in his thoughts and was determined to buy a column in the daily. He launched 'Art Corner' with the help of 'R' man in his premises. The idea was to teach young kids the value of art in their lives and help them develop skills at a very impressionable age. It did take off and lo and behold there were little kids from all over the city joining in. There were inquiries made from all over the world for giving real value to the little kids. Pretty soon Augustus sabotaged the centre doing very little work or nothing towards its normal functioning. 'R' man was disgusted and pretty soon dislodged the 'Art Corner' board out of his house. Augustus was enraged. There were many who were vying for his tutelage especially young kids. Primary among them was 'R' man's son Robin.

It commenced with a desire but burst forth hastily to a need. He wasn't a wayside Guru with his unique ideology but a messiah, a saviour for suffering masses. When he uttered a word the angels sang in heaven. He was christened the lone arbiter in heaven matters. His lips were like a soft whiff of breeze on a rose petal. He held the ultimate dictum of 'seen it all' and 'done it all'. White bosomed and pristine, cleanliness was his religion. He never let a blanket of dirt settle on his holy floor, his dome of worship. He was generous with his ablutions and sometimes let his landlord grimace, hoisting buckets of water over himself too many. He was far away from smoky joints when pictures of distraught lungs charred of black soot brought him to his senses. However he didn't mind the occasional scotch whiskey or a pint of beer with friends at a loud party. On those cold hunky nights by the shallow light of his room he sat on the periphery of his veranda with a bottle of chilled beer and gazed at the darkness. He put on an earthly demeanour when on that shady night he stepped into manhood. He was no more that white lad twiddling his thumb under a shady tree waiting for his parents to fend for him. He left home to satiate a hunger that beats hard on young boys, of uniting wholly with the other sex. Augustus had seen many dark nights with different partners and was no stranger to women with libido. He honestly proclaimed that God had sent his children free and that they might practice any faith or belief bereft of the thought of others. Hands were free and be put to any use as desired. His austerity was a testament of peace that surrounded him. He was on a crash diet of beetroot and sweet potato and all the heavenly greens on earth. He barely touched the cow except on those ravenous bouts with friends and kin. Ornamental chains, pendants and bracelets of exquisite kind were reminiscent of his dabble in the desert. He braced his touch on meagre possessions like the stereo, refrigerator and the television. He was too possessed with his possessions and cuddled, caressed them with utmost care. Had life made him what he was or was it the circumstances that elicited such genteel behaviour, he never knew. He was light as a feather due for his weight in the world. He was a party animal alright but knew the way to a simple and good life with his sagacity. A stranger would readily be taken in for his looks and righteousness. He had been through hell, all his own doing and now was mentally ripe for the other side of life. Seldom did he realize that the habitual drunkard needs no excuse or season to satiate his senses. He is a creature of habit and must thus comply. Yet he pretended to turn a sage with alacrity and effectiveness. He believed that life had phases and one can undo whatever one may have done in the past. The road to salvation is the most difficult one to follow but it is the only one there. Augustus had read about it but thought practically impossible to hold.

Robin could see his dreams and stillness of the wind call out in whispers at a wondrous thing called Augustus. He had met his match in a subtle thoroughfare to bliss. Eloquent, calm and worldly he gathered all his senses to exchange ideas with his messiah. Augustus accepted him with open arms and sometimes reluctantly to show off his weight and stature. He had a vendetta against 'R' man and thought his son was the perfect ploy to set things on an even keel. Robin willingly got sucked into Augustus' convoluted trap. Augustus was a guru to Robin who abided every sigh and grimace that the holy let out. Thus their long and fruitful meetings commenced mainly in the evenings and sometimes in the morning. Robin felt safe and warm in his abode and declared him to be the best man alive. His touch was so soft and soothing and words like a sweet rhythm of saints. Augustus enveloped the desire to make the world his home and help the broken. He sailed on the treatise that the world belonged to the poor and downtrodden. He let out an aura of grandeur and was celebrated for his actions. His words were pouring through the daily each day and he sought complete supremacy. His infamous colours were aglow when he defamed the name of 'R' before the daily newspaper editor. 'R' man withdrew from the paper with dignity. He blamed the very hands that gave him bread and dignity.

Robin, the young lad was struggling with confidence and self belief, in Augutus' words. In a vibrant resolve he opened up to Augustus and sought his help in the matter. Augustus put on a persona as delicate as the breeze after winter rain. He was adamant at pushing his placebo down Robin's throat. He was a self proclaimed leader with a delightful posture who had boyfriends in the deserts. His mind suffered a weekend lag when he missed his buddies the most. He turned a rant homosexual later in his life when he closed the doors to women. Robin seemed a sizeable stock given his looks, husky voice and tall built. Robin was more in tune with the honest man's deliberations and drive for goodness and humility. Augustus had the do it all remedy to soggy socks and a wavering radio to a choppy stereo. Augustus believed in a pacifier's idiom and never locked horns with the disgruntled directly. Instead he was adept at playing games and strangulating the prey most subtly. Robin felt like the chosen one in his umbrage. Augustus called it 'sessions' of self improvement and alleviating low self esteem. He was playing on the young lads psyche ready with butchers' hands to slaughter when the time was ripe. Robin could grasp the subtle thought that he was a complete zilch and nothing could be worse than this. He felt a disconcerting pain that he could fit nowhere. His voice would break and body trembled even in everyday conversations. He was a convict in heavy chains asking for mercy to his dear lord. He was like a drained soggy cotton wool when not in his master's presence. The very presence made him fluffy and cheerful like the evening bird. He wanted him like a child needs abacus to learn counting. Augustus fast became the child's crutch and was followed by Robin everywhere. Robin realized that he was deep in his conscience and couldn't do without his company. Sometimes Robin couldn't understand why Augustus played hard to get. The impatient knocking on the door could be heard for miles but the master wouldn't let his subject in. With a grimace master declared that he had better things to care of and had no time for someone whose father had let him down. He had somehow swallowed the pejorative standing of 'R' man but would never forgive and forget. As his most forceful and deadly ploy he extolled and empathized with 'R' man and how to strive to be like one. He would furtively cast his nets to softly catch his prey and become the centre of wise thought. Deep within Augustus was jealous given the man's intellectual vivacity and his firm hold over the English language. 'R' man was pool of ingenious ideas with a charisma few could match and had served the government for twenty odd years. Augustus had never worked at an organization for more than three years yet commanded the same amount of attention and worship. For Robin, Augustus was synonymous with purity and gentleness and a colossal intellect protracted to the duration of a man. He had completely lost himself to the fine odour that permeated his house and candle lit deliberations from those holy lips. Augustus spun a world order rampant in thoughts and felt for people in China and Congo. His views were like hot flashes for Robin and he did well to huddle up and listen to the man speak, in silence. Robin was mesmerized with solitary life of Augustus and how as a one man army he lived on his own terms. Augustus believed that one must provide for oneself and that there was nothing like a free lunch.

Robin was hard at catching the vibe at college. He was lagging behind since his rendezvous with mighty Augustus. It all seemed in grasp when suddenly it slipped away. He wanted to follow his messiah who had abandoned college and all kinds of structured education. College for him was complementary and was never a pivotal point in education.

Dry leaves scattered on the tuft of dry grass. Robin balanced himself on his bicycle, panting. Deep within emboldened a certainty that he had gone wrong somewhere. His thoughts ran haywire sometimes to his childhood and sometimes to his encumbered freedom sans Augustus. Had he hurt his father for the inflicted violence and insinuation? His hair was a dust ball and sweat poured from all over. Was he pure in his drive to lessen his burden on parents by taking small steps to freedom? What kind of freedom was he vying for anyway? He was on the road to drive his conscience clean and usher a holy bend for the creator and provider. He seldom missed classes and when he was all greased up the college closed sine die. Slowly he turned an innocuous stranger and his eyes shied away from friends. His drive to conserve his conscience hampered good health and he grew weaker by the day. He felt like a scrounger and sometimes the foolish hermit spreading the good word around. The million odd cells in his brain were in constant conflict and he felt he was growing old. He held on precariously to the dictum of self reliance and freedom. Night entailed walking on dead roads far from the hurly burly setting of the city. His thoughts fed him and he missed regular meals. He grew skinnier by the day and days were spent in a search that had no direction. He would ride on the decapitated seat of his bicycle for ten miles to college. On the way when hunger broke all barriers he would stop by for a cup of curd. An offshoot of the Flavious nest, Augustus had filled his brain with famous lines from popular books of psychology, art and literature but had no inkling of what they meant. Had he let the noose off the thought that all accomplished had flown in their dreams? One sweltering afternoon Robin shut his hurting eyes and was just about to drift off when it happened. His frail framework touched the sky and floated atop his football playground in a dream of the afternoon nap. He saw marching men of English hierarchy, armed and singing a blurry tune. He quickly opened his eyes and gasped for air. Augustus talked about doing good things for the family, at the same time looked at ways to ruin 'R' man. It was hard for Robin to hold on to his ramshackle exterior and storm of thoughts diluting his efforts. Times were not good in the 'R' household. The main concern was Robin's health. His mind was a driving pinion obeying its motion. He strove to capture borrowed senses. He set sail on a fidgety verve each day to turn a grotesque tangle of nerves with dwindling breath. He sat on busy grass just beside the main road forming a puddle when college proceedings were a shot in the arm. Robin's scary plight forced him to collapse after every bicycle ride to college on home turf, his skin turned rigid black and bones protruded from all corners. Augustus was bent on giving a taste of the new world to Robin as he cajoled him into believing the unthinkable. He declared 'R' man's affirmation to desert his family members, leaving them to perish, as emotional blackmail. He cleverly juxtaposed his lines with a dastardly claim that 'R' man wanted to end Robin's life.

Why then did 'R' man lay pleasantries after bouts of smacking and indiscriminate slogging? Why did the assailant banish his own family while displaying bonhomie to outsiders? Why did his preaching and offhand views have underpinnings of annihilation of the world? Augustus loosened the noose off his subject offering some time to ponder. As a serpent in heat he wallowed in contradiction,

"When will he die? I have seen many fathers' die and it's but natural and healthy".

Entangling nerves worked at a frenzy pace. The day peaked in constant squabbles with 'R' man holding him responsible for a lost self. Robin had turned into a cradle of curses as he begged for a clarification for insanities, constant spanking and a lost temper. It was hard walking on a road with no kind words.

'R' man's outburst was more out of his own life's misadventures and inflicted pain from his near and dear ones. He feared the borne scathe take a toll on his young ones. Robin drifted away with time from 'R' household. The harbinger of freedom, Augustus instructed his disciple to follow the road out of the house.

All greatness has evolved from serpentine pathways. The blemish of plot triggered his senses and swamped his up surging mind. On a cold dark night holding a soft caressing breeze he stepped into oblivion. He ambled to the sweet whistle of trains. He trivialized a runaway train leading up to a serene shack in the mountains. On the roads he saw vagrant puppies snuggling up to a doting mother. He vouched for himself and wanted to drift away in the moment. He could hear ranting and bitterness of a lifetime clanging in his mind and clouding his vision. He sought to walk up to the other end of the world. He gave up the fleeting train and instead decided to use his foot to cover the distance. Dilly dallying on the marble floor veranda he had heard the rooster for years. Sunken eyes could now gauge the sobriety of the situation. Robin had now entered unknown territory yet his feet never did cave in. Cattle running haywire embroiled the situation and muddled his saunter. His rugged feet touched the edge of the city. His torn shoes were a crater of mud. Mud peeped in through the indiscriminate holes on the sole of his shoes. His nerves were stretched to the limit and the thought of a halt was non committal. His dangling arms swerved and twitched with sudden pain but feet never stopped slamming the ground. The road was pitch dark ahead and rambling lights on either side. It was getting quieter with every passing moment and he could hear his own puff of breath pushing through his nose and mouth. Now the only companion by his side was the moon that spread its silvery warmth on deserted land. This bird had flown to a different land pushing boundaries even further. At the eleventh hour his feet caved in and refused to budge. There was a tempest building up as the wayward clouds gathered above when one could hardly hear a leaf rustle. The dusty leaves sang in willowy mirth when a soft breeze purred in from nowhere. The moon cast a blurry silhouette of lone man drudging in the dark. The swinging rooster on its haunches was on its nightly sojourn with a whiff occasionally clipping its striated wings. The purpose of the flight seemed blurry. Robin decided to rest a while under a tree. Everyone was on a nightly tranquilizer into the surreal world. The sole of his feet was chapped and unnerving pain eked in his body. On a bed of dead leaves he sat down, hands around his knees. The moon spread its silvery light into black charred sky. It gleamed on Robin's temples and eyes holding back tears. The scanty streets bemoaned with the odd surprise stranger ambling across, all covered up, to his warm bed. Robin's mind felt a tremor that never seemed to subside. When he closed his eyes, his mind was the bucket of outpourings from 'R' man. He wished he were in a wise man's shoes who knew the road to redemption. Augustus seemed pure and direct in his timely assimilation of critical matters and Robin was primary subject to his assertions. Robin's delicate mind was a soft target of spiteful words by the forceful and adamant hands of 'R' lasting a lifetime to a possible annihilation.

"I will follow you even when you turn forty and will never step into your home then, you can count me out on that, chicken"

He had seen those nights of skirmishes, bedraggled and torn all over, hurt and beaten, crucified for the words spoken out of turn by the slaughtering 'R' man. His frame trembled in paucity of nourishment and tongue had forgotten the taste of food. The spiting spurt dillydallied into the futile zone to the line of clothes in Robin's wardrobe, which didn't have enough variety and colour to fit a bright day, Robin often professed. Amid the entire hullabaloo Robin's college attendance was hampered as classes were missed. His overworked mind was on an eternal wake up mode and never flinched even for a second. Added to that Augustus' diabolic sermons rang true in his ears and he swore to abide by the manifestations of free and unhindered soil that the leader strove for. The night lay silent in an echo of darkness and stillness. Robin could hear no birds or familiar movements of the soil. He could hear calmness and echoes in his own mind. He pouted at the thought of being fed bananas after an honest spanking by the hands of 'R' in his childhood. The venomous belt, blind and held by the ambidextrous, had died down and paved the way for abrasive verbiage. The sinister lay fast asleep, contended in his tent far from his subject. Robin smouldered with rage and helplessness beneath his calm exterior and challenged his rickety frame for a walk back home. The roadside hawker agape lay listless like in a drunken stupor. His body was fire with umpteen bruises that lay open to grime and dust. Life to him seemed like vagrant clouds carrying a blurry image to be deciphered until they disappeared to a different formation. Robin lugged his body of bruises and the screech for destination seemed overwhelming. Lo and behold he could see faint light of dawn peeping at the corner of his eyes. He had never known the countryside and took the opposite direction heading homewards. He intermittently gasped, parched and forlorn, he had never longed for home thus. The struggling voices in his mind had parted momentarily and he could hear his own panting and footsteps. He dragged his lunging footsteps to the final bend. The morning light spread all over and environ seemed soft and wavy. With misty eyes he clutched his lower jaw pressing his teeth together. His rambling escapade did manage to churn an ounce of sweat in a drop that readily mingled with soft mud. Tattered and bemused where miles transpired, the sporty shoes wondered when it will end. He was out to build an edifice of his dreams only to find to be incarcerated by his own thoughts. This was the longest journey on two feet the size of a marathon. Early birds were out of their chirpy nests and created a fusillade of cantankerous sounds.

His eyes were wide open holding sharp spasms of sleep in its inner core. The solitary saga had ensued the entire night echoing with thoughts of encumbered freedom. Little did he know that the extravagant martyrdom would eventually leave him at the gates of blemished existence? He swore his belching of thoughts were aimed to make him head for the railway station but eventually he let his walk to nowhere emanate. He was en route to the other end of the sky lest the heavenly father intervened. Sanity dawned midnight when his mind was far away from runaway thoughts that fed on him to push him to ruin. Did he have to fall into an abyss for a garden of fruits and lilac? He could be dead and gone, traumatized, undernourished, or let sanity drive him to equilibrium. He wished he could lie flat on a carriage for the remaining distance, too tired and worn out like the shoes he wore. He didn't want to speak but simply put an end to his suffering. He wished his body were swamped by the warmth of the sun within the abundance of 'R'.

His joy knew no bounds when he finally reached the gates of 'R'. He realized that he was not too disgruntled with 'R' or the house to think of running away for good. After all 'R' man had been just and kind with the thought that Augustus was an unnecessary addition. As he pushed the gate to its extreme and trotted within boundaries of 'R' he felt he had never stepped out. For 'R' man this was not the first glimpse of torturous spell the young lad had been through, so to react was trifling and waste of time, he contrived. He let the barber make his definitive cut and bid so long to a hail and hearty seeker. 'R' man had seen life in its many colours and he didn't go as far as singing eulogies or calling it a disgrace. He was of the firm belief that the sun no matter how bright will cast a shadow. He let Robin jump in and went off to catch some sleep. On his way he muttered, "*He needs a gla 'f wo (glass of water), that'll get him moving again*" Sombre, Robin's eyes were heavy like sleep accumulated over a thousand nights and body was still as a grave. Robin's college was hardly regular. He spent most of his time at home. When he somehow went to attend classes the lag in coursework would make him start all over again. Sometimes the classes were held in a rush with a promise that the course would be completed on time. In such cases there was a world of time spent within the confines of the campus hanging around for classes to begin or shuttling between labs. The labs were hardly ever ready for the experiments to be performed. Sometimes the lab instructor would be missing, and when everything was in order the machine would break down. He sat under the banyan tree and wondered how its coiled branches shot vertically from its basal branches. The number of such shoots could foretell the age of the tree. Some roots tethered around the bark and held them in crucifixion. Some gangly shoots embedded themselves on the ground and made prodigious circles. It was easy to dismantle their snugly movements in a gibberish plot to dismember the abstract sketches but hard to resurrect. The munificently spreading branches bore the toll off the hands of destruction, oozing with blood sticking onto dangling limbs, lithe and stolen. People hung onto the shoots until it collapsed under the weight as they uttered a nonsensical smile. In awe of their strength they fell to the ground with the branch in hand. It was harder to let them be that to destroy the delicate wonders of creation. Some shoots hung on to barks and branches in a raging leverage with small dank alcoves and even formed streaks on the parent. Some appeared twisted in knots neatly with a smattering of a joyous birthday or wedding gift tied with glossy ribbons. One could be totally surrounded and hidden, sitting under such a tree in retrospect. There stood maze of thin branches, circling around to form goblets inviting rodents and birds to seep through and rest in a circle of warmth. In its many manifestations it was critical to enjoy nature's unique creation from a safe distance lest it may hamper its natural growth. The abstract ensembles existed until human propensity drove him to destroy and investigate convoluted paradigms of perpetual mystery. There is a denial of human sensibility and kindness towards flora and fauna. Some abstract manifestations will still be riding, untouched from the genesis perplexing human mind. Human endeavour to harness mysterious misfits of creation has hampered nature's urge to express and permeate the gamut of existence. Still they continue to breathe in air and water and stupefy the imaginative and perfunctory mind. It was home to vacillating squirrels biting on nutty objects and scurrying away at sight. Their bulbous behind, with black stripes glimmered and wobbled in the sun. They could climb a tree, sink their teeth into hard nuts or play peek-a-boo all day long.

The college had no canteen of its own within its premises. Instead there was a makeshift tent serving the purpose run by an old lady. Her children and grandchildren worked in a different city while she had Bholu, youngest grandchild. Bholu would work odd hours to be in business. Prices of eatables were fixed at a penny less than the market price. Business thrived at the subsidised rates serving a potpourri of delicacies under the banyan tree. Each heated afternoon cast a melee of discordant voices with reaching hands, some for food and some with change. Robin's thoughts were interspersed with those reclining days spent under the banyan tree sipping hot tea, watching those dainty squirrels with shrieks of euphoria and pain. The daily newspaper was segregated into pages with each page in a different hand. Some eyes skimmed through the main headlines with patience while some had to go through the bank exam results in compulsion. There then ensued a spat for capturing the section with the main news making matters worse when someone's tea or food mangled the print. It was a welcome break time far from the rigmarole of academic session when eyes gave a cursory glance to the rumblings of a nation in tandem. Some were more persistent at the breaking news and left the rest for the swarming eye catchers. Bholu's name rent the air, some faint from a distance and some too loud in his ear, for prompt service. The engineers-to-be drank a toast to Bholu who hardly knew how to read. He was however happy and contended with his flavoured hands serving jauntily. He magnanimously gave up his academic pursuit pretty early in life to offer swift hands to his ailing grandmother. He was a one man show yet sometimes felt the heat and unending mayhem, wanting to quit. Deals mismanaged and discrepancies in calculations haunted him deep into the night. These were times when there was no one with him and he consoled himself and oft blurted out his grievance to his grandmother. She was cold as ice with such outpourings and let matters rest with a sigh. She always reminded him of the good work he had done so far and should not be worried about minor glitches. On cold dark nights when the day was done she ran her crooked finger over Bholu's hair and let the pain dwindle. She was proud of her child as the sole link to this harsh and ever changing world. Although her baked hands and her fragile body could only budge a little all day yet she had her words and blessings for young Bholu. She could sit in prayer for a lifetime and no one could suggest a son like Bholu. All those turbulent years dissolved before her bleak eyes when her near and dear ones came and went in a dazzle. She hung on like a timeless herald to his young ones withering and unfolding in the fervent sun. It was the stark luminosity of the game that held the lines and wrinkles on her face with facsimiles of obdurate. She wondered if it was brave of her to weather the storm or the breath through the staunch silence in which she did not budge in her igloo, insurgent. Her faint heart never missed a beat when she would rather escape into total silence. These were the times not her own and she could not find her way out. She now desired to see Bholu grow up and maybe stand at a place where she once valiantly stood. Bholu exuded cheerfulness reminiscing a time when he spent his days in jobless slumber. Slumber would carry the young lad way past lunch or even dinner. It was heaven calling when opportunity beckoned and they won a contract for running this makeshift canteen. She wanted to work till her last breath and see Bholu off to a start in his life. Bholu was the lone purveyor of a meagre livelihood, keen upholder of the house in the ambit of dedicated service to his old grandmother. Bholu tended to hollers and little whispers with equal aplomb and dexterity. His clientele were mostly students with the odd groups of ruffians for pickings from the basket. He made sure all dues were cleared within the day but did not entangle with those bent on delaying the token. The makeshift canteen was placed beside the river Ganges. Every morning or twilight strong winds gushed from the shores and swept all in its current, harbinger of a new day and darkness. There were storms with billows of waves pushed by strong winds pounding on the shores. One could feel it at any time of the day with rushes of gargling waves and strong winds that slapped the face at will. Every day Robin would sit by the waves in between classes and lunch break. It was a pivotal point to reflect and ponder on a life gone by and will be. He could hear the oarsman swivel the oars and hum a nostalgic song with wonder of what life is all about. It symbolically ascertains that life is like a river that we have to cross and get on the other shore. Silence pervaded the ambience and Robin would flip pages of a book he borrowed from 'R' library. It was based on life and times of the great sculptor Michelangelo. His dainty designs for a man lost in pursuit inspired Robin to adhere to singularity of purpose in narrow brook of life. One could hear the distant oarsman emanate in a sombre tune past the patchy skies exulting over life and its many colours. They reflected on life as the combination of the prosaic and the bewildering. The constant current pushing the waters were like desire and ego that seek the endless mind. The flippant squirrels rambling across trees and the noise of birds perched on them drew his attention. Robin temporarily took his eyes off from his book and listened patiently. He left the intricacies of the novel for a while and attended to other matters. Thus he covered the book in slots and the end was far away when Michelangelo's life would reach a conclusion. But that could hardly happen, given that the last few pages of the novel were missing. He was slowly drifting away from coursework because of his obsession with other things that excited him, including his novel. His college never had regular classes and even the term exams were delayed or postponed indefinitely. The college came under the ambit of a sick university with scarcity of adequate funds to develop its disciplines and cater to the swinging demands of student body. In such a scenario sessions and classes were called off with lack of payment to its teaching and non teaching staff. Getting a degree was a prime concern for all new students and makeshift teachers were appointed with dented repertoire to overcome the lag in coursework. Robin's fragile mind found a reason to enter a world of his own, slain by inadequacy of his college classes. He took to the streets, the mud and cacophony of mindless clanger. He ignored the pleas of 'R' man to check if the college classes had begun once again after the long break. No one noticed him in the 'R' house except when it was time to sleep at night. Robin overworked his mind once again, never missed an iota of thought that would throw him far away into oblivion. The sun beat down hard on his face and body, and he was ready for the end, as prophesied so many times by 'R' man.

Robin had grown frail and too weak to hold his own frame. His college attendance dwindled and he met it in seasons. 'R' man pushed young Robin to college each day and failed mostly. Robin had grown too weak to move. Once a brave rickshaw puller proposed to drop Robin and 'R' man at the college from 'R' house, which was far away. This was a skinny old man with tar complexion. He tied his lose dhoti around his thigh, ready to help the weak to the pillion. This was a crucial day of an internal viva voce at college and 'R' man was adamant at pushing Robin to at least show up if nothing more. Insipid and moribund Robin felt a pain in walking up to the rickshaw. He perspired from his hairline on his forehead to his feet covered under folds of trousers. He uttered his refusal with force, shrieking with all his might. 'R' man planted a resounding slap on Robin's slippery cheeks. Robin stopped blabbering and never moved an inch. He had almost lost the verve for college, emboldened by the fact that he was lagging behind. He gathered all his strength and lugged his slight frame to the rickshaw. He was unkempt, unshaven and could hardly utter a word. 'R' man accompanied Robin on the rickety rickshaw down the flat road and on boulders on muddy track. Robin's head crashed intermittently against the woody margins of the canopy of canvas around the rickshaw.

Two different people upset for their own reasons never looked at each other. Their eyes were juxtaposed and peeped in opposite directions. No words were spoken in heated discussion or uttered out of rebuke as each one held a silent posture. Inspite of the bitterness each one knew that they cared for each other, especially

'R' man for his child for none of his fault. Occasionally 'R' man would raise a hand to show the rickshaw a shorter route to the college. It was like patience and solace were tangibles that Robin could ask for, at will. He did feel a sense of peace with 'R' man around. He stretched himself, dropped all his concern and worries, like a child taken for the evening circus. 'R' man would often utter in disgust of how his own life had lost direction, stifled in a place he didn't belong to. His youthful peregrination had taught him that it was a sin to like a place being pushed around by job demands. As soon as he started to like a place, he was immediately transferred to a new place. Lo and behold he came to a place to settle but found it off key and slovenly. There was not even a meagre manifestation of like company and spirited night with friends. He found the crowd rustic, not ready to speak his language. He found it hard to find someone that he could relate to. In his eloquent writing and oft misleading demeanour he expressed cantankerous silence and holler to a lonely sky. So he expressed the desire to flee to his rainbow valley where he would stumble upon his people at will with flying reindeers in Christmas. Civilian life was abrasive and wild, farfetched from the peaceful and protected environs that he had become accustomed to. He mostly kept silent in his room, shoved from pillar to post by family obligations. He prayed often and had the holy Gita (holy Hindu text) by his side. Sometimes he broke the discernible barrier and descended to a lower plane sharing a light moment with all and sundry. For him the ship that carried the weight of all humanity had capsized. The world had ended and we were suffering in the aftermath of total annihilation. The air had grown thinner with more humans than ever before and lunacy pervaded the choking atmosphere. Only the vile and reckless gunners could survive the onslaught. He remembered a time when there was room enough for civilization to exist. Now he searched for an oasis far off from the desert of lost reason and impoverished humanity. The nation had disappointed him as he groped for security and well being of his family in the abyss of total darkness. The prevalent conviction had an adverse effect on his near and dear ones. Robin too, could feel the heat come summer like a burning cauldron. He would rather be a falcon spanning the livid skies. With trembled hands he could feel the end of existence. He accompanied 'R' man on trips to different cities. One particular summer felt like burning coal on the skin with the sun far away faint into non existence. There was dense smog over the city and the eyes barely pierced the distance. People had thick skins and the virtues of love, kindness and nobility did not seep through. Crime was an everyday word and was rampant on every street and corner of cities. It poured down profusely on city gates, cathedrals, stretches of gardens and almost all public places. In this scenario of living dead, where does Robin go and how could he survive?

People usually took a faster transport to go places and this rickshaw seemed rather time taking and slow to hit the final bend. Eyes were locked at the centre and mind was looking for ways to save time and make it in time for the exam. But the slow churning of wheels meant that Robin would easily miss the exam. This could be a telling blow to Robin's college performance and he could flunk his exams. He was totally out of sync with his studies and due to lack of regularity he lacked understanding of the basic principles. For Robin life was bathing in silver on a soft moonlight night when the breeze sang soft lullabies of tears and joy. The iota of contentment lay in illusions and farfetched thoughts with subliminal pleasure in a surreal world. He dreamt of serenading on those nights by the swaying trees to a lover of his own. Now lost in the din, harsh noises quivering the atmosphere and the impending doom were enough for Robin to think of carnage and destruction. He reached out for his hand and found sweaty palms trembling out of nervous energy. With every push on the pedal the rickshaw man was slowly crumbling to pieces. Sweat poured all over and his skin dazzled under the sun. He somehow raised the final bend with the college gate stone's throw ahead. The college stood at a quaint little corner and not even the shop in the vicinity knew that it existed. The college had lost its name to a gazillion other colleges that were recently born. Yet it was the only engineering college by the Ganges and many famous people had walked its premises. Robin was proud of his alma mater. The city had lost its colour that it once had. There was a gradual decay of the city with lackadaisical temper of its teeming millions and the narrow outlook of the rich and wealthy. The college had also suffered with its wounds inflicted indiscriminately and astoundingly harsh. The lab equipments had lost its vigour with age, made exasperatingly loud noise, irked by disturbed sleep. The same equipment had seen three generations pass by with its nuts and bolts seldom on an even keel. Their readings were awry and failed to sit in the laws and postulations. Many had survived beyond their lifespan, capitulated and worn out with no room for repair. Such were then infested with cobwebs dangling around blunt blades and dormant motors. Yet students graduated with the same infrastructure and locales as engineers even with the dilapidated equipment, to lucrative jobs.

One fledgling envied his senior who was through the jungle of lost reasons and severe circumstances. Seniors were epitomized as heroes, battling uncertainty and helplessness, praying by the Ganges. Brave warriors made of steel descended from a different planet and would patiently see a seed blossom into a tree in the pensive silence. They surfaced every now and again, from their remote rooms, to monitor the dormant proceeding almost dead under the rug to a coughing laughter like nothing ever mattered. When storms marred the season they peeped out of their windows in silence. When classes ensued in obscurity they raised their hands in approval and wholly embraced the weather which was rather hot and humid. Sometimes they turned blackboard blind not ready to submit or dig and guffawed aimlessly. They belonged to yesteryears and had seen many seasons sweep under their feet until they saw the rainbow while they were all cooped up in their rooms. They slithered in the mire and salvaged some dignity when they were awarded the degree. But that day took ages to arrive. They packed their bags with zeal and headed down the barracks homewards during holidays and when the college closed down for no good reason. There were shades of happiness and despair, not knowing when they would be heading back. They felt ousted and grey when classes and exams were prolonged sine die. There were other matters that screamed to the fore, and they were lost forever in their own world. They then heralded as heroes of war of a different kind, with a humble confession, "*What have we done?*"

They had already consigned to flames the torturous times spent by holy waters leavened by a song of prayer amidst the dazzling light. They didn't want to even think about their pitiful states. They sang as one to a new year and were astonished to find rookies swarming the campus with innocence and gaiety. Umpteen times had the dotty birds squabbled, the occasional parrot nonchalantly utter sweetly? The old lady beckoned for another tandem stroke of tea and faculty urged them to guard their degree and not flounder. Every passing moment was ascension to higher plane as they drifted away from college peers and tough times ruled the roost. The lone tree had dressed itself many times and nitty gritty squirrels danced in its arms. They would rather beckon far away hills with random notes on a flute squashing grapes in a bucket. Sometimes lost in the mist, and uphill road too steep to manoeuvre they lost all hopes of graduation. They closed their eyes and let time do the talking, watching it pass by. They exhorted the new students about the perils and misadventure that lay ahead and their tarnished resolve to better the prevailing setup. All effort was wasted and they advised them with a low key sojourn, aiming for the final degree and trying to dislodge the interim from their minds. They had seen the Ganges rise in vociferous anguish and calming eddies brushing the shores, yet the melodrama never ceased. Yet they were here on merit unlike those far away colleges that took heavy donation. All had cleared a state level entrance examination and thoroughly deserved an opulent brush of brisk years. Yet they grew anaemic by the time they reached halfway and didn't know where they were headed. They had lost all hope and only time, the healer, could make them strut. Some decided to forget the difficult moment and tied the knot in the interim keeping alive and stepping out of the arena, partly.

Some would precariously count the days of bed rest because of severe influenza or a cracked bone. Some would hone crisp grey hair washing down the temples. Yet the seniors revelled in the celebrity status around the campus and even helped the professors in college affairs. They had weathered the storm, assorted yet with a singular mission. They had seen it all, and heard the dwindling oarsman in the haze that life was nothing but a daunting rhythm. Robin had lost his way and couldn't fathom where he stood in the pattern. He was too preoccupied in a whirlwind of a tormented mind and college matters lay awake on those sleepy nights for not being tended to. He was turbid and blue as he reached the gates of college. 'R' man promptly got off the rickshaw and brought it to a complete halt with his hands. With a blind gaze Robin sat there breathing heavily and dreamy with a mind lop sided. In gazing moments he forgot that he had reached college to appear at his viva voce examination. The rickshaw pulled up in front of the classrooms and Robin was helped out with 'R' man and a few others. 'R' man rushed to the classroom to meet the professors conducting the exam and Robin reached for the corridor sinking in a stiff and sick gaze. He could see his advancing footsteps, weak and tentative. Paltry dogs hindered his sight and he stood there trying to avoid them. They screamed for help looking at the ghastly sight and ran haywire. Oblong face dotted with unkempt beard and unsavoury hair made him look frightful. He'd rather hide his face from himself and let the comatose magnify. He could recognize familiar voices and sighs round the bend and prying on him. He was like a helpless dummy being dragged around from pillar to post. Rest of the piquant crowd was salubrious and garrulous converging in short gasps to Robin's plight. Robin stood there like an earthen statue draped in faded linen, botchy at places, face buried deep into the ground. Rotund flies circled the length of his stricken body gaga over doting Robin. They vacillated in excitement when someone brushed them aside vigorously from rugged beige. 'R' man sometimes whacked Robin under the chin with his index finger urging him to look up and straight but in vain. It was like a bob that always swung back even after plucking it to its extremity. He was a colossus of inactivity and morbid ruminations who didn't try to fathom or take interest on the other side. Sometimes he did catch a brain wave that made him gaze upwards and catch the world but it was short lived and fleeting. His abysmal state made the crowd knit their own stories about him. The most obvious tale was that of probable trouble by the opposite sex. Probably, as few surmised, Robin had lost his love to someone else or his love had disappeared into the woods on the sly. There were as many stories floating in the air as minds set to work. Yet no one came close to the burning saga that had made him sick and the odd one among the crowd. His body was supple and he stood there listless seeking rest for a frail frame. 'R' man sought permission to present Robin before the examiners. They didn't want to see more than what they saw at a distance and advised Robin to take some rest. They did call out his name once again, yet they had gotten used to his absence and hence crossed out his name on the register. The exam was a lark yet he missed it making his situation at college critical. 'R' man was insistent begging for a round of quiz but to no effect.

'R' man kicked the air in disgust and prepared for the retreat. He ran his soft hands across his forehead and chin facing some awkward rows of questions. He was forced to answer questions that did not matter just before he left.

He was treated like a new recruit at the turnstile facing his first real bout of interviews. He was furious and rebuked people not even half his years of battle and experience. The candle flame was indeed just a colourless sheath before the mighty sun and could not dare question its magnificence. Their questions were derogatory and didn't touch the actual subject matter. 'R' man didn't want to be rude and let the people talk with narrow minds. Sometimes, enraged, he wanted to give back a hefty blow of words. Yet for Robin's sake, he kept quiet and let the town talk about his life in the Army and his family. They saw this as a perfect opportunity to talk about frivolous matters to bide time and recreate. 'He whispered insanities in a tight corner and let nobody know. He read the ragged contours on their faces and knew they were pushing it too far .He blamed Robin for the scathe and the damage to his sense of pride and dignity. He had strongly guarded his virtues of truthfulness and honesty and let no one tarnish principles. He had to step back for the sake of Robin and not show his seniority and the respect he had among his peers and junior officers. His life was like the abundant sunshine that had learnt only to give. He could forgive them for the blue moon, the tides, caress of the whiff on a cold winter's night and the soft echo of the nightingale that brought peace to this lone heart. 'R' man had envisioned immaculate snapshots of an evening tea by the Thames River or picnicking the countless rivulets in France, subtly rejuvenated at Champs Elysees. Life for him should be lived on the lighter side; after all it was all but a joke that made Him laugh until he pulled a fast one. Kings may fall and beggars may crawl but to our ludicrous delight the clock keeps ticking over and out. He was not a dream monger stepping skywards into a subliminal world but had his foot on the ground, knowledgeable, conversant with the law and matters of a bulging nation. He wanted to build a fortress around him, aloof and adrift in total seclusion. He waited for the kaleidoscopic mirage with soft coffee on one end and his literary abandonment on his finger tips.

Faint rays enveloped the tardy old college building and the sun slowly dwindled away in the chill. The twosome was on their way to their very own 'R' home. On the outskirts of the college suspicious eyes greeted them as they were partly covered by billows of incessant smoke. 'R' man was irritated by their peculiar laughter and a gaze at the sky for a high five. The crowd was as fragile as brown leaves strewn in autumn dust crushed in the fist or under the sole of shoes to dust.

'R' man had reconciled with life sometimes completely forgetting what he was after. Thunder and dark grey skies, banging head on the wall when things went out of control and reading oneself a sodden poetry was all that remained in his life. Life was indeed a collection of moments, good and bad, when the bad seemed to outlive the good like a scrounger too meagre in his offing.

R' man's dream of a villa by the desolate hills had reduced to piles of garbage in all corners and the common street mayhem. He had been planning to move out for quite a while now, yet his intentions were dismissed by family considerations. He swore by his erstwhile black locks it took a dramatic sequence of events, an acute mental drain that forced the grey to blossom and prey. It was not the heat from the harsh sun that did the damage.

CHAPTER FOUR

'R' PERSONA

'R' man's father never had even a single strand of grey hair before he passed away. 'R' man lugged his way forward to the mighty gate, watching the long nights pass by when the moon softly baked the pristine environs of 'R' house. He felt he had erred grievously somewhere and was ready to lend a hand to redress. He knew somewhere in his heart that he was as pure as the cuckoo in its evening melody and it was the tardy Ferris wheel of life that elicited bad behaviour. He surmised it took an erudite genius not to notice the ups and downs of life and the hindrance it caused to a normal happy living. Yet he held himself responsible for the hardship his family faced and words too heavy for his little children. Inspite of the ordeal he still stressed on happiness and well being in peace times and called for a healthy diet. He sometimes even crossed his boundaries and stressed on his boys to pick up dancing or helped 'R' lady to prepare '*kebobs*' for the evening. He placed the cutlery for luncheon on the table, forks and knives, assorted fruits and vegetables for dinner with grace and exuberance. Dreaming of a perfect 'English life, 'R' man had learnt a lot in his Army days, and had nurtured his mannerisms and etiquette. He had developed a taste for poetry with sublime diction. He empathized with the highland lass and could feel the pain hidden within the lines of poetry. Pretty soon he hypothesized that literature was his reason to travel thus far in life with glimpses of the absolute. He could hardly live without it. Striking off the bane of everyday life and saving the family from perilous cliffs, living without literature for eternity, had made him sound like the enemy. Within the tunnel of darkness there glowed a soft effervescence that freed him of all the sorrows. This happened only after he retired and spend all his time with books. From the dazzling orange morn to when clouds swarmed in to grey noon he spent a magical stretch of time with books, his passion.

Fresh out of college he was about to sail overseas to the USA. Yet caught in familial obligations he slung his paltry bag around his shoulders and turned homewards. Retirement meant a period of honesty and indulgence following the lofty bird in the sky, a silent dot. Twenty odd years almost on enemy lines sneaking in a line or two at evening parties about enemy intrusion, the Army had left a void in his life. It nurtured a haunting resolve to quit prohibited lines and raise a farmland with a rake and a hoe.

He'd rather bank on artists hands to create a subtle beauty of words with the depth of oceans than deal with paperwork that kept on growing. 'R' man was the model of selfless service and an expert at official liaisons and paperwork. He was at ease with unknown people, and hence he was entrusted with meeting foreign visitors. Foreign delegates were elated to meet 'R' man as he fiendishly blurted some pithy lines of the foreign dialect. They amassed great pickings from their tour courtesy the stolid 'R' man and even prolonged their stay as a gesture of friendship. Evenings were drowned in clinkering wells, caressing bushy moustache and hurling invectives piquantly in good spirit. 'R' man showed qualities of leadership and camaraderie, becoming the sought after and celebrated. Very soon he was the one beckoned for intricate missions with touch of risk and calling for careful thought and action. Sometimes he was thrown to enemy lines, escaping safely with revealed secrets, and his feats were flashed on the evening news on television. A dangerous mission, life threatening when all officers were absconding before the lull of war, 'R' man was asked to report immediately and he did the trick. His juniors did climb up a tree when the rigorous discipline in the Army left them gutless and hinted at eloping with dear life. It was 'R' man who dragged them out of burning and secretive holes and resolved a flurry of grudges. He made them feel at home and urged them to fight their way out with gusto and pride.

"Dandy, when all seems too hard to chew then just go around, right boys, get on with it" straight from 'R' survival guide. They pressed their caps over their heads with affirmation and sometimes could not outdo a sinking feeling like a capsized boat. They pressed their toes in tight leather shoes and marched forward. On those dark nights at the mess party they wore those stiff ties rejoicing at feeling like one with the battle. With the morning siren they rose with a soft headache but left no

Efforts sag in drills and letting the cap off after a rapturous salute. Thus many lives were saved from the disorderly civilian life when they looked for extreme challenges, like in the armed forces. They were the chosen one living in protected country with discipline and decorum were the order of the day. They were recruited at a time when the country needed the best of youth to spread the reach and strengthen defence. Within their vineyard even bees had their names, world revolved around garrulous neighbours and the morning siren was the harbinger of a new day. Friendship among loved ones was as pure as a digressing conversation without giving heed to the passing time. Yet just like the pitfalls of any kind of refuge, for 'R' man the duty was too intense with little time for and in between. He could bet he had seen beauty in pearls on red roses or stealthily watched the night go by but lost it in voluminous and stained files. He was a standard when it came to rigorous office work working out solutions in a jiffy and shaking the burring roof, of a dozen ceiling fans, with his unusual cursive. 'R' man was even delegated extraneous tasks hard to handle and carefully hidden below files of a regular day. His hands moved in perfect synchronicity with adlib of his concern that even his seniors followed in a stunned gesture. He once nurtured the thought of appearing on the huge silver screen. In his early days he had even discussed his developed script with a famous actor of yesteryears as a vent to his creativity. Yet the wind blew his desires away and he found himself with a tight summer shirt, top buttons off, with stripes on the chest. The pages of collectible books once crisp and entangled in blowing air, caressed and longed for, now spoke to moth and termites in subdued voices. There were trying twenty years of service in the Army and then the thought that retirement came too soon, causing his children and family suffer in a dismal civilian life.

The seething sun with blurry boundaries in the dead afternoon made the living escape to shady dwellings. The birds circled the sky in dots chirping and slowly disappearing to their homes. Some would swish away the water from coats after a dip in a pond or a pool of tap water. The sweeper caressing the same spot rhythmically with a huge broom could hear the sweat pour from all corners of his body. The machines stood silent like a colossal statue. Suddenly the evening arrived. There was a soft music emanating among the trees whispered in tiny drifts. Eyes of the non teaching staff seemed heavy and parched after a day's work and limbs grew tired, not willing to move. The burst pipe issued endless angled water for no one with the occasional bird burying itself in its puddle or squirrels prancing as in a game. The finely mown grass was totally dry. It grew in patches, bare at places to trails made by human intervention and tall and green at others for creatures to hide. College stood like a Goddess with a promise of timeless education and a chance at a bright future. There was an ingenious war sundial of clay stamped at the centre on the ground floor. The sun ended another day in oblique silence with a rumour that it's going to hide behind grey tomorrow.

There was the usual rush in stinky rooms sinking with loads of paper. The head clerk extorted money from all who had pending paperwork to be administered by the office. His meagre earnings were not enough to fulfil the insatiable need to keep the house warm. In pilfering pickings he could at least keep the lamp burning and feed his children. Sometimes the sudden swelling of the trees in a thick breeze momentarily would let the ghost out of his contorted action. He swallowed the bickering with demanding people with tangy tea down sore throat. The heat of the room chopped in slices by the ramshackle old fan smeared faces with dark patches and swarthy wrinkles. Every new student was a source of unbridled income for a period of over five years. Every student, throughout his course could not do without a visit to the office and rendezvous with the clerks. With trembling hands the clerks let the rabbit off the hat and fleeced a large sum. There was a tall photo frame of Mahatma Gandhi on the burned brick wall. All swore that times had changed and Gandhi would be reduced to penury if he were alive today. The only similarity with the leader was their proud loin cloth tucked luxuriously around tight waists. The old officials were like dead paper weights with only so much to hold. It was only when a titillating cough rose up their noses that immersed eyes noticed the populace gathered with forced grins. Their eyes popped back to where they left off and quips went floating by unheard. They only got out of their chairs for a visit to the principal's chamber and patiently waited for Bholu to arrive with fresh tea. Their aching backs and stiff necks was just another job hassle and their overworked eyes were constantly fixed to blurry print lest they lose the rhythm. One had to cry out loud, to be heard, and a mere whimper was not enough to bother the stone gaze. Sometimes the old men were embroiled in a tiff with students complaining about absconding certificates et al and matters remained unresolved. The officials were as stolid and gray as the humanity of brisk politicians and never gave in to a game. They had no letters embossed with their name or have the confines of a separate chamber, yet matters tended to hold ground and stay there in their premises. There ensued a profusion of irritable visits for the fleeting document and the clerks assumed a larger than life figure. People who could sense a pattern would invariably slip some cracking notes of currency for starters. Not only did they elicit unequivocal attention but a promise of perusal at the very earliest. The next smile would see them being handed over the papers or certificates for signature and formalities and bid a smiling goodbye.

Robin found it hard to break the ice with the clerks, let alone getting the work done. He moved around in circles sometimes even forgetting the purpose of his gaze at the clerk in the middle of his request. In stiff fingers the clerk would let out the documents never shifting the steady gaze downwards and even blessed poor Robin. Robin could never understand how people got their work done so easily without uttering a word. He further believed that all the clerks and staff, so lean and thin, with a dark complexion were all honourable men. He often ended up with the same clerk who always appeared to be busy. Robin would stare at clerk for fifteen minutes, whispering, subdued, and unintelligible. Then he decided to walk away for lack of response, wee bit scared and revulsive. He would be sent back with greater resolve as he walked back with confidence for another shot. This time he mumbled in confusion and let the stifling air in the background do the talking. As luck would have it the old man, with a thick pen between his fingers, drifted. The clerk stared at Robin and didn't want to ask for the obvious, yet reluctantly laid down the rules of office. Robin offered whatever cash he had to raise a smile on the clerk's hardened face. Yet against all odds certificates/paperwork had to be collected from the nagging clerks.

Robin could sense a tinge of love in every eye of girls that walked out of the girl's hostel. Yet Robin denied such signs to himself and stayed away from the perfumes issuing off young girls. He ironically suffered under an undying pretence of unfinished obligation, before vanishing into the thin. He adored their smiles and radiance of rose lips. He was tight lipped with deft footsteps right from the beginning to avoid any collision. He would rather suffer a blister in the urgent stampede of his own making than soak up the smile and exchange pleasantries. He didn't believe in inhuman flirtations when one side in bent on causing harm. Also there was time enough to absorb the bride to be and there were other pressing matters facing him. There were some who openly courted, sometimes more than one at a time. On such meetings Robin often wondered why the couple kept so quiet when together, just going through the motions. Maybe they were surrounded by the crowd around them, yet they acted like total strangers, which amazed Robin. It appeared that there was something serious to be discussed like the falling smog or diminishing water table. All eyes would gaze at a young leaf plucked in haste as it was rolled and rubbed time and again. Robin had a friend who courted one girl for some time. Very soon he became the big brother, a perfect shield from the radar of the raunchy and wild. Rush would take Robin to his grandparents home and show him his room. Robin would ride on the pillion and Rush with his colourful hand gestures to friends on the way would drive the beast out of dirty and vulgar intentions. Rush had more lovers hiding in the Girl's hostel behind closed windows and stuck under quilts than Robin knew. Rush was a budding engineer and his drawings would often be reach the hands of his growing female fans. Sometimes he patrolled around the girl's hostel to ensure that no vile or vagrant intentions harmed the girls. He believed that young woman were perilously holding ground on a slippery thicket and there is a great evil force trying to dismember the quiet aroma and the music of pensive eyes. Rush kept his dignity intact and never bothered about those who thought that he was violating the rules. He scratched, squashed and even chewed the bitter of eucalyptus leaves when a plaguing matter played with his senses. Rush rubbed with the party disconcerted and would not dawdle with rambling thoughts until a solution was scripted. He embarked on a fresh morning with no touch of previous night's unfinished sleep, resolved and made his point softly. Rush believed in balming sounds knowing that reckless and loud effrontery was not a solution to priceless utterance of truth. He knew he had won the battle when his voice was the only one heard amidst a gang of stokers and ring leaders loosening limbs. He had dispersed many crowds in his heyday and was always done before the morning siren of college broke out. Rest of the day was a rambling flute with friends' et al with giggling Robin sharing tea and toast. Robin was amazed at the penance and the extreme perseverance and dedication shown by Rush despite other obligations. Robin had no inkling of half of what Rush did or manoeuvred during the time they were away from each other. All he could make out was the jocund Rush helping him with information regarding books, and a brief history of the faculty and departments. Robin was like a lost soul, not knowing his way in the world, taking things for granted. Rush on the other hand was grounded and well versed with ways that make a balanced mind, worldly and well informed. Robin had to be shaken out of his poverty and the lost sense of reason and purpose. His friends bet he could not swallow morsels of food on a healthy day and his mind was utterly disorganized. They choked on a deep sense of pity for Robin and tales were rife that there was a lunatic in the house walking heavily in corridors. They covered their nose and dragged themselves clear of unwieldy and unkempt Robin. 'R' man pushed Robin round the corner and they somehow managed to reach home after failed efforts at appearing at the viva voce. 'R' man was through with the ordeal of trying to save a career and lay in his bed loosening up and closing his eyes. He was too tired lugging Robin through the crowd and to be the subject of ridicule and banter. He would rather sit beside a shady tree, and watch yellow oleanders drop in the breeze. 'R' man cared too much for his young ones to the point of being obsessive and absurd. He was more curious about Robin and found Reuben all too cold and stable in his career. Reuben found a leeway in abiding by manner and speech and never irritated the old man. Robin on the contrary was born with a foot in the hornets' nest and would break rules for no rhyme or reason. With his short temper 'R' man would incessantly and impulsively turn livid blissfully unaware of the damage done. His show of affection was bizarre. 'R' man would run his cold hand under Robin's shirt frequently over the fat of his stomach to check for any fever. Robin would be asked to climb onto 'R' man's back while he lay on the bed for a foot massage. 'R' man would lovingly stamp Robin under his weight, lying on the bed until Robin raised a squeal in protest. Or after being smacked hard Robin would be coaxed for truce with oranges and bananas. Yet 'R' man was a disciplinarian of thought and action like true Army men. His house may be rummaged and disorderly yet his principles of honesty with no room for compromise were well known and admired. Robin would blush when 'R' man used the official lingo with fellow Army man or a young officer in starch with his cap pinned up around shoulders. At this point of time, Augustus had been a dream far flung and deserted like the old city at night. Yet Robin kept him close and decided to rejuvenate the warm camaraderie like lovers do. He quietly slipped out of 'R' house after twilight to bring back the warmth of the days gone by. Augustus dodged his eyes at the door for a while before calling out Robin's name. Robin could not bear the numbing silence that ensued after the utterance of his name. Augustus had stopped persevering with this lost cause ever since the last rendezvous was called off. He didn't want to revert back but was not keen on losing out on idol worship and the thought of having some fun. He gave out the new rules of his house which included not spreading legs on the mattress lying on the floor, while sitting cross legged on it. Also Robin should try and speak succinctly to avoid wasting time. Given the limited area, following him while he carries out his chores is certainly not allowed. Also that he will talk while he works. He reminded Robin that he was allergic to the yuppie culture, while he did coin the phrase he never learnt how to live with it. He despised using the words coined by the two minute culture. Strictures apart they slipped into a warm refrain before cursing the surroundings in one voice. They sailed on the lively and stimulating of how an old man in his dwindling strength was playing with mixed signals. Augustus called it a farce, laughed and clapped his hands. Robin backed the loud guffaw inciting silent walls and the feverish guppies in tanks. Augustus finally invited Robin for a trip to the mountains of white snow caps, out of sympathy. He let Robin off the hook pretty early that day and urged a sense of honesty and obedience towards his college studies. He let the patient out, breathed a sigh of relief after succeeding in creating more doubt in Robin's mind. Another day will bring another way to mock at the family and its falling leader.

He could never leave his slipshod subjects alone as they were just another medium of laughter on sleepless nights. He braved in his experiments of tampering with brains by planting questions that hurt their psyche and created doubts about others.

Robin had a lot to chew that night and was drifting far away from his college. He sank in thought trying to figure out the real enemy. Robin felt happy to be the blessed one to be a part of a famous life to which the world flocked to his doorstep for wisdom and protection. Plethora of racing thoughts would not subside. Sometimes 'R' man tried to calm him down and make him relax and enjoy the evening breeze instead. One gusty morning when the winds kicked up with force, he was sitting and brooding over lost matters of the past when his nerve close to his brain snapped. He could hear the pop sound and tried to reach out for the epicentre. It seemed that the wind would blow him away, and he would die losing out on the real culprit. In an illusion he could see a hand of white smoke with a pointed index finger. The pointed finger zeroed in on a garlanded portrait of the two famous people in his life. With gentle hands the couple blessed Robin for all the sins he may see. Robin was all perked up, jubilant as he impulsively opened his eyes. He couldn't wait for the evening when he would meet the expecting eyes of Augustus with hints at walking together on the mighty hills. They met with radiant light pouring out of aquariums and decided to break free, together. The following dawn would be perfect to close shutters and bid farewell to life itself. They would run away to escape land in the shadows of the mountains with mugs of frothy beer. They would run free from chains that checked their motion in sombre hearts, perishing in a dearth of love. Robin went back home, elated and couldn't wait for the day when they would be free. Augustus was an expert on catharsis would slowly unfold the true meaning of life to befuddled eyes. He was the curer out of curiosity with no professional certificates and practiced whatever he preached through study on his subjects. He would utter a toast of jargons to throw his weight on unrelenting patients. He worked on their primordial fear in utterances too rancid and gibberish for their own good. His questions would dig deep into their lives with no room for privacy. Sometimes it he would push it too far with objections ringing loud and clear. He garbed his petulance with gaiety and calm definitude and a brotherly touch. He bloomed in the thought that in the end of it all he had nothing to gain. His uninhibited guile would not be talked about for miles by outraged Samaritans and sometimes never at all. He had no bristles of grey on his beard and was way past marriageable age under no compulsions for a better half. He believed that married life was like living in the aftermath of death or sickness.

One stormy night Robin covertly slipped out of the gates of 'R' peeved at the harsh treatment of 'R' man over some trifling matter. He buried his cold feet in deep water that submerged the whole area due to incessant rains. He waded through water in quick thrusts of anxious feet to meet his messiah, Augustus. He felt like an ostracized stranger when his eyes met with Augustus's cold eyes that had seen enough of him. He wished this moment to pass and he could snuggle up in the corner of his allotted space. He managed to avoid collision and was allowed in with a slight slamming of the door. This was the opportune time for Augustus to lash out with tyrannical words for a deep sense of betrayal at the hands of 'R' man. He had grown even more jealous of the man lately. No one could match 'R' man's command over English language and literature like the sound of heavy rains from overcast sky. To win over Robin he expressed a deep sense of compassion for 'R' man and how be genuinely cared for him. The door made a click sound and Augustus could see 'R' man standing through the dying door slit. He hid Robin in one of his rooms and shut the door. 'R' man had come looking for Robin, but was turned down.

"How do I know the whereabouts of your son? Your dear son is not the only thing that matters in this world. I have better things to do. He may have been squashed by a high speed truck or run away from home for good, I really don't care. Please don't waste my time."

The water level had reached knee high due to incessant rains. The water was dirty with the colour of mud and sediments making it hard to wade through. The drain was easily dissolved in the water at places and home to creatures that liked to float freely and cross all boundaries. 'R' man was in a hurry like always and ignored some splashes of water colouring his face and neck. After a lot of effort he managed to reach home, disappointed and tired. Robin came back home late into the night and quietly slipped into his room. He was asked no questions. It had become the usual practice for Robin to stay away from home for long periods. It didn't matter to 'R' man any more, as long as Robin returned home. Robin waited for dawn. The rains had subsided. The street lamps hung loosely, wet with patience. The frogs croaked randomly and the insects made a deep sound in sleep. Robin was out on the streets again, the way it was meant to be. The rest of the family was fast asleep. The sound of shoes wading through muddy water disturbed the intense silence. It was like the people had deserted the city, birds never chirped, trees were still. He was finally free from bondage, to elope with a heart that knew him well. He was leaving 'R' house for good, the yellow oleander tree that stood at the entrance gate. He was leaving behind his rummaged bedroom and a sick wardrobe with trousers that never fit. The slackened red roses hung their heads in submission after the deluge. As he walked by, he looked at the chandelier with pearls glittering like always in the bad days and good. It was way past midnight when a snowy apparition of God pushed him out the out of sight of the gates of 'R'. His raced away to Augustus. He ran as fast as he could before the bright of the dawn could shine in his eyes. The rusty gates of Augustus's house were askew and Robin just walked in. He promptly rang the bell to find all asleep. He paused between his calls, lest it annoy Augustus. Augustus, woke up suddenly, thought the noise was just a figment of his imagination and went off to sleep again. Robin persisted, increasing the gap between calls and reducing his clinging push at the bell to soft dabs. The breeze had picked up, pulling Robin away from the bell. Robin was getting sick of hollers. Augustus had probably forgotten about their plan or else he would have been waiting with open arms in the dead of the night for him. Robin could sense a whirlwind pushing him away with force. The wind formed a grey apparition that led him out of the gates to safety. He obeyed the wind in its priceless dictum and regained posture after falling to his knees. The night was about to end. Early rays of morning had hit the leaves to usher a new kind of light. A stagnant train whistled in the distance. It added music to the dead silence, indicating that the good had prevailed and life had awakened. Robin was pleased to have been saved by divine intervention. He never knew there was more life to be lived. He had doubts about the happenings of the previous night. Was the apparition an illusion or there was actually someone trying to save him. The whistles of a train, the darkness and the unheard door bell were no figments of imagination. He even remembered the fragrance of flowers that he met on the way. He was occupied by the thoughts of the previous night. The world had woken up to its usual noises, the trees vociferous, and the skies the brightest. The army of ants was on rigorous resolve to trespass enemy lines and the mighty rodents slow in manoeuvre, loaded with ill gotten food. Moments of hush and reticence was replaced with total disturbance like all rogues had been pushed into service. Robin lay on his bed, half asleep. Suddenly like a déjà vu he jumped out of bed in delirium. He hollered to all and sundry in the house and streets. 'R' man was in the middle of an absorbing novel, with a slight smile on his face.

"Not again",

He threw his glasses hanging on the nose bridge and ran to Robin. Robin had had another breakthrough and looking for ears to hear the discernible sound of recovery and accomplishment. This was a case of levitation with his body perched high in the air. However, this was all in his imagination and 'R' man was not all that interested in his story. He concluded that speakers in a debate on television uttered gibberish and could feel the emptiness in their gestures. He could recollect playing cricket with Reuben on hard ground. He swore he had tasted those red berries on wild trees, too flashy to ignore. He longed to hold the stick of drums that played loud in the evenings. Robin blushed under spotlight when the darting tennis ball reached his hands and his elders gathered for a game of tennis. When his turn came for badminton he quietly looked the other way for volunteers and gladly offered the game to the next one in line. The Army station was guarded in all corners by sniffer dogs and watchmen. This was Robin's colourful childhood and he sat on the pavement, carefree and gay. He had outgrown the fixation with bright caterpillars hidden behind green leaves. The music teacher at school engaged the pupils in a soft rhythm of the morning hymn with a resolve to mend ways and strive for purity of thought. The English teacher repeatedly rubbed whatever she wrote on the blackboard until she produced immaculate calligraphy. Robin could not play the guitar so well, yet learnt to play a particular song that he never forgot. Robin was too short for the basket in a game of basket ball and was elated when the ball thrown high reached the height of the basket. There were no seats in the huge truck that drove him to school every day. The truck was covered by a canopy of canvas and children held the steel rods that formed the frame of the truck. The children invariably fell on either side of the canopy as the truck drove through the tricky road, jerking and swaying to and fro. Older children stuck their head out in the open to squinty eyes and loud grin at the storm of wind. Ties blew in the wind and glasses faintly hung on the ears were thrown far away into the fields. Robin had often heard of the swimming pool but never considered a plunge, too shy to bare his skinny frame. So he tried to divert the attention and run away whenever 'R' man brought the subject matter to everyone's attention. 'R' man would invariably catch Robin's deception and quip

Look who's running away, sleeping rose, Rockefeller"

Afternoon would find draw happy faces with a pointed piece of abandoned wood on mud. Come a slow and peaceful evening Robin would swing his open arms with the action of a fast bowler or a spinner in cricket. When approaching the fields loaded with kids for a game of cricket, his hands hardly moved when he was asked to bowl. He loved the way spirited uncles played the harmonica or the flute. He enjoyed hearty picnics with uncles and aunties, friends and the 'R' family. They went to the forest bifurcated by railway tracks with a brief canopy of elaborate trees and shimmering beads of leaves. Robin wanted to wear the collars of the school band marching with triumphant sounds but didn't have the seniority to push himself in. It was the modus operandi to catch the young boys when they were overloaded with course work to elicit greater vigour and strength to carry through. He sure hummed the name of his friend Raj in sleep. Raj was a chivalrous young lad, honest and simple who wore boots with dysfunctional zipper and who belonged to a poor family. His simplicity and openness impressed Robin, smartly dressed with top two buttons unhooked on his shirt. He paraded the grounds like a brave and adventurous lad and Raj often reminded him of Baron Vonder Trenck. He laughed sparingly but spoke his mind when it was required. Robin tried to avoid the wily Rajat, the teaser and bully. Rajat called him names, holding his collar and coming too close for comfort. Robin usually quipped, "*Do I look like one?*"

Reuben once overheard Rajat and dragging him by his collar, one day, asked him to stay away even in the truck or the bus stop. Robin avoided Rajat who would smile looking away and never confront the 'R' kids. Rajat was drifting away in silence and was nowhere to be seen one fine morning. He probably graduated and left after his father was transferred elsewhere. No more pain for Robin at being insulted and humiliated, Robin could breathe freely. The only thoughts that stayed in his mind were that Rajat was a member of the school band, a proud drummer and Robin had seen him flying. Rajat had probably found another troop elsewhere and was bullying someone new.

Reuben was in his final laps of his college far away from the gates of 'R'. Friends collided in groups and flourishes round an ardent tea stall that levied debt but never an inch of rebuttal. He filled his world with thoughts about the extraordinary students and professors and the good fortune of attending the best college. That was five years ago when he suffused Robin with bright geometry boxes and ingenious pens and pencils. He sat in the corner of his dark room of the hostel with glances out of the dark window. He combed his wet hair and felt feverish. The same songs English songs were passed on to Robin that he discovered. Robin hummed along for most because he couldn't catch the words. It became the anthem for those carefree encounters when Reuben would relax and unwind at 'R' house in his summer break. Reuben would exchange notes with 'R' man when he came home for the summer whining in a seesaw battle. Engaging in conversation was the first thing Reuben did on entering 'R' house after a very long journey. 'R' would prematurely put forth the happenings in the right order like he had already read the book. Hot tea would lose its vigour food would just about turn rancid when 'R' man never seemed to stop. Reuben would gape for hours and sometimes show lines of tiredness on his forehead wanting to stretch after a long train journey. 'R' man would drift in his words mentioning about Russian roulettes, swarthy Eiffel tower at twilight or elaborate Buckingham Palace. He was a man with the rhetoric with words that excited the senses. Sometimes his words sounded too heavy for the audience. They simply sighed and let it pass.

Reuben worked hard in five years of the degree course and would invariably hang his head in air to reconsider a chain of thought. Even though his college had the most beautiful campus yet it was too rigorous. Inspite of being the best the students never spoke highly of the college with the horrid demand to be precise in ones duties. Sometimes Reuben went red-eyed and lethargic to class from watching a late movie in the previous night. Sometimes he was claustrophobic sitting for hours in the library comparing notes and reference materials for maintaining good grades. He had not seen the entire college even after years of study but got accustomed to the medical centre and its striking roof, he fell sick often. Sometimes he despised the warm lapping of winds on young leaves in the distance for being too loud and jaunty, sounding burdensome. At times a meditating leaf would drop from the open window onto the book being read. Reuben would look up in wonder to find someone who cared and looked at him while he nudged his way forward. The college was home to the best brains in the country. Some drowned themselves into unsavoury course work and some walked the tight rope of superior intelligence to earn a place in the institute. Some who pinned their hope after unending hours of practice and study sometimes had a perishing feeling. It was like their hard work was not enough and there were people far better than them. Yet to their delight their hard work paid off. They mustered top seats in the institute and were proud of their effort. Reuben had cleared the test and now it was Robin's turn to fly past torturing questions. Robin kept a picture of top hundred people of the nation who had qualified for the exam in the year Rueben qualified. He rode on their mysterious smile and dwindling eyes, sometimes in pain. Some wore a smile and cheer, some grey with thought while others too young for their accomplishment. Robin knew a friend who had found a place in the college, determined and clear. He was the topper at high school, full of life and tireless energy. He braved the uphill storm too early while Robin wondered how such questions were conceived in the first place. Robin turned obnoxiously blind that day of his exams, nervous and crying for help. He died a sudden death not ready to even consider the questions with a balanced mind. He found a place low down in a lower class college after tottering his way home. Robin appeared at the entrance exam for three long years but could not qualify. Reuben sometimes rued the fact that he had to spend his summer vacation entirely at his home. He'd rather hook a pleasant spot by the mountains that sang in a strange hilly native song with the dangling of the hips. He would rather slap the pearls of morning dew in some far off remote sanctuary in the frost than sizzle in the heat. It was a hearty send off each time summer arrived when all students camped together and bid each other a warm good bye. Home trails were the happiest and magical and all gathered in the best robes to watch warm trees and yellow rings of the sun on their train journey. They huddled in the train compartments and played a game of dumb charades or playing cards. Reuben found himself rather subdued with 'R' mans infinite questions trying to dig out the details. He helped Robin in coursework. By the crisp wink of his eyes that wobbled, 'R' man would pull out questions from nowhere and keep Reuben excited, on his finger tips up to a point. Then eyes would suddenly shut in the middle of the discussion and tired limbs slackened. Reuben later realized later that the discussion with 'R' man was priceless compared to going to the hills to escape the heat. It gave him a chance to exchange notes with a doting father and 'R' man's advice was always handy in keeping balance in a lopsided world. 'R' man would relate wonderful tales from Panama Canal or the repercussions after the bifurcation of erstwhile Germany. He would drag the morning for tales from his cavalry days when he would rode horses in high boots in a game of polo. Incidents from his own life were revealed at the very end of the talk when Reuben would be fast asleep on his chair. 'R' man would invariably end up talking to the wall, unheard. Hence his children dramatically constructed his past life form the bits and pieces disclosed to them but it never fit a perfect rhythm. When someone asked a direct question about his earlier days, he tried to avoid the question,

"I have seen a lot of life, too many twists and turns, but why exactly do you want to know? Eat, drink and be merry, got it, rosho kharosho?"

He couldn't be taken to the doctors on turning sick. He had his own set of medicines prescribed by an old doctor long ago who had passed away. He never spared his own father with his admonitions and point of view. He often retorted

"I have no father to take care of me. He's gone and will never come back. Besides I know the root of this sickness and I will find a cure with my own set of medicines, trosho"

Reuben's last two sojourns had seen him scampering home from the railway station to see how his folks were doing. His motto of travel home was to rehabilitate and sow the seeds of sense of individuality in Robin. He felt sad for Robin, troubled and forsaken. He had never seen the streets so brazen, thoughtless and merciless. It was like the yellow oleanders on the boundary of 'R' house, in surrender as though they had nothing to say.

The cloud hanging low was speechless and would not let the heat escape. Just like in experiments where in one proceeds through a series of logical steps Reuben knew there was a remedy to distraught mind. He had heard of Freudian principles that could cure an unbalanced mind by conditioning and forming new associations. Yet he was no professional with tactics and tricks to see Robin home. He would lie on his bed gazing in the distance for hours sometimes disparaging the unearthly news gathered in newspapers. He would hold still, unmoved when 'R' lady brought him some tea, lost in the silence. The sun would gaze through tortured windows and bake the bed with its slanted rays. All the members stood together in the room, speechless. Reuben had carelessly planned his last ever visit to his hometown. Reuben was reluctant to leave and rather drown in the peaceful environs of his college for good. The professor would load him with unbridled assignments and tests and he would come up with excellent grades. Lately he never knew what this was all for. Reuben would raise a forced smile at lunch or dinner with friends and he couldn't help talking about Robin. He would fervently cling on to telephone calls with the hands tiring in the pressing of the receiver. He had a glimpse in his eyes about a poor lad led astray. Reuben walked off the booth with a lot on his mind. He was sea sick of magnificent halls, elaborate corridors, and lush playgrounds. Wide roads, tall green trees, setting sun were a burden. He felt happy after performing an intricate experiment and ordered snacks with friends. But not for long. Discussing details of Robin's plight with friends late into the night was all Reuben could muster to help him sooth and stay focussed. He felt Robin had fallen prey to the evil Augustus. He believed that some people deliberately caused harm to others because of personal reasons and usually hide their true self from others. He would close the book mid-chapter in excitement when jubilant senses would envision the final send off from college. How like a snail he climbed each day little by little in a palatial dome and danced about in light and shadow until the final bend. He had fought his way to glory and sometimes in midterm there were moments when he had no inkling of sunshine and rain or how the clouds waited so low. Sometimes pushing his eyes across text in voluminous books his senses would drift to the square drawing room of 'R' house, tranquil and fulfilling. The day would dawn in auspicious light sans culprits like Augustus who words could damage the mind permanently. He was persistent with class work long after the classes were over to complete coursework in a jiffy. He ran through his study material repeatedly on those warm nights under the lamp. He wanted to walk into the next day and the next until he could free himself from the mundane coursework. He would drag himself out of his bed in the afternoons to the mess for lunch, unwillingly. He sat idly until someone pushed him to try the new dish highlighted for a change. Very rarely his face would glow in resplendent energy when he found someone reacting like Robin did,

"Did you see that, he does the same thing, how could you?"

Once he saw a friend having food with the same resolve and passion as Robin. Robin's eyes brightened at the sight of good food and he would blankly swear at a thought while progressing through the meal. At this time he had a prominent person in his life by the name of Prof. Rabindra Chatterjee, his guide and teacher. Reuben did his final year project under his guidance and professor was prima facie helping him in getting admission to a US University. Prof. Rabindra had a track record of helping deserving students with good opportunities to prosper in their profession in the nation and abroad. Well versed in his subject he sat for hours with his PhD. students delving on postulations and theorems. Reuben would join in with doubts on his mind,

"Intruders are in plenty, what was your job today, come we'll tackle all, give me a moment" jovial Prof. Rabindra invited Reuben in the soft evening light. He had a cheerful face with cheeks puffed up and shining with gaiety. He chuckled chewing the evening snack laboriously. He was one with the plight of students on warm evenings when he took a detour to their rooms. Helping a grievous situation and encouraging the students to fight the battle to make them heard out of the roster was his panacea to success. He drowned his senses in fragrant flowers and walked on dead leaves

crowding up pathways in awe and wonder. Walking round the block in laid back evenings was his ritual as the noise from the hostel died down in the walk back home. He would perch himself on top of an easy chair at home, close his eyes and listen to his spine. These moments of thought and relaxation were valuable to give him a direction in his efforts. The daily routine would take a lot out of him and he sometimes stopped in his stride revaluating and sinking deeper into essential matters. The management was playing games with him and had stopped his promotion. He didn't let it bother him for long. Reuben never knew how to present his problems directly to his guide. More than coursework, it was the thought of Robin that was bothering him. Dr. Rabindra fortunately had read his mind. He already knew about Robin, *"You don't worry son, Robin will find his way, he has reached that point I dare say, don't prolong your stay here, get on that plane and fly away for everyone's good. Besides do you have the results for yesterday's point of digression, the Ptolemy way?"*

Reuben felt like home. He smiled, gathered all his books and notes in a flurry and in a heaving shake of the head on either side resolved to fulfil 'R' man's desire. 'R' man had a dream of moving to the USA right from his college days. Surrounded by familial pressures he curtailed his wishes and wanted to send his children instead. Braggart and tipsy he uttered the forsaken word to friends in parties, at how the statue of liberty had become the farcical truth. He had already pictured America in his mind and knew what he was talking about.

Reuben lunged for the bed with his writing pad and penned a poignant letter to 'R' man with plenty to conquer overseas. He would peep out of his window intermittently for inspiration. He noticed how the weather had changed and some new flowers with vibrant colours had blossomed. His window was trapped in the shade of a huge banyan tree in the morning but he could still see the sun through its leaves. God's decree is sometimes lopsided and only time could read His mind. He governed his lips with caution when speaking to his guide Dr. Rabindra or when discussing the plight of Robin with 'R' man. Final exams were almost over with just one more day left. This would be the final homecoming and he vividly reminisced the last four summers spent in his hometown with family. He noticed how the excitement and vigour died down in Robin's eyes with each passing year. The college may offer the world to a casual visitor but students felt trapped within its boundaries. The limitless skies enveloped in peace and dead silence was eating up his senses. He wanted to scream down the road and vandalize the place with his friends. His finals were over now. He circumvented his usual that day and never bade goodbye to Rustamji the manager of the canteen. He sat in his friend's room early in the morning checking on the details of the train they were to catch later that day. This was his last day at college and he would rather gather his belongings and stash away the remains into bulbous bags and prepare to leave for good. He didn't want to loiter about talking to trees or branches for gratefulness or blessings. So when the time arrived for a move on he dumped his luggage on a rickety rickshaw and never turned around to things he would probably miss forever. The trees roared in the background and there was honest utterance of depleted tunes from delightful birds. He had turned into a stone with no room for worship of a college and its folks that had walked with him to graduation. There were staff members, officials who ran the boy's hostel would be sad at the sudden departure of a dear student from their chequered lives. He had no bills to pay. He had no obligations to be met and he would rather quietly disappear than face the past. He didn't know if he was excited to leave, with Robin, the biggest challenge awaiting him. When he was about to exit the main gate forever he thought he heard a shrill cry from the wilderness. He turned around in a daze and unmistakably got a last glimpse of his temple of knowledge and devotion. The wind was calm and everything took its place to perfection until a fine young lad who hailed from far off land would conquer them altogether once again. He sang no dirges in remembrance but did recollect how he scampered through his final exams defying earth and gravity.

He was thankful to his alma mater for giving him the skills to find a place in this bellicose world and for a certain Dr. Rabindra. He didn't want to look back for days spent under the fiery sun with the dogged heat too hard to bear. His persistent effort had opened up many possibilities for career advancement and becoming a scientist like Dr. Rabindra.

He was now in the hurly-burly of the city with an insipid landscape and chaotic existence. He wanted to turn a blind eye to the commotion and waited for his time within the peaceful confines of 'R' house.

The roads were being emptied in the late hours of the night. Street lamps were in full glow as they washed the traffic with dull urban orange. The whirring heated engine of the scooter shrieked loud for help. 'R' man shifted gears of the old scooter to manoeuvre a sharp turn. The loosely tethered helmet slipped forward to partially cover 'R' man's face and hindered his gaze. He shook his head vigorously upwards as a short remedy for an irritating helmet. He was in time to receive Reuben and gather moments of prayer at the temple just beside the railway station. 'R' man was in need of helping hands as Robin's recent behaviour had saddened him and he was certainly looking for hidden clues to resuscitate Robin. For him Reuben was the benchmark from which an ideal behaviour could be assessed. Reuben being more of a friend could easily talk to Robin on the subject of commitment and responsibility. 'R' man could pray for hours before the good Lord as ask for atonement of sins he never committed. He was sad in the end with his confessed perversions to family members. He was drifting away from Robin or rather Robin was drifting away from him to his own land of delusions and illusions. He would often arraign in discontent

"He is out to self destruct, he will listen to no one, and look he managed those lines astutely disparaging me and his mother. This is an insult; I will not take it, anymore"

Robin had the struck the match for self immolation and no one had seen him with his meals for many weeks now. Food in 'R' house went floating by and some never touched it out of a certain condition of the mind. When they tried to eat, they were too distressed to entertain wholesome pickings. 'R' man felt rather weak in the knee and somehow lugged his weight for a slice of hope at the railway station. It was like the 'R' house set on flames and the end was near. Robin was not in a position to even look straight, chin up or stomp his way to any place outside the precincts of 'R' house. He swore he saw the lake bubble when it was frequented by frolicking ducks or droves of cattle rattling boundaries of shallow puddles to quench thirst.

'R' man landed up in the wrong platform waiting for the train that never arrived. After swiftly changing platforms he found Reuben keenly looking in all directions at a particular platform.

"Look at the darn heat; you've really melted down, haven't you?" 'R' man looked concerned.

Reuben placed the huge bag on his lap up to the chin in the pillion seat of the loud scooter and they pinched their way via shortcut to 'R' house. 'R' lady sat excitedly away on the taut sofa with a smile she could not resist waiting for her son to arrive. She was the valiant torch bearer of the house and if not for her the house would have never seen new mornings. In 'R' lady the children had found a voice that heard them in violent uproar and took their side. 'R' man uttered in vehemence and disgust at being tied down by job and responsibilities. 'R' lady did do the patching up when there was no one to listen to her. 'R' man invariably found himself on the edge of emotion, with the lamp shade et al in his disgruntled hands ready to be flung with great force. 'R' lady would hear him out and cry at the emptiness and helplessness and build the house of cards that had been shattered to pieces, with her own hands once again. She could finally see the little boys holding their corners, crying out of fear and 'R' man's projections of doom. She waited for the ebb of every storm in her house and then stood up like nothing had ever happened. She would play the jester on those radiant evenings to her little boys to see them off for a game with the boys. 'R' man's thoughts always centred on the day when he could leave all and go away, but 'R' lady simply prolonged the duration for its arrival. She saved the frolic and grin of her little ones and never let it die. Yet she rarely spoke a word in retaliation to 'R' man and ran haywire after the storm subsided and damage was done. 'R' man forgot his last minute hostile outpourings like a blimp in the night sky. He studied his action in silence, more too often repenting while 'R' lady was always ready with baked cake to hold the house together. That was the time for titillating senses, for Robin to rapturously bite on a guava and to run around in gaiety. It was also time for neighbours to share good fortune and who never knew what ensued in closed rooms or in darkness. It was time for 'R' lady to spread her wings and learn new crafts as a stimulus to embellish her four walls. She learned how to embroider wall hangings of jute and draw pictures on frames of charcoal. Sometimes it could take her late into the night and with tired hands she lunged forward to finish the job lest there be a storm anytime soon. Sometimes she corrected 'R' man bent at imploding a storm out of nothing and matters conveniently digressed to a hot cup of tea. Robin vividly remembered those tangy fests, climbing on mama's back and arms swinging like in a dance. 'R' lady brought sanity to the house in a mind muddled and apathetic towards life and what it could bring in its course. She worked resurgently with broken glass or spilled tea on walls smudged with patches from the past. She bravely passed words of commiseration to her young ones. There was the latest line of saris she saw at the marketplace but let her friends do the talking while she stood speechless in one corner. Sometimes the playful mind sought these earthly pleasures of adorning oneself with costly wear but she dare not ask 'R' man for it. She ransacked her wardrobe over and over again to search for something new but in vain. She patiently waited for auspicious occasions like festivals and anniversaries for her father and mother to buy her the world and feel the sense of colour all over again. She lost all her strength in holding the storm while she played the game of survival in the wee hours. By the time she could think of the colour purple or pink the house was already in flames and she threw herself at the behest of imploring children. 'R' man stood in the corner breathing heavily repenting the wild streak and studying the lines on her face. She would implore 'R' man to be gentle while smacking the young ones and couldn't bear the shrieks of children succumbing to violence. Yet he dazzled with all his force pouncing on the kids like trampling an irritant insect under his feet, stamping the rogue long after it was dead and gone. Yet the boys adored the two good people in their lives. They would cry deep into the night when their parents were out for a party in the mess across the railway line. They waited with patient breath when Reuben flung himself with joy at noticing a thin dark boundary of two people approaching in the distance. And after it was confirmed that they were indeed their parents then each one would wipe the tear from the eyes of the other. Their parents were happy to see them as much as they were far away for the world of superficial and false dazzle. This was the tender world of children, so innocent and tender. Truth was the order of the day, pure as bedtime stories. 'R' lady always professed the belief that this world could be despite the clouds and violent thunder to undo its strong roots.

She didn't have the intellectual capacity or the pervasive understanding as 'R' man but knew how two and two make four. She was well grounded breaking the world to granules to her understanding and taught good things to her children. She used the two edged sword of good and bad to cut across humanity and the principle was pivotal to her understanding of a virulent world. For Robin she was mother epitomized, wholesome, amiable and soft like evening breeze through the prim window. She effused with plates and bowls in her balancing hands and abounded by elegant ladies of laughter and frolicsome demeanour. She went as far as the post office or the roundel by the railway tracks to give her hand at negotiating work outside the four walls. And then there was 'R' man to take care of paper work and all official liaisons. She was the kindest word heard in ages when it came to dealing with house maids and others workers around the house. They adored the lady and would go to arduous stretches of the mind to see her contended and leave a slick house, shining and unperturbed. They boldly paraphrased their plight before the lady of the house and she gave them clues to a keen and delightful existence. They happily bent some extra notches and extended their duties towards the lady and the house and did vent out their angst with the lady when all work was done.

Laxmi the house maid was older to 'R' lady by a whisker. Her mouth was spoiled by the redness of betel leaf with condiments. She had puckered cheeks and constantly smiled to no avail. Every evening at the stroke of four she was greeted with subdued laughter in the lady's eyes while rolling out fresh betel leaves. The tactile floor would soon then be swept with outreaching laughter on both ends, within minutes. Laxmi would press the floor to rise in a rush and prepare glasses of milk for the young lads. Her light saunter to the kitchen would be cut by jostles of young boys. They would shy away drinking the milk in her presence to unmet scenes of adventure. One afternoon she was the unexpected guest with 'R' lady's eyes accustomed to seeing her in the evening. Out of her soft hands rolled out a white puppy with brown patches. It smelled its way to safety and comfort sticking out its gracious tongue in acceptance. It was a precious gift for the boys who could discover a whole new meaning of love and affection. The dog was aptly named Rover after the hero of a tale Robin read at school. The little creature wiggled it back, would climb on slippery shoulders and give a rapturous hug, with tongue lashing out and nose digging deep. Then it would suddenly ricochet from the show of archetypical love and consider the odd contours of a stone lying in the open terrace. Rover would seldom bark at the utter dismay of the boys and would only do so only when a stranger was seen near the compound. Rover stepped back some distance while hurling an attack at the stranger to leave some space for encounter out of fear. The first thing on the mind of the boys after school was to see Rover, bored with a dying curiosity in the simmering terrace. He luxuriously wiggled his back with a short tail that lashed at the discomforting air and would not stop. Rover pertinently thrust his nose in the Robin's face when he was barely ready with his outstretched arms. There were whimpers and arbitrary licking for his sappy tongue to reach out and conquer. Sunday was the bathing day and Rover turned into to a reptile with wet hair sticking to his slender body like glue as if it was nonexistent. He looked different, lost all the gloss of fine dry hair over his body. He was shrivelled up and carrying a bathing grunt, in a mass of crackling bones. He grudged on his state, waited for dryness, when his skin would wear the fluff of his coat and he would be cuddled with greater intensity. He would bathe in powder with the surrounding air charged with white dust. The powder aroma became the smell to identify Rover. He salvaged some pride in being treated so well as compared to his extended family loitering in the streets. He too was from the streets; felt clogged down, sometimes, in closed quarters and not allowed to flourish in the wild. Yet those thoughts rarely ever occurred to him after accepting a different kind of upbringing from infancy. He felt a void when he saw a lanky stray dog stealing around the parkway and was adamant in scaring it away with spiteful bark close quarters. He would then calm down with two hoots after the stranger disappeared with a realization he was better off than those unwholesome creatures. He would keenly unearth a plateau of porridge and rice in the evenings and grunt low at being bothered when engaged in a serious business. When rotund and comfortable he jumped in air and stand with his paws in air covering some fair distance for someone to dance and frolic with him. He knocked on the stones with his swarthy nose when there was no one to play with him. He would then tear down waste paper with his sharp teeth and curse the thing to the hilt. He had quickly learnt sitting and standing commands but disobeyed when he had too much to eat or felt pestered for no reason. He ardently chased a bouncing rubber ball in the distance. He grabbed it under his sharp teeth and never thought of returning it to its rightful owner. He had to be coaxed to release the ball with teeth marks all over lest he rues over dinner. He let go in a gruff sound and catapulted for the next skit of the bouncing ball. His amusement was short lived; very soon he had his fill and was ready for other intriguing exploits. The nose was the compass and the mind reader in the sense that he could gauge the happenings around him with this piece of weapon. He was astute at matching imprints of smell and voice and knew if he had encountered a particular person before. If he found the matching sensation then the meeting could go either way, bring roses or venomous thorns, beguile in warm thrust of the paws for starters. He was hard on obnoxious strangers and little rats that roamed the insides of unknown holes and on the corner of walls. Rover would sometimes circle around to catch his own tail to reach an itch tucked far away in oblivion. It would take a plunge into the heat lying down in the terrace in hot afternoons with a hanging tongue, sticking out for some air. Rover put all the fear Robin had for dogs to rest. Robin had been bitten by a stray dog before Rover. He had to suffer, for demonstrating surfeit intrusion, fourteen injects in his stomach next to the naval. The truth behind uncertain animal instincts leading to deviant behaviour had not sunk in Robin and he was seldom game to the dodgy creature. Yet he was one with Rover but sometimes took his hands off him when he attacked showing his sharp teeth ready to be sunk in. These were however rare occasions and easily forgotten in the good times spent with him. Rover was not allowed near gypsies and stray creatures as per 'R' man's strict orders.

He would be dragged by the collar to safety when he smelt a whiff of those gangly and diseased creatures. Rover would certainly pull the harness with all his force towards a duel. The stray dogs were cold to the thought of an encounter, for they had seen plenty in their lifetime and just wanted to vanish from the scene. This would excite Rover even more thinking that the perpetrator put up his hands in defeat. The street dogs had the effrontery to appear before him and entice him. He would oblige with a huff and would whimper in his persistent urge be left free of the tight leash. He longed to go near those creatures, smell them through and attack them in retaliation for showing their teeth and the seething anger. Once Robin looked the other way for a moment while taking Rover out for a walk on the streets and lost the leash from his hands. Rover had held the animosity for those low lying creatures for pretty long and this was the opportune moment to vent out his grudge and anger. He jumped at the rogue totally disregarding the impulsive reaction from sharp teeth creatures, savage and unkind. This was the last time in Rover's life that he was cuddled by Robin. The dog was rushed to 'R' man for he had spots of blood on his sharp teeth. Rover was put was under the care of the best vets the city offered, vaccinated and tranquilized to numb the senses. The intruder was searched at the same spot and at the same time of the evening with bread crumbs and dog biscuits. It was essential to trace the wild thing to understand his habitat and if he had been infected with any kind of disease. This would then help in the proper diagnosis of Rover. 'R' man harped on the possibility of a fox from the nearby jungle being forced to roam the prohibited area in excruciating circumstances. Yet he could only surmise and would rather scatter bones in the neighbourhood for the intended prey. Only Robin had seen the creature that enticed Rover that evening and had already forgotten the look and built of the fiend of the streets. 'R' man had no time to sink his teeth into the matter. He would sometimes randomly pick out dark holes in the night in his walk in the wild in an attempt to discover any wry creatures with unusual steps. He would pick a few with his discretion and give out fake calls to end the night

"Look I have found the damn thing, pass me the net will you, tacky and perverse, come lets push off, it's too dark in here"

Rover was quarantined and barred behind closed doors of the servant's quarter. He would vehemently press his claws against the netted door. He sometimes cried out softly to the sunken air when there was nobody around to elicit empathy.

"You're done old chap, we can't have you in, yet we'll have you with us till we get a call from your brethren. Listen boys, you've got to step aside into the calm when feasting on a friend who has gone bonkers lately" 'R' man was stern.

Rover would sing in rare overtures to attract human hands. He couldn't understand why the world wouldn't look at him suddenly and shun him from lurching in the open. No one was allowed in the room and Laxmi felt sorry for the footsteps of folly that once deftly alighted from her fingers in wonder. She would pass on food quietly when Rover was not in the mood to confront his situation. Robin sighed in grief and wanted to touch Rover on the other side and take him blindly for a walk down the block forsaking common sense. He could feed him cold milk with cereal or watch him drag a dubious ball catapulted high into the air. Yet these were mere desires that were hard to fulfil. Robin wanted desperately to free the fluffy baby from the cage. He couldn't hear the wailing of submissive loner who had been lured by the stray dog in the first place. Sometimes Rover sat on his haunches at a distance from the wired mesh watching the restorative gestures of blokes from the other world. His existence was just like a zoo animal that had been reticently inclined lately to spend most of his time in his hole. There were no decorative medals for accomplishing this feat. Instead he had found a way to pester the 'R' house by not showing up for urgent calls at the entrance door with the mesh. It would be fairy tale come true for Robin to find him at the door fence and desperately wanted to know when Rover quietly roamed in the vicinity. Sometimes it would be days when Rover was nowhere to be found and common sense contemplated an early expiration. All anomalies had been carefully considered and plight of the creature confirmed after days of confinement. He was probably dead. At that juncture curious hands broke the door open and to find Rover reminiscing in one corner and licking his claws as dessert. The door would be forcibly shut with a sigh of relief. Perhaps this was his ploy to escape the clutches of his masters for good and it very nearly paid off.

One morning 'R' man decided to free Rover from his confinement into the outside world. A dog trainer was aptly appointed to do the job that tied him to the leash and walked him to the busy marketplace.

"Say ol' chap I could see rigor mortis on his face, he's got to face the brunt, I feel, let him go and be one with the wild, yes, we had done a great service, he was never one among us if you ask me, he was a scout,

trafficking the busy roads, one with the melee. Let's not tamper with roses or hem in the bushes for one with a kiss of the wild." 'R' man was succinct in his remarks.

That was the last glimpse of Rover the family saw. With a sinking heart they let go off the chains of a dog that wanted to be, live freely in a place where he aptly belonged. Laxmi knew it and the family knew it, yet the love and affection crossed all barriers of birth and existence. He was one with the billows of smoke, standing in knee high gutter water not knowing where the food would come from, castigated and whipped to the bone. This was the preferred life to dwindling in warm houses trying to break free from the twisted leash for hours. He could never taste the world in narrow glimpses, walking that restrictive road. Sometimes Rover thought he was overdone with sympathy and freedom down wild streets. He would rather belong to, than trance in the open with no caretaker.

He had smelt the warm tinge of leaves and grass on those laid back evenings and believed nothing could ever come close to that sensation. The servant's quarters was cleared after weeks of closure brimming with stringy cobwebs. A thick coat of dirt was piled up at places and stifling smell of Rover permeated the ambience.

The quote by the fatalistic 'R' man had sunk in and the 'R' family gave up the cause of the fat little cuddly stranger called Rover. Robin's blue eyes sometimes searched for Rover at places where he liked to sit and dismember old shoes. He searched for Rover on the road he took oblivious to abetting enemy. The warm smell of dog powder that enveloped his smooth fur was all over and he could almost see Rover wiggling his being. He could feel the touch of his fir and the way he ran his hands over them dissolving them with a kiss on the cheeks. Months passed and impassionate Rover still gasped in the conscience of the 'R' household. Far from forgotten the children often thought of buying him in. Then on an evening walk by the marketplace Robin noticed Rover listless and walking languid, opinionated. For a moment Rover was hard to be placed for he had stretched into an adult and lost all the fat around his midriff.

"Say ol' chap that's what I call a joke. Take a gander, thought Rovi would not survive with no one to feed the old thing. Honestly I don't like Rovi living on leftovers and thrown away food. Yes, he does look handsome though, doesn't he? He's lean and thin, mean, healthy too, like he was meant for these colours. Ladies and gentlemen, introducing our very own Rover. Sail along trooper, a gypsy family waits for you in the marketplace. Good riddance you don't even seem to know us. It's your last life, remember? Both of us are a part of each other. Tie a thread my son and don't leave this time, the odds are in favour of you and you seem to love it. Rosho Kharosho, carry on swindler"

Robin turned back in the far distance to catch a glimpse of the tireless warrior. It would be a sin, indeed, to tie a strap around his neck for someone born on the streets. Turkish bath with dash of dog powder would be replaced with mites and ticks on his fur coat with no brush to straighten the hair. Maybe he had already sniffed his way to lost family, the protector on swallowing and unearthly streets. Rover had by fair chance found his way into the dome of the wild, where all are free to face the weather, and survival, the biggest dilemma. He sure had to start from scratch but found his way, flayed, and disliked. He had been driven from pillar to post until he found the streets more hospitable and swanky. Yet he had learnt to wallow in the debris and luxuriate at a soft beckon from a stranger, when the world was kinder by night. He was dragged way from townships and assorted dwellings to finally run free, roll on to sand or coarse mud and in a state of torpor breathe the squalid stench. That was the day when the last chapter out of Rover's book ended and each one vowed never to tame a dog again. Robin could feel the cold blister on his foot which did not hurt much. He remembered a time when he was all too harsh to Rover.

"That is indeed an honest send off; we don't have to worry about that ol' chap again. Gee, he has found his family, and Oh! A true love, I see. Let's not blow foghorns in the night, look how snugly he fits into his hole. Calls for a drink, I hear ya, we'll call it a day early tomorrow and raise a toast in celebration, not for you young kids, I'm sorry. Carry on ol' chap, the night's young"

Last night Reuben had a dream. He opened his eyes to a warm cup of tea being offered as a tranquilizer to fleeting thoughts. He was in a transitionary stage coming out of illogical summers spent in the precincts of a mother of all colleges, not knowing where he would end up. He sometimes rued the purpose of his fight, caught up in trammels to books thicker than his fist. He sometimes felt like writing poetry on discoloured pages and pour out his heart when the sky was cold and grey.

'R' man tuned the final bend on his conferring scooter and Reuben found himself enticed to a familiar surrounding and voices heard before like déjà vu. There were similarities in the long stretches of roads of his college and his home town. He often asked a question to the streets of his college with a desire to be at home, warm and safe.

"Do you hold the same streaks of endearment, can you take me there?" He was often reminded of the wondrous foliage and wide open spaces of his college. He was sparsely intimidated by his surroundings at college but 'R' house was a balm to tortured senses.

The yellow oleander was all dressed up as it spilled yellow in its dance to the gentle wind for an auspicious home coming. The streets and the drain, too dark in the night were aglow for a reason they never knew. The stray dogs were in total disarray to the gush of the smoke from the scooter engine past them. They frantically turned around and disappeared into the thicket. One could see the clouds above even in the dark, yet it never rained. Perhaps it would rain after Reuben was back home safely. Reuben never really spoke with dad around even when he had a word of two to say. But this was special and he tossed in his seat before breaking the usual silence. *"I am so happy to be here. It seems like ages when I cried round those hedges, or prayed under the yellow oleander for good results. How can I forget the first taste of lather? Or the tangy plastic ball up the rubble and out into the streets. Yes, I am a fleeting monger and hate to count days backwards even in this trip. I am like one with the tide and never had time to decipher what life meant for me. Can't take away any bit of excitement coming my way, I have slogged in the dark and in the too obvious brightness to earn my day of leisure. Don't worry about Robin. This is just a phase in his life and he is just muddled up with questions he has set out to answer. I will take care of him and pray he finds his way back to where he belongs, in the college and come out triumphs with his studies."*

'R' man acknowledged with the shake of his head and sometimes felt he had totally lost Robin to his unique expression of love to his children. Reuben never had the time to peep out of his room to revel in the spell binding architecture of the college erected by American architects. There was no time to play the casual visitor, just figure out a solution to the newly arrived assignment. 'R' lady was ecstatic to see her son back again. She could not hide her emotions and there were tears in her eyes. 'R' man threw himself on his bed while mother and child enjoyed moments of gaiety. Reuben had finally weathered the storm that furtively rang on his windows late nights. He had graduated to a new life and to something big if he could. His dreams were as pure as the colour of spring in a new world of light and softness. He was halfway through the pudding with cherry on top when his chin dropped to hear Robin crying out for sanity. Robin had the healthiest pattern of his growth and development in his family from the very beginning. But now Robin was trying to disturb the equilibrium. Yet he walked upright and swung open the door to find an impervious Robin with eyes staring walls, crouching in the corner.

"Somebody, can we have some light in here. Why are you sitting in the dark Robi, do you even know that I have been awarded the Master's degree. So what's happening over here? Any new friends or someone you might have met while I was away? Forget that, Robi do you even look out your window. Look out to see fulfilling beauty of flowers, creepers, hedges and shrubs. Do you hear that little bird Robin crying for friendship and the love in its big round eyes. Look as it doodles away in hind sight over grains and mud. We have so much to learn from its carefree gait, wobbling left and right. That's the way to go Robi, carefree and not perturbed by things that are beyond you anyway. Hey Robi, I'm no coach and expert at life matters yet can throw some light

on you that may make you get up and seek.

Am I speaking to the wall or what? Say something and let's give it a push. Look I have arrived and we are all dressed up for the frolicsome fest in the last few minutes of the night. Let the party begin."

Robin did get up holding Reuben's hands with a simper but sunk back to his spot after Reuben was done for the night. His arms and legs were tied to a hook not allowing him to drift though he desperately wanted to. He was thin as a needle, low on words with trauma stricken eyes. Augustus always found Robin with a low self esteem and rather depressed. The doctor checked Robin for cholera and jaundice that had bitten the city. Yet he was suffering from the symptoms of an ailment that anyone could guess. It was more to do with the mind than an under nourished body. Everyone in the 'R' house was fast asleep except Robin. Reuben was tossing and turning in the heat on his bed and made irritant noises looking for a place and posture to sink in. It was way past midnight when he finally got up for some water and almost choked to find Robin losing precious sleep over nothing.

"Robi, what are you up to, please sleep, it's too late to consider and populate, see even the grass outside has slept. Go on buddy we'll discuss it in the morning; let's not pull out pages right now. I have a lot to share, be good, and just gather what the night has for you. I got to sleep, please Robi, we need you".

The following days found Reuben busy as a bee in preparation of his maiden journey to the shores of the US. He remembered the time when Robin wanted the answer to his unsettling questions,

"What is it like to be a twenty year and something old, I sure like to be one" Robin often asked Augustus. Augustus did pop in to the chagrin of 'R' members and headed straight for Robin's room.

He lay down flat on his bed as a ploy to offer help like he had done for some of his sick patients before.

"This then is your canvas, the empty wall I mean, and you have to make it breath by filling it with kaleidoscopic colours. Life is yours if you want it dearly. Enjoy. I've got to rush, catch up with a friend you know and maybe a party tonight at my place, want to come. I was joking. Take

care. Ciao."

Augustus was gone like an ugly blister on Robin's toes. He didn't know how to feel. Questions arose in his mind; was Augustus responsible for his present state, should he be antagonized against him, or hold him in awe for befriending a low lying stranger? He first had to learn to acknowledge a warm cup of tea on a cold morning, he surmised. He wanted to and even made an effort, but somehow learnt not to. What was he holding himself for, the thought beckoned, when he could easily help himself with a cold shower, cut across the breeze into the woods? Why was he contriving his own disaster? The river had never been glossier, time was ripe to roam its edges but he settled in his corner and never winked. Robin never realized that he hardly ever slept, suffered with lack of hygiene and never had food until it was forced down his gullet. Days were spent in preparation for the Reuben's grand odyssey skywards into 'R' man's dreamland. They would be out on a last minute shopping buying the bare essentials for the trip and gathering information. Robin was stuck on the walls considering the hazards of taking a step forward arbitrarily. The family members were treating him softly with every gesture to challenge him on his foot back again. 'R' lady was busy with her fingertips calculating time and money with all the clothes and other necessities on her mind. 'R' man was busy accumulating cash from petty sources which could barely add up to the amount required. Sometimes in the excitement, busy lips and fingers would stop and the jubilant atmosphere would become sad and all efforts seemed worthless. They could never forget Robin and his plight and furnished his wardrobe for him to look dapper in collectible dresses. He had almost run his whiskers and dug his nose onto them but not too close to consider them. There were moments when 'R' man would lose his cool and try to find a reason for the loaf gathering moss on Robin's table or the tea running cold in its desire to be relished. College matters would be attended to at the turn of the century, he surmised. There were a few years left before that moment. Yet it was critical for Robin to live like

normal people and have hopes and dreams like all do. 'R' man held
the cure all for his family always but this one was a thorn in the
flesh, hard for prognosis. Time was running out and the family,
muddled up could not decide if there was a reason to celebrate
or to be sad for Robin. 'R' man was looking for the curious jump
from decrepit state to a state of indulgence and merry making. If
there were such a pill 'R' man could bring it even from the deep
seas. Somehow he found himself too exhausted at the end of the
day to carefully think of alleviating Robin's plight with no room
for indulging in art or literature. He was too busy arranging for the
trip and found himself rendering the word around the corners of
the city. He swore by the uptight winds pervading the premises
of offices he visited there was room enough for laughter. It was
a classical example of how the family had turned into one of the
specimens of Freudian postulation as per Augustus who had done
extensive study on the subject. Augustus was given his partying
gift, caught by the collar and slapped on the cheeks by 'R' man.
Augustus changed his route of adventure and never crossed those
streets that had made him a star overnight, in fear. Reuben couldn't
bear a passive Robin anymore and decided to consult a psychiatrist
with 'R' man's consultation. He was a best in town and Reuben had
to wait for a week before their turn arrived for a check up.

It was about two o' clock in the afternoon. It had rained in the
morning and it was greyish and cold. The trees were adorned with
young leaves that reflected dull light. The vibrant birds were settled
in the dry patches of trees enjoying the wet weather. The sky was
choked with white and grey and eyes could not penetrate its depth.
There were fresh puddles of water torn apart by racing wheels of
heavy vehicles and rampant cattle. There were weeds and shrubs
getting ready for the next deluge.

They were incessantly thrashed by street urchins and devoured
by munching cattle. The wet garden in 'R' house was stormed by
a flurry of wildlife with toads, caterpillars, grasshoppers, crickets,
snails and the occasional bird kissing beads of water on the thick
grass. They were all bundled up together as a jester to save the

sick man from ruin by stoking the hidden fire. They had seen the hanging head for a handful of seasons and had come out in the open in pleading for sympathy from the Almighty. They were ready to fall prey and decimate in the hands of the hunter but would not submerge in darkness and scamper for dear life. As an involuntary reflex action they stayed away from humans hiding behind itching leaves shining in the grey weather or camouflaged corners. Yet their prey stood glaringly before their eyes and they couldn't hold ground for long. They prayed for Robin in their effort to save a life and disappeared. Robin was unaware of signs of nature and sat hidden in his room. Robin lost count of the days he stayed put in 'R' house before deciding to visit the doctor.

The clinic was located on the other side of the town. Robin and Reuben had to borrow their way in short bursts on dilapidated auto rickshaws until they could reach the doctor.

Crowded street was a witness to the warm tussle between light and dark, with the dark enhanced by the hanging clouds. These were meant to be happy times with a picturesque weather meant for a picnic. Robin was silent, indifferent, with the stench from his body disturbed by the fresh smell of detergent. His head was buried deep into the ground and he patiently waited for nudges and hooks from Reuben to hold a different posture. He had to be lead by holding his hand like a child who never knew where he was being taken. Reuben feared Robin could be impaired for good and wanted to forget the nightmares he had lately in this regard. Robin never realized that it was not just getting up from pangs of rest and moving forward in life. It went a lot deeper with his condition deteriorating with passing time, something that he was not aware of.

He had developed a sense of fear of the world around him. He found the world callous, wanting to defeat him in his purpose and cause harm. His questions were weird that even the best of people had no answer,

"What is it like to be a normal human, and more specifically to be twenty and something years old?"

He found people moving around with confidence, healthy, happy and focussed. He had no clue of the true story hidden behind faces. They walked differently and uttered a different language. They were persistent with what he called a life that he had denied himself. 'R' man had the perfect solution to this debacle

"Ol' Willy let this period be over then, by Jove, I'm going to call a female nurse and hook him up, right-o carry on, atrosho"

Robin felt that his days were very soon going to be over when he would collapse under his own weight. His breath didn't actually push through the nostrils. Limbs took a world of time to react when he tried to move them and he felt they were not his own. So in order to end it all in frustration he practised holding his breath. He nearly toppled sitting on the railing of the terrace, holding his breath, when there was darkness before his eyes. He had held his breath for too long and a smack on his shoulder by Reuben shook him back into conscience. Or when he found phenyl that could slowly induce the sleep of death, mixed with coffee and pleasure. He could go for the quick snap cyanide rather than opting for a tedious end yet didn't have the gumption to ask for it from the store keeper. He could hear his insides echo blue and black like his organs had seen enough of venom. Sometimes he thought his body reacted to some outside force and all his actions were in fact not his own. The undeniable force kept him in seclusion, away from the hurly burly of a high pitch afternoon. He felt he had spoken to the walls and paint for too long and even they couldn't elicit healthful tips to make a day in all its glory. Coming out of darkness of the end he decided to live. That day 'R' family members were overjoyed and thought there was an easy way out of the problem. If only Robin knew the way to break the shackles holding him, he would run berserk in the rambling town. It would be as though he had found the magic potion and was suddenly akin to the ways of the fastidious world.

There was sand and water in his shoes when Robin arrived at the doctor's clinic. He was held softly at the elbow by Reuben and sat aloof in the waiting room. The clinic was located in the interior narrow lanes thick with mud and slush where no human could ever safely tread. It was hard to walk past the sludge without the toast of wryly creatures to be confronted. Reuben had a hard time with Robin and sometimes planted his foot in the middle of the slush to be one with it in the passing moment and to rue over it terribly later on. Robin was unmoved even if one of the creatures were breathing in his shoes. Faces of patients and their relatives drooped in passive submission. The walls of the dull waiting hall needed an overhaul. The patients were literally dragged from their seats when it was their turn to meet the doctor. They were not misled by intoxicants or the like yet their gait and inaudible words in confusion showed that they were indeed into drugs or the like. Some of the people holding their disturbed relatives turned happier than before after emerging from the doctor's chamber. Some came out even more confused than before, worried over the fate of their loved one. Still others were just about keen to observe the rules. Reuben was suspicious of the doctor from the moment he stepped into his clinic. There was a deafening silence pervading the hostile atmosphere. There were too few patients, each wanting to round off their sessions in a jiffy. It seemed like the world was least interested in the doctor and his shanty clinic in a far off desolate corner of the town. At one juncture he even tried to walk Robin back home without a check up. Yet he decided to persist for the sake of curiosity and the desire to see Robin dapper. He wanted Robin to feel the subtlety of life and seek happiness in simple things. He felt something dragging him backwards when it was Robin's turn for a check up. He defied good reason walking into the doctor's chamber. The doctor was ready with his stethoscope with a cocky face never giving in to his patients or being happy to see them. His ill humoured view of his profession indicated that he was averse to meeting some of the worst people in this world who would probably never be cured. It didn't take him long to diagnose Robin and he struck his pen wildly across paper in a missive and uttered,

"How long has this been going on? You Sir, why don't you eat and go to college. No response, I expect that, don't you? I have checked

his body, there's nothing in there. Very soon he could go bonkers if not rejuvenated and reenergized. This is what I do to such patients, and you can check my track record that it has worked miracles in the direst of situations. We must give him an electric shock and that's how the bubble will burst. Let's not tamper with him by giving him strong medicines. That can only put him to sleep. You can get a cost estimate at the counter outside. Let's do it for the general good. He will be up and running in a week's time and do the first thing that needs his attention, go to college. You may go now, thank you."

"Here Sir, I want you to gargle today before you go to sleep and spew all the venom you have inside of you. Thank You anyway, I haven't seen a doctor like you and make no mistake, I will never. I should have known this. Let's go Robi, we'll go home now" Reuben walked out of the clinic in disgust. There was a storm building up and they rushed home before it burst its seams. Robin returned with his tireless gaze into voids of null. Reuben set out finding the expert in the area to hear the final word. However he stood clueless and pensive like 'R' man trying to justify rumours in an area they were not familiar with. At the same time Reuben had other pressing matters, like running to the bank and shopping big for the occasion. Robin was once again walking the same lines he did before. He thought the world had designs on him, so he presumed, to see him begging for a wee bit of home. So he sat there, blissfully unaware of what was going on in his home, not fulfilled with his crouching pose.

Three months went by and Robin's shoulders still dropped down in submission and he had shown no inclination towards life and its colours. Robin opened his eyes to Reuben one morning,

"Robi, what on earth are you up to. Do you know three months have elapsed and you are still clutching that corner as if for dear life? Why don't you take a breather for God's sake? Look Robi, I am here for you right now, but you won't see me when I am gone. I am leaving Robi. You've been warming in your seat for too long. It's time for some tea and to get going in your strides to live a day and a life in style and to conquer them all. I have part conquered, so I know there is no point in being pensive and sad, fighting glances in a closed room, look there's

no one listening to you. Look they have brought out new hair oil, old company but new name, and a new range of soaps and cosmetics. You must try them and their fragrance will remind you of me and these last days that I spend in my home country, probably. Take a quick shower and sit with me for a while in the thick of silence and abundance. Yes we'll make it with our own two hands. I need you; we need you more than anything else in this world. Join me."

Reuben had reached the brim of his last stay at home. Preparations were almost complete when a niggling thought on everyone's mind as to whether Reuben should leave for the US, given Robin's condition.

"Should I leave now or stay? I can't leave Robi in this condition. I must consult Dr. Rabindra. I'll talk to him tonight" Reuben sorted things.

"You need to study the corners of this room. Robi is indeed ill, as he has been over the past six months now. He will go down even further but don't worry he is in good hands. I shall try not to amuse myself with beads of fine poetry or absorbing prose and I swear I never clipped his feathers. He is free to do and act the way he wants to. But we want him to talk and do a good job with his studies. We are there for him, Reuben, so don't forget to catch that plane and fly to distant lands." 'R' man was direct.

Somehow Reuben was not convinced and he sighed deeply and hung his head in submission whenever the thought sprang up in his mind. He could count the steps to his library in college or the flowers that toppled each day from the yellow oleander, but he could not tell how long Robin would take to get going. Like a lost soldier he walked the corners of the house in utter disbelief. He was liable to think otherwise. It was hard to adapt against the seeds of negativity and the frequent heart burns were an indication that there was something cooking inside of him. He could slacken in his take on scientific matters but he was never wrong when it came to Robin. They knew each other well.

The day arrived when he had to make a decision. He had already decided to forgo his trip and was convinced of a miscalculation on his side. He called up Dr. Rabindra to apologize for declining his offer.

"*Nice to hear from you son, I was waiting for your call. I have already promised those people in the university over there of the most capable and intelligent student. You shouldn't step back right now. For the well being of your family members, you must go. I had faced a similar situation back then. My father was terribly ill and I was adamant at quitting. But my father advised me otherwise and I have gained a lot by that decision as you can see. It's a cycle my son, the grey will turn into bright sunshine and the trees will flaunt a new dress. You can call your brother over there when things settle down. I'm sure he'd love to go there. So don't feel the prick, and trust me you are doing the right thing. Be brave and after all it's your father's dream you are going to fulfil. Steam away delightfully, whatever's gone will come back tenfold and you will think of this day. Give my regards to Dr. William, a dear friend as always seek his help in any matter you wish to. Go on son, this day was made for you and let him clip away on doses until he is strong and full to write you letters and talk to you. Don't miss this chance. I will pray for you*"

Reuben decided to take the plunge for the good of his family and to do the justice to the years of his constant effort.

ALONE AGAIN

They were to catch the evening train to New Delhi for Reuben's flight scheduled after three days. Robin was skimpily dressed, bottom of his trousers covering his shoes, loose shirts hanging like on hangers on a deprived torso. Last night he was dragged from his burning seat by strong hands to the shower. He had denied himself a cold splash for months with an urge to starve in the decrepit state. He cried like little children denied of food, detesting cold water. The constant stagnation had taken a toll on the hair on his scalp and skin. He derived pleasure in denying himself comfort and would rather wait for the end. He swore he had heard those jovial eyes in the distance but didn't know how they managed to pull it off. He wanted to study the voice of silence. He longed for a void so dear to him and always near him until he could listen to the sweat pour all over his body. Lost in silence forever, his wish was far from being granted in a world obsessed with noise and anarchy.

They held him by the arm on their way to the compartment of the evening train. He walked rather hurriedly and didn't try to know the reason for being stopped frequently. His eyes were hooked to the toe of his shoes and he could count the blisters on his foot by walking on them. He never had an inkling of where his luggage stood in the swelling crowd and couldn't tell which way to turn. Eyes turned into that of a toddler except that he didn't cry when the crowd got to him. He missed the perfume of almond oil that was locked in his room out of Reuben's shaving kit and the town of familiar footsteps. Now there were obnoxious faces before him and he ignored them. It was hard to put away street urchins and hawkers selling their teeth out of sweaty windows. As a child 'R' man would shove the two brothers into the same sleeping bed of a fast moving train to engender a feeling of oneness and warmth for each other. Their shirts and trousers would be stitched from the same cloth and even their talk and behaviour showed a little bit of each other. They were friends for good, letting off the steam, in a squabble, sometimes, with a show of fist power to dominate over the other. Later did they realize that they were more of twins, one and the same? The boys were essentially trained by 'R' man while the lady of the house braved in not letting the ship sink. She was the sandwich lady never forcing herself on her children and 'R' man. She was always ready with bandage with searching fingers to wipe all the tears. When the time was right she would hold round cheeks of her little ones in limitless gaiety.

Robin's mind would often throw a blank question for his mother, for which he had no answer,

"What do you do mamma?"

The heavy train pushed against strong winds and climbed onto corner tracks of polished steel, lunging forward. His desire to sit the entire night earned him a spot by the window. He sat still and had not given in to forty winks for the last many months. 'R' family let him have his way and they slept away to bobbing motions for a bright new morning. 'R' man woke up at halts deep into the night and urged Robin with squinty eyes to try to sleep when the train starts moving again. His face had the imprints of the design pattern on the seat it didn't bother him.

The train pushed around the final bend on a new morning and no one knew what it would bring for the 'R' family. There was not enough leg space as new local passengers got in to make life hell with Robin's legs extending out of the seat. He somehow held his position by pushing the seat in front with his legs. The swinging motion of people holding on to dear seats was reduced in intensity as the slow motion train was about to reach New Delhi railway station. Some held sleep on their eyes, some were fast asleep totally averse to the fact that final destination was a few winks away. Most were locked in a gaze out of the window. Moments spent together in the morning and the night before had made them into a family with all hostilities forgotten. They helped each other with water and some space to hold and remember. The coiling train stopped indiscriminately at paltry stations with the buzz of insects holding onto spikes of wild grass. People got excited when the train moved again from stagnation ever so softly to whistles heard for miles. People were already crowding the exit doors and some were enjoying the vacant spaces in the train compartment, suddenly. The passengers were locking up the aisles and the 'R' family would rather crowd the doorways than be left behind.

The train kissed the platform and all stood up queuing crookedly and tightly gripping their belongings for hopping on to the platform. There was a sudden gush of noise as peering eyes on the station brightened to the big train approaching them and ran with her to catch familiar faces lost in the crowd.

There were hawkers selling refreshments and tea with excess of oil and spices for a bite to remember. Then there was a stampede at the door even though all knew that the train was not going anywhere after its last stop at New Delhi. Some maintained a logical distance from the crowd. They would rather take a nap before there was no one at the gate and they would then saunter with someone to carry their luggage like kings. 'R' man was in a hurry anyway and didn't wait for the storm to subside. He first helped Robin off from the high gate followed by other members. When all was done they sighed in relief and 'R' man ordered fresh round of tea for all its members. 'R' man loved to travel and the thought of reaching a new destination excited him. Their top priority was to get away from the commotion and the sweat that made it unbearable to stand and gather a peaceful moment. They rushed onto the exit door to board a taxi for the hotel. Robin was finding it hard to keep up with the rest and sometimes would race to safety when he was lost and one among the crowd. His condition was critical and his body was in dire need of nourishment and rest.

They booked a room in a hotel in the vicinity of the International Airport and Reuben and 'R' man set out to find a hospital. Luckily there was one located near their hotel and Robin was immediately rushed to the doctor. The diligent psychotherapist had dealt with more complex cases before and Robin posed no threat to his repertoire. It was a simple case of tortured senses complicated by lack of food and rest. Robin entered in to his room, smelling of sweat, pensive and lost.

"Hello gentleman, now would you please look at the ceiling and tell me what you see. That's nice you can do it, there's nothing in it. Your father is very concerned about you, why do you do this? So do you see anything? Let's slowly check your weight now. You seem to have lost a lot of it."

Robin looked at the ceiling and was lost in his gaze until the doctor asked him to let go. Robin stood on the weighing machine.

The psychotherapist looked at the weighing machine intently to the extent of losing himself. The weighing machine had probably malfunctioned. The doctor looked puzzled, knocking the machine with his fist and took off his glasses in disbelief. He gazed at the machine, speechless, not knowing what had gone wrong.

It was then that it came out. Robin actually smirked at having made a fool out of the doctor. The doctor tapped the instrument several times to notice a digression from normal swing of its needle.

When all was done he smiled and asked Robin to relax and the right treatment would take him back to his old days of glory. 'R' man and Reuben were called in,

"Sir, it's a case of acute depression. It does not usually happen but it can happen at this age. Young children sometimes lose their way trying to figure out things and over working their faculties in the process. They lose interest in the daily grind and look for peace in things far from the normal bent.

This will however work out, you lad is bright and yes kid I saw you smile even though I know you didn't mean to. Here is a list if medicines to be given regularly except this one which has to be swallowed only in

case of an emergency. He will be O.K., trust me. Give him some time"

The word was out. This was far better than electric shock that could hollow his insides for good. It was a no touch treatment that revolved around oral doses and nourishment that would very soon knock him off into cinema halls for the latest flick. 'R' man knew it was serious and his past suddenly flashed before him. He had been rude to his boys especially Robin, hostile and persistent. When the assault was more than Robin could bear he took to the streets like a gypsy in the search of love.

"Why does he irritate me so much?" 'R' man would often ask when he over reacted in certain situations.

"Where is your dancing friend after all? Where is he and why is he not with you if he really cares. Say ol' chap he's really left you to the dogs. That scoundrel tried to destroy us by first taking me for a ride followed by you. Why am I talking about him anyway?" 'R' man let the lid off the jar.

The hotel room had confined space, quite different from the 'R' house with many rooms and where one could change the ambience at will. 'R' man and Reuben were out giving final touches in the preparation for the journey abroad. Robin was feeling uncomfortable and walked to and fro in the room, head down and bent over. He suddenly stood in the dark and started wheezing with convulsions and 'R' lady helped him with water and orange juice. Breathing became even more difficult and Robin was making strange noises. Matters took a serious turn and this was no fun 'n games. Right now he wanted some air and didn't want to close his eyes too soon. 'R' lady took a good look at the prohibitive pill and decided to give it to Robin. Despite being notorious, it could put an end to misery and constant dart of uneasiness. So it did and Robin was relieved. He started breathing easy again and sat in the corner of the room pressing his chin against his chest.

"Relax Robi. The worst is over. Have some juice. Let me pray. Just hang on, papa would be back soon and then we can go to the doctor. I hope that pill doesn't harm you" 'R' lady assured Robin.

Robin continued to deny himself a full gaze of his surroundings. In it lay his first step to recovery, albeit simple, it was never conceived. Looking down continuously had become second nature to him. He had not looked into the mirror for ages and failed to keep up with a changing reflection. Coming back into life he had to learn more of this callous world where people hide their true face. There was a lag he often felt he had crossed the line when odds were against it. All he wanted was a house of love so that he didn't have to seek those magical sounds elsewhere that could make a sick man healthy again. With 'R' man love seemed like an illusion sometimes making it hard to breathe and at other times bringing the family closer together.

"That's my way say ol' chap. I may seem rather rude to you, but that's the only way I know, just the way I talk to my friends. They don't mind at all and take it in good spirit. So why don't you lighten up and catch the message instead of the tone. I don't mean to harm you and I am sure deep down you feel the same. So carry on ol' chap we have a battle to win and it ain't over by any margin." 'R' man laid down the rules. It was too late for any kind of explanation, redress; the damage had already been done.

Robin jerked his frail body and suddenly discovered that he couldn't move. He tried to walk or stand on his two feet but they were stuck to the ground and won't budge. His body stiffened suddenly and he tried hard to swing his arms or stand up and tried to form words in his mouth but in vain. His tongue stiffened, he couldn't speak, and he was soon crawling on the floor. 'R' lady was darting the room in confusion trying to figure out how to take him to the hospital. She was about to call for room service when 'R' man appeared at the door. Reuben and 'R' man carried him to an auto rickshaw and was immediately taken to the hospital. For a moment the ominous sound of death seemed daunting at the 'R' doorstep. 'R' lady was crying and she never thought that his condition could get this serious. She always felt that with ample nourishment and care he could easily slip out of any kind of medical condition. He was pushed into the taxi with gentle hands with a danger of deteriorating condition and possible permanent handicap. 'R' man cursed himself for his failure to elicit some kind of emotion in Robin's eyes, carrying soaked almonds in the morning for Robin who was as rigid as the walls of his room. For a long time Robin had been kept away from the midnight owls that romped the dark of trees in his garden or from the shining pearls of dew in the early hours of morning. He missed the quiet ambience of the 'R' house when morning peeped into the night and the night darkened the day and he breathed in spasms of procrastination. He missed the gleeful hands of his childhood when he would let those men and women twice his size rule the world.

He missed those windows through which birds would daub the insides of his room with refusals singing a song or two in return. Now he needed a lantern to search for those bloating birds or even for an open hearted window with no bars. He could feel the drippings of yellow oleander with whistle knobs with the breeze that played around in with it in circles.

His soft head touched the roof of the taxi, as he looked down trying to feel his thighs with his head.

The first sound that echoed out of his mouth was that of his father and mother if anybody could hear it. For them he had drifted far away and would lose him too soon but for him they had come even closer. The taxi bent around the curve for the hospital entrance in an emergency. Doors were struck open; 'R' man rushed out for a stretcher and hospital staff ran haywire trying to bring the situation under control.

Robin was rushed on the stretcher and taken to the doctor in his ward. Robin was immediately put on saline water and his condition improved. The doctor had the last laugh,

"Sir, I knew this would happen. Remember I gave you that pill and warned you to use it only if his condition got serious. It is because of that pill that his whole body had stiffened. There is nothing to worry. He would be up and ready for college in no time. The bubble has burst and I encouraged you to give him that pill so that we could feed him through tubes eventually. Just look at him, like a big baby and you can

even speak to him. Go ahead."

Finally the stiffness wore off and his body was supple again like before. His innocence was trapped in the over head saline water bottles and he took to them willingly like fish to water. His gaze was almost perfect peeping into expectant eyes that rued over his condition for a greater part of a year. His forced affinity to the ground soiled by ubiquitous ants was weighing down on him and he wanted to trace the skies with his trying eyes. It is a hard time for the one shying away with plenty of action missed and giving up the desire to indulge in the excitement building up at the corner of the eyes. Yet for most part of Robin's life it was shyness that did him in. Even now his eyes never dared to capture the complete picture although he did touch the sky when no one was around. 'R' man was equally delighted at the progress,

"Say ol' chap, you are looking much better. Coming here was the best thing that could have been done and now you are under constant care and monitoring. We couldn't do any better what this team of doctors and nurses have done for you. I don't believe my eyes; you are actually looking at me.

You have done Reuben a big favour by not clanging in a bizarre note. Complete your studies son, then we'll find a nice girl for you"

The doctor was in town and turned up for a spot check up,

"How's my son doing? Here let me check your pulse. Are you taking all the medicines I gave you?

You are improving son. Sir, give him adequate food and I think the best thing for him is to get some sleep. He will feel much better after that. We are almost done here Sir. You can even take him back him in a couple of days. But please talk good things to him. Just try to make him a happy and I am sure he can make out between a dull moment and a bright one. He needs all your support at this juncture and he will be on his feet with a normal string of activities in his hands. He is a bright one and we must not lose him. So carry on junior, you've done a splendid job. Nurse, feed him some nice pudding will' ya. Poodli-doodli I'm on my way, bye"

Robin wanted to survive in dire circumstances when he had been reduced to a vegetable. His strength sapped and his heavily bandaged wrists connected to an overhead bottle with saline water trembled in spasms of pain with protruding bones on clenching fists. His eyes closed in the early hours of the morning and he was off to a different world. It however did not last for long with noise and grunge of a working day ready that was hard to swallow. The overheard tube to feed him had been removed leaving behind blood stains on swollen veins of his wrist. He couldn't remember if he had slept at all the previous night but was feeling much better as compared to the previous day.

Focus drifted once again to Reuben and his preparation for the big occasion. The family moved on to the hotel and the lady prayed for the hard bargain for giving back Robin and taking away Reuben far away from her eyes. Reuben was busy in preparing for the trip and sometimes flipped a dollar bill to Robin and exclaim,

"Look here Robi, this is a dollar bill. This is what American currency looks like. I would sure like to have you there once I get there. Don't worry Robi; this one is for you and 'R' house. Rejoice in milk and bread and please do write me letters, are you with me, Robi?"

The thought had been stamped on the minds of the children of 'R' house long before doses of music and culture of the land of the free. They tried words that were hard to pronounce in broken lines of English to outdo 'R' man. With time they picked up the language and could go as far as fetching a meaty sentence of the language rather than prompt yeses and nos. The children taught table manners and hints to follow 'R' man for a decent gait while in motion. 'R' man gave a piece of himself to his children and God hinted at ways by which he could realize his dreams of sending his children to the US. He decided by all means to see that Reuben flies away free from all restrictions for honour, dignity and pride. There were constraints and roadblocks on the way but there was time and room enough to come up with a solution to puzzling questions. He could blame the dilemma of how his life had shaped for his despair but not let it ruin the feast of the season and get in his son's way to triumph in glory.

This was the first time for Reuben. He had travelled to distant corners of the country in trains that had gathered speed over the years. He had seen an aircraft, played around with them as toys, but never occupied its seat to actually fly in thin air. And this was no small journey a forty wink long. Hanging in air for long periods one would suddenly realize that a whole day had elapsed. The crowd at the airport never spoke about air turbulence and unforeseen disturbances in air that causes havoc to the smooth flight of the aircraft. They just wanted to have fun in air. Reuben simply believed that the aircraft simply ballooned up in air by some strange phenomena and passengers went high on candies and juices while the plane then converged on a narrow strip of runway. He couldn't help being a little apprehensive yet clung dearly to the logic that not many people would be flying had it been unsafe. He decided to close his eyes while in air, pray to God while the airplane gripped the air above and get out of it as soon as possible. He wanted to look at the rising sun with the perched window and hear its huge engines as they generated thrust and power to navigate the aircraft to the desired direction. The machine would jerk differently as compared to trains and would touch the clouds and fly miles above them. Robin once again nailed his eyes to the ground and was swamped with grief and solitude.

He never uttered a word but his sadness was written all over his face and it felt like he would miss Reuben forever.

"Robi, why don't you see? I will be back very soon, whenever time permits. I too don't like to go right now. I wish I could stay with you until you were fit enough to attend college and live happily all over again like you used to. Hey, I am sad too. But my going will not only serve me, but it will serve all of us. So please don't weep, just wait for me. And please give me a smile before I leave. I am as unhappy as you are, in fact even more, but I will not give up my dream and our dream so easily. So cheer up and let me get you some refreshments"

Reuben proudly displayed the boarding pass to Robin. Robin ignored it just like the dollar or any piece of paperwork that Reuben wanted to show him. And then parting ways, Reuben suddenly disappeared for security check and Robin wobbled looking all around for Reuben, like he had never left him. It was then that Robin lifted his head for some space and behaved like a tepid little child quailing who never knew what he was missing. He suddenly realized that Reuben had scrambled to the precipice of formalities to finally board the plane.

"Da has left; can't I see him for the last time?"

They rushed to the huge glass window from where the planes were visible. The huge nose of the airplane which would take Reuben away was locked to the front gate. The aircraft appeared to be like an impudent young child being severely punished. Its huge wings hung down low as if it would kiss the ground and made it look attractive. It could hold proud mamas, uncles and aunts, grandpas and grandmas in grief or gaiety. It could set them free of petty indulgences and fly them peacefully across the starry skies and through the hot flashes of the sun. It still ruled the minds of plenty as a scary invention that could actually hang in the air with no support for hours. Yet the laws of nature enforced such a design and were true as the air that surrounds us. All minds were laid to rest while in flight. All that the people could do was catch the clouds and some sleep or enjoying a drink down memory lane or flipping through the pages of a book. Yet there were many who even after the advancement of the human race were still sceptical about taking a flight for a desired destination. They would rather ride peep through the window of chugging train nailed to the ground, or take on a ship battling through the waves to see them through than comment on an unstable airplane.

They bet their pennies on mother earth that would not give in but could not believe the wind driving an airplane that could not even hold a feather. Airplanes are here to stay and not hard to figure out.

"Count the roses in our garden, pudding, close your eyes, he will be there" 'R' man reassured Robin.

Their eyes were locked to the entrance of the airplane and the passage to the aisle. Robin didn't know how to react when suddenly 'R' man pointed to the aircraft's front window of the cockpit where Reuben stood waving his hand.

"Look I told you Robi, we'll find him. Come let's give him a final goodbye. Don't be sad, let's make him happy and send him off like he was always meant for the high skies. Don't worry you'll be there too soon, cheerio"

They waved and waved until their hands got tired of bearing their weight, yet they still didn't stop. On a special request the pilot allowed Reuben to stand just outside the cockpit and wave his hands to his dear ones. Like every sweet story comes to an end, this was near its climax and the players had to part after a very final goodbye now. So Reuben gently indicated to Robin to hold back his aching arms while he entered the dome. One last sailing hand would leave him alone in the world, yet he had to move on. Time was up; the little Reuben had finally grown up, this time it would take longer to turn up, maybe a year before expectant eyes would have their fill. Robin lingered at the glass view long after Reuben bid him goodbye and the airplane languidly rolled over to the empty part of the runway for the final lift off. There were shrieks at the final burst of the engine as the airplane climbed up the hill to touch the skies. It was all over and 'R' house was in tears wishing they could enjoy a cuppa together or taste those delicious mangoes.

"That one's gone, say ol' chap. We must not despair. Look Robi he has gone there to study and make a name for himself, so please hold your college more passionately. But if you think it's too much for you then give me a buzzer and I will fix it for' ya. That said why don't we get out of this place, get a cab and see what the evening holds for us." 'R' man picked his nose by his pointed finger in a jiffy hardly giving the impression that he had actually reached out for it. Robin just wanted to be there knowing that there was no point in looking through the window for nothing and watching the people hastily pour out with tonnes of luggage. He was finally led out of the airport with eyes looking back that never knew where

exactly to find him. Reuben would be gazing at the skies, excited, yet sad at the same time for not having a titillating conversation with Robin when the two sides held rather reserved opinions. The two were hard pressed for a dual, like childhood, with loud voices that dangled in the halls that would often result in random dislodging of household objects. Then in the climax the parties would come together with a clear conscience and rejoice as each side had won over a friend. Where was that Robin that everyone desired and failed to understand how he had turned to stone? 'R' lady often declared the culprit behind such mysterious situations to be a magic pill that Robin had swallowed numbing his nerves and making him a door mat. And Augustus was responsible for giving him that pill, driving Robin to hallucinations. Recursive denial by Robin would not convince 'R' lady. Robin was pliant and easily brainwashed by the convincing assertion that his own people were trying to disown him. Robin would find it hard to listen to others, except for that solemn voice that rang true and held him astounded, forever it seemed.

Back at the hotel, 'R' man and lady threw themselves at the bed while Robin peeped out the window.

He was in a state of shock and thought that Reuben was around and he just had to call out his name to be near him once again. Then a huge plane whooshed in the air just above the hotel's roof top. Robin cried out for Robin,

"Da, can you see me?"

Robin's pointed finger followed the bird until it was one among the clouds. The 'R' house cried a silent tear of two lost souls that had parted ways to match up to the ways of this world. He would not budge from his posture long after the plane disappeared into the June sky and one could view mocking birds finding their way back to their homes in haste. 'R' man and lady used all their force to pull him back

"By Jove, I didn't know he had so much of strength. Come along Robi, get some rest. Right now Reuben would probably be hopping over the oceans. We'll give him a call at his university, do you have the

number? There, no worries come sweet lie on the bed. Let's get rid of these mosquitoes first."

The remaining family returned to 'R' house, like missing something dearly. This time Reuben had flown really far away and could not be summoned from the neighbourhood. They were astounded at the young man's courage and bravery of doing it alone and going to places that 'R' man had never been. One could only imagine how worried he might be about Robin's health and negligent response to a normal way of living. They crowded the phone one evening when the phone rang. The receiver was swiftly handed over to Robin,

"Robi, is that you. Yes I have reached safely but I absolutely dislike the ambience and the college. I am missing home and want to be with you. Can you hear me Robi, tell me what to do"

Robin could hear Reuben cry and it didn't stop him from doing the same. Robin's condition was an ounce better and could flatter all concerned by his mobility and untimely blabber. Yet to the extent of discomforting his legs he never took to the seat like yellow bees so despairingly close to the human skin yet shy of settling down and biting.

Robin was gazing down the streets with tonnes of psychiatrists ready with the remedy even before the sick landed in their bay. Most of all they were thick skinned and treated their patients like sheep and cattle or those dumb rodents in bell jars, played with physically and psychologically in the name of experiments. The patients would be written off with strong pills that made the mind numb disabling logical thinking. This pill played on 'R' man who swallowed them to understand their effect on Robin's mind. He went off to sleep with the windows shut, silently snoring away, and would not wake up. Dr. Ramsi, the friendly physician and a neighbour whom everyone called a quack, tried to wake him up by yelling at his ear. He even smacked the head and wiggled 'R' man's toe, but failed.

"Feed him with lukewarm water once he gets up, he needs a blood check at my pathology centre and then we can lay it all in print and

exactly know the state of his mind. Don't worry he'll come through, after all I am the doctor."

'R' man slept the whole day and woke up late into darkness. The air looked quizzical and rather uptight. He walked into the drawing room, looking for a book that he probably wanted to read and very soon he swished the air with his palms not knowing what he was up to. Suddenly the phone rang. It was his father-in-law on the other side to check up on the condition of 'R' house.

"Who's that? Do I know you? Sorry Sir you just dialled the wrong number. What's that? What did you say my name is? How did you know? Get some ice Sir, it's too hot"

There was a temporary loss of memory. With heavy movements he tried to remember the word he had read some time ago or even what the word 'literature' meant. He once again gazed at emptiness for hours that had taken a good part of his life. He had swallowed a pill not meant for a normal person but he believed that there was nothing wrong with his son. After all he was the healthiest child at birth that he had ever seen. Like a normal child Robin played with grime and toys, festoons, with a sense of fear in coming of age.

Robin was ripe for learning and bending his back for a day of pleasure. It was not his fault to have fallen prey to an unfulfilled civilian life where the insightful poke at each other for a piece of flesh. 'R' man had known evenings, sunshine of thawed ice mixed with drinks, wondrous evenings by scandalous light and a cheer up the mess gates. 'R' man now struggled to look for reasons to make his retirement well worth living, accepting civilian life on his rickety scooter. He looked for some solace, cashing on deals meant especially for ex-servicemen.

'R' man reacted rather slowly to the environment, trying to remember anything he could,

"Say ol' chap, I have forgotten all the words in English literature. Looks like I have to go to school again. Blimey, I need to go back to the place where I belong, on my nice cushion bed. Ta da" Robin lost count of the variety of pills he had swallowed including half a bottle of laxative yet was untouched by their side effects. He

would frequently stand at the window or walk a few paces to and fro in introspection, but could not sit or lie down until his body collapsed to sleep. He finally could talk to his friend Rankin who knew a similar case where the patient could live a normal life on pills. Rankin with his flashy motor bike was all the rage in college, especially among the girls. His marked simplicity had even followed the footsteps of a girl he nearly loved. His suave gestures with good looks could make the evening shy and were openly discussed and much admired. His grades were not a question when he was a subject of discussion among the ladies and he could grab anyone he wished like the morning sandwich. He talked for hours under the shady tree to his beloved and all were curious if he actually popped the question. He would go to the extent of straightening her clothes or hair to show his care and undying curiosity of breathing closer to her. He was graceful enough for the lady to have a home with her and burn candles of togetherness. Yet he touched all the girls living in cluttered hostels and surviving on garbage food. He even knew his juniors who could not keep themselves far away for far too long. They crowded him by stealing the moment guilefully in huge numbers like dry leaves blown away to the bark of a tree by a strong gust of wind. If only he had a guitar to make the crowd go wild to satiating pulses and a jig so loud, Robin often thought. What happened to this stylish, debonair man, Robin never knew but he did know the advice Rankin gave him. He reminded Robin of one of his distant cousin who was doing fine living on this doctor's pills and advice. The doctor had the hands of a magician and was an expert at curing these kinds of ailments. So whenever Robin called, Rankin would reply with words that sounded like a sermon,

"This is the right doctor for you. I know someone who is living a normal life living on those pills. Just go to that doctor and he shall give you an easy fix for your discomfort"

"But for how long do I have to take medicine?" thus the soliloquy went long after Rankin hung up.

Robin called up Rankin so many times yet Rankin never desisted from speaking the same words with verve and resolve.

Dr. Rishi was a practicing neuropsychiatric specialist who had his own clinic and fifteen years of experience. He was one who put his book aside for moments and looked at the patient closely for future course of action. Doubling the dose was never a scapegoat for him. He dominated his field of practice, had won several awards for his contribution to medicine and believed in sorted action rather than pompous words. Robin had descended on that scorching evening on an arm chair in Dr. Rishi's clinic, with no grip over himself. He wanted to fly away with unresolved steps to place he was yet to know. He would not sit, constantly groping for space. The doctor asked 'R' man to relax, as very soon Robin would start behaving normally. This was the beginning of a relationship that would last for decade. The pills were to be taken for a very long time. They may be tapered giving the impression of their absence.

Dr. Rishi prescribed some doses and asked Robin to come again in a week. That year Robin could not only attend college but try to catch up with lost coursework. He had to club with the junior batch after flunking one year at college and he found it hard to sit in the same room with his juniors. He sometimes met his own batch mates and saw them smirk and mock at Robin's face,

"Go to mamma, she will sing you a nice bed time story, we'll graduate until then while you languish errr.... in the third year, or was that second year. Get away loser"

So he decided to avoid them. He turned around when his eyes met their exuberant gait ready to plunder plush jobs through consistent academic performance. It was hard to lose old friends to muffled pleas. Robin blended with the new group at college, young and ambitious.

"Say ol' chap, read your steps. I have a fine pair of hands in the Fine Arts club wondering at a piece of clay, or a ripe brush swinging in gay abandon speaking to his painted pine trees and flight of birds, there's got to be another reason. Don't lose heart son, if it doesn't hold on to you, change tracks and follow me." 'R' man was discreet. Robin went down memory lane when on one lunch at the table with family he was moved to tears when he couldn't unearth the mystery

behind a maths puzzle. It was the first time he did not read the sign that the seeds for the artist had already been sown, although in claustrophobic silence. But Robin was busy head down on a soggy lap and despaired at having lost everything. So when the time came to decide a career, no wonder his mind was muddled up and he finally ricocheted to a path everyone took, to a degree of success, he thought. Yet he was too deep into his chosen career and would rather restore pride in graduating to an engineer, than aspiring to be an artist. 'R' man saw the futility of the exercise somehow and believed that passing with a degree was a matter of crucifying himself. Yet Robin was out of the claws of clumsy doctors who treated people like rodents in a tight shoebox. Dr. Rishi had the panacea for Robin just in time for the final lap of his degree and had made him pant like the usual milieu. Robin covered the same distance to his college in dust, grime and heat with pride raising the handkerchief for comfort. He smiled at the other end when it was all done. It did unnerve 'R' man for the broken journey of Robin on tight lanes on rickety auto rickshaws that hardly moved. The rickshaw held more passengers that it could with a fear that it might topple over. So at the right time 'R' man decided to introduce a brand new scooter into the family.

"Say, ol' chap, we are willy-nilly there. This is the key to your future. And if you ask me frankly son, you should cast your nets at the surging tide and hope, fingers crossed. Go there and black out like you did in your matriculation and always remember you are as normal as can be with a decisive edge over the rest" 'R' reassured Robin.

'R' man had no longer to meet the haughty bunch of professors, only to be guffawed in hindsight. 'R' man had twenty of them bent down in salute as he passed through the road to his office each day. This was far from slightest tinge of respectful. 'R' man wished he never had to go through those parched moments and Robin could hold his gait and walk like a man.

Robin started attending classes and labs to the harsh sounds of the motorbikes racing away when classes broke off. The students painstakingly listened to lectures with Robin at the rear seat and welcomed the newcomer to their gig. Robin soon found it easy mingling with the new group and discovered that they were just as desperate as he was to graduate. They would then spread out in all directions for organizations that might fetch them after getting an honourable degree. All had battled their way, coming from meagre villages dotted in the outskirts of the city. They lived in packed hostels that urgently needed a lesson or two in hygiene. There were dead rats whose stench emanated from hidden corners. Bathrooms left no choice but to be one with their terrible odour, enough to make a dead man walk away. Rooms had scanty light with broken furniture that couldn't hold plenty. Despite the acutely dysfunctional environment the students somehow found reasons to enjoy and had plenty to write home about. They were reborn after a fresh bath and tried to avoid the stained rooms for the rest of the day. Many focussed on their coursework and guided their steady progress instead of counting reasons of why the place was most unfit for habitation. They would hang on to their beds all day on a holiday making notes, singing songs soon joined in by roommates. A heavy lunch down the aisle of a smoked canteen with coagulation of spices could brighten a day. After a heavy lunch, it was time for a powerful nap. One such man turned up rolling his sleeves one evening that proved to be the saviour of Robin. Rick, the man from the planes took a peek at a man in distress. It was a strange coincidence that Rick knew Robin but not vice versa.

"Hi, I am Rick. I saw you perform at the college fest. I like it very much. Ask me if you need any kind of help. I am indeed a big fan of yours"

For a moment Robin was in a daze, trying to recollect when and how. After all he did give a solitary perform at his first college fest carrying a guitar. The hoodlums and the rowdy chunk that held the college captive with arms hidden in their closets had cheered and almost fired a bullet or two in air. Robin had to refer to his notebook for he had forgotten the lines of the song, while singing and playing his guitar. Finally, out of frustration of forgetting lines, he threw his notebook away and sang out the title of the song which he clearly remembered. Thus all cheered including the disheartened who had turned up to watch something exciting. Rick was in another room and was pulled by the loud sound of Robin's voice on the speaker. He ran to the concert hall to find his hero, singing. God works in strange ways and who knew the same Rick would meet Robin one day and be his only hope of graduation. Robin was low on energy and had almost given up the chase. He needed someone to closely look at his present level of preparation and suggest a remedy.

"Say, ol' chap, Rick is a good proposition. I would like to meet him and discuss how we can prepare for exams and win a degree. I am hopeful, Robi after a long time. Yes, we'll make it. We'll meet this Rick guy for sure" 'R' man blissed-out in admiration.

Rick was up to his neck solving mysteries of engineering logic while Robin found time to swing his arms and go high on music. He calmly stood at the door of Rick's room, hands on his hips watching a fidgety Rick. Sometimes fever, headache, body aches got the better or Rick who always thought his preparation was lacking in depth and never found time to be on his side.

"Hello Sir, nice to see you. I need a glass of water. Lot of work has to be done Sir. So please let the books guide you and I am here if it all goes beyond you. Hurry on Sir, we don't have time and I need to dry my clothes out in the sun and rush to the cobbler if I can. You can wait for me while I count my steps"

The final internal assessment was in a week's time. These numbers were a booster for the final score and the students worked hard to score high on these exams. This was a time when cheating was the order of the day and the professor's themselves encouraged it so the student didn't go low on marks unnecessarily. Robin had the will to succeed. Yet he had lost so much time that he found himself fingering his shelf for the number of books he had, never knowing what's in them.

Rick could help Robin with engineering drawing which carried the chunk of the marks in the internal assessment. So he did with Robin not having the slightest idea of how busy fingers could create an intricate design masterpiece. Robin walked the space tightly behind Rick never questioning him, quietly abiding. At one time 'R' man happened to be in the neighbourhood, after sitting for hours by fresh bougainvillea dropping in large numbers in his garden. He decided to holler a voice of help to Rick who was fast becoming a friend and guide of Robin.

"Hello there, I was just passing by and thought of passing on my good wishes for your exams. By the way I am the father of Robin; yes the one kinda lagging behind. He will catch up, I'm sure. At least he's come out of his terrible sickness. Say ol' chap call me if you need anything. You are a saviour."

*"Sir is doing fine uncle, he needs a potion of your spirited service that saw you become such a senior and accomplished officer of the Indian Army. Why him, we all need it. I am just showing him the way and I am pretty sure he will do it all on his own. So don't ever worry about him."*Rick let out a fitting dialogue that made the old man sigh.

The final exams commenced just before the monsoon rainfall. Students were all geared up for the final bout after suffering the delay, for no good reason, sending their academics for a toss. It was the same story with Robin's original batch although the delay had narrowed down with the passage of time. He remembered going on a hunger strike once with the previous batch for the commencement of exams and subsequent classes.

There were students hard at work in the shadows of the toppers and some that hardly worked. Robin was not among the toppers, neither was Rick but Robin didn't like to be called a back bencher. Others pleaded with the professors to decorate their near empty answer sheets, the professors willy-nilly obliged. He wanted to avoid such circumstances. Robin could produce a little more than an empty answer sheet, always. He felt the void in his preparation for he had missed those foundation lectures that are essential to understand higher level coursework. The omniscient talked of flying numbers, grafted scientific principles and phenomena that could be comprehended by mere signs on the exam paper. He had Rick for solace and a look at the picturesque weather outside his window with a certainty at getting at least the pass mark. So for the first time he prepared narrow and long strips of paper with a world of information for cheating. Come exam time he found it hard to pull the reams of paper out of his pocket lest he be expelled for corrupt practices. He dodged the eyes of the invigilator smiling away in ignorance. Someone raised a holler when the obstructer was out of the room for a while and students freely exchanged ideas and answers. Robin pulled the conning sheets of paper out of his stuffed pocket and hardly found them helpful. He would rather prepare for the exam than live on outside help to justify the purpose of exams. He was very much like those blokes from the hills who hardly ever opened the book. They looked fashionable in their leather belts and sung along with 'Eagles', 'Guns N' Roses' and the most recent sounds that fizzed through their lager beer. He wanted to script the perfect answer without any help and have healthy strips of 'asides' on the corners of his answer sheet like those toppers had. And when the bell was about to ring he rummaged his answer sheet for one convincing answer but found none. He let out a wry smile. There were cheers in high fives and pompous arms skied into the horizon with a healthy amass at the marks table. By now the cheating reams were in a horrible state of mess. They had been thrust viciously into the pocket with their curves flattened by rough hands. Robin would think twice before carrying them again. The onset of the monsoon brought the drooping head of Robin out of the exam hall, whining and irritable. He could see the flatulent smiles of the hilly blokes with their effortless copy book reproduction and constant reconciliation to their own hide outs. Robin had hummed with them, holding hands for a life that the rest of the oily hair, check bush-shirt and fountain pen geeks detested. For once he wanted to be like those geeks and follow their gait to a deeper understanding of critical principles in engineering. He wanted to copy them and carry all the thick books slung back on his shoulders regardless of the incessant blows on his spine. But he could never understand them. They spoke a totally different language, shaking their heads vigorously for whatever written on the blackboard by doubtful professors.

Robin had come a long way overcoming his nemesis, mathematics. He had grown progressively strong in the subject intending to submerge in intricate and convoluted mathematical formula. That afternoon at luncheon the bugle sounded too soon before he could connivingly manipulate seemingly complex mathematical problems. There was indeed a hidden trick to solve every problem. This was higher mathematics categorically denying prodigious school kids. Its never ending stipulations outdoing foolscap would invariably lead the pursuer to burn the midnight oil. Even though he had attended the classes at the beginning of the term, he could solve the problems to some extent. He set out breaking up a complex problem and counted on his knuckles to do the rest. Most of all he outscored himself at the beginning of his college and was among the best, as lofty as the pines. Now after the deluge he was looking for reasons to escape the tussle when he never knew what the game was about. 'R' man and Rick hinted on Practical work that could win the battle to a huge extent and Robin would at least pass the exam. There were a string of viva voce exams and Robin could easily incite the mercy of the professors gaining enough points for a big help in the final tally. Robin held onto fits of laughter, when the sharp rebuttal from the conning professor stumped a student at his wits' end, though the answer was very simple. And when he could not bear the air tickling him to the bone and he was about to let go restrained gestures, he pushed himself out of the room with due permission. He shared the laughter with Rick that he had despised for a long time like a dry spell with no inkling of the grey and storms. If only some camera could catch the many moments of togetherness with Rick. Like each wave had to proclaim its way back to the waters after kissing the shore, Robin knew the banter didn't have a lasting pitch in the subtle noises and whispers of life. For moments the two held each other's arms softly. Wondering what they had at the moment, packed in like glistening sardines, betting on the light that hardly emerged. They elicited moments of bewilderment and gaiety that hardly surfaced. On the other side of the river bandits of weapons polluted the still and serene air. They exuded fire like their weapon and expended their energies so brazen to a bizarre sense of humour. A voice beckoned each morning at the pool table that it would take one encounter to shut their eyes off.

The critical and convoluted drawings required an artist's keen effort. The simpler ones were handed over to Robin for easy disposal. Rick soaked in the chill from his broken window and his fingers would often freeze trying to fit the curves to symmetric proportions. His perusing eyes would often drift in the haze of parallel lines and peak at erroneous locales. He would then palm his forehead in disgust or even smile on a bright day for his fetish. He had to soften his pencil for two identical drawings conjured up with keen senses, one for Robin and one for himself. Robin could only point a finger at the emerging billows of smoke at the tea stall and lead Rick to warm escapades. Sometimes he towed his dear friend who gave into the sweet petition, wanting to divulge in the rendezvous. Sometimes Rick never wanted the break and bemoaned his fingers in quandary at unfinished strokes of imagination. A blink of seriousness brought to attention would often leave its chartered course to anomalous gaiety and rank stupidity. Just like people holding their noses lest somebody steals them, like the fulsome fart of the professor in mid lecture, the stupidity was a rage. The weather was grey, damp scattered leaves on the ground were muddy brown under the footsteps trampling them. Robin was sure he had not heard enough from the skies. Sometimes coming home for burning under the eclipse of monotonic books was like the yearly vaccination one must endure to keep safe from helluva different kind of diseases.

Pawan, Rick's fast friend, with a tinge of the hornet's nest, wily and contemptuous, was trying to cut across familial ties that had swarmed Rick and Robin unknowingly. Robin was through a period when he was remonstrative, little more vocal and spiteful at the evil he saw around him. Robin was livid to find Pawan in his undergarments one day rubbing his bare thighs with a towel when a girl happened to look up Rick who was a friend. Pawan's gestures, undone and lascivious bothered an uptight Robin who indicated with a grimace and hand on his hips to strike him off Pawan as a friend. This was a period of a mild episode for Robin. In this period people often change, become more outspoken and confident. Robin swore he could ramble on the guitar for a packed audience and strum in the middle of a rapturing number. His words were holy for Rick and served the words of an astute commander who had suddenly erupted from the damp and grey. In the whole incident Robin was yet to utter a word. A mere grit of teeth and forward strides followed by quick recoil in trying to tip off the rogue was enough for Rick to end the age old friendship with Pawan. Rick was like a brother for the girl from the hills. Pawan befriended her, to the extent of take advantage of her for she was made of very loose soil.

Robin warned them for the worst and they crowded the busy tea stall for a round of tea and a token of thanks to Robin for addressing the problem. Robin knew his heroic deeds would dwindle very soon. Under the effect of doses he would be reduced a commoner. He then wouldn't dare to utter a word when people spoke of common everyday occurrences. He felt stunted and forlorn at not being able to make people laugh. Robin raised the raison-d'être to his breeding when 'R' man expected perfection from nothing young lads in speech and action. He discouraged them from being their natural flowing self. The confidence and self belief had vanished.

He was ready to slump to the ground sans his episode and hoped Rick would still have some tea with him. Robin literally saw clear skies through his mind's eye. He felt that Rick saw the same when he gave the nod. Later Robin realized that Rick might have been referring to something else. He would feel safe if he could ask a relevant question in class amidst all the students. But the college was all deserted with no classes in revelation of his skills. Rick handed over the drawings mostly done by him to Robin. Robin was happy to find his name printed in astute boxes to bring home the belief that he too had an identity. The score gathered from these drawings was crucial to see him past pass marks in the final tally.

Viva voce exams passed off when he was not his own or when he was truly himself as he sometimes put it. Now the burst of crackers in the neighbourhood wedding would make him jittery with the feeling that someone pushed the trigger on him. He called on Dr. Rishi one afternoon for his check up and confessed that he was not himself when he met him last time. But this avatar of being scared to hell, not ready to drive off the dry leaf that happened to pop onto his head from the overhead tree was more like the true Robin.

"By Golly, we don't need ghosts in this ramshackle town. We need softer men to live by who fear as they must out of respect that out of cowardice. Hold on to yourself son, you sound much better and that is a nice shirt". Dr. Rishi cleared the cobwebs from Robin's mind.

He was to walk like others did in the heat of the day and work their sweat in earning a day of reckoning. He could not sally on witchcraft lending him tokens of confidence and his worth; he had to learn to stand on his two feet. He felt helpless without the magic potion that could make him rule the world. He abhorrently accepted the touch that was all too real. He longed to be that famer who with his sweat and toil raised a crop and carry heavy loads of grain on his back. Someone who would sing in the season of sweat even though his house would turn turtle in the gusty storm. In it perhaps lay the road to self discovery but he placed the bookmark at this juncture in his book of life and moved ahead. Nearly all students, including Robin had scored almost hundred percent marks in the internal assessment exams with gaps for the obvious discrepancy. Rick roamed the darkness that day looking for Robin and wished he could be the first one to break the news.

Robin was still Rick's hero and perhaps would be for good. Robin denied such claims, and would rather hide himself somewhere from the crowd. Rick did break the news and Robin jumped in happiness.

These were the last few days of college with a gap of two weeks before the final university exams. Robin skimmed through the tree branches and the tall grass where he spent friendlier days to see if they knew his name. He had known the waiting room outside the principal's office, sitting in silence to meet the principal. He outdid his part at the machine shop with lathe machines and the like holding on to blisters without a whimper. There was limited apparatus in the lab and only a handful could be permitted to try their hands at a given time. Rest were urged to come at their convenience and bribe their way to not just quality time on the machines but to some grace marks in the exams. It was a sad goodbye with all the tears and good times he spent, sitting on the lawn until his trousers turned green. He remembered rushing with Bholu for a quick tea in the little time between classes. He would lift eyes tenderly to girls in the common room and hoping someone would allude to his ways. He promised that one day when he had bridged the gap and become a wondrous find he would include his alma mater in his gripping tales by the Ganges. He watched the sunken river go by, sometimes lunging in sorrow, sometimes stroking fresh waves in its womb. It was a huge relief to watch it flow by in its expanse far away from the daunting burrows of books. It was hard to ignore its abode to fabricate an irksome life of an engineer to be. The Holy river wanted to keep an eye on Robin, to watch him grow, experience life under his own eye lashes, triumph in his day of glory. She followed him in school and now in college. He was sitting right next to the spot on the holy banks where Gandhi happened to sit and ponder one day. He came to her shores for the last time asking for her forgiveness for not being close to her with the worldly ties making him confined to boxes in infinitum. He held the fragrance of the soil in his breath. He heard the sounds of a busy day, peaceful by the Ganges and a raging fury in those dark chambers at a distance. He hardly found a reason to visit his college and watch the Ganges. He could come and visit his favourite professor, sit by the banyan tree. He could watch poor Bholu swing his arms involuntarily for a delightful cup of tea. He needed reasons to visit the little cuboidal room they called the Mechanical department. Robin had developed a liking for the long trip from home to his college. He was in a totally different frame of mind when he covered the distance on his bicycle. His original batch friends had already graduated and occluded the passion and the sense of excitement they had for Robin. He was once the highest among them, rightfully deserving the final robes of graduation. They sat decidedly before Robin holding his green mark sheet to roger a twist of fate only to find that he had actually flunked. They then epitomized a feeling of pity for hence forth he was ostracized from the clique of the chosen ones. He was forced to be one with those worthless blokes of the hills for whom studies was a scapegoat to feel the grunge and rife exploits away from home.

Robin didn't have to allude to hostile milieu of the hostel. He would rather suffer the dust storms riding on a riddled and uneven auto rickshaw. He was mostly a day scholar who once most horridly decided to take a room he was entitled to in the hostel. Hostel life meant freedom. The harsh life outside would see the hostellers honk musical instruments, blow with all their might through the holes of a harmonica, or divulging a tune in the six strings. Robin was in tune with the hostel life and cringed at the sight of the rancid soil of the environs. He shuddered when he walked those tight and dingy corridors leading up to the bathroom or the crowded mess, opting for cheaper food. He was granted permission to try out the hostel for some time on the grounds of collaborative study and discomfort of commuting to and fro to the college during exam time. He chipped in with songs on his lips and often found insufficient lighting to study at night. He rang true with the boys, lithesome and spiteful, uttering rubbish and unholy. He came precariously close to raising one jocular rhyme with the wild and unwieldy thugs of the day, but curbed his way in and abated from an encounter. He didn't want to get too close with the unlawful. Robin found himself in his room commuting through difficult problems, eyes past midnight stretched and kept alive, in neat and silence. Now he had an inkling of the hostel life and its strenuous ordeals in the dark. Robin stayed awake for four nights not in a row just for fun. He found that there was a total freedom of expression in the hostels and one could grin for no good reason. He started swinging his arms more freely and listening to the gist behind laws and hypothesis that ruled the book after returning from the hostel. Some of them were too engrossed and burdensome to register. He was at work most of the time with deft strokes of his pen, chewing over the portion he had denied himself for being too involved. Sometimes his medicine intervened in lengthening the hours of his sleep late in the morning. The medicines were in the right dosage. He didn't want to push Dr. Rishi for a reduced dosage lest he turn too voluble and suffer from episodes all over again. If that happened, then he would frantically reach out to lost relatives who had turned cold with differences, and childhood friends who may no recollect the days gone by. Very often he would visit Rick at the college hostel, his ears open to the dust storms on the way. Robin was ebullient when he met Rick. He felt they were making good progress until Rick reminded him that even a twenty four hour vigil would not make him budge close to completion or a mere distinction. The sorry tale dallied on everything he had ever tried before but invariably fell short of perfection. That was Rick's preparation level and Robin was way below that like the water in a well. Like the toss of the grey weather that haunted Robin he coiled away from Rick until a firm hand on his shoulders of his best ever friend brought him home with a tangy grin.

"Like the shine on the leaves after a healthy downpour you will shine Sir, just borrow a few sentences of the book and you don't have to grapple with the esoteric and unkind. And then it's a mere strike of the pen on that decisive morning, revelling in presenting a long and convincing answer in unintelligible letters down at the periphery to let them know what they already know. Remember, we need a first class that not only sounds good but will make you eligible for a plethora of jobs, auspicious and stingy, government and non-government, field job and sedentary as long as you have age and the numbers on your side. So cheer up, don't turn cold at the sight of logic that defies the senses, carry a smile and that first class is well within your grasp." Robin held onto these words like a musician to his piece of music.

The centre for the final University exams had been decided and it was a neighbouring college a few hundred yards from the engineering college. There was going to be an unprecedented tight security at the centre with no corrupt practices to be allowed. The examinees were to be totally free of belongings once within the ambit of the exam hall. The exam area would be freed totally of birds, rodents and insects that obstruct a healthy deliverance at the exam hall. Ample pitchers holding cold water was placed on straw mats to satiate any thirst. Exams would be held on alternate days with a rest day to consider and prepare for difficult questions. Rick was assigned some other centre and he dived in to the morning newspaper blurting out in streaks of nonsensical. It was perhaps the most important exam of his lifetime. Hard work had almost brought him closer to perfection.

These exams could decide his future. The degree earned would be most critical in any kind of job he could undertake at anytime in the future. There was a handful who had failed good five or six times at the exam. This was their sixth or seventh appearance at the exams. They had turned into uncles in their mid thirties, rambling the corridors in a weighty gait. They sweat heavily, barely fitting in double desk and chair half their size, asserting themselves in beige Ascot caps. Engineers in these parts were a status symbol and plenty pursued it until streaks of grey appeared on a balding head. The degree could land them plush government jobs besides a hefty sum as dowry in marriage. Robin was a trifle intimidated looking at those oversized, taut males in feline goatees. He never wanted to sink to their level. He would rather be gaunt and famished for traces of fastidious memory. He wanted to appear just once at the exams and let fate not play peek-a-boo with him. He was always on the safe side of all exams that he had ever undertaken, except for flunking once when he was terribly ill. He didn't have to strike the damp matches repeatedly for a flame that never existed; he had not gone so far. He just had to reproduce what he had read in a year's preparation in his next appearance at the exams.

He had never seen the face of supplementary exams on the face of the earth and fate never declared him to be made for one. After every bout of strenuous effort to capture the essence of logic, he added a few ounces around his waist. The fat around his waist shook like jelly when he walked into the queue for the prestigious exam. He knew a friend as a kid who flunked in school and was shocked at the lack of preparedness and alarm when matters could have been controlled. The ones that fail to trounce the red perhaps clung to other pursuits that made them succeed immensely. Yet few were adamant and wanted the college degree at all costs. Rest of the students feverishly turned pages to starchy glances, like they had not even started. Their tall fingernails glistened of oil, their subtle snort, late in the night came in their way of pointing their finger to the heart of the matter. Robin quizzically didn't find him to belong to those oily hair geeks or those disgraceful few. The middle aged ones were lackadaisical in their saunter, carrying alias names like the changing cap on their distended heads. Robin worked on his own with his books and barely approached someone for help. And when the problem got out of hand, he let out a whisper and let the awakening dawn, adjudging him the master of high seas. He trounced such benchmarks with great effort, raising the bar for a sudden high of understanding and reaching a crescendo never seen or heard. It was calmly put down by experts including Rick as something they had always known.

The University exams started in a hurry and the first few days were spent in getting to know the new environment. There was a huge gate at the entrance of the college. The exam room was at the top floor where one had to rush through damp stares at the call of the bell. Students had to stand in line for checking, holding bare essentials sniffed randomly by the police force. There were corridors of wait and aimless banter by the affirmative who rued over not enforcing a dot after every answer. Robin spent a lot of time at the corridor, sitting on the stairs, going over painstakingly written text to capture the inimical. He passively watched students cluttering up the corridors, their mindless cackle and their jocular disposition. There were friends together in the toughest of times or just to walk past the afternoon levied on them. Robin was prepared enough to answer bread and butter questions that sought simple definitions and behaviour. He organized diagrams that fit the asset of a school boy but rued the ones that waited on him with esoteric dimension. His picky hands poured out an abstraction as an answer on the sheet for the tough ones, holding his forehead in ignorance and walking home an incomplete man. The ones appearing for the fourth or fifth occasion at the exams seemed perplexed for most, chewing the pen, their grown up limbs feeling the pinch in suffocating space. Their pens lost their way, hanging in the air long before the final bell. They had heard those bells many times and it didn't bother them at all, carefully considering an investment in real estate and the like. Each passing year brought new responsibilities and commitments with limited time for adamant pages of the book. They were like guests no one knew and they walked their own isolation to their allotted seats. They pushed the flap of the cap backwards each time the cold wind blew and pressed their lips in subjugation. They were like a drying well where one can hardly see ones reflection when getting pass marks was as easy as writing ones name. They were the talk of the town although the regular ones never came near them to holler a token of friendship or seek advice for the future in the most trying times.

Robin tossed and turned in his bed at night putting together an answer the way it ought to have been in his mind. The laws and assumptions were burning in his mind. With sleepy eyes he got up each morning with ubiquitous lines of stifling text books on his mind. He missed the kindliness of a warm fire. By the time realization dawned that he had to appear at an exam later in the day, he was alive and daring to paint a picture with articulate hands. 'R' man aptly called it a miracle.

'R' man rued over his hands, contemptuous and indiscriminate, haywire at ill-treating the brave Robin. He knew that Robin was now walking on his own and jutting out with emotion and gestures. The body had recuperated to a normal pulse and heart beat but the way he had flayed his body, this was indeed a miracle. He was on the verge of graduating. The two together would call the popcorn man, or taste the spicy concoction made of puffed rice and lemon tossed into the air unconditionally making a perfect day. The afternoons after exams smelt of the aberrations, ruing over points remembered in the aftermath. There were meted out lines that were meant to be somewhere else. For all these ills he softly touched his forehead with cupped palms. He whacked his head softly with his fingers and smiled at the tug of war in his stimulus mind. Sometimes he could feel the breeze after rain, when manipulating and manoeuvring was an arduous task and he scripted the prefect reply. He looked pensively at horse drawn carriages for inspiration. He had some dues to clear speaking to the trees as they uttered their songs in the voices of birds. They swayed, offering their longing arms of togetherness. He had some words for those desolate streets around his house in which he walked alone, singing to their pungent ears. He knew that he always had the roads to fall back on when there was no place left to go.

It was his last exam and he rejoiced on the streets, nonsensical at times. He was sometimes desperate for the missing lines and mistakes that could have been avoided. He joined hands in prayer at a temple with no uttered words or wishes and offered a flower in devotion to the Lord, turned back and went away like he had no more to say or imply.

The last one was a piece of cake and he would rather enjoy the happy homecoming than rue over mistakes. He felt empty somewhere deep inside in the dark shadows of blue that crossed his desk. He felt there was room for more. Had he not turned off the light so soon in those quiet nights and dug into a few more lessons, he would have had more to say. There were many who left the exam hall pretty early. They were getting ready for the party and celebrations but Robin hung on until the bell made the final call to disperse. It was a near empty room with the invigilator standing next to Robin, hands on his hips, waiting for him to give up and follow the crowd. Robin soon handed over his answer sheet. He had surely heard some butterfly swing its gleeful wings with streaks of black in beige on flowers of nectar. He smiled at the old man selling guava that squatted each day with offerings of red and green coated with salt. He wanted to bathe in the holy Ganges, brush the yellow oleander's in the confines of 'R' house until they traded their secret with the severe ground to kissing in a soft rhythm. He wanted to look like himself before the mirror decided to distort his image. He wanted to pray to the Emblica tree in the courtyard planted by his grandfather. He wanted to hold it like a rock in his mouth until the sour turned to sweet in fringes of childhood. Its round hard fruit could be blamed for the growing cricket frenzy among the boys, using them as cricket balls. Robin discovered a new meaning to life in the interim.

It made sense to him feeling the warm hold of tea on the lips in the morning, writhing his hands after a shock that perished in haste. This was life as it will be and he rejuvenated in its experiences. He flinched from pain no more in a world his own, marred by illusions and delusions. His eyes went to Rick who was waiting to hear from him.

'R' man was as happy as could be. He broke the silence of the wind glistening in a thoughtful moment through the pages of an intriguing plot of the evening novel,

"Say ol' chap, come sit Robi, so you've conquered 'em all. This is graduation, the bit that I have been talking about all these years. Now you can take a step back, relax and see how the bees daub themselves with pollen and polish the flowers as they buzz around with all their might. Haven't you seen those caterpillars lately, ones you had in your shoebox when you were young, hiding in their skins and trudging up mountains only to open their wings and fly away to places they know. Get me a pen and writing paper, I see a picture emerging of courage and triumph of a boy caught in web of an indifferent world and how he miraculously traced his way back home to curious gazes at life and its many colours. No son, you really don't have an idea what life is all about. You are just too young and I do want you singing in the perfect melody. Get a job like polished people do and lend some lines to the symphony of lofty words as a hobby. I will find you a girl. So let's move.

We owe one to Rick. Why don't you come along and we'll just look him up."

The persistent river tossed its thick waves munching away in eddies. The oarsman far into the depths of the river was a tiny dot churning the waves and singing his tune that could not be heard. The college was silent with the irregular sounds of hammering, sawing in the distance. Bholu was the first survivor that Robin shook hands with after the great storm. Robin somehow thought that the University exam was the final event in all eternity and that the world would end after it. Trees would lose their dazzle, squirrels would go nuts and jump into the river, brooks would lose their shine and rivers would swell after the exams. Months had passed in anticipation of the final exams and every grain of sand, whiff of breeze, abstract pattern of clouds in distant skies had a story to tell. They foreboded that the exam day would probably never appear and if at all it did, no one would see its end.

Lo and behold it did and there was a huge relief among the boys. They caught up with lost sleep, rejuvenating their bodies with lost nourishment and care in the last few months and planning holidays far away into isolation.

Rick was happy to see 'R' man and family. He missed his family and wanted to be with them and tell them how he kept awake late into nights when it was hard to keep eyes open. He had won the battle setting his own standards. He stood at the brink of a possible distinction while Robin would be lucky enough to get past first class. He greeted 'R' man and Robin and made room on his cluttered bed for them to sit.

"Say ol' chap, we were in the neighbourhood and wanted to look you up. Both of you guys have done very well in a short period. You have my blessings and trust me this chapter is over and you are never going to hear about it ever again. You are now free to do whatever you may have desired to do. Isn't it a nasty pre-requisite to practically all jobs in the world?

Don't despair and think about the result and your future, life brings moments of speculation and one is forced to think of what will be. But hey, this is a tiny speck of your life, albeit crucial and it certainly doesn't matter if you score a little less. On that note why don't you come with me to the Officer's canteen if there's anything you need?"

'R' man assured the boys.

"Uncle, is it possible to have a pair of boots? These old ones that I have are torn and its nails hurt my foot when I walk" Rick asked for something hesitantly.

"Let's not wait ol' chap. Get on the scooter and Robi why don't you find your way home while I take him to the shoe centre in the Army camp. Ride on. Why did we wait so long, you should have come around earlier?"

They were the best pair of shoes in the rambling town, soft on the inside and hard and sturdy on the outside. There was a fine dividing line near the toe just like the Army men wore in the heat of duty. He bet the sleeping squirrels woke up from their nap closing their eyes for moments in an undisclosed shade of the tree. The glistening crows stepped back to utter hungrily in harsh decibels. The ants just danced away in parade when the sleeping giant appeared on the streets with loud knocking sounds. Its formidable appearance turned everything blue in delirium.

And the shoes would last for many seasons with little or no care. It would pompously stamp its name after a flirtatious shine on its tough surface. Just like the Army men, soft and kind, decent yet strong and unrelenting to enemy pressure, the shoes didn't have a lot of shine. Passing down the streets Rick would often stop to check its zipper and walked with grace. The thick leather didn't give in to the cold winds and its surface shimmered in the light ever so delicately. Rodents, ants and other creatures under the sun kept away from the pair, obeying a sense of awe and wonder. The trampled dry leaves that let out a deafening shriek when the king of the road walked all over them. Distant ears could project its arrival in rhythmic and striving beats as the sound of friction deepened to reach a peak.

'R' man had worn similar shoes in a parade marching before a distinguished audience. Rick wore a different pair of shoes when it rained heavily to avoid the dirt and slush which could ruin the texture of the boots and scar its surface for good. Then there came a time when the earth was dry, Bholu repeatedly transferred tea across two tumblers, and Rick pressed on his boots to meet the world. They were a jewel in the master's eye. Rick rubbed his nose across its leather and spent hours shining it and removing the debris of a conspiring world. It was being prepared for a long journey ahead when it might be forsaken for urgent matters clouding the mind or when it starts disintegrating with age. But right now it was the only thing that mattered. It made Rick feel special, far above the ordinary like a king in a walk each morning to meet his subjects. His friends, looking for reasons to break into laughter, would give a patient ear to the sound of footsteps. Rick's boots was their only target. Rick enjoyed such talk among friends only to the point when sarcasm stepped in. On such occasions he quietly left the crowd and saved the shoes from malicious intent.

The only thought on his mind besides his new pair of shoes was the University Exam results. Robin was hoping that he had done enough to earn passing marks and if the wind and the earth were on his side, a first class would not be impossible. Robin didn't know how he had performed, given the blank spaces in his exams when he could not produce the answers. He would be proud enough to pass the exams. He remembered the time when he was so sick and weak that he couldn't find his way to college. He couldn't understand darkness and why it fell in the first place. His books got stiffer from neglect attacked by moss and there was no one to flip its pages.

But now he had changed and being normal was not an illusion anymore. He could prepare for any exam adequately, sing a song in the evening with decreasing intensity lest someone heard him.

The college results were finally declared. Robin was all excited that day. In a pink shirt he drove with 'R' man on his scooter to the college premises. On his way he stopped at the temple on 'R' man's request. 'R' man was happy indeed with the turn of events and the happiness that Robin had found in his struggle to bring sense to his existence. 'R' man asked for strength for Robin to accept his results just like they were even if it were to make him a trifle dissatisfied.

The clerk was all muddled up with exam results crowded by students waiting to hear from him. He took a long time to pull out Robin's result and once he did, he hands went out to accept any kindness from Robin for showing him the results. Robin quickly passed on some cash and there it was in bold letters. Robin had secured a second class and the final tally showed that he had missed first class by a whisker. Had he not turned out the lights so soon that night and struggled with the theorems and laws a little more, he would have easily crossed the first class mark. In all sincerity he believed that he should have been awarded grace marks. Concentration only lasts so long in exam environment. It doesn't take long to be lost and be one with the noise that may appear to be insignificant with the nature peeping through windows that hardly ceases. 'R' man was overjoyed and remembered the time when he was called by the class teacher at school to collect Robin's result and the happiness it gave him to see Robin pass another exam. The scooter on which he rode had changed and also the bleak fact that they were now civilians. For the first time in his life Robin had secured a second class in his exams.

'R' man was moved to tears and he was happy to see Robin clear the final hurdle in his life with flying colours.

"Say ol' chap. That's a miracle, I dare say. Who would have thought that you would finally get on with life? After all, your condition was critical and you had totally lost touch with college and books. Yet to come home with passing marks and making it as an engineer is quite unbelievable. Hats off to your effort and determination to pull off a seemingly impossible task in an extremely short period. Man, you need a break and rest those brains. Yes, you have graduated and now you can colour the world the way you like." 'R' man closed his eyes in solemn prayer. After all, the lag in Robin's college studies had been overcome to a large extent. He was just as adept as any other engineer given the burst at the last hour. This explained the purpose and secret behind engineering studies to almost its entirety. The days Robin spent in this college, harsh, apathetic yet balming were forever in his memory. He felt nostalgic sometimes

thinking about those times when he roamed those corridors looking for a purpose. This was the first place that gave him a taste of failure pushing him to work even harder. The old friends whom he trusted and depended on left him with a sense of pity for Robin. They didn't want to walk the same road as that of a failure. He too left them after a while with a dose of the new ones in Rick and the extended family of friends. Yet he had some memories. He remembered Bholu's warm cup, the old lady's persistent smile, tossing squirrels earnestly looking for some clues to the hidden treasure and mother Ganges with no ebbs in its eternal flow. Time had come for rest and rejuvenation. He let music fill his ears and novels be the order of the day. 'R' house was truly blessed and for once the members were happy in the morning bliss and watched the pensive evening birds return to their nests. Life was beautiful in the sunsets with the sights and sounds of the nature filling up senses. The crisp walk down the deserted road didn't make Robin feel forlorn as its serenity and divergence to a place unknown made him feel excited and peaceful. Robin now looked for a change of place and environment with some new friends.

It was a sad send off. The old gardener had developed a liking for Robin and his resolve to stand up on his own each time he fell on his knees. He cried a silent tear that morning on hearing about Robin's decision to leave the city in search of a job.

There were times when Robin locked himself in his room, not wanting to hear from anyone. It was the old gardener that coaxed Robin out of the locked room and taste the pudding of the day. Robin easily refused 'R' man in all his pleadings and urges to leave the windows and doors open for fresh air and light to seek his room. He wouldn't allow them to touch him and talk to him. The old gardener remembered the time when Robin walked out of his room and helped him fix the cacti in sand. Robin loved watering the coleus watching rows of its coloured leaves shine in the cold water and look fresh like morning blue skies. He even recalled the time when Robin bought a slate and chalk for him for teaching him the alphabet although it didn't last for long. He recalled cutting across the main field one evening on his way to work to watch Robin running round in laps. Robin sank low in his panting and sweating while others were lost in frivolity and a lack of depth. He remembered his own youth when he dictated speed to the passing wind, running for strength and blessings from above with no room for complacency. The old gardener pulled his gear over his face and looked blankly at the skies, sad at Robin's decision and the danger of losing his laughter forever. Robin's remarks often made him wonder and astonished at the purity of thoughts and intentions to go miles in pursuit of hidden code. 'R' man would be pushed into loneliness once again and there would no visits to Robin's room to exchange notes. There would not reason to be angry or assure Robin that he was half way through the process of finding a girl for him. The afternoon would be spent staring at the walls when the eyes would not be heavy enough for a sound nap. There would be nobody to jump in excitement at discovering something new and run up to his bedside to let out the new idea. No one would make him a hot cup of tea in the evening when eyes barely opened after the afternoon nap. There was no one to express his point of view to on a laid back evening and polish his own views of the economy and government. Yet he couldn't help push Robin out of the nest for greater destinations, getting a job of choice in the city and most of all getting closer to sending him to the USA. He didn't know how he would accomplish the latter yet his faith would see him circling his bed with joined hands in devotion. He sprinkled holy water on the Gita each morning and prayed to Sai Baba hopeful in a spread of the boys to correct his failures. Reuben had already reached the preferred destination for a higher degree and it was up to the Lord to help Robin on his way to America. 'R' man was saddened within to see the big old house deserted and once caught up with job and the like there was no way that the boys were ever going to return. They may have to come for marriage but even that was not certain if they were stationed in a different country. He felt his end was near, incarcerated and forlorn all over again and waiting patiently for the voice above to appear and take him away, far away. Yet he still felt he had to hold himself until Robin, with a stormy past, a difficult child living on doses for sanity, found his way to distant shores. He wanted to live and help Robin find his way and wanted him to grow in strength and vigour standing taller than the rest. Robin searched for companies that sent its employees abroad for training purposes. Usually a company sent its employees for training only after the employee completed a certain term at the company and even after that sending the employee abroad was very bleak. Yet that was the software era when people were being sent in large numbers for training or other purposes. He started working at a software company with crammed rooms that could ill afford to have another employee. He was in the training period and would become a regular employee very soon. In a small room packed with trainees he learnt the basics of computer technology and how it had evolved and continuously changed over the years. He swore he heard the clock race past the leaving time each day when he felt the excitement of going home, carefully putting forward his deduction to discerning ears. Then he would race home and find a quiet corner on the way to absorb the twilight and awakening night life of the city. Sitting beside a peaceful flickering lamp he could see the natural fading light blend with it to produce a hue soothing to the senses. He lived indeed for such moments after he spent quiet moments of struggle within the office during the day. He tried to keep up with his reputation and obeying orders to their entirety like he had always done throughout his life. Very soon he purchased his own silvery motorbike. The city now was in the palm of his hands. He could address any corner however deep and distant it may be with a slight push of the accelerator. He learnt how to manipulate the foot gear at top speed. Also when in the middle of stifling traffic in an effort to skip his way to safety before being allowed an easy ride without obstructions. The engine worked like magic, hardly making any sound even when on the run. It was different from the scooter that he had driven looking for reasons to emit black smoke and make a noise too harsh to hear. He kept a close watch on his motorbike. He didn't let flakes of dust settle on its steel body and hid a clean shining cloth within its crevices for a coat of shine on its body. Robin was a careful driver, letting the fast and the furious go past him even if hard pressed for time. He never circled around thick traffic as in a circus like bikers often did on a red light in order to get ahead and stand next to the traffic signal. He would rather stand in queue behind a line of cars or motorbikes and wait for the heavy traffic before him to move on a green signal. He drove it just like the scooter, slowly and carefully, perhaps not the way bikes should be ridden, where the push to the bike by a sensitive accelerator is put to maximum use. Robin recollected his tedious bus rides when he had to wake up early to get on to the right bus and see it stop too frequently on the way. The paper tickets were a nuisance. One had to cut through the crowd, stolen and harassed on the way. It would take some time to reach the very end seat where the conductor would be seated, tidying his moustache or counting folded cash jutting out his fingers. And when the brakes were applied, people fell on each other like they were helpless. The ladies were the worst sufferers who couldn't even complain for someone falling on them indiscriminately. The seats were occupied quickly and there were more people standing holding bars and supports. One was closer to sitting on a seat being a lady than a young boy who seemed like the ostracized lot, too strong to sit and too weak to have his own palace on wheels. It took the bus forever to move and it invariably tilted slightly under the load appearing to capsize any moment. It was far from a jolly ride with the sweat and grime where the destination looked like impossibility. People were stranded in close proximity, each one desperately trying to avoid others gaze.

Robin rode those tight buses many times and sometimes was late to reach the exit gate when the bus stopped at his destination. He was always among the standing as he got up for the ladies even if he found a seat. He strongly felt that one should avoid the buses and look for alternatives. Yet many preferred the form of transport because it was cheap and sounded more sensible for extremely far off locations. Now Robin could overtake a bus, to find crushed people within fighting for space. He forgot about the times when he was among them still not sure of how to get a ticket. He wanted to call 'R' man for a visit to the city. He would like the place and get a break from the peaceful confines of 'R'. It had haunted him on cold nights when he tried to break into the rhythm of sleep. 'R' man never failed to remind Robin of the dream he had and that he should look around him for the appropriate call for a sojourn to the US. 'R' man was pleased about his present job and new motorbike and promised to go for a ride when he visited the city.

'R' man toured around the city on his scooter with a wobbly helmet earning small amounts in odd projects that exploited his expertise in a variety of areas. There were many who offered him full time positions given his balance and command over the subject and the English language. Yet he refused tonnes of such offers sailing on the wings of an eagle, wanting his freedom dearly when he was far off from the busy times of early adulthood. Besides, his thinking mind was constantly evolving new ways for a progressive nation that was somehow trampled beneath the wheels of bureaucracy. He didn't feel like going too deep into newspapers or novels and wished Robin could find a company of his dreams. Search was on by all concerned and Robin sometimes wished he could fly away from the silent torture of computer jargons that somehow failed to become the common language. It left one wondering for their precise meaning for long, and when the trainees would be directed to move ahead, irrespective of their grasp, because of lack of time. Yet it felt nice when passing moment reached its zenith in a coffee break, break for lunch and most of all when the day ended. He swore he had seen some ladies at work, but all were lost and hardly visible during the day to even think of getting close. It was mainly a boy's only show and the few girls that stepped in were lost in the crowd with their feather weight hardly occupying any space in the office premises. He did admit that he was learning new things and the very basic computer technology that would not change for many years to come.

Robin was getting close to a permanent position. He had completed a few months and was slowly becoming an expert in matters that once felt alien and too much to comprehend. He could now think of earning and make his parents feel proud.

On a usual day when Robin was enjoying his coffee break, one of his friends informed him about this company called Sofrek India Pvt. Ltd. that planned to send its trainees to the US for higher training. 'R' man heard about this company at just about the same time as if by telepathy and called Robin that evening to deliver the exciting news.

"Say ol' chap, did you hear. It's our dream and you must go after it with full strength. There is a bleak chance although I haven't heard about the company at all. I think they are brand new and what an attractive proposition to have to start with. Don't waste time Robi, put on your best when you go to meet them tomorrow and don't forget to show them your degree in engineering" 'R' man had seen many such situations in life when opportunity beckoned at his doorstep. He was certain that Robin would finally find his way to the land of plenty. He was a man who kept to himself and would decisively point to the unfinished work to Robin and Reuben when they held their nerves asking him about his past life. His father knew quite a lot about him, in fact more than anybody knew about him. Yet there were things that happened 'R' man after he joined the defence forces that only he knew. He never shared with anyone never denying rumours that he was marooned and sick once to the point of no return. Yet he kept those thoughts hidden deep within himself and never disclosed it to the mirror. He would let the light fall on him blinding him to a squint and soon enter a new world. But that was yet to happen and there were things left for 'R' man to take care of. There was a cacophony of apathetic horns ceaselessly irritating the senses from bicycles, scooters and four wheelers in a city. The city was prone to street violence and he was never safe until his scooter turned the final bend on the quiet lane beside his house. Yet the entire family needed him and Robin sometimes wished he could leave all his concerns and obligations and sit next

to him all the time. Robin was sacred of the thought of losing him and couldn't believe his eyes sometimes to still have him by his side. With 'R' man, Robin had known love for the first time in his life and in spite of all the apparent differences they were one family with members who genuinely cared for each other. The way he rushed with fruits and goodies after a bout of violence and torture, moving the rest of the family to tears, was something that 'R' man had perfected. 'R' man even went to the extent of calling himself the most despicable person that could ever be, who had spoiled the evening and entangled the rhythm of a normal existence. Yet this violence and hatred had never ceased in so many years even though its frequency had dwindled. He couldn't hold back his anger resulting in astronomical blood pressure. In such a case it was important for him to rest and stay calm and breathe normally. He was advised to avoid bouts of uncontrolled panic when things got out of hand in an erratic world. He was asked to avoid salt in his salad and space his talk with deep breaths. Robin sometimes suggested a rush of green vegetables for better health and to practice Yoga first thing in the morning. Yet it didn't go beyond bringing a smile and false assurance that he was already in it.

Robin took the taxi the other day flashing past unseen parts of the city and carrying his qualification and achievements in a file, pressed close to his body. He would somehow convince them and plead for a position if at the end they decide not to hire him. He had a hard time figuring out the location of their office and the coiling streets and buildings hardly spoke of the company's name. He was about to give up when this stranger hinted at the location and it turned out that Robin had already crossed that street and building several times yet didn't know where to look. Robin reached the office exhausted and anticipated a soft interview before the offer. It was late in the afternoon and Robin didn't want any trouble in deciding his fate helping himself with water to stay alive. Finally he was called in and it was as if he was ready to face any eventuality and circumstance and ardently press for an opportunity. He had been trained by 'R' man to be tough like a military man making him win any battle and never rattle a nerve even in the face of humiliation or a rush of disparaging words. They were to test him in a short exam where the questions had a taste of what Robin had studied in a course after college exams. He just had to push his brains a little for a picture of the logic he had already known in his mind. Robin forgot about his discomfort for a while and let the evening roam with its shadow forgetting about time and how he could miss his favourite pastime at this time of the day. There were many questions that were beyond him and it was very much the story of his life. He had tasted denial in all too many ways and failure was just a way of life. He wished he could take his mind off this sudden sadness and follow his senses. His results were not satisfactory as expected and he found his way back to his silvery motorbike, job and sudden desire to stop by for a warm cup of tea. He never called 'R' man and couldn't get over the cloud of sadness and helplessness. His enthusiasm and desire to make a life by learning new things by focus suffered a setback and the girl with a purple dress and an attractive hairdo didn't matter to him. His friends heard about the sad tale and couldn't breathe life into him by their frivolity and silly jokes. They knew that Robin could not catch the wave of laughter and slackening of tension with nonsensical humour like he used to, fresh out of a setback ruining his life's plan.

"There will be more to follow, Robi. Say ol' chap this one gone a begging. Why don't you tie your shoes laces and enjoy the moment. I want you to buy something exciting with the money I am about to send. How about that I-Pod you are so keen on. And forget about the rest. With your effort you will find more opportunities. C'mon son you can do better. There are plenty of fishes in the sea. Really son, please be happy, I am running out of time. I love you very much and you are the reason why I fight this world" 'R' man held him close.

Robin let the noise cease him. He carelessly kicked his bike with a firm whip of the legs, nudged the bike through tight corners he should have avoided. He blew the horn as if to summon the traffic, flying past them in a dazzle. He acted brave with his friends, looked into their eyes when his grammar seemed odd and new. He mellowed in a quiet humour that took time to sink in and a gait portraying a strong self image ready to flip the world with his hands. All was normal and Robin looked at the bigger picture when going to the US seemed rather small and trivial. It could be accomplished any time in the future and there was no need to despair if a plan failed. He instead was worried about his father's health and couldn't understand why he talked of the end which was due someday anyhow. 'R' man had only done good things for his entire family, being the eldest and never received anything, not even a word of love from anyone. He was bound to be upset and his story of self sacrifice went back to a time when he lost his mother at a tender age. He almost drowned in the river trying to save someone from the strong currents, the loss of a dear one playing on his mind. He searched from pillar to post for the love of a mother but found none and there was no one he could cry before or find someone who would accept him unconditionally. His heart was broken at times and he found a way to let off his grief by banging his head on the wall. There was no one to disclose his plans to and how his relatives sometimes would not let him live in peace. He found a way out in uncontrolled rage to deal with conflicting issues and it had driven his whole family to their knees for a piece of undefined and quiet earth. There was so much pent-up anger and disgust in him that was let out to his near and dear ones. With the passage of time his violent spurts reduced in their intensity and number as he slowly drifted to his books. He let the children breathe in peace and come to him for precious advice with no fear or hesitation,

"By Golly, Say ol' chap, if I were your age, late twenties and early thirties, I would have conquered the world. Now these grey locks, panting after little exertion have tied me down and no one needs old hands that lack the agility, if not the skill. Walk into the office of the CEO of that multibillionaire and multinational company and say that you have plan. Work with him and explain to him he couldn't afford not to have you. I wish somebody could put me in my prime once again. I

would have tossed those high aficionados like peanuts on a high noon with a nip of salt on the tip of the tongue. Jolly good, carry on son you will have your chances so just jostle along the crass, dandy" 'R' man wished for a lot more.

The phone rang and Robin was in the middle of a training class late into the evening. He immediately hung up and slipped the mobile into his front pocket acting as if it had never rung in the first place. It rang again and the polite instructor asked him to step out of the class and receive it, after all it could be important.

"Mr Robin, this is Immanuel from Sofrek India Pvt. Ltd. Thank you for speaking to us. We have scheduled another test for you at the same location. Kindly reach our office by five in the evening tomorrow and we are most happy to have you. Thank you once again for receiving our call and we are most fortunate to have you as a most deserving candidate. Please do ask any question that comes to your mind. Good bye and we'll see you at the office." He returned in undecided footsteps with no notion of whether to fly in the air or hear the folks in tacit approval. He couldn't handle the moment and walked the desolate corners of his office, hands possibly holding his bag, past the purple lady with a tossing bun of hair hanging on her back. There were no hollers to dissipate his angst, his eyes of stone never blinked as he headed for the reminiscing corner by the tea stall. He sat on the bench trying to recollect the words that seemed to understand his ability and value for the first time albeit hidden beneath business protocol. For the first time he was nudged with a tea cup, instead of his lunge for it, and its heat blew his fingers in disarray trying to tame it. He called up his father as the first one to whom he would disclose the sudden rainbow in his cloistered horizon.

"Greetings Pa. Sofrek has called me for another test tomorrow. Chances of getting hired look good. It looks as though they are keen on hiring me. My degree has helped me for the first time. There was a time when I was sick and all looked impossible. But thanks to you and your timely interference in setting things right at the college, I could attain a degree and I promise you getting a job would not be difficult for the rest of my life. How is Da? I haven't talked to him for quite a while. Please

take care of yourself and God indeed has a plan"

"Wo-h what good news. *You have made it like I always thought. My experience tells me that they have already hired you or else they would never have called you. Say ol' chap you have done it. Remember in life always think 'what next?' If one plans fails think 'what next'? That way you'll never run out if ideas. Well done, my blessings and love. Carry on"* 'R' man was ecstatic. That day 'R' man found out a reason to rummage his cluttered room. He dispensed with all unwanted paper and letters from friends and colleagues at the forces that once sang of promise and togetherness for a lifetime. He glistened his bedside with his favourite books after getting rid of the impurities and the accolades that once made him feel like a true officer and now sounded spurious. He became the man of the moment and his room was a pool of tatters, letters that once iambically moved his lips, drew him closer to himself had been destroyed. And now he was lonely as he silently toed his slippers in a walk up to the living room or his study. He was sick of hearing the same words in his letters and would sometimes dull the ink by sprinkling holy water on them after every prayer. He could hardly remember where he had been or the turn of events that morphed him into mellow grey. His being was meant for the hard sun, torture to black soot and a torrid frustration that hit him like stones on the bare chest. It was not a surprise then that he was the most talked about officer in the forces, as he nonchalantly mingled with the chiefs in a party and excused him for being so brazen and downright honest. His seniors would rather hold a double face encumbered by the high office. However his chiefs were impressed the most and wanted the truth. He had words to say at any gathering be it a birthday of a friend's child, or a group of ladies at a party blurring the idea of a male chauvinist. He would invariably reach a high. He got home too early in the day when he was asked by all concerned to serve for the family and kids but he was instead glad to reach the minimum age of retirement. It haunted him in the vicious streets of civilian life when his children found it hard to talk the talk and squalor and stench of dead animals, left untouched, and played on their minds. In a state of paradox he convinced all that retirement was all for the general good. The drainage malfunctioned, gutter poured onto condemned streets, softening the soil. Pondering creatures sprang up, thick with black muck, fattened over years of being overfed in seclusion and now forced to blink at the new world out of their hide outs. There were dumping pits at almost all street corners where house maids covered their mouth and nose for the overpowering stench and dumped garbage hastily before running for cover and a safe smell. Besides there were other reasons that would have surely piqued 'R' man and made him change his decision. The lawless thugs carried arms hidden somewhere within them waited to be irked by all and sundry and pumped a few indiscriminately. How could he hold his children from meeting the ghastly world, tormented minds that sought blood. The family was glad to be way past the preliminaries and now carried minds that were used to the filth and stench and spread all over the city without a wobbly nose. The ghost of Caesar was nowhere in sight and the family smirked at the friendly murders in the neighbourhood that was not enough to undo 'R' man's pleasant siesta. There were processions with gala crowd atop busses and cars singing in a street rhythm striking cymbals and in communion with the mud, slush and squalor around and the dank tops. The ladies even broke into a dance without a care for the glancing crowd. The years spend in childhood with those familiar streets, shops and dumping grounds evoked nostalgia for young Robin. He yearned for a taste of the city lost in the penchant to drive his way forward in cramped corners. The big city had all the jobs and opportunities and the punitive exodus began a long time ago from the gates of the deferred city. It left behind retired folks like 'R' man and marginal businessmen whose wares were not displayed on national television. This was the sad tale of broken homes, separating fathers and mothers from sons and daughters, in a place where days perished in thought and hands and feet fought for a reason to be kept busy. However there were plenty of courses offered in the forsaken city that could keep someone busy for a while just like in the case of Robin. Yet their culmination threw a world of questions and the clever and the bold took a decisive step in the right direction. Staying put in the old city seemingly failed to add to their repertoire. It unnecessarily stalled their progress when they could easily be an apprentice in a trying company and sow the seeds of grandeur and achievement when they would hold high office. The old city in its wavered cosmology never thought of resurrecting an ambience for the chic and urbane. Its streets were still lost in swinging heads of bullocks driving carts of men and bulbous loads too hard to carry. The language that seeped in through the villages and those narrow congested and borrowed lanes captured with dwellings and pool of slush, grime that made living a sin. No wonder the city had lost its sons and daughters to far off places. They were sometimes misled by the glitter and false hope of riches that never seemed in their hold and they saved their pennies for some tea and left their worries behind. Yet the conditions of living were far better and never lost hope for potential success if they held on for long enough.

The same questions appeared in the exam the next day. Robin submerged deep into them battling out the mystery to the point when his answers sounded sweet and whole. It was strange that the same problem that once seemed irrevocably invincible now was the rabbit off the hat of a magician like a prank played on the mind. He had gone too far into certainty and it was like the company was desperate to have him and played a little game of peek-a-boo. They would call him again until he could get over the suspense. These moments were far too few when he could crawl out of his naiveté and give a winning blow at an exam. He could now handle questions that sometimes incited random breath and uncalled for sensations when he would annoyingly beat around the bush. It happened at the University exams so many times and especially at competitive exams that he appeared at in plenty when he realized the futility of digging too deep when there were no answers. One exam to remember was the one that got him into the engineering college when he could answer almost all questions like his lips in a déjà vu read the questions before their completion. He knew where to turn, unlike him, carried out a lot of calculations on his mind and like school children painted the question paper in huge block letters screaming with formulas and complex multiplications. He was ranked among the best, a perfect fitting to the hard work in school when he almost lost his eyes. His teacher, then, was a bundle of bad words with the ill advice that his mediocrity would put him out of the picture in future endeavours and make him suffer like hell. Miss Grover had been a spinster in all her working years and the boys joined in a soft banter of how her fat posterior had driven away all the eligible bachelors of the town. She failed to touch her toe even though she tried while standing with straight legs each night. She further explicated her own disclaimer that she would rather revel as a bachelorette all her life than to be tied down in servility and be at the mercy of masculinity. She had a hardened exterior too uptight and rigorous in how she dealt with students and parents in PTA meetings. Very few knew if she had a softer side encumbered by the sounds of unknown people and the impending duty in her stern voice that travelled far. She probably teased and used common folk language in staff rooms turning into a harried and coaxed young girl who sought attention and let out feminine sounds in earnest, wanting to be that girl of college days all over again. She weaned until someone twisted her ears and sealed her lips all over again and be heard in soft dabs on her forehead by pressing fingers. She wanted someone to hear her in her whimpers lugging through a dull day. The lethargic questions that her students asked her ready to outwit her yet could never challenge her command over subject matter. After all she worked at her subject after school hours loaded with matter way beyond the years of the school children who perhaps could never muster an eluding question. The students affirmatively tossed their brains, scratched their heads with a sumptuous dose of Science to come up with a tricky and an out of the box question not too obvious. It was as if Ms. Grover had been waiting for the rogue and set matters right in a jiffy with sweet lips. She was good at her trade, enjoyed principal's keen eye on her loading her with perks and fresh batches and even gave her own cubicle. She was an instant hit with the students, boisterous and vibrant connoting in crisp and perfect English, speaking in intervals for easy assimilation and even pulling a lighter one off her joke book. Many thought she was too good for Science and perhaps English would tip over the scale for the perfect balance. Yet she followed her first love and would often shake her head after a perfect day that there was absolutely nothing wrong with her life and that things were meant to be this way. She sometimes forgot about how the pliable chair seat got dented under her weight and how she sometimes found it hard to fit in a car seat. She could run for miles with her mind or her foot and not find an answer to her overpowering weight. The fat would hold still over her body and spoke in voices of carnage when the gigantic mass wobbled when she walked or when she shook the amassment for pleasure. She was losing her hair on her head; her lips couldn't carry the sheen of lipstick for long. She often got tired climbing up stairs or when was hurriedly summoned at the Principal's office. She panted when the class was too demanding hurting her vocal cords, the chalk was getting too her and she squinted too soon trying to make sense of the black board. She had waited too long for her Mr. Right and wanted the rains to go by when she promised herself to finally be game to brute masculinity. She had saved enough for a rainy day and even promised to forgo her passion and dazzle the four walls for her beloved and family. She could teach her children to be the perfect students and how hard work seeks its own reward and one must be honest and truthful to a cause. She was proud to hold the senior section when boys are on the verge of becoming assertive men. Their questions of totality brought out a thirst for the potent force that could satiate their undying curiosity and the great desire to be a part of the whole on the fringe of the cosmos. She meant business, caressing the topic in stops and starts at the beginning. When the onslaught was too heavy for the average, her gaze shifted to the chosen few in the front benches, habitual toppers softly held by the palm on the back of their heads. She believed that Robin was average, was happy to point out his awkward cursive at the terminal exams. She ardently believed that mediocrity was the bane of modern society and one had only to feel the fit of the glove on the hand by putting a little effort to forge ahead and get ones due in life. Mediocrity as a culture was stagnating and sporadic. Education in the true sense is when these sharp kids racing ahead in time grip their pens to bring out the true meaning of books and studies and carve out career in the upper strata. She believed that one could be ordinary, yet foster the impeccable by sheer hard work. She stopped short of the back benches while in a class not wanting to spoil her mood with a glimpse of the average. Robin too deserved to be at the very top but somehow reclined to an average performance in the exams. 'R' man was a nervous wreck constantly losing temper and creating a havoc that inhibited natural growth and development. How could Robin decipher the complexities of mathematics, or elicit the silent imagination in science or recite verses in English when the 'R' house was constantly tense. 'R' man wanted to move out of the city yet couldn't convince 'R' lady and her resolve to stay put. When in a flow and totally submerged Robin silently turned his head to the violence and cacophony in the house repeating the words of the book that had almost melted in his mouth. It would take a big effort to re-establish lost flow and sometimes it never happened enforcing the label of ordinary grass. Robin could count the dew on the roses in his garden, doggedly check the flow of the stealing breeze by standing on its way, and climb on horses. He could walk for miles like in penury until his feet indemnified by converging into priesthood, be the grace of lips for ages in God's own desire. Yet he could never fathom the word that would embellish ruled paper in obnoxious exams, with total pandemonium in 'R' house. He had seen those toppers and their fathers, joyful and calm, allowing growth and development in thick and quiet. Their parents hardly lost temper and allowed their children to have a say in matters that allowed a shade of their interference. How could the flower blossom if someone constantly tampered with its bud? Reuben the quieter and defensive had seen blessed pathways elsewhere and never questioned authority while

Robin always played with fire. He was one with the glittering grey on 'R' man's head that was the result of Robin's own experiments on wisdom. The toppers at a very early age had a developed a sense of their self. Yet the children at the 'R' house struggled with the tone of their voice, stomped at uttering a harsh decibel and when sometimes trying to break free in an unconventional rhythm. The result was their quietness and a growing affinity to the wall in its wholesome void and stillness. It was like their natural flow of feelings in words had been checked and 'R' man often rued over his offerings in their younger days. He couldn't carry on with the same intensity prying over them when his strength had reached a plateau.

Yet he did have the premonition that his lads were the best. It transformed his effort in grooming them to the utmost, sometimes to watch his skin turn to black soot under the hard sun in the effort. He didn't endorse Robin's getting up late in the morning after he was done with his college exams. He often banged the door and grimaced to get the message through. Everyone tried to avoid 'R' man in his violent outpourings but not Robin who felt an unusual peace in his presence. Robin's absence had dragged 'R' man into loneliness and could only feel a touch of his presence through his letters. 'R' man's life had no reason; his days were spent softening his bones on his bed with the occasional newspaper, book or sleep in his hands. He had lost the purpose of his life long ago when the children sang their preamble in shorts in school and when he totally forgot the way his shirt was buttoned on his chest. He sometimes felt his family had tied him down when he could have driven his motorbike around the hills and far off places. He could have read the evening news and stopped by at the film studio with his script for a grand movie. Yet his flippant wishes disappeared when he saw his little children crying out for him and 'R' lady groping for words with the evening tea. Life had a meaning in their shining eyes and was the only reason for a strange way of showing love. There were torrid times that the family had to carry given his erratic loss of temper. He kept a golden ring under his pillow and wore it occasionally for the good of his little brothers and sisters.

They were little children when he got married who had hardly gotten used to their names and their identity. 'R' man held the first job in the Army among his siblings. He frequently roamed the country with his duffel bag on his square shoulders with barely enough money for snacks on the way. The death of his mother when he was a toddler had a seismic effect on his tender mind, morphing him into a stone. In medical terms he lost the balance, looking to weather the storm in his mind over little things he did not understand. His upbringing had thus been lop-sided looking for love of a mother who had gone too far. His children had not been denied a father and mother and the smiles in eyes with a sweet desire that greeted them each morning.

It didn't take long for the results to be out and Robin felt he had walked too far into certainty to be denied a place in the company. They had pushed Robin's paper into a bulbous stack falling off at the cliff into oblivion like his effort didn't matter anymore.

"Mr. Robin, you have been hired in our company, congratulations. We'll train you for a while before you leave for the USA for higher end training for a period of four months. Please join us next week and we are happy to have you with us, so long". The director summoned words that sounded scripted. It was a gamble, empires crumbled and priceless dreams ruined at the failure to procure visa. But that was stashed away for later and for the moment Robin couldn't help smiling even though it sounded rather absurd to the spectator. He never realized that he would make new friends as there were many who willingly bought the logic that the company indeed had tie up with an American university. He devotedly touched the cold floor of a nearby temple that evening and bowed his head. He was in thankful for a dream dreamt by him and 'R' man was truly on the brink of fulfilment. His urgent need didn't push him to ask for more than strength and protection from the Almighty like he always did. Yet his joined hands said it all in their prayer and he didn't need to mention the obvious. It was His wish that brought about a glimmer of opportunity in the first place. He felt that someday he would open his mouth and say what he truly wanted when life demanded

such a proclamation. For now he was pleased at being finally heard, anointed with vermilion paste on his forehead with fragments of rice grain to the sound of a bell perched on top of his head with basil leaves, crumpled and fragrant. His day would be spent at his favourite tea stall with crossed legs on his radiant motorbike with a tinge of sadness at quitting his current job. He had almost crossed over the gestation period for a permanent position. He called 'R' man to cheer him up and give his sad eyes a reason to rejoice and urge in ardent voices that America was not far away. 'R' man was ecstatic,

"Say ol' chap, didn't I say so. You were bound to make it. It's our land even though we are not its heirs, we were born there and I wonder where s it's been all our lives. We have been decidedly chasing it just like my brothers and sisters all over the world and some will never see it sit before their eyes. Do I sound too sombre for my soliloquy? I have wanted to get near Piccadilly street for some cakes and coffee, getting on the Greyhound around the cottage street, ruling out pancakes for some strudels from that Danish Bakery, a land so light with few people that you could blow it away with a mouthful of air. I surely like to sit beside the statue of liberty at dusk to see it mellow into a towering silhouette at twilight and count my dimes for a visit to the White House. There are so many places to go but I would ideally like you to join Reuben and stay with him when you get there. So long ol' chap I need a break, grief has struck once again amidst the rambling and I need space to breathe". 'R' man's mind was racing in thought though he was happy for Robin to finally find a reason and a promise to fly west. Robin calmly eschewed his triumphant emotions in the customary meeting with his aunt and uncle who lived in the city and extended their kind blessings for a brighter day. He was always a stranger to them and found it absurd to go beyond formal correcting posture when scripted pleasantries were entertained in a strenuous interlude. His eyes hardly met theirs and he roamed his insides for a reason to distract his eyes far away. Maybe to the unknown weather outside or the tiny dot of salt that had descended on his spotless trousers, or the exquisite architecture of the drawing room. He looked for

a reason to end their discussion. He made excuses of some urgent work in the area or the engine of his silver motorbike requiring an overhaul or sometimes as wayward as a visit to the local church. The end was always pushed to the extremities of darkness or a sudden build up of black clouds or when there was nothing else to say. Although Robin had a huge family of aunts, uncles, cousins and many that he had never known, he had kept way from them as per 'R' man's instructions and never been on talking terms with most of them. His relatives were not used to seeing him and often broke the silence when they met by voicing his identity umpteen times as 'R' man's son, like they had never known it before and sometimes even found it humorous.

"Like he is the son, is that right? Lord blessed us for this day, for it is fulfilled, I don't need the toast of that kitty party tonight. That was a good one though" his aunt was surfeit with pleasure. Robin and Reuben were not quite popular among kindred folks. After a certain age lost their goodwill and admiration of being the sons of such an illustrious, flamboyant and charismatic father. They were just too mild, donning a frail and lifeless exterior and who had not matured with the passing years. It was as if their growth was stunted and the metamorphosis into young men was hindered. They were speechless wonders and couldn't hold the crowd in awe and delight with their keen diction like 'R' man. They would allow themselves to be flanked on all sides with varied and distant adlibs. When their turn arrived they would push the word with great effort out of their mouth and be ignored. It was not emotion or the apt intonation that could make them worthy sons but more often a slip of the tongue that would be rued over by them the entire night. Even their frequent smiles seemed inappropriate as if they were just trying to pay their dues and widened them to the extent of appearing to be a normal conversation. Then they would suddenly be silent and furtively slip into the abstruse and appear rather scholarly and pensive over the state of affairs of the world itself. 'R' man was a darling with the crowd as he gracefully plonked on the witty, humour fresh out of his reserves. He delivered with

a relaxed and easy smile and suddenly turned as serious as the sound of someone dead and the crowd ruminating in a spell, waiting patiently for him to finish. Robin was just happy to have him as his father and would stoke the genius in him by carefully nodding to his claims and assertions. He felt one with the raging inferno and the state of affairs. 'R' man spoke to the young and grey with equal aplomb. He raised a stiff index finger and clutched his hands together in mid air after densely darting them in symmetry to make his point visual and expressed persuasively. He would promptly elicit their approval in his frequent stops. He made sure the audience was with him all along. Then after his talk he would swing about in totality lunging forward for his tea that has lost its steam and the snacks that had been forgotten for fresh ideas and unheard voices. He could hear many voices together like his words had hit them somewhere deep inside. Robin listened intently to his father and intervened to the extent of a pondering smile and hoping to dazzle in eloquence one day likewise. However he wasn't much of anything before his relatives. Robin had questioned his growth looking into the mirror for child who had been denied adulthood in his looks. He had learnt the English way of life with forks and knives, tray the glasses and bowls while serving guests, excuse oneself before leaving the dining table. He learnt to greet people on meeting them, never to run the handkerchief over the mouth in a rush but to gently dab away the food or liquid form the lips. He learnt to greet the family in the morning when the day starts, in the evening when darkness descends and finally at night before preparing to sleep. He had all the virtues that build a character, honour and pride at being the successor of a distinguished family. Yet there was something that was denied and he couldn't change the image on the other side of revealing mirrors. How could he be not having something that was served on a silver platter to every human on this planet? His wrists were thin as a stick; he stood at six feet from the ground. His eyes were most penetrative as they could ever be, his legs were tall and lanky, yet his face had the pretentions of a school boy even though he was way past college. There were some relatives who accepted him just like he was. There were others who raised the obvious question making him feel hopeless and wanting to drag him through a hundred years in seconds for that enhanced look. He walked safely and carefully out of the local cinema hall thankful to God that he was still intact after watching the unusual happen to the characters. There was nothing to worry for it was not happening to him or his near and dear ones. These were the moments when he fully embraced himself and cherished all the good things that he had in his life instead of going after distant drums. There were moments when he would rather hide in his closet. He would abstain from a holler to the mirror wondering how to change the stagnant thought when he knew that certain things were not in his control. Reuben was on the same boat but never bothered to think about it constantly. He was on a mission of doing justice to his hard work back home and 'R' man's pledge to show him the best in the world. He adhered to the feeling that he was indeed pretty and his young looks cast a spell among the new and old positively. There were greater disabilities in this world and Robin thanked God for being the healthiest child in the family.

On a Sunday Robin decided to look up his place of work which was at some distance from his room. He wanted to decide and eke out a route that was the shortest and the most comfortable so that in following trips he just had to manoeuvre along a predestined path. This was an easy step because his new office was not far away from his old one. All was locked and barred at his new office once he reached his workplace as expected and he was considering a surprise to find the makers of the new company at work. He wanted to go around town shopping or jump into a classy restaurant for the evening but longed for company. He desisted from occupying a single table at a restaurant. Couples and families would stare at him while he desperately tried to keep busy by fidgeting with the glass of water in hand. He would nervously wipe his face with a neat napkin to make matters dry and clear. He would squint his eyes at pensive thought, holding chin with warm fingers and swish hands in air to the mysterious music like a musical conductor. All this just to show that he was indeed busy and enjoying just like others even though he had no company. He would rather go to a wayside stall where one had to stand and eat and throw away one's plates once finished. The buzzing flies would look for a place to rest and circumvent the swatting danger. He never liked the idea of window shopping believing that it made sense to buy something that to look at it from a distance. It didn't take him long to select something with subtleties and hidden beauty that his eyes could conjure in no time.

He always thought that he would take no time in selecting a life partner because friends just happened and his choice would be as true as the summer or the winter. He wanted some company that could coax him on young and nascent evenings that there were more possibilities than to just sit in one's room or being the lone stranger roaming around shopping arcades. He was bored of watching evening shows of romantic films when it felt like stealing from one's own bucket of popcorn. He had walked around the corridors of malls, sounded and appeared uppity, suave and modern in the hope of making some presumptuous and accepting friends. Robin had walked alone too long and believed he was like this from the beginning of time. He had walked alone in the din, cutting the silence through his sweat and incessant footsteps in the hope of seeing more than the normal eye. Sometimes he gave up in the thickness of silence and the futility of roaming the callous earth, sat on the evening chair in a park to watch the young and the not so old frolic. He then invited the other in his imagination who could be a friend, guide, man or woman, who would ask questions cutting through the numbing silence. They would ascertain the general direction in which he was headed and offer priceless advice to help him combat any challenging situation. His invisible friend would lead him through a defiant maze of thought to a clear solution and a conclusion making him lighter and ready for laughter at the silly. Sometimes the friend reasoned his loneliness and his battle with the void in his life. He/she advised him to let it be as it was just a passing phase that was temporary just like the feeling of the tongue and the gums after swallowing chillies.

Sometimes his grief was so upsetting that no illogical friend could surpass its intensity and in such cases no help was sought from the figment of imagination. Robin had gained all the weight back and was regular with his meals. There was a time when he remained without food for almost six months. His drought had affected his brain and his nerves twitched for the lack of food. 'R' man sometimes described it as a desire to self destruct but there were sound reasons for his ruination. His mind was muddled with thought- whacking of 'R' man from a very early age and then offering apologies with apples and bananas. The very recent Augustus encouraged him to disown his father, and walk on the road away from his house to find his own way. 'R' man's slaps from a very early age had a deep effect on Robin and he was forced to think that something was wrong with him. Loaded with such conflicting thoughts and Augustus wishing 'R' man be dead and gone created a tumult inside Robin's tender brain and what happened was a result of those daunting thoughts. He didn't sleep for three months and was close to an electric shock. But now new leaves appeared on the old and dilapidated tree and the branches hung in the spring to fruits touching its knees. Augustus might have dropped the whole matter in a family where his discourses didn't work. He hid himself in deep down crooked and unknown roads far away from 'R' house. He practiced social welfare hardly knowing if he had actually changed a life and capitulated to his homosexuality. 'R' man slapped him one night while he was on the road to celebrating a new brand of cognac or a new perfume in his closet with boyfriends. He dropped by, shrieking in delight to find 'R' man and quietly disappeared like a cat shooed away. There was no reason for Robin from that point of time to go anywhere near Augustus. Yet Robin did for he still had a soft corner for him. The serenity of the place attracted him besides his soft handling of objects and words like angels treading in the clouds. Augustus' view of life was intriguing and wholesome. Every sound, every word had its weight and substance. He was concerned about tea marks in his old cup. He held the broom like in an emergency to drive away the sheet of dust from his living room floor and listened to the small white light that peeped in through his window in the afternoon. His deeds however didn't make any sense and Robin had turned a nervous wreck in his tutelage.

Robin's visits died down until finally he forgot to walk on that road and never turned that way.

CHAPTER SIX

YELLOW OLEANDER

The yellow oleanders dropped on the ground with the same frequency with which they blossomed. Tender, even a slight movement slit their throat and they tumbled like bells on the floor with hardly any sound. Its fragrance eluded plenty even to the keen and discerning nose, dipping into the hollow of the bell, but was diligently captured in scientific books of horticulture. It was a symbol of courage and stood tall amidst all the storms that 'R' house saw, dwindling yellow dropping like plucking strings on a sitar(Indian musical instrument), yet no one came near it because it was highly poisonous.

'R' man would sit in the open and count the droppings in an hour, sometimes coming close to a magical figure. He would suddenly forget all about his effort to the phone ringing or a whiff of the boys floating in the air. The soft and bright flowers reminded him of his children who richly deserved all the rest, peace and happiness in the world after the storm that just hit them, unintended. He never crushed them under his feet and listened very carefully for voices from its hollow. It would help him decide how to control his raging anger and hold words on a tight leash lest it harms someone without their fault. It was indeed a lucky charm to finally see Reuben overseas in a quest for the highest and Robin to follow soon in its subliminal forte. It sounded sweet on Christmas appearing as tiny flames lighting up a shiny tree and chanting words from a perky Santa but with no children around. It constantly reminded him that all that the world was continuously changing with the environment and one could not afford to sit on a single bunch of flowers for long. Old ones were supposed to give way to the new ones with no excuses to stay or delay the arrival of new ones, just like thoughts. Sometimes he would stand hand on his hips next to the tree for some answers. Yet he found no movement, no wind to whistle to its shiny leaves, no critter to force its weight on its branches while he sauntered in his gloom. The yellow oleander is a life giver enough though extremely poisonous in that powerful medicines to alleviate fever are extracted from its poisonous fruit. It was symbolic of the life at 'R' house, breezy and a stunner in beauty from the outside but venomous and unkind from the inside and the venom a life giver in the bigger picture. Robin had suffered a lot in his past but adversity and hardships had made a man out of him. It had made him realize the importance of a good friend and relation and the dire need to uphold a relationship.

Robin had seen and heard things that a normal person would never do albeit in illusions and delusions. May be this was not an end and there were more corners of the mind to conquer and experience. He remembered his childhood on the firing range and his encounter with poisonous pods. His clothes were painted with their poisonous sap and piercing his skin with their sharp thorns. He had grown an affinity to the wild. The venomous and the yellow oleander was just an abstract addition to the family, reassuring and senile from a distance with no spines on its body. Sounds of movement of its shiny leaves could be used as percussion in a musical stanza and flowers could be offered to the holy Gods in devotion and prayer. Their poison was far more subjugated and submissive never exhorting or inviting anyone to its periphery or swallow it's venom in spite of the knowledge. It carried a shield of venom just to protect itself. What then can be said about humans?

He followed the darting pigeon in twilight from the point it flew off from the roof of a building. It picked on its bulge of feathers with hard and pointed beaks and making low noises like it longed for friendship while on the roof. The warm evening tea was thick and it delightfully stuck on the insides of his mouth like glue and gave a feeling of fulfilment. He wondered how a single tree could give up all its leaves to look so barren and skeletal. He had watched this tree every evening from his window and how it slowly lost all its children one by one until totally alone to the passing wind and storms. He wondered about 'R' house and how it might be empty in a similar way with its children far away.

Tomorrow would lend a new shape to his future. He expected to meet like minded people and make some friends.

He got up a little late the following morning as he had found it hard to settle down the previous night with all the excitement in his veins. He hurried through his tea and tore at the loaf of bread and omelette with heavy teeth before jumping on to his two wheeler. The morning ambrosia gave him the strength and the will to perform at his best and outdo plenty, armed with his rigorous training at college. He had seen the worst and the best and was totally adept at handling in-betweens. For once he wanted to be the best. In the past he had allowed others to outsmart him too many times when he was deservedly the best.

He skipped the temple and hurried through the traffic. The bike exhaust gave out white smoke that smelt of burned fuel while he pushed the accelerator too hard. They would probably make him sit at the back bench from where he could neither see nor hear the instructor. His words would softly fall on the instructor's ears that would gladly ignore it. Or worse he would be asked to find his way back as a punishment for not showing up on time. He was travelling faster than he imagined sometimes negotiating tight corners with shut eyes. Matters came close to a nudge and a negligible distance from the other vehicle saved him. Yet he realized that traffic happened in a jiffy with hardly any time to react and congested traffic always had one hand in danger. This was a 'make do' milieu with the light and the heavy traffic squeezed indiscriminately onto narrow roads. Vehicles almost caressed each other and a miracle made them waddle free of one another. Robin had been there umpteen times and nervously closed his eyes ruing over each narrow escape. This day was the same. By the time he coalesced his thoughts into a diary of his mind he had hit the final bend to the gates of the company building. He put on a smile to appear fresh and cheerful and swept away all complications of the mind. His eyes were fixed on the doors and windows of the building as he gingerly raised his motorbike to its stand. The officials had already arrived before him yet he there was no one at the lobby who could be safely identified as a trainee. He was later informed that the trainees were yet to arrive but the management didn't mind given the distances they had to cover, some braving the weather and the traffic from outside the city. The people at the helm of affairs had been very patient in selecting their employees, allowing Robin a second chance. He had almost forgotten his appearance at their entrance exam on the first attempt. They were quite calm sitting in their glass windows dispensing files. Fingers were busy over keyboards of their laptops with the occasional frowns and peep at the huge clock on the wall. This was after all a custom to never turn up on time. Robin had turned stiff with his hair blown under the torrential vestibular fan to a mess and he was through reading the glossy magazine on the table. One more moment of waiting and he would readily change his ways, running late for all summons like condescending kings to consenting subjects. He didn't want to walk up to the coffee machine too many times lest it sound rather trite and rude. He had just entered the dome and the officials were yet to be befriended. So he talked to the officials for a while. They didn't want to give away too much too soon and left a huge part of their itinerary to surmise and common sense. Yet they were quite clear, open and warm about today and how it would shape up to the extent of happenings in a week. It was a gamble that few would partake with fresh ones out of college or career people crazy enough about the land of free. They would take up this job even though quite unfamiliar with the technology offered. There would be no immediate benefit to their current profession or any permutation in the future. They would then grit their teeth in anger, or tear down the place with incendiary intentions if the venture failed.

In walked a hefty man with a bulky carry bag in one hand that was a shade heavier than him. It was beige in colour, crashing with his rock thighs that probably no one would consider lifting even if challenged. He was probably a family man, who seemed to have lost hair on his head to years of experience and disgruntled bosses, trying to meet tight deadlines. He already had alimental job with a taste of the latest technology. This would be a fitting extension to his repertoire. He would truly benefit from this experience, hiding the idea of a trip to the US in the secure palm of his hand. Actually it was not that he didn't think of this trip at all, his face turned red when he thought of driving down the highway. He imagined walking the sparse streets with his kind of shops, or merging into a discotheque with his bird forgetting about his three children and wife. Abba (father) sometimes alluded to the grandiose America where the air was clean, where even the poorest had a respectable life with a share of the amenities enjoyed by the rich. He was curious and certainly couldn't be counted among the poor. He blatantly followed the corporate protocol by shaking hands with all and sundry upon his entry with Robin the first on his list.

"Reman, reporting for duty, nice to meet you, when did you come....."
Reman was a little surprised at Robin's decision to join this company given that he was fresh out of college as an engineer. There would be tonnes of jobs on the roadside with people eager to have him as an employee. Robin felt ashamed to divulge his greed and quietly smiled indicating that there was indeed some other stronger and more viable reason for him to take this step. Yet no one could deny a hidden desire to experience the land of the free and be excited about exploring the place where the world converges. Reman's bag was stuffed with loads of paper collected over a lifetime. He didn't believe in discarding obsolete and unwieldy papers that used up leg space and bag space and was a soft target to rodents and insects. There was a dedicated bone in his wrist and upper hand to handle such kind of extreme pressure. It had become even stronger and adjusted with every added block,

with a gradual increase in tension. He was a sort of leader and wanted some space and people to deliver his dissertations and iambic addresses. Then he would part ways with the ordinary grass and it didn't matter to him that they existed and were a part of his enamoured crowd. He would offer them a grim face at being mistakenly applauded or when they appeared to be dozing in the middle of the resurrection. He would go an extra mile with his bosses, with an effeminate bow and seconded them like they were the last and final word that would be executed even though they sounded absurd and stupid. To the chaff, he was the invincible, someone who could gauge the problem even before it occurred. He was the man with the words in all occasions and could never be taken for a ride. Robin was certainly one among the crowd who never questioned the higher authority and shook his head vehemently in total surrender when a 'yes' seemed like a 'no'. He already drew the line from the very first time he met Reman. He stopped completely after a certain point and felt he had to grow in his shoes to pursue matters any further.

Still in the bigger picture they were strangers who happened to sit under the same roof and waited for orders from the chief for further action. In walked a short man with a toothbrush moustache and a politeness that couldn't be bought. Roshan had served the Indian Army but had to quit given his limited reach with his head scarcely popping out of a tank. He was closely followed by Rank, a shade taller with a long and thin moustache, caressing it softly and it hurt when someone pulled them for fun. The two were like shadows, Rank right behind Roshan with a synchronous thirst and hunger for each other and merely enforcing common ideas and belief. If at all there was a difference in their impressions in matters of interest they quickly changed tracks to match the other. If finding a friend was like looking for a needle in a haystack, they were the lucky few who had found each other. They were identical in many ways, comforting each other and were destined to dive in to the facade of walking on Columbus land. The weather seemed to be warming up and the day was finally alive after Robin hardly found anyone around on his arrival earlier. The coffee machine began to jitter and echoed varying tones. The coffee was beginning to spill on the table top and disposable cups danced on the piled trash container. Everybody seemed happy and delighted to explore new possibilities. Robin found his own corner kissing the soft coffee and elaborating on his repertoire as an engineer. At this juncture all agreed that this was indeed a next step to their career and they had been looking for this kind of technology for ages. They plunged into the nitty-gritty of technology and gulped down large volumes of hot coffee, hiding their true faces. Robin stood in the corner, handling a score of people that were not his forte. He would rather be alone in his 'R' room and let music cross his ear over the patterned tiles. He put on a smile when things got out of hand and never denied the intention of choosing a program that would give him chance to substantiate his dreams. They talked about and fun in the US and stern resolve to make it in spite of the luck factor involved in vying for a visa. Somebody would hold their ears and bring them home to talk about technology and the possibilities in a fast changing computer age. The computer geek would raise the bar and all would agree amorphously like they had already known the facts. Some walked on borrowed intelligence and the jargons hardly made sense. They were poked in by the management cutting across the voluble air and announcing the address of the CEO within the next half hour. There were more to come and the management didn't mind refilling the coffee machine with fresh coffee beans. The trainees took leave from the officials and stepped out of the building. Robin stayed put and didn't want to risk being absent for the all important meeting. He crossed his legs on the sofa and decided to read more about the new technology that was still emerging. He could then fervently hold the centre of attention in rampant discussions under the same roof. He swallowed in deep discussions, knowing full well that in the final analysis it all boiled down to ones mathematical skills.

Robin was just beginning to shuffle his feat, wanting to roam around the corners outside the office like others when a trainee stepped in. He was heavy footed, thick chest, thighs and not too tall. He talked with his eyes and had a cunning smile when he met Robin,

"Hi! This is Roni, I guess you are here for the same program and I don't suppose you are the only in the program. Where are they? Gee am I late? I tried but the traffic won't let me"

He had a sparsely appearing goatee that lend a speck of maturity to his face. He smiled always, talking softly and hardly ever losing his temper. He had his own simple apothegm that he stuck to, always

"Make others tense, but never be tense"

He walked the mile in trickery and guile, never gave a straight answer and retorted that it was all for the amusement of the listener. His spread gaiety and laughter by never engaging in a simple direct talk. He was fresh out of college. A shade younger than Robin, he did demonstrate some seriousness when Robin dug deep into his life and his dreams and ambitions.

"All of us have some sort of ambition, but it is the peace of mind, tranquil flame at the Gurudwara (Sikh temple) and the teachings of Guru Nanak (Sikh Guru) that shall conquer and keep us sane. Rest is all dust.

I am a Sikh, like you can tell but I go to the temple each evening and offer sweets for solace and ask for peace when I turn in sleep each night in my room. Rest is all utter stupidity and we are up to our necks playing games and there is a humungous stampede for things that hardly matter. But people don't let go and you can hear them wage priceless wars of freedom.

Money can't buy me freedom, it is just to show to others and I am rich. But am I really rich?"

Robin surmised that within each lies a corner of thought, commiseration with a philosophy that helps them shape their steps in a general direction. Roni for one wanted to kiss the girl whom he saw at the bus stop everyday who was like an angel with snowy, plump cheeks. He showed great interest in woman only things like shopping, cooking, gossiping to the extent of knitting. He wanted to learn them all and understand their psyche in the bargain and was a touch feminine with a heavy posterior and thighs. One could hardly find him serious about anything on a bright day and even warnings and prejudices were directed towards a mid day guffaw. Robin had begun to admire him for he seemed to be the leader of his ship, in total control and never be brought down by the city blues. Sometimes the sun hardly dazzled, grey skies gave no clues of where to begin. Things that people had to say hurt like a carcinogen eating the insides gradually. For one, Roni was happy with his life, his motorbike which required servicing like children need milk, putting it off out of laziness. He smiled quite often in his paltry existence with a tremor of panic each morning on reading the newspaper. He loved to read the news paper and it was his interface to the outside world helping him in forming his own ideas and opinions. It gave him words in a friendly discussion with all and sundry. He propagated his own brand of stupidity and filled up the air with nonsensical utterances, trivializing the gravest of situations. Robin always believed that despite his hidden picture behind the veil of stupidity and stale humour, he had a plan. It was just that he believed that life was not a serious affair. After all and we were all in this bus that never stopped no matter what. We had to sing along or tantamount to nothing in the passing moment. Yet Roni was curious about Robin's family, its members and how each got along for reasons beyond Robin. He wished them well in a moment of devout seriousness. He never suffered the tremors of sadness like Robin, pressed his lips constantly in a smile for others and was as light as cotton. Yet like any young man or woman he had dreams. It made Roni drive down homewards on his pampered bike which was at least a hundred miles away on dark nights and bright afternoons. It gave him a sense of accomplishment and purpose. Looking after his near and dear ones was the greatest dream that he could imagine. The journey begins from that point that ultimately leads to bigger things.

There was one more trainee who happened to walk in rather flustered and looking around nervously for clues. This was Rodney, the last addition to the group of trainees in Sofrek India Pvt. Ltd. for this program.

"Hi, Rodney, are you......? Is this supposed to be...? Sofrek?"

"Relax Rodney you are at the right place. We were waiting for you; the meeting is due to begin any moment. You've made it, my friend" Roni brought some sense to the confusion and conundrum infused by Rodney's entry. Rodney was of the silent kind, with a soft beard, mostly unshaven with a fold of seriousness constantly guarding his round face. No one had ever seen him totally relaxed. There was a perpetual frown ruling over his face. He appeared devoted to his work and disregarded any nonsense that came floating to his desk. He was not a prodigy by any standards but guarded his intelligence with his quiet and reclusive demeanour. He neither challenged nor expected any clarifications or questions. He did come on rather passionately, with a fleeting smile to topics of discussion that he owned fervently and would agree in a vigorous shake of the head. To the rest he was this ambling stranger jutting his head in ignorance. Robin always looked out for such people, yet it did come as a surprise when Rodney was not in his list of best friends. Rodney was too quiet and repulsive, never loosening up to fun of togetherness and laughter over a cup of coffee. He was not ready to look into the eye of the beholder, turning his head in the middle of a conversation, denying the message of gaiety that connected people. Yet he walked the line of seriousness and when colleagues lost their track a trifle to frivolity and nonsense. They came to him to put them where they ought to be.

He saved the ship on umpteen occasions, navigating it across the rough seas. His eyes were fixated on the screen, never one with Roni's nonsensical wave or when the instructor pressed for a round of coffee.

The meeting began as scheduled and all were present after hours of dawdling around tea stalls and overdone coffee breaks. The room was silent with smell of books and the breeze knocked the window softly. Each one was keen to know the about the plans of their sojourn west to the land where the world longed to be. They wanted to skip the training part. The imminent trip was discussed but the focus was on the training part. They would be roaming the building and its corners for the next three months, reconciling with the basics of computer programming. They would be trained for the visa interview after they dig into the basics of their training program. This would be followed by a competition to outscore the other in the mock interviews. But for now they were required to relax, to get to know each other, make friends and look for a place to eat in the afternoon during lunch breaks. Some were adventurous in that they rode for miles to reach their favourite joint by the side of the road. Sometimes they drove their vehicle too fast, twisting their bikes in tight curves given the dearth of time. Some stuck to the home grown recipe in a food stall or a dingy hotel with bland food nearby. Robin joined all of them in a group and followed, given limited choices. There would be random tea breaks. All would then descend to the stall downstairs break and into an absorbing discussion invariably started by Roni. He had keen eyes and senses and had the answers to practically all questions. Those questions that escaped him were the ones he chuckled to mindlessly. He was quick at grasping someone's intentions in the way the words were uttered and the facial expressions that were thrown into the discussion. He was the parody king and had this bizarre knack of entertaining all present. All looked up to him for a laugh in a dull and ruminating day. There was just this missing aureole to celebrate his presence. Robin still felt that Rodney could be the friend he had been looking for ages given his silence and the right choice of words in speech. He intentionally drifted away from the crowd. Yet he nonchalantly ignored the warmth of friendship that Robin often felt. So Robin found Roni, and obliquely narrowed down on his companionship and found his smiling face in the fields of gray and forlorn. There were a lot of things that Robin detested in Roni. The very obvious irritant was that it was hard to elicit a direct answer from him for any question. He would lower his head, staring until his eyes twinkled and an answer issued with not the slightest bearing to what was asked. He would laugh everything away until a higher authority demanded some seriousness. Even then the frivolity prevailed after moments of silence and thought, as the modus operandi with him around. The second irreconcilable thing about him was the way he drove his motorbike. He was in a state of agitated frenzy when manoeuvring steel across heavy traffic, hairline away from disaster. He swung past the bumpers of standing cars like a coiling snake, knees almost touching the ground on the slanting bike and everyday was a lucky day to be untouched. He was a trifle immature to realize that accidents have just once. One was better off without the display of exuberance and recklessness on the streets in traffic because they belong to no one. Perhaps age would make him mellow, Robin concluded. Rank and Roshan detested Roni and always thought he was a bad influence on Robin. Robin disagreed, although he kept some distance from Roni, avoiding extreme hero worship and devotion like he once had for Augustus. He parted ways when he had to, never lingered in thought even when disconcerting and smiled freely when a good one got to him. This meeting in short spells never had a voodoo effect on Robin's psyche and didn't stop him from keeping his stomach full on starving afternoons. Every training class elicited a new conversation among the boys with unforeseen possibilities and a furtive disclosure of company's plans and proposed structure of the program. They appeared ebullient and in the very next moment their eyes and mind were wandering at the sight of their next plunder of an eating joint in the extended lunch break. Roni never consented to the group and was usually absconding to his very own eatery far away where no one could see him. Robin had started staying out with Roni in longer spells much to the amusement and chagrin of Rank and the rest. Roni and Robin would ride on Roni's bike till the tethered end of time to the bridled corners of nowhere. The smell of spicy kebobs and oil on fresh 'parathas' (dove preparation) would make them stop.

"Don't waste your time with those old fogies. Life is here and now and meant to be enjoyed and not sulked in depression. There is so much to see and absorb, we are not horses after all that only knows the smell

of hay and the sound of whip on its body"

Robin couldn't agree more and gave into even the flimsiest of ideas from Roni's mind. Robin was astonished at the agility and the intentions of scaling this world with the precision of a wanderer. Yet he derived plenty from his insane excursions and had made about fifty friends in the process. Robin had struggled to find a single friend and even then the longing seemed to be slipping away with time. It was remarkable how Roni balanced his world in his busy lips. There was a busy tone on his cell phone for most of his friends who couldn't get through to him on a soft and delightful evening.

The group never knew where they stood in time. Months passed by in study, preparation for spot tests, buying expensive books with a hole in their wallets and persevering culinary adventure. The thought of America almost slipped out of their mind until one day after completion of three months the management had some good news for them.

"Gentlemen, time has come to start your preparation for the visa interview. We have called upon Rudra Associates that specializes in preparing students and others for visa interview under the guidance of Mr. Romesh. They will tell you exactly what you have to say and do at the Consulate, your etiquette and mannerisms will be closely scrutinized and evaluated at the end of the day. I wish you the very best of luck."

The group was happy to sail through the preliminaries not as convincingly as they ought to, given the back up of pricy books and experts that knew everything. Robin sometimes rued over his lack of understanding of the basics. He denied himself the effort of getting under the skin of extempore lectures by burying the thing that muddled his mind. He didn't go far with graces of clearly defined problems and their solutions. He wet his tongue with gripping coffee from a noisy machine on a fresh afternoon and changed the topic of contention. The premise of the management sometimes seemed absurd and ridiculous as getting visa was like winning the state lottery. Yet like true gamblers no one ever gave up until the last roll of dice that sometimes dawned too late. Roni didn't hesitate in inviting Robin to move in with him. It would not only save some money but give him company on long evenings with silence ricocheting off stones and dark and painful streets. He kept busy with his cell phone friends only for a while and very soon he found himself on his own, looking for corners on the newspaper that his eyes had missed. He could go to the temple only so many times, have a huge glass of his favourite warm milk with cream on top or rest his thoughts on sweet '*gajra*' (sweet dish with squashed carrot) with cashews. Robin kept the offer in his mind for a long time, until one day he called up 'R' man for some advice.

"Say ol' chap, that's a bright one. You two have been together for some time and he sounds reasonable to me. Besides he's going to be around when you two fly off to the US. It sounds good to be with someone whom you could consult and who could help you prepare your visa papers. Go for it son, you'll save some at the end of the day and don't forget very soon I'll be there soon to look you up and help you in all possible ways. Cheerio!"

Very soon Robin burst through the gates of Roni's meagre room making it noisier and hospitable. The room was rather small with just one bed for guests to sit and no tables. At nights just one could occupy the bed and the rest had to adjust on the floor. The room had a front porch where one could sit with a chair with enough leg space. There was a '*dhaba*' (eating joint) at stone's throw that offered bland food, hard to swallow on a regular basis with a danger of damaging the taste buds. Yet no one forgot the ice cream stall just around the corner after a strenuous stretch of the stomach to accommodate rancid food.

The soft cream spread rapidly on the insides and very soon the culinary debacle was forgotten. But Roni went there now and again because it was cheap, available at odd hours and was at a walking distance from his room. Robin arrived in the evening, hands fully engaged with heavy bags and carrying enough cash to survive. Roni would share the rent with Robin. On lonely nights he would drive down to the local bar for drinks or be one among the crowd in the lobby shows of distant malls. Robin had never tasted beer in all his growing up years. Once he ran away from home following the Augustus dictum to a hilly place on a bus. It was a fleeting and rare expression of freedom in which he didn't know how to act. He thought of collecting souvenirs which were in abundance in the valley and maybe try one of those roof top restaurants for a pleasant evening. There were plenty of foreigners occupying almost all the tables soaked in beer and the like. They smoked their way as a soft interlude to the popular songs played on the stereo. This was the time to break free and experience the very thing he had run away for without informing his folks, carrying his world in a handful of cash. Yet by the time he could ask for beer, the song had ended and the evening turned into darkness. He helped himself out of the restaurant, sober and disturbed. He had tasted beer once before in his life and was not particularly fond of it. 'R' man once was off to a holiday with family and had a bottle of beer in the refrigerator that would have to be thrown away lest nobody drank it. So he asked Robin to drink the beer instead of destroying the bottle with the beer.

"Glug the monster will 'ya. It's nothing but plain water, you'll love it. Say ol' chap without it the party goes nowhere. I have had plenty in my time, no harm if you did some. Want me to join 'ya?"

That was the first occasion of his taste of adult life. He thought of adding fizz to his sandwiches but the word never slipped out of his mouth even in a 'beer only' place.

But now it curiously seeped into the colloquial language and then the blood stream in a bar with soft music when being sober was a sin. Roni was crowded with his so called cell phone friends like they had been desperate to meet over a decade. Robin could hardly look into their eyes and utter words to strangers. There were no restrictions to the length of the night with the bar open into the early morning hours and the DJ playing popular requests. The soft light would soon turn dark when folks lost control over themselves with the alcohol mingling with the blood stream. Robin would rather rest in his room and prepare for the day ahead than hear the rooster crow and listen to the broom swept across the pavement in the early next morning. The continuous chat seemed to be never ending. Robin did his best in distracting them once in a while, yet they were swift in snatching the point of discussion where they left off. When Robin had too many, he decided to quit and bury himself in bed. Roni decided to leave but not before deciding the sight for their next rendezvous and grabbing a fist full of salted cashew. Roni was tipsy and he curved his bike repetitiously on a straight and empty road on the way back to his room. He sang songs of freedom and rejoiced in his delightful life. His songs fell on the patrolling policeman's ears but he was too fast for them.

"Have you seen those ducks in water? They are so lifeless, almost in a coma when they are out of water. But when they get into water, they hardly need a clue as they read the water precisely with passion and sing their own song. Life and love have the same effect on me. I love every moment of it when I'm in it. Hey Robi, have you ever fallen in love? I almost have but can't say for sure for it didn't last that long. What happens when you fall in love Robi, do you have any idea? I want a lady Robi, because I have never loved love this way before. Can you help me; I'm sort 'a crying." The effect of beer gradually crept onto their senses and balance. Roni almost walked onto the footpath with a spin of the wheels of his bike.

"Is th....is the ri..ght way, hell I thin..k so? Robi you're ....a good ma....n would you pass me the binoc...ulars? Why is the street s...o bare and derserte...d? Any clues?" Roni had one too many. They collapsed on their beds with heavy sleep on their eyes that. The day thus ended and Robin remembered the night guzzling beer in a tight corner with hardly anything to say or laugh about. He would sometimes be forced to smile back when a stranger's eyes searched his face for some kind of a response.

The next day the duo sharing the small room by the wayside hotel woke up with a mild headache. They rushed to the office, buttoning their shirts on the way to reach late, yet there were some who had still not turned up.

The two felt better as the day progressed as they looked into each other's eyes intermittently and smiled.

In the afternoon the team assembled in the offices of Rudra Associates for visa interview training under the guidance of Mr. Romesh.

Mr. Romesh was quite experienced with visa interview matters. He had been to the consulate twice, once for his MBA degree and on the other occasion for his MS degree in the US. He had never been refused visa even though his college was not well recognized. He was a sensible and down to earth man, eloquent in spoken and written English. He had been in this business for the last ten years and knew effective tricks and tips that could make anyone succeed at the visa counter. He took up the challenge of training ten trainees from Sofrek India Pvt. Ltd. to make sure that no one is denied the visa. It was a daunting challenge as the success of each trainee depended on their skill to communicate effectively with common sense, presence of mind and agility. Mr. Romesh stressed on mock interviews. Each candidate would be called in his office one at a time until he could hear the perfect answers to all the questions asked by him from everyone present. There would be a score awarded at the end of the interview and candidates were supposed to improve on their previous scores. The first few meetings would be the warm up sessions when trainees had to go through the printed material handed over to them and make some noise in the process. Mr. Romesh was open to any suggestions or doubts by the restless trainees in his office while he had other things to take care of.

"Gentlemen, it's what you say on the final day that matters, it's how you feel then that matters. No amount of training will ever speak to you; it's your own firm resolve to triumph on the destined day and your commonsense that will conquer all. This is far from the real thing and is just an added advantage. You must pray on that precious morning and the night before and my aim is that all of you present here get the visa."

The office was on the top floor with a large room to accommodate the trainees on desk chairs. There was a white board with random strokes of multi coloured ink pens from a previous session.

It was hardly ever put to use for the trainees. Like impudent children they destroyed the sanctity of the white board by scribbling on them like the walls at the roadsides or subways. The management didn't mind as long as they were not out to destroy personal property. Sometimes in their laughter and fun they forgot the very purpose of their training and going to America was not the important thing on their minds. It was only after they were inspired by the success stories of individuals from Rudra Associates that going to the US seemed to matter. Reman would be the first one to get into Mr. Romesh's office for list of instructions lying in the table. It was supposed to be passed on to the group before the start of each session and on this occasion he appeared to be rather stiff,

"Be at your very best, the interviews shall begin right away and I hope you all have prepared well with all the anomalies and exceptions in mind. Remember he can ask just about any question under the sun. You need to know the basic stuff like the back of your hand and further apply your common sense to counter the remaining. I am the representative of this group and if you have any issues please come up and discuss with me. Chill guys, don't be so tense, it will be fun, allow the light to come in and let's break off for tea and snacks. Don't look at me that way, let's do it"

The word was out with fingers chilled in nervousness. There was a tense silence in the group as each one was lost, feet hardly moving. This was the first time that the group felt the dividing line. They had grouped together like one family and now they felt separated from one another. What if a few members of the group didn't get through? Reman was surely an easy pick, given his vast repertoire and his expertise at extemporaneous dialogue. The rest would pout at something new thrown at them at the visa counter. How could a team member bear the thought of someone actually making it while others were being left behind? So each one started calling out names of the rest as projected successful candidates while leaving themselves in dark. They felt the need to go it alone, hiding tantalizing secrets from the rest and spreading to their own disparate corners. Rank and Roshan, Roni and Robin, Rodney and....

Robin wondered how everyone could blossom on the same day. Some were bound to have a bad day, maybe the traffic would get to them or a niggling family matter hard to ignore. Maybe everything was perfect, the weather, the clothes, the knowhow, the location, the interviewer, yet the words just won't come. The candidate would grope in the silence leaving the listener guessing. What if it was just like any other interview or an examination when all the answers suddenly drop on someone, like a déjà vu once outside the hall of interview or examination in the comfort of one's home. They were a stack of silence at the tea stall downstairs with the only sound heard was the slurping of hot tea. Roni suddenly turned livid for no good reason,

"Sorry but that's not how you sip your tea. Get a hold over yourselves guys; we need English to save us. Those of you who can't can bid good bye to their dreams. High time you learnt the English etiquette. Stop making those noises and try to construct meaningful and ripe sentences of English language. I mean how can you get something when you don't know how to ask for it? I don't want to be harsh but you very well know who among us is going to get through" Roni addressed dumb faces.

Reman caught up with perplexed trainees,

"You know Roni has a point there. There are many who can't speak a word of English or for that matter any other language but still get the visa. The reason is that they are old and would probably never think of settling in the US. But we are young and we need to convince the officials that we are not going there forever. For that, yes we need good command over English. Don't be so adamant guys, relax we will peak at the right time."

There were some who could speak their heart out but with incorrect English and some who never uttered a word even though equipped with the right words. Robin had the right words but was not conversant with the technicalities of the procedure. He could deftly handle the initial stages but when the story stormed into ifs and buts he got caught up in the weather. He could differentiate blue from orange colour of horizon but couldn't decipher what caused it to happen. As a young boy seeking admission in the first standard he accidently wrote the neighbour's name when each boy was asked to write down their names on paper. His mind was sharp but had time blurred that incident on the lunch table when he couldn't solve a mathematical puzzle, and 'R' man uttered in disgust that he never could. He was like 'R' lady who believed in handling problems that were as simple as addition in abjuration to the complex and mystical that was passed on to 'R' man. Robin enjoyed simple things in life and tosses of the esoteric had made him cringe and pursue something that sat nicely into his head. Sometimes he devoured children's stories in a children's book when the mind could paint a perfect picture and the words never entailed a second opinion.

The trainees of Sofrek India Pvt. Ltd. regrouped, rejuvenated by the refreshments, sitting together although within boundaries of their newly formed teams. This form of alienation was essential. Closeness could bring remorse to the members given that some were bound to sail through leaving behind a bucket of friends.

There was much lesser noise in the room, white boards were left in peace and the member gazed ahead in silence. They all bent over reading the material before them on the desk chairs like good Samaritans. The first one was called in after a long wait. It was Rodney who just peeped into the classroom with colleagues and chuckled like it were a piece of cake. Reman was a neutral member and belonged to each of the newly formed teams equally. After all he was the leader and couldn't be biased with some. For all good reasons he was already through and was scheduled for an interview at the very end. Mr. Romesh was very confident about Reman and believed that he didn't even require practice. One could hear Mr Romesh's voice only, loud and reverberating in the room. It appeared as though Rodney was absent, only few could fathom his subtle movements, talks and gestures. The interview didn't seem to end and the peon pushed in with glass of water with hyphenated signs. By the time he could place the glass on the plate holder and force himself out of the room he saw Mr. Romesh referring a book. Rodney wet his succulent lips for a response in full steam. Some of the trainees were so exhausted with the wait that they walked off downstairs for some air. Robin placed his elbow on the desk, palm on his chin and passed time by soft dab of his fingers on his lips. Rank and Roshan didn't waste any opportunity to break into soft whispers, and giggles. It disgruntled plenty until someone stared at them with a tight index finger on lips. Roni was getting late for his evening visit to the temple and a large glass of milk with cream. He was a man of instructions which he gave out to anyone appearing at an exam or interview. He had filled Rodney with his ideas and strict instructions. One of them was to strategically divert the attention of the interviewer to a totally different direction so that the person gets lost, forgetting where he was at initially. That way he could finish off the interview in lesser time and speak about things that he knew well and could handle with ease. He practiced it all the time, never answering directly what was asked but adroitly changed the destination of the speaker. He tried to make every conversation interesting, jovial stretching his humour as much as he could.

The pigeons had flown away from the ledge long ago to a place no one knew. It was getting darker and quieter with every breath of the trapped trainees. Some of them even started yawning when the body started to crumble under tiredness. Reman was getting fidgety and didn't wait any longer to walk into the office. He realized that there were some who had to cover large distances and the buses and auto rickshaws won't be plying around dead streets forever. Even those with their own two-wheeler won't find it easy to wade across the dark streets with a wobbly front light. They couldn't avoid those unimaginable pot holes with no lid ready to gobble even the bulky. All were relieved to see Reman walk away into the office so that they could leave for home soon. The room was a shade noisier and with greater resolve of the trainees to fight their way to the US and even learn the language all over again if they had to. Rank and Roshan saw this as a perfect opportunity to break the silence surrounding them and fill the space with murmurs with a tinge of warmth echoing in their bodies. Robin often wondered what the talk was all about. Even ladies would find it hard to gabber restlessly for long periods. They would rather wait for an entire day to fill themselves up with things that could be discussed.

Roni would mischievously call them a couple in love with each other.

Even Roni who had fifty odd friends and a world to discuss often felt the silence creep into his talk to which he quietly obeyed. He didn't put his lips to rest without a gibe at the pair with a relentless stream of words when the world groped for words to say. Reman never seemed to emerge like he had been trapped in quick sand and was done and buried long before he could cry out for help. He had probably been preoccupied with some activity thrust upon him sharing the helm of matters which Mr. Romesh vociferously assigned him.

A bell rang cutting through the silence and the frail peon rushed in with a glass of water and cup of tea. Rodney finally emerged with a distended smile and beating the pile of paper in his hands in air more out of excitement than to drive off the heat or the invisible horse flies. He was closely followed by Reman with his warm hand on Rodney's shoulders. All were agape with tension and excitement to hear Rodney and Reman speak and felt they had been unnecessarily kept in suspense, to hear their teeth grinding in a grin. None of them said a word in spite of the barrage of questions at their doorstep. Somebody had to stop the mania and when matters were about to be out of control, the two started speaking together. Rodney gladly handed over the floor to the boss, and Reman cleared the air with his short statement,

"Folks, it all went well. Mr. Romesh is quite happy with our preparation. There are certain areas that need to be improved upon. But remember this is just the beginning; we still have two months before the visa interview. Mr. Romesh is very experienced with visa matters and trust me our visas are safe with him. He is bound to make us think out of the box, like he did with Rodney and don't expect him to be happy

by just learning your name, whereabouts and how you were doing. So as for Rodney's result, he scored a six out of ten, which is a good score. Folks, sorry to keep you waiting and we'll meet again tomorrow for the next few rounds of interview. Be careful on your way back home and remember to get some good sleep tonight. Always remember that we are in good hands. Ciao!"

There was a burst of cantankerous sounds of engines drawing heat in tandem bound for distant corners of the city under the fading street light and silence following them. Roni and Robin didn't have to go far, so he reached out for some tea and hung around long after everyone had left.

Roni could even visit the temple next to their room and offer prayers with Gods in diadem. The temple was lucky for him and he believed that all his wishes had been granted and would be granted in the future. All he had to do was ask for it. Once his mother was terribly ill and had probably seen the end when the doctor gave up on her. It was raining cats and dogs that day and on mother's word he stepped out of the house to the temple, a few kilometres away on his motorbike. He was as wet as the earth underneath and he squinted his eyes to manoeuvre the strong current of the rain dancing on his laps and beating on his chest. How could God take away his breath and the only reason for his happiness so furtively and silently? His tears mingled with the rain and he never found himself so alone. His loud cries appeared to be a whimper in the dark and the thrashing rain like punishing him for his sins. The rains seemed to intensify peppered with lightning and thunder as the decibels of his plea in cries overwhelmed him. He couldn't do away with someone he loved so dearly that was the only reason for all his conquests in a burdened life so far. He broke into a convulsive cough like he would throw his insides to the rain and slush. He had never been so wet in his entire life. When he reached the temple the bells were swinging in the wind and the rain and playing a note of praise for the Lord. He jumped out of the bike, throwing it away like he didn't care and held the bells with wet hands, swinging with them and closing his eyes for a moment.

He bowed deep and touched his head on the ground with hands on the sides. The Hindu priest was singing songs of devotion and performing 'aarti' (Hindu ceremony); the air was filled with a sea of sounding bells. Roni closed his eyes and let the priest sway to his own songs that was a shade louder than the thunder and lightning and the adamant rains. Surprisingly there was no one else around and Roni felt a warm hand on his head urging him to rise. Roni was completely wet and shivering from his head down to his toe. A flower dropped from above to his outstretched palms as if to ascertain that his wish would be granted. His wails reverberated in the idols of Gods and stoked the devout senses of the priest who rang the bell even harder. The priest looked into Roni's wet eyes and asked him to sing along and leave the rest to the good Lord. He shook his head in sticky solidarity and was on top of his music and song. Roni never knew the words but joined in the song beating his hands softly together. Suddenly there was a loud noise of thunder and lightning like the sky would split and swallow the earth in its anger. Roni couldn't help interrupting his prayer with a spasmodic gaze at the spectacle. Luckily there was no damage done and Roni asked for leave from the priest. It had been a long time since he left his mother and wanted to be near her. The priest offered him 'prasad' (holy sweets offered to the Gods) and blessed him for his wishes to be heard. Roni was quieter, although completely dripping wet. For a moment he couldn't find his motorbike that was lying flat on mud and the water had seeped into it completely. He wiped his face with wet hands and raised the motorbike to its stands. The bike had turned cold and wouldn't start with soft kicks. It was only when he spun his might at the lever that the engine started to come to life and be ready to budge to finally carry him to his mother. It seemed like a never ending road in the pouring rain. The bike ricocheted off turns hardly visible even though Roni took the shortest route possible to his house. He had turned silent and pensive even though the sky won't cave in. Suddenly there was a loud noise from the engine of the motorbike stopping completely. Water was fully filled in its insides and it was unable to generate heat with the water and fuel mixture. He started walking slowly holding the wet motorbike handle with his hands and felt the pangs of sickness within. He had ambled through these streets in many a victory march, recklessly caressing the streets on his sturdy motorbike with no tinge of worry with mother beside him. The same street resisted his movement making him trudge in sorrow when he knew that there was a lot to cover. He sat on a rock by the roadside helping his motorbike balance on the stone by the side and let his breathe settle down to a softer rhythm. He tried calling home with his drenched mobile but the instrument failed to transmit given its wet paraphernalia. He had never felt so alone, there was no one on the street to console him or even allude with affirming eyes, egging him to carry his struggle to its very end. Moreover the rain never stopped to allow life to get a better grip over itself. All was blurred and diluted in its volubility and spell of disaster. This was the moment when his eyes opened for the first time in his life, he suddenly felt 'responsible' with a sense of duty to his family and people that mattered. He felt that he was indeed an important element in the scheme of things and that he couldn't run away from himself. He didn't waste another moment thinking and sulking over life; he rose on his feet and pushed the motorbike with all his might. She heard a sudden miscalculated rush of blood in her veins and the stumped doctor called it a mysterious trick of divinity to be aptly recorded in the journal of medicine. She was freely breathing again calling out for Roni in the stymied darkness. Her hands were caressed softly by her husband imploring her to hold on to the moment for Roni would be rushing home. When Roni turned the final bend, he felt he had been walking in the rain for ages and he would turn into an old man by the time he gets home. Slight drizzle had taken over the heavy rains in an overcast sky and the steady build up of dark clouds eastside indicated further heavy showers later in the night. Roni raised his motorbike to its stand, was happy to see the doctor around and rushed within to see his mother.

"It worked mother, it worked! I am so happy to see you. Please don't do this to me anymore. I was scared to death. Don't ever go away or you

won't find me alive either. I love you mother, you are the reason I fight this world and torture myself to a victory march in the culmination. I am ready to fight once again, with you beside me. I can never forget the temple and its priest, they are indeed life giving. I am so happy to see you again. Did you have your dinner, I'm hungry too..."

"It's a miracle son; I have never seen such a thing happen, ever. I had lost hope and gone home, rummaging my cupboard in vain and disgust for a possible cure. It was then that I heard your father call that she had revived on her own; I just rushed to your house in delight. I am not much of a stargazer, but will become one if you insist. Take care my son and get these medicines whenever you can, no hurry. I'll leave now" doctor's eyes were hopeful.

They were united as a family once again and Roni had changed forever. He understood life even better and a sense of responsibility was uppermost in a conscientious mind.

Roni stopped by the temple late into the night and reminded Robin that He had a plan for all of us. He had a lot of things to take care of and that we unnecessarily waste our time and His in deception and sins. Their last stop for the day was the eatery joint by the side of the road that was bound to rip the taste buds with its bland and irksome food. The food looked even more repulsive when dull light fell over it making it hard to guess its true colour. They somehow swallowed the food with glasses of cold water until it was time to disperse to the room awaiting them. After a few moments they didn't even realize what they gobbled in silence and they forgot the smell of what sat in there.

The next day the team arrived way before the start of the proceedings. They could still be found in groups although they were loosely packed and were all ears to a common word. Rank and Roshan didn't miss a single moment in making each other heard and holding onto heartfelt emotions. Reman counted the total trainees present and made some notes in blank ink on a register.

The round of interviews started at the allotted time. The interview time reduced considerably and the classroom was kept busy with trainees walking to and fro.

Robin was one among them and he honestly believed that he understood the gist of the matter clearly, with precision. He walked out with a perfect ten and all were astounded with his performance. Mr. Romesh was elated with Robin's interview and thought that there was scope for even further improvement. There were a few more ten point grabbers to follow yet Robin was still the first among them to achieve the figure.

When all struggled to construct a harmonious English sentence in the flight of a conversation, Robin added a warm gesture in his fluent digression. Thanks to 'R' man and his training when he didn't allow any other language to fall on his ears when the boys spoke to him. The boys were forced to toss words in ignorance until they were meaningful. It was a different matter that 'R' man had a bag full of questions for them while they twitched in a reply. Very rarely did Robin walk up to him and ask for something that required his love, attention and perhaps some money. The boys in their childhood kept away from him, mostly. It took them a while when they stepped into adulthood to form fuller sentences in their own opinions and become friends with the mellow 'R' man. English had helped them indeed and 'R' man realized the dearth of spoken English in the country. People hastened over learning the language in a jiffy when it was a slow conditioning of ears and mind that could make the language sink into their senses, just like his boys. If not the B.B.C. then the English news on the television in the evening that brought the family together to encourage thought in English. When 'R' man resolved to utter in English only, all were taken aback and uncomfortable because they had seen it at a distance and never practised speaking it. He spoke the language to everyone- his relatives, mother, father, officers, children, even the downtrodden helpers who were a trifle scared of the language. He was sowing seeds of English in the family to make someone rise in the distant future with a perfect tooth ache and echo an English suffering.

It won't be long before the boys would be queuing up at the Consulate office and wonder in desperation about the missing documents even though they carried them in surplus. They had started enjoying their sessions with Rudra Associates under the guidance of Mr. Romesh. There was a gradual improvement in the mock interviews even though their scores sometimes dipped for no good reason. Roni would push for a drink in the night at the local bar when the world turned a blind eye to their existence and even Roni's ubiquitous wire friends seemed like a distant ferry. It was a rest day, Saturday, and the lads were feeling restless trying to cope up with a home away from home. There was nothing to hold on to except some old newspapers, in and out glances at a stodgy mirror with a diagonal incision that distorted the appearance on an indulging Saturday. The sun was a jewel in the afternoon sky with recurring waft of cool breeze over pampered faces. Roni had heard of this great store in the far interior of the city where they were clearing off the stock by selling branded shirts at throw away prices. Robin pre-empted with his usual rebuttal without even an inkling of Roni's grandiose plan. Robin desisted from riding on the pillion with Roni, given the maniacal contortions of the bike handle as if under a panic attack to someday get comeuppance for Roni's wild streak. Besides it was near winter when the soft birds disappeared without notice and the air got darker in a hurry as if the afternoon never existed. He could stretch himself to the tea stall or revel in choicest rendition of snacks that could make him squeeze his face and eyes in delight. He could even visit the temple if Roni so desired, but never allow Roni to dictate the wheels of the motorbike. Robin had his own motorbike that he carried with great caution and couldn't perturb a random horsefly settled on the pillion while in motion. Robin did not budge in his defiance and was not ready to walk into danger blindfolded, just to appease the rough waters of friendship.

"Hold on nugget, why don't you take me instead of my way of dealing with heavy traffic? You can sing da-da and have it your own way. Try my bike for a change and see us get to the market place in no time. Why don't we hurry until the night hustles in and sings a different tune altogether. You don't have a problem with that, now do you?" Roni

had countless plans on his finger tips. Robin willingly agreed and life, he surmised, could mean a lot many different things instead of the freak incident that one somehow expected. By the time they reached the temple Robin could feel streaks of darkness before his eyes that pushed him to hurry a trifle with wobbly eyes. The streets were as usual, hurried and uneasy with people trying to save seconds when being pushed back on the busy street would mean defeat and ignominy. They were worse than street dogs fighting over a disputed bone wanting a piece of road like it belonged to them. Robin put the jar on his movement whenever there was a moment of doubt allowing stillness to cut through ungainly traffic and usher his way forward. He was not riding on his own motorbike and it took him some time and fair bit of understanding to apply brakes or change gears. Besides it made a louder noise that was sometimes hard to bear in addition to the cacophony of the traffic. Yet he had quickly adapted to the new machine. He was in the process of perfecting deft touches by foot and hands that could elicit a programmed disturbance in its inner core. He was a few metres from the market place; Robin was relieved and wanted to unite with the colours and the din in the market. The engine was close to a final shut down and was deliberately dying down on him. Roni popped his head on the side passing remarks that Robin could hardly hear with his ears covered by the helmet. There were more people on the streets excitedly fringing its sides, swinging their holiday bags and bargaining volubly for objects that stole their hearts. There were no traffic policemen around and vehicles crossed each other at frantic pace.

Robin was just a few paces away from the turn to the market place when he pushed the accelerator to its extreme upper limit. The vehicle didn't respond, there was a huge lag in transmission with the speed reduced to a whisper. He kept on working on the accelerator trying to push the bike to optimum speed. The grazing motorbike reached a cut with no divider where vehicles appeared suddenly without notice to cross over to the other side of the road. As luck would have it, a car appeared before Robin, and his hands were still clutching the groove of the accelerator. Within a split second the motorbike raced ahead with full throttle. The machine did respond but at the wrong moment. The motorbike slammed the car ahead at full speed and its occupants were thrown off onto the loaded street. Robin didn't feel a thing besides a sharp pain in his limbs. His feet got trampled under the load of the motorbike and Roni was already up on his feet not allowing the culprit to run away. Just then Robin's mobile phone rang and it was 'R' man on the other end,

"Say ol' chap, how are you this afternoon. Listen, we just received the results of the English test you gave some time ago as a qualifier for an American University. You have done extremely well, jolly good. I am coming there soon, well done ol 'Sunny we happened to be very proud of you. Are you OK?

"Fine ...Pa, I'll talk to you a...gain".

Roni had no bruises on his body except a mild scratch on his elbow. It was the intensity with which the motorbike hit the car for a head on collision that did the damage. Robin tried to stand on his feet but couldn't. His knee cap of the left leg swung freely in an oscillating motion like it was never attached to the rest of the leg. The moment he tried to put some pressure on them to stand erect, it dithered away like the linking bone or support had caved in. Luckily he was not in a lot of pain but the abnormal behaviour of the leg bone put him in distress.

Roni was livid and demanded compensation from the owner of the car besides dropping Robin to the nearest hospital immediately. The car owner was too scared with the huge crowd gathered at the sight of the accident and agreed to help. Robin was helped into the car by Roni and a few others. Robin would have been happy trotting around the neighbourhood and watch the beautiful night settle in followed by the rising canopy of city lights. He could kiss the winter night air and watch the trees and the dust in deep slumber. The lofty birds would be hiding in their nests, quiet and contended in their world of plenty. He could sit in the temple for some time listening to *'bhajans'* (holy songs) to bring peace to eyes in devotion. He could gladly agree to drink milk with cream along with Roni with the upper lip soaked in white. He could stay a while in the neighbourhood, safe and warm instead of crouching on the dastardly streets raging with speed and mayhem. The shortening day and a toss of darkness had done the damage. There was someone to take care of Robin in times of adversity and he just had to listen to his friend who somehow thought that it was his own fault. *"I wonder if it's a fracture, Ron. Something is broken inside for sure; I don't know what it is. Do you have any idea, c'mon Ron I want to hear it"* Robin was desperate.

"Don't worry Rob, we're almost there. This is the nearest Government hospital; uh... take a right from here please. We'll have the doctors help us out of this uncertainty, perhaps an X-ray is the key, just relax" Roni held on as a true friend.

Robin could sit but not stand as the unsteady knee cap rocked to its own corner on either side and lacked the stiffness and solidity as in a normal foot. The sun peeped in for the last time that evening with its faded light rather desperately. It wanted to see its son through the ordeal. Robin was carried into the hospital with the help of shoulders lifting him slightly in the air. His hands rested on them on both sides in the absence of stretchers or wheel chairs. Robin broke into a different tune altogether, far away from his pain and the discomfort limiting him to total stillness. He had had his own share of pain when he had been bitten by street dogs twice, once when he was only seven and on the second occasion when he was eleven. He had to suffer a painful bout of fourteen injections on each of those occasions just below his navel. Those were the worst fortnights of his life. The doctor tried to softly distract him out of the pain with a cartoon show playing on the television kept in the room or ask him about his favourite pastime if that did not work. Some doctors didn't even utter a word, heartless and egocentric the needles poked in roamed the insides for more than five minutes. It happened twice to him and he made sure it never happened to him again in his life. There was a second occasion when he jumped from the second floor as a child with a curiosity of heights. It did hurt but luckily there was no damage done. He was in pain when he had denied himself food looking for answers that were hardly etched on the countryside. He had reached a point when his body couldn't bear the sound of the dagger and had nearly collapsed. His mind had reacted to the pain in illusions and delusions and his life had been reduced to pills that elicited normal sensations in the mind. He was in pain in those railway journeys across the country tied to the edge of the seat for most of the journey. The pouring sweat and the stench of the general compartment with 'R' man's erratic loss of temper made the matters worse.

Friends started pouring in to be with Robin and offer any kind of help possible.

Robin was in tears when a sudden thought surfaced in his mind,

"How will I go to the US now? My life is ruined. This leg would probably never be healed in time for the interview at the consulate. God spare me, I need your kindness in this hour of need, where are you? My dream has been ruined, my father would be so sad, I can never join you guys, help me someone" Robin mind entertained a single line of thought.

They all stood dumbfounded, like a lightning had struck them, in a state of shock. No one uttered a word; they hung their heads in despair until Reman joined them and broke the silence,

"Who has asked you to think, Robi, just relax and get your strength back. Remember, no one can stop you from coming with us; there is enough time before the interview for you to recuperate and start running again. Stop thinking otherwise. And you gentlemen standing there, don't be so gloomy and still, get him some fruits and where is his X-ray report by the way?"

Robin's left leg was plastered and one could hear people breathing normally back again as night fell. Roni promptly asked for Robin's permission to call his father. The X-Ray report was not very clear and asked for further tests although it did ascertain a broken ligament. Roni pressed for a discharge so that better care could be taken at home. The hospital doctors were reluctant to let Robin go and insisted on putting him under observation for at least forty eight hours, until such time the plaster would dry up too. Yet it was a government hospital with not enough doctors and care and the doctors on duty had a faint grip on their statement. So they let Roni have his way, but insisted on further check up at the hospital. The owner of the car that caused the accident was asked to pay the hospital bills and drop Robin home. The boys helped Robin into the car and Roni and Robin drove off homewards. Robin looked at Roni's legs or any other healthy leg he could see and envied their state. For a moment he couldn't understand how they could bend their legs at the knee, walk and run without any discomfort, while he couldn't touch his left leg.

Robin got the chance to see the caring side of Roni, who was often inclined to make flippant and controversial remarks about everyday things. But his eyes opened from the time he met with the accident for someone who didn't run away when his friend was in distress and cared like a brother.

"I've given a call to uncle; he will call you very soon. And yes he was shocked to hear what had happened. I'm sure he will be here pretty soon. Are you OK? Nugget, hang on we are almost there. I will drop you at home at go to the temple for prayer. I know it would be closed by now but I can always utter a word and the Gods will positively hear me. Have faith, God willing you will be on your feet again very soon and then we'll enjoy America together" Robin was static on the bed peeping at the darkness outside the door. He longed to be one with the sheet of cold hanging outside, in complete unison with the darkness and the stillness of the dark trees. It was just another longing to be normal like so many times before and be walking. He couldn't fetch a glass of water and was limited to puzzles and crosswords on the newspaper or some exciting news creating a ripple in the psyche of fellow countrymen. Whenever he tried to break free from his shell there was something to pull him back and enslave him in the passing moment. Yet this time it was a physical inhibition when his mind was intact and not burnt out from overwork with no twitching of the brain cells. He didn't have to run miles trying to hide from himself with opposite psychosis

hitting his brain leaving him in massive quandary and indecision. All he desired was to be up on his feet to fulfil his father's dream and at least touch the land if not settle there for good. The question was if he would be accepted as a part of the group at the eleventh hour. He could barely make it to the Consulate on the destined day and hide the lag in the preparation for the interview. The plaster itself would take forever to be taken off and by such time the students would have started booking air tickets before procuring visa. 'R' man had an inkling that something untoward had occurred the moment Robin talked to him in the afternoon. He had been cross legged, lying silent on the bed, staring blankly at nothing ever since Robin went away. He had watched how each one had popped out of the shoe box one by one to be one and lost in the illusory world- first Reuben with the big leap and now Robin disappearing slowly. How he sighed deeply sometimes in anticipation of launching his dream venture at home with the help of the boys which would indeed be a good reason for the family to be together. He had lent this voyager's dream to their hearts in the first place even before the boys could trace America on a map or realize that it was a country. His lone companion, yellow oleanders had conquered the ground once with their yellow flowers, few of them plucked for offering in prayer while the dropped ones rotting in the changing weather of the day. On any given time, as 'R' man noticed, there happened to be four flowers hanging loosely and some of them out of those were fortunate to cling to the fragrant basket. New flowers were manufactured in a haste to replace the lost ones to give the impression that the tree never ran out of flowers. Two of the four flowers parted too soon and would be carried away by the wind in close knit dances before they disappear to places only they would know. The remaining two were witnesses to the parting and it won't be long before they are carried away to the pages of some holy text, or devoted to the Gods in prayer or may be snatched away by the high wind. 'R' man noticed that at any time there were four flowers on the tree and the story was oft repeated. He could hear the music of the leaves, shimmering in the daylight after a group of four had withered and there was a fresh troop on its way. He was a silent gazer to watch them come and go in the shades of night and day; he could not touch them or coax them to stay a little longer while he pulled out a tale from his bag of the past. His spurred indignation of yesteryears, recklessness of his youth, wanting his young ones to come of age too soon by giving them the diet of grownups in words and ideas, he had somehow lost them in daylight too soon. Yet he was not going to give up on life and somehow waited for the time when he could be with his young ones. He sailed through imagery in chosen novels and books and penned some new possibilities of sentences and thoughts with a rare imagination. 'R' man called Robin, trying to be soft and kind in moments of distress than unnecessarily remonstrate in a bad temper. *"Rob, say' ol chap, we didn't need this, how in the world could this have happened when you are as careful and alert as the circling hawk with its eyes constantly gazing the target. I feel umbrage at the turn of events, yet no one can avert the hands of time that sometimes lifts us and on other occasions brings despair. Also each one if us meet with some sort of accident at least once in our lives. This kind of completes your quota. Anyway, I will be there in the evening, hoping to catch the early train tomorrow. Don't worry, I will take care of you and make sure you are aboard that aircraft that'll take you to America"*

"It's always been a serious medical condition for me, calamities and disasters have never left me and I have fought my way in and out of hospitals. Remember the time when I had an allergic reaction as a baby and my whole body including my face was swollen. You were in a train, as I was told, at that time and a railway doctor attended on me. My life nearly ended then, as it had on many other occasions in my life. This is not as severe I guess; my legs will feel the ground again"

'R' man genuinely cared for his family members and so did the family members for each other. His caring enveloped his brothers and sisters, aunts, uncles and surviving mother. He attended frequent emergency calls from his family members outside the three his own and one could frequently find him bobbing on a weekend train, holding on to a support and resting head on it for some sleep. It was time for another journey on that busy street and he wondered sometime where his life was taking him. He looked for answers in his books and the frequent diary that he wrote in unintelligible handwriting. He carried lofty words in his sensitive mind for a while but lost it completely in the melee. 'R' man had attended more emergencies in his lifetime, dressing up with a close look at the mirror for the afternoon train, than the books he had read in an eventful lifetime. There were fewer lines in mellifluous and urban couture dropping off from his pen to make the reader wonder in amazement, than the frequent rides. He never managed to get a confirmed ticket on the train unless he was travelling with family. But he somehow managed to scrounge a seat in the end even at short notice under the defence quota. Almost his entire life was devoted to railway platforms and train journeys. He would suddenly wake up in the middle of the night, at home, to the sound of whistles of trains, loud and imaginary, lunging for some water at the dry awakening. He remembered how a sardar (Indian Sikh) officer received him at the station even after twenty years. The Sikh had helped 'R' man twenty years ago when he had received his first transfer. Wrinkles on his face barely allowed him to hold a smile and grey hair and beard gathered over the years not allowing him to be recognized. Fate brought 'R' man back to the same city after so many years. It was not long after he decided to follow the sardar that the thought dawned on him that he was indeed the sardar he had left behind with teary eyes ages ago, it seemed. That was long ago when the sardar had black hair and beard and 'R' man didn't have a soft paunch. He never tried those tea stalls or eatery joints at the platform with ringing loud voices of hawkers selling their products with enthusiasm. Their food was too oily and replete with chemicals that could harm the body and cause addiction. He pushed the stricture on his children to avoid train food and platform food at all costs even if their aroma were srivinting and people could hardly resist a titillating tryst with spicy food. He could just walk into any train at any point of time and expect the TTE to provide him a seat by some minor adjustments. Robin had been cross with him once when 'R' man came to drop Robin at the same station. Robin looked the other way after finding his reserved seat in the train to New Delhi. 'R' man tried to gauge the weather by breaking off into innocuous chat with fellow passengers seated around Robin. The train started moving and 'R' man rushed in with a glass of cold drinks in his hands for Robin. He handed over the glass, patted on oblique shoulders of Robin and rushed out of the train. Robin had suddenly felt pangs of desire for his father and rushed to the barred window for a glimpse of 'R' man waving his hands. 'R' man was allotted a quiet sitting chair by the window. His mind was totally blank, for a moment he totally forgot where he was headed. He knew all the intermediate stations having travelled that route umpteen times. He just had to call out the name of a station to a fellow passenger keeping a track of the stations on the way and he would precisely know where the train was chugging along and how long would it take to reach its final destination. He didn't have to peep out of the barred window in frenzy like little children do, struggling to keep the names of the stations on their supple minds and raising questions in plenty to clear the air of doubt of their whereabouts. He had a deep relationship with the customary lights and fans in the train. He had seen the half moon lights and fans running at lightning speed many a time and found him at peace ahead of an unknown adventure and turmoil.

On many a trip as a young cadet he would poke his comb onto the fan blade through the metal grill, whisking them to motion. And the fans and the lights wouldn't usually work and required adroit hands to see them in glory, turning into a tale to hold close to heart. There was the harsh yellow light that pinched the eye giving the impression of daylight. The soft blue blended with the night darkness, was a sleep inducer making people swallow in deep sleep. That was the fixed pattern of the lights and fans on the train compartment and 'R' man hardly noticed a change in his long years of travel. The burning eyes of incandescence up on the skies, the roof tops, were enough to give him a spirited company and carry him lightly though the meandering journey. He remembered how he often travelled with family of four across the northern plains and how little Robin gauged the steps that lead up to the bathroom for an abnormal urinary condition. 'R' man would be peeved at the frequent calls to run up to the bathroom, sometimes in the middle of the night and painfully obliged flinging obscenities into the night air. 'R' man's irritant mood made it worse and Robin's body sometimes responded in deep panic, asking for a release at frequent intervals. Robin had lost partial control over his motions being emotionally stretched with 'R' man's wavering temper and often required a bathroom in the vicinity to come to his rescue. Robin would poke his finger in the form of rebuttals whenever 'R' man lost his cool, crushed like a pinch of salt, crying and dissuaded with his inner organs reacting to the turbulence. Reuben had found a way out of such situations long ago when one fine day he decided to fight the pandemonium with his silence. His silent voice detracted violent outpourings from a defied 'R' man. Very soon 'R' man looked the other way gritting his teeth and wondered why he lost it again. 'R' man saw no season or reason to lose his temper. He would start at his young ones or 'R' lady just about anywhere, even on front of a crowd in a train or any other place or an evening with friends in the serenity of the drawing room.

CHAPTER SEVEN

MENDING DREAMS

One traumatic day had passed. It was that time of the day when the ill fated motorbike rammed against the stubborn car a day ago. The winter sun was faint and powerless just like his thoughts .He couldn't find hope hidden in the dying trees and winds as the day ended and realization of his soggy dreams. He waited for 'R' man with open arms. 'R' man was laden with dust and tiredness and stank of the typical train smell that often clung on the body with hardly any warning. Robin had hurried through his afternoon lunch and gulped down big chunks of tasteless semi solid food just to keep him full. Robin requested Roni to pick up his dad from the railway station and bring him home. Roni had talked to 'R' man earlier and carried a photograph for identification.

"I am on my way Robin, don't you worry. And it's going to be my bike and not yours. I know it was my bike that went berserk a day ago, but my friend, although your bike is brand new, I can feel the grip better on my bike and know exactly how to tame the beast. I will reach the station with my bike in a jiffy and then we can get together under this dangling tree and muster a plan that would lead us out of the maze. So long, my friend, don't try to walk out of the door, I will be with you again very soon" Roni's words were reassuring. Robin shaved the dust off the box of sweets that he had especially bought for 'R' man and straightened that day's newspaper for his dad. The sun had set and darkness roamed the trees and his room. He was relieved to be out of moment of horror and total disarray when his

vehicle was doomed. 'R' man was the lone saviour when his kids were in a dire medical condition especially young Robin with an affinity for hospital wards and tandem strokes of sickness. Reuben was steady as the pole star didn't sink in any kind of disease after a certain age. Robin fought his way through sickness through his entire teenage and even now when he had grown a beard and come of age. It was as if he was longing for love and care, more so from 'R' man and wanted him by his side at all times. 'R' man looked for the cause and a permanent cure, Robin let it be and calmly listened to 'R' man's disgruntled outpourings. He was willing to swallow all the pills tossed to him and don any kind of gear to fight the ailment. So when calamity struck, Robin was kind of relieved to fall into the arms of 'R' man with a firm belief that he would be reenergized with the powerful synergies of medical treatment. 'R' man's worry on his lips was enough for Robin to feel the force of struggled muses on 'R' man's sensitive mind and the haste to be cured soon. Even a slight sneeze by Robin was enough for 'R' man to raise a synchronous protest and suggest a check up at the local clinic. So when Robin had lost his mind, he read all the books on schizophrenic unrest. He questioned the psychiatrists for feeding Robin fat pills that mingled with the blood and didn't do more than causing sleep. He had doubts if Robin had any abnormality at all in the first place. He wondered how a normal child with no history of mental distortions suddenly start hallucinating and foster a chemical imbalance that could not be corrected for the remainder of Robin's life. The neuropsychiatric specialist was clear that pills could only correct the chemical imbalance on an ongoing basis and the paucity of such drugs could cause rampant episodes with erratic behaviour. 'R' man wanted a higher word after not being allowed in by Dr. Rishi for creating a ruckus outside the clinic premises, refuting his treatment. 'R' had read about some new findings in a recent medical article concerning schizophrenia. He slumped to the mundane, breaking his bed. He didn't have reserves of unleashed energy hidden in his thighs or arms that could make him hunt for the man with the highest accomplishment of the day in the field of psychiatry. He sure was not contended with his morning cup of tea and bread and wanted eternity to push him into his youth, to dance in the sun as a man in his thirties and capture the cynosure of life. He was after that undeniable force that would keep his loved ones sane and clear the sun for their gaze out of their windows. He got tired too soon. Sometimes he blankly looked at the glittering yellow oleanders and how they had the perfect dimension and character of a true flower. They were not too fluffy, gay, showy attempting to attract unbridled attention or too placid to pass by untouched. They were tender and graceful, longing to find their way in an uncouth and unsavoury world and were tainted as the forbidden fruit. Much like life of 'R' man in all these years, easily deniable, bitten if smitten, yet a trip meant to be made. He saw the first of these flowers when he came home after retirement and how these mighty flowers never failed to plonk on his musky courtyard in all these years. His hair had turned gray and his resolve for a new day, dampened by his waning strength. Robin was still, listening to the sounds of the city at night through his door which was ajar. The news in the paper didn't make sense to him as he struggled through the vivid tales of the swindlers and their telling scams when his own life was heading for a dead end. He starved himself for supper with 'R' man when he arrived with his penetrative point of view and plans that could almost make a dead man walk. He was guarded by a strong Hindu faith and nearly had his way through life when his sole purpose was the good of others especially his near and dear ones. After many years had passed all had spread far and wide.

"Hey Scotty, look who's here. Say ol' chap you need to put on those dancing shoes and break free of your plaster for good. Don't be too sad Sunny, life is nothing but a gig, got to live it, and try not to think too much. It's a glorious day, mum has sent you some gifts and I will see you off to America, all too soon. Let's see, not too bad Eh! It happens Robi, happens to everyone including me, pray to God, He is our life support system" 'R' man arrived with the bright colour of a new morning.

As soon as 'R' man started to chalk out a rough plan for the next day, Roni interrupted him,

"Uncle, before you go any further, I'd like to inform you that I have to leave for my home town right away which is about two hundred kilometres from here. So, I will be on my way with my motorbike as company and I apologize to leave you alone this way, but my mother is sick again and she had called me, I just can't ignore the call. Give me a call for directions, I know these streets pretty well and I know you do too having stayed here long ago. But a lot has changed since then and I am just a phone call away. Take care Robi and I shall pray for you."

"You drive carefully son, it's going to be cold and the darkness is going to sneer at you like a scary ghost as you ride along. Take a breather when the stray dogs get to you and you don't have a clue what the fiendish night is up to. Be fully alert whenever you decide to take on the road." 'R' man had a bag of instructions from past experience.

"I will, bye all, I will see you soon" Roni was on his way.

'R' man had owned a bike once and covered almost the entire northern plains up to the foothills of the Himalayas.He didn't rue over the day that had turned rancid negotiating official rigmarole, lost in jargons. He kicked the bike with colossal force and a streak of wild and roamed the countryside in carefree gaiety with 'R' lady. Where he lost his mirth on the way when his flamboyant motorbike turned to a rickety scooter and a dodging helmet, unleashing tufts of grey hair jutting from his head, no one knew. Dreams had died a sudden death with whistles of a far away afternoon train lingering with lurching passengers on board.He was left with the pretensions of a fulfilling day when he had to lug his way throughand go through the motions. He swore he had laughed a million times on the other side of the deluge and now looked for reasons to be calm and appear satiated. Robin swore he had seen his father laugh once with friends in a party. The image just withered away in his mind like the summer wind that suddenly died down and his father's face was constantly contorted with anger. But that was a long time agobefore Robin gained consciousness of maturity and brimmed with thoughts of a grown up.'R' man had so much of discontent bottled up inside him with no one to vent his angst and life swinging by in a hurry. He felt he was being sucked inby the city and his people.He was like a bird whose wings had been clipped by the strong winds. He did manage a stunted flight never failing to touch the people stricken by numbing grief and emptied the last leaf off his pocket if it mattered.

"Say ol' chap, how did you manage to ride with him, he is a despicable, horrendous driver. I mean the way he negotiates traffic is the least dangerous. He nudges around traffic like a snake, never too sure of him and one of these days is going to pay for it dearly, one is forced to think. These folks think they have mastered it all, presuming the streets to be a circus as they swing about out of control. Do you know when we as cadets were taught slow marching, we were asked to push the air ever so gently after we felt its weight on our legs. We had to wait patiently between the shifting of weight on our legs and would pay a rigorous penalty for mistakes. A bike should be steady and a shade on the slower side, still as the wings of an eagle circling the skies, just like your drive. You drive like magic, and you know I don't ever flatter. Leave that rascal, let's eat. Let me walk out, get us something to eat and then perhaps we could plan for tomorrow. Just hang on; I'll be back in a jiffy" 'R' man walked out into unfamiliar streets.

'R' man didn't have the answers to Robin's doubt of making it to that airplane to the US, but had faith that had carried him through most of his life. As officers they were taught to be in silence, emotionless, for a critical missionand look for clues in their very own investigation. They were trained never to read the writing on the wall even if it all seemed to be a waste of time. Robin tried to adopt the painless strategy in his own life. This one required quick decisions and cure. His sessions with Rudra Associates had terminated and the lads were sent off for a break to their respective homes.He was short of a few sessions with the group lending final touches to their planned repartee with a degree of politeness and etiquette. Reman touched on all corners of the visa procedure with the inebriated, bulky bag of beige dangling on thick fingers doing the rest. This was after all a pilot project and the company had stretched its resources to make it a success. The picture was bigger than the boys rejoicing over brownie points earned over test sessions yearning for the customary pat on the back for consistency. The real thing would bring altogether a different challenge, with remnants of a bad day or the irritable ways of Indian traffic peeking its way out in the interview sessions. They had no inkling of the storm ahead when they could be discarded for being rather too polite. That didn't dissuade a hearty bunch from walking that road and longing for paradise where dreams begin. 'R' man figured out the temple the next day and prayed for strength and poise. He was up before Robin opened his eyes and felt the beginning of a bright new day. When his eyes did open he had no clue where 'R' man was and was a trifle worried given that 'R' man was unfamiliar with the streets and its ways. He noticed a pattern when 'R' man would disappear in thin air, leaving his family behind before anyone could notice. He would mingle with the bizarre and new like it were his own home town and be gone for quite a while. The trained hawk eye would appear with hand full of essentials that the family needed and a few articles that were better off resting in the shop. He was sure forming a link, criss-crossed and busy with all the shops in the neighbourhood. He not only got what he wanted, but elicited warmth with few and triggering a vendetta against those that were rude and derogatory just like foes. Most of them in these parts walked the thin line between being humane and street smart hoodlumism. Their stern resolve to create anarchy and intimidation in a terrorized society had the backing of people at high places. They were the face of future leaders and were best left to hold the streets in their diabolical grip. 'R' man was familiar to the weather and wondered where his generation had gone wrong to allow proliferation of the religion of ruffians. Committing a crime in these parts was a blessing in disguise, a harbinger of an unmatched career at higher places. Yet not all could hold a gun or spread terror with violence and wars and vouched for civility in their quiet saunter on the streets. 'R' man never torched such acerbic outpourings with the breed of ruffians who couldn't bear an uneasy tone that was bleakly disparaging. Yet he carried his life in his pocket, like he often quipped, and didn't really care if he were not there to welcome tomorrow. He would give it all if it could make a fledgling crawl out of its nest and soar away to perfection. He would vaporize in the effort to pay his dues and honestly dispense his nickels and dimes and emerge as pure as the chime of the wings of a swan as they flap. He had the essentials that made an exciting English breakfast. Robin was the helpless host with a plastered straight leg that won't budge and required shoulders when he decided to get up to attend nature's calls.

"Dress up Robi, we'll go to that private clinic a few blocks away and get some tests done to know exactly the real state of your leg. I'm sorry we can't move around much but I know pretty soon when you start walking again, you'd be taking me places I have never seen" 'R' man was reassuring. Dead leaves crackled with the change in weather as they sat face down, swollen. The chirrupy nest looked deserted to be disturbed illogically and haphazardly by its many children, enhanced by the moment to lift the load of another day. 'R' man had made his clan proud by earning his commission very early on that blessed day when his siblings had just about started walking, following warm and open palms the size of their faces. His father had called it a day after years of service as a distinguished civil servant. His remuneration was not enough to stoke another fire for food or entertain guests over an extended lunch or dinner. 'R' man was not very ecstatic with his new found career and wanted to follow the footsteps of his illustrious father. Yet caught in the excitement of landing a decent job in the forces, he let go his desire to be airborne to the US or leaning in his civic duties towards a reprimanding soil. Henceforth there was not a single day when he didn't squirm like a fish out of water wanting to breathe again and break the shackles of forced duty. He had no choice but to see the day through in a manic and crowded office with confidential work hidden in ubiquitous files. It would not let him have a deep sleep at night. He was a big help to a proud father who passed the word around to practically everyone in town that his son was

sworn in before the President himself as an officer in the Indian Army. 'R' man bought a swinging arm chair for his father who knew that his son would redress the piece of earth he holds with honesty and fair game. He even gifted his father's favourite pack of cigarettes that his father would immediately tuck in his pocket to hide it from other members of the family and issue a warm smile. There was enough money for the family to survive. 'R' man's father often desisted acceptance of large sums of money from his son. He knew that 'R' man could sleep in the cold or stay without food or hide torn clothes just to see his family together and happy. His father had tasted the rich aroma of priceless gifts crowding him on weekends from high rank dignitaries of the day while serving as a civil servant. There was a sudden death of events and pomp and show. He wiggled his fingers all day in those relaxing slippers and hopped his spacious rooms throughout the morning and afternoon after he was forced to resign. The courtyard was bare that once held a fidgety crowd trying to get a glimpse of the high rank officer. They were lost on their grievances and hung around till sundown until they were heard. There was some iota of respect left among the crowd for the officer that was, allowing his car to pass by unhindered when competing with others. Yet the respect was disappearing into faint gestures in bows of the head that seemed rudimentary.Inspite of that he was still the lord of the house and wallowed in the respect of a handful. There were plenty to help him with the door when he decided to take a walk out of the premises, with his diamond studded walking stick. The world swung around the corner of wayward streets wanting a glimpse of the high class. Time seemed to have knocked him down when he wandered the streets with unbearable heat in a torn 'kurta' (traditional male Indian dress). Even the wayside barber forgot all his appellations. It was worse than before. Earlier he had commanded respect and admiration, mollycoddled by his staff for the daily set of duties, leaving many unheard and unattended. Now he was a free man not knowing what salutations and obeisance stood for. He was once blinded in their light not knowing where to turn for honesty and truthfulness. Before holding the esteemed office he sang a sweet song on his bicycle and wandered around carefree. He made short stops with all and sundry, high class and mundane, and unfolding a glimpse of tomorrow. With the hope of 'R' man and a brighter day he dwindled with the passing entourage of time.

The MRI report came in the way of a sumptuous dinner. Each party tried to forget that they were in a makeshift arrangement in an effort to feel at home and the warmth could only carry them so far. The report stated in precise language loaded with medical jargons that made it sound rather technical that Robin had multiple fractures on his left leg.

A major operation was on the cards to reverse the damage and load the leg with metallic support on sensitive areas. Robin sat on a wheel chair under the faint yellow light of the clinic. He was flanked by Rank and Roshan on one side and Reman on the other. There was nothing to talk about as disappointment hung low in the air and helpless glances rued the ominous silence. There was no way out and a touch on shoulders, wanting to fill the void that Robin found him in was nothing more than doubling the pain. No one seemed to agree that Robin would be cured just before the time of the flight. Yet they did utter words of consolation. They didn't even try to hide the reality. They faintly indicated that there was indeed a dying miracle that could concoct the prefect recovery in record time. 'R' man earnestly consulted rather obstinate doctors trying to find a flickering opening in the diagnosis. He tried to read between lines and find a way out of surgery even though the papers indicated the obvious. He had challenged many a doctors before to the extent of questioning their practice and was successful in averting the danger and complete ruination in many cases. He had an extended discussion and discovered that the report could not be disputed and a decision had to be made for further prognosis. He stopped his calculation after reaching the zenith of his mental strength and decided to call it a day. The operation was scheduled on a Sunday, two days from that day and his primary focus was to arrange for money. He stood before the boys of Sofrek India Pvt.

Ltd. and softly requested them to disperse.

"Say ol' chap I'm sorry to keep you waiting guys. You know, you have been a great help and come down here to ask for Robi. I'm touched. I'll let you know about further developments. If everything goes as planned we should have a successful operation. Take care guys and don't stop praying like I pray for you. Bye for now and we are headed for home too."

There was darkness outside. The leaves stood rather still to the soft whistling wind. The skies seemed brighter than expected for this time of the night. It was as though the skies had heard the beckon of a new day. The twining games of the boundless traffic had subsided and the scene was not scary enough to put another one down. They seemed to have respect for each other with room for their free passage and not wanting to fall off a cliff at this time of the night. The auto rickshaw with 'R' man and Robin knew exactly where to go and the two found peace and unheard voices when life called upon a truce. 'R' man placed his warm hands on plaster and its hardness paved the way life was meant to be for Robin who hardly ever found himself out of danger. In all his sickness he always had 'R' man by his side and their expeditions stank of the hospital smell and syringes. Robin often wondered what the game was all about. 'R' man was getting old and wondered about the state of health of Robin in times to come and where his sickness would eventually take him.

'R' man decided to exhaust his savings of a lifetime in the form of a neat check, crossed and signed at the bottom for a life that would be saved.

All were up early in spite of a Sunday. A cold wave of wind hit Robin in his upper half while the lower half was covered and he shrivelled up by folding his hands. 'R' man stood pensive before a broken mirror, screwed to the wall. He was confused and doubtful, ducking underneath the cut for plain surface of the mirror to shave and rinse. He was not in favour of a surgery and believed that tampering with the insides of a body could change its natural proclivity for good it may lead to complications later on in life.

Nature's replenishments were complete and lasting and the wounds and injuries were soon forgotten with time under its shadows. Robin never knew that his ramblings and experiments with a fragile health would one day lead him to surgery. He urged his father for a second opinion,

"Pa, can't it be avoided. I don't think I can bear it. I know all the preparations have already been made for the operation but can't we go somewhere else as well?" Robin sounded desperate.

Robin was not sure about those private surgeons with the cost of surgery through the roof. With medication too expensive, too private, it was not known where fickle hands would lead him in unconsciousness. Performing surgery was a business after all, playing around with the hearts and kidneys on a daily basis. The breakfast didn't go down well in both concerned. They could not feel the warmth of the sun on a cold morning and were looking lost and in despair. 'R' man took the long walk to the temple followed by the main street to holler for an auto rickshaw. He somehow struggled with his steps and looked for the faintest of reasons to digress. The auto rickshaw stood warm and ready outside the door. 'R' man purposely delayed the ride to the private clinic by clearing up the room that was already clean and pushing paper plates in to the trash bag. Next he had to carry out the final step and carry Robin on his shoulders to the vehicle parked outside. He somehow delayed this step until the auto rickshaw driver blew the horn urging them hurry up. When there was nothing left in the bag to delay the ride, he decided to have a short discussion with Robin, asking him about friends and Roni's future plans. It didn't work and very soon he found himself bending over for Robin's soft hands on his shoulders. Robin started hopping to the main door balancing most of his weight on his body and trying not to fall too much on 'R' man. For a moment in suspension he almost fell on him completely but somehow controlled his motions by reversing his action in mid air.

They had almost bounced off into the hired vehicle when the mobile phone rang. 'R' man would have severely damaged the phone if it had been one of those useless sales calls that had too much faith in its customers. He made Robin sit in his room and asked for some more time from the pesky auto rickshaw driver. He looked at the screen of the mobile like someone who had not lost faith and would triumph on the slightest of hint otherwise. He walked up to the window for some light and noticed that it was Reman on the other side. He was about to hand over the phone to Robin when Reman sounded peculiar, carrying a strange intonation. He cried out in a loud voice that appeared subdued as much as the tiny receiver of the phone could hold and wanting to speak to 'R' man.

"Uncle, before you take the next step, I have an excellent Orthopaedist in mind, the man who is known to have saved countless operations by nature cure and rehabilitation. He practices in the Government hospital and is open on Sundays. I feel we should take his opinion as well"

"You are a life saver son. You have rightly diverted my mind; I am ready for any second opinion. Something was stopping me all this while, and I feel this is the voice of Almighty and I am an aimless wanderer without His eyes. Thank you son, I am indebted indeed, now could you please also let me know the address". The table had probably been decked with new sheets and elevated, trays laden with dust free instruments, tools and equipments. The surgeons sailed on cups of coffee, stretching and relaxing before plunging into flesh, bones and blood. 'R' man bent a little lower than expected, helping Robin into the auto rickshaw. He brushed the invisible dust off the plaster with the hospital address uppermost in a resolute mind. His hands were stretched into space holding the driver's shoulders for navigation, approved in many ways by the driver, shaking his entirety. He negated the driver stiffly by prodding him with his sharp index finger for taking a turn too early when he should gone straight for a while. Robin could see the meter speed up like the rushing wind past them and was concerned for every rupee that escaped their pocket. 'R' man hoped that this was the last of set of emergencies that he had to attend. He hoped Robin would discover

a still and peaceful life far away from dangers to flesh and bones and inner body. Sometimes he couldn't make out if these dangers erupted because of his over protective nature with his boys. He had faced the wind and life with an open chest with danger always lurking on hindsight and learnt to make a life that way. The boys were loaded with that extra gear to keep them safe and warm, lest the inhospitable weather get to them. When danger sneaked up on them they were hospitalized for repair. Their bodies had never tasted the true warmth of the sun or shivered with goose flesh in the biting cold wind. They were far from survival tactics when one had to bite the neighbour at times. 'R' man wanted to avoid the very danger that they would be entangled with. The birdies were not allowed of the nest, given the love and protection, warmth driving away the harsh world not knowing that they were meant to fly. Yet the birds were slowly creeping out of the nest now and facing the hostile world. They were frequently in despair and out of breath with the father, 'R' man slowly turning grey and incapacitated. The children would take many years to undo what 'R' man administered and Robin's US trip would prove to be the conditioning in the right direction when 'R' man couldn't follow him. 'R' man had already acknowledged the damage he had made to his children in so many ways yet Robin could not bear the tear in 'R' man's eyes when he indicated his futility. There echoed a voice of his soul in his cries, so pure and honest, so lost in the raging war to make ends meet in a lop-sided justice to self. The birds could learn to fly, albeit with difficulty, but where would 'R' man hide or run to when his whole life was spent in service to others and he denied something vital to himself .By the time they pushed into the last turn to the government hospital, they were loaded with hope of escaping the knife and the curse of stubborn doctors that won't budge in their decision. The entrance looked rather deserted with no wheel chairs or stretchers in sight and helpers lost on the insides attending crippled patients. 'R' man helped Robin with a rock shoulder and they entered the waiting room of the orthopaedist.

Dr. Randal on duty had people coming in from all over the country for check up. He had a long list of VIP's consulting him and vouching for the best treatment in the world by his skilful hands. He was from the same land of bandits, dacoits, anarchy and filth like 'R' man. He had seen many cases in his tenure, complicated and dicey but had never knelt at joining the private bandwagon. He was the doctor for the poor who didn't have the gumption to try the private clinics where the bills exceeded their incomes and they sounded too rustic for the ambience. There was a huge waiting hall with all seats occupied except for one. 'R' man gently pushed Robin to the vacant seat and walked up to the counter for an appointment. Robin believed he had been to the place before. There were hanging heads in anguish and pain, waiting for a sudden call from the doctor and breathing in spirit and other chemicals floating in the unhealthy air. They were a few with thick turbans round their heads, clad in dusty 'dhotis' (loincloth), peeping into eyes and seated on the ground. They looked into sick eyes that had a fixed gaze and were bent in a certain posture that caused the least pain. There was a general air of discomfort as is often felt in such surroundings, life had pushed Robin into the abnormal zone all too many times and all too many ways. 'R' man counted the patients in the room to confirm the number allotted to him and surmised that it would probably be dark before Robin's turn arrived. Dr. Randal suddenly emerged from his room, annoyed and irritated followed by the group of fellow junior doctors. They huddled around him in a circle, heads down in total submission. The whole ward rang with his loud reverberating voice, scalding and spiteful. It was as if his instructions petered out previously in an esoteric language to his juniors was totally misread. He abused all in a row and slapped a few for insubordination and missing out the core of his instructions that he had so clearly conveyed. They all hung their heads even further in humiliation but no one uttered a voice in dissent. They had a deep respect for the doctor and were bound to learn even after being caned. They were like little school children who had cut their fingers while sharpening pencils and didn't know how to deal with it. The doctors dispersed in different directions after the tonic and Dr. Randal succumbed to his chair handling emergency cases. There was a man lying still on the stretcher being rolled in on a trolley to the doctor's room. Robin was told that he accidently jumped from the roof of a tall building and hurt his spine. He could never ever stand on his feet with the broken spine and could view the world only from a supine position. Robin realized how these bones help us live and breathe, yet we never realize their importance until they are hurt and disabled. He shut his ears and didn't want to hear about any other such accidents. He just wanted to be guided away from surgery and let the broken part heal naturally. 'R' man, who had been standing all this while, hopping to the various counters, peeking into the doctor's chamber, stepping out of the room for some fresh air, finally found a chair to sit. The operation table on the other end had been deserted and the doctors probably had a stretched night of poker with friends under the protruding bulb of a suspended lamp shade from the ceiling. Their expert hands were itching to cut open Robin's leg and make the decisive incision. Yet Robin was in the hands of the final word, a world renowned surgeon who had made a crowd of people rush to him for a cure and left those private igloos rather cold and forlorn. The waiting room looked empty with only two patients left besides Robin. The doctor had walked up several times to the waiting area to assure the remaining patients they will be attended to. 'R' man sat cross legged, left hand on his chin and dropped off to sleep occasionally. He was satisfied at the proud entourage of an accomplished doctor and the patients that swarmed like bees with a story behind broken bones. He fetched some lunch for Robin on-the-go and hardly recognized what he had been feeding on for the last few days. Tea was most comforting in these times and both felt the warmth of togetherness and called for it whenever the mind was clogged by discouraging thoughts. The doctor was due to call them in anytime now. The last patient before Robin had already made his way into the doctor's chamber. 'R' man swept his face with sweaty hands and forced his eyes to open and be alert to doctor's observations. Robin sometimes felt a faint itch on the insides of his plastered leg and feigned a cure by scratching on top of the plaster. The doctor had already read Robin's history and studied his test results including the MRI scan before he was called in. Robin was helped by 'R' man as he skipped and jumped to the doctor's chamber after being called in.

"I have studied all the reports of Robin including the MRI. It does show multiple fractures and there is nothing much I can do. Your son has to be operated on and I suggest getting it done without delay. I have had a plethora of such cases in the past and I keep getting them all the time and we must obey the results of the MRI report and act in the best of interests of the patient. However, I would like to take one look at the leg before it is operated on. So please get the plaster removed and come to me at noon tomorrow and I promise that you don't have to wait this long. And I am sorry to keep you waiting today. Let's meet tomorrow when we shall decide on the future course of action"

Near hopeless faces emerged from the waiting room of the government hospital and they had nowhere to go and didn't know where to look. Robin whipped the dark dust under his feet and he skipped along with his right leg. 'R' man dropped his shoulders, with shoes slithering in despair on the mud in a total surrender to fate. He remembered his Army days when he was not over burdened by the responsibility of a family and he would snap his fingers in delight to summon his official car to take him away. Now he had to wait for an auto rickshaw on a busy street and make earnest requests to carry them. There was not an iota of respect for him in the civilian brew. He was back on the streets as a commoner, just like he had been always before joining the Army. 'R' man slept on the cold floor that night while Robin struggled for sleep to set in. There were no words tossed about in lethargy or just to fill the empty air and warm it enough before both parties were submerged in sleep. 'R' man was up early the following day, lost in the blinding white light before anybody could notice him. He had fixed the route of his saunter and knew exactly where to go to fetch the desirables and sometimes deviate on a well directed path to a catching light.

They were at the hospital early in the morning. Robin lay still on the hard bed while the doctor ran a pair of cold scissors through his plaster. 'R' man was nervous and smoked half a dozen cigarettes to calm down riveted far away from the room where Robin would be freed of a straight leg. He did find his way in after a while when Robin's eyes were searching for him and stood next to him, hands on his hips.

"Say 'ol chap, I don't think you can walk yet. Don't move your leg much, we'll rush to Dr. Randal and I am glad to see you off that irritating plaster. You must be feeling a lot lighter and I hope it turns out to be a minor injury. Let's go jeopardy"

Robin sat on a bench outside the hospital while 'R' man was lost in an underground tunnel in the vicinity lined with medical shops. 'R' man soon appeared with crutches in his hands so that Robin didn't have to vacillate on one leg and succumb to the dust on his way forward.

"These are your wings, now you can fly. Never seen you with them before. Stand straight and walk like a king. You don't need support anymore, you can even run with them" 'R' man encouraged his young lad. Robin was almost moved to tears. He couldn't assuage the pain and fight of one father for his children, to be their shade in rain and abhorrent sunshine.He peeped into Robin throughout the night when Robin's body simmered in fever and palpitation. The children studied their parents in the same way the parents kept an eye over their children. Robin was born in an emergency table and 'R' man had fixed his eyes on him ever since his first life threatening emergency. Nothing had changed ever since then except that now the frequency of admissions to emergency wards had dwindled. 'R' man had hope that this be his very last calamity before Robin left for the US. He wished Robin to get checked up thoroughly over there with the best of physicians and/or psychiatrists and stay fit for the remainder of his life. The 'R's' were conveniently ushered into the doctor's chamber without delay with 'R' man's gentle hands on Robin's shoulders. Dr. Randal made Robin sit on the stool while he took a good look at the incapacitated leg. He twisted it to Robin's

loud shriek of pain, pulled it and shook it vigorously. He flipped it sideways to gauge the general health of the leg. When it was all done and settled he pushed back on the cushion of his arm chair, soft fingers on his chin and gave out his diagnosis.

"Gentleman, your son has no problem at all. Whosoever said that he has a broken leg is a crook. I can tell you this MRI report is doubtful. This is just a simple case of broken ligament. He will start walking and running in a week's time, just in time for his US trip. If I twisted a fractured leg then the pain would be unbearable. His pain was within limits when I played around with the leg and it disappeared as soon as it erupted. I can gauge the depth of a fractured leg and one with a ligament injury and your son requires no surgery. That's why I say these private clinics are dicey, they do give you five star treatments with all your money but their diagnosis is doubtful. Go home son, relax, do some exercises, get some wax treatment done and you will be that happy swan singing over a quiet lake"

'R' man felt heaviness in his legs and the peace of a log. 'R' man purposely left the tainted MRI report somewhere and never bothered to hold it as a token of survival, carrying traces of future course of action. He held his boy by the scruff of his neck gently as they ambled their way to the exit door, sliding his shoes on soft marble in a scattered queue. Robin on crutches stomped home with spike of energy and resolve, trying to straighten his crooked left leg too soon and writhing in pain often heard by the now cheerful 'R' man,

"No worries, ol' chap, let's take one step at a time. Your interview at the Consulate is still one month away and we have plenty of time to recuperate. We should rather wait for nature to take over and you would be surprised at its quick healing process. Don't you think that if God brings misery then He is the one who shows us the way? I say the Mighty Ol' chap is up to his games once again. Cheerio let's eat something."

Robin welcomed the strong rays of the winter sun through the entrance door. They were straight and firm wanting to reach out and exude the warmth that could heal. Robin tried to lift his left leg with some weight tied to it. 'R' man was in and out of the house burning his pocket under the warmth of the sun and filling the coffers with supplies too many. He had cared all his life for whosoever came within his ambit and with all his heart to bring them warmth and comfort without a care for the nickel or dime. He did get back the love and concern that sounded genuine from some quarters. His energy was sapping but he still found himself to be one with the dust and the grime. He bravely walked on the streets in his home town mid afternoon to a temple that was located at distances the size of a marathon. All for the reason that he didn't have enough cash in his pocket for the not too flashy auto rickshaw. He sometimes wondered when is a man appreciated or rewarded for all the work he has done. Is that Army man heavy with medals all over his chest been rewarded enough? Is money all that matters in this world and can it buy the love and the care and the feeling of oneness at times of calamity?

Roni, the swinger was in town. He circled his way through the forest and the highway on his motorbike across hundreds of kilometres with panicky hands. He reached astoundingly safe that evening that was pushing towards darkness. 'R' man was in the house and he welcomed Roni, who was so curious to know what had happened in his absence that he forgot to take off his helmet. He finally did on 'R' man's request and his dust laden eyes seemed all too happy to see Robin off his plaster. He was happy to see Robin swinging his effected leg like little children on a table with room to spread out their legs.

"I knew it Sir. There was nothing serious about it from the very first moment. Moreover, he was not in too much pain as it is in the case of a fracture. Thank God, for a moment I was scared too, isn't it Mr. Ligament, should I call you that Robi, I think that seems just right. Now we'll all go to America together and there's now worry when there's Roni by your side. We'll work together and make it happen. I think that it's time to hop to the temple. I'll just be back. Ciao."

A tight whiff of breeze enveloped Robin as he felt the soft pinch of pain that felt like it hardly existed. He put his hands on 'R' man's shoulders and was like a fledgling fresh out of the nest learning to fly all over again. The wax treatment did hurt feeling the burn with every brush stroke of hot wax on his soft skin and his leg turned into a candle once the wax dried up. It was like a shot in the dark and the pain dragged itself into his inner whole just like those callous injections just below a puffy navel. His only reason to stand by and bear the pain was that 'R' man was by his side. 'R' man was often perturbed by Robin's weight gain in the absence of movement for quite a while.

"Say ol' chap, you need to chop some wood or tire after a short distance run or maybe walk around aimlessly for miles just like I do back home. Burn that baby until you turn into wood. All is not lost though, my son, let's choke on spicy to celebrate your recovery"

It was like the interim never existed. Robin could put all the weight on his legs and walk like normal people do. He could select the places to visit, the streets to roam when night faintly touched the evening and 'R' man stumbled on some sleep back in the room. Very soon 'R' man bid adieu to Robin and Roni with the folks back home wondering at the plight of the storm that came from nowhere and plenty of phone calls from people searching for the man with the ideas.

"Say ol' chap I have to leave now. Take care Rob and Roni please be by his side at all times. Give me a buzzer when you need me. I am awake always and sleep is like the next door neighbour, in and out stealthily. I am alive always even in my dreams and reality with opened eyes is a different kind of dream, isn't it? Robi I want you to dream and do divulge if possible. Roni , boy, take care and please take Robi to the temple as much as you can and drink one extra glass of creamed milk from my side. I better leave; I can hear the train honking, so long boys. I will see you once you guys get the visa, I guess, Ciao". All the current employees of Sofrek India Pvt. Ltd were asked to assemble in the offices of Rudra Associates by night for a final session. The interview was scheduled for Monday morning and there were a lot of sorting out to be done, doubts clarified before the boys benignantly took the plunge. Reman was the first

to arrive early that evening considering a third round of hot tea to cut through the cold. He manipulated a hand held device and a bobbing bag that was like his lifeless child. Roni was very careful with Robin's bike and decided to keep his own bike in the shed when it came to lugging Robin around the circuitous roads with irregular traffic. He took Robin through roads with the least traffic and mostly pedestrians respectfully clipping the corners of busy streets. A precursor to Robin's new found life and freedom the duo stopped by at the friendly mall for a quick snack. Roni had a knack for the city traffic yet his erratic driving hushed Robin in complete silence. He closed his eyes for split second manipulations and tight manoeuvres, near misses ringing loud on everyone's ears. Robin often wondered that someone flouting every rule in the traffic rule book, cutting across traffic like an animated trapeze artist, danger always lurking in the shadow, never ended in a disaster.

There was no time for offbeat sermons in place for the employees for the interview the next day. Mr. Romesh wanted to ride on positive vibes exuded by the boys for the moment as he patiently waited for his ship to fill in. Roni managed like always to furtively find his way in, followed by a rejuvenated Robin ready for the final words of wisdom. Rank and Roshan, closer than ever tossed their arms together in a tight grip and were tied together by a common language. Rodney was perhaps the last one to join the group, because he lived at the farthest extremity of the city, serious and poised as ever. When the classroom was noisy again Reman stepped into his shoes for a parley with Mr. Romesh. Today the boys would not be entertained on a one on one basis but Mr. Romesh would address the boys in a short session. Reman, the exhumed captain would be the first to enter the Consulate to fathom the weather and gauge the general mood of the esteemed counter officials. He would then give out specific instructions for his brethren and the preferred language that could make them the most effective.

"Gentlemen, thank you for coming down tonight at short notice. You see we had to meet for the last time before we send you off to show

your colours. Remember don't put all your eggs in one basket. They can ask you just about anything including your passion that has shaped you. They may like to know your favourite colour, or the bird that excites you the most. One question that will be common is bent towards an assurance that you will not settle down in the US for good and will return soon after your visa expires. Remember there is a provision for extension of Student Visa, if you decide to study longer. Don't forget to get good sleep tonight and be yourself tomorrow without trying out a false garb of somebody else. My company Rudra Associates has a good past record, most of the aspirants have passed the visa blocker with a few exceptions. This is a good group and all of you are well equipped to pass the test. I would like all of you to disperse in a queue and enjoy some tea and snacks I have arranged for you on your way down. Take care. Best of luck. Bye." Mr. Romesh was hopeful.

Robin pressed his file with a stern palm that was loaded with papers to be presented at the window. Some of the papers were not the standard size, too large for the compact folder, jutted out to his displeasure. He didn't want anything to stick out while he carried the papers in his hands and made sure he could balance the onslaught with one hand. They had a rather unceremonious evening, grabbing dinner at the bland corner just to be full and little or no words to exchange. Roni skipped the newspaper; both had knelt in prayer at the temple earlier that evening. Roni broke the silence before both were about to drift off to sleep.

"What do you think Rob, are we too loud for comfort. Are sailing too high, ignoring the obvious and the simple things that sometimes matter the most?" Roni blabbered almost in sleep.

"I don't think so. I see no reason for denial. But, yes, it is risky isn't it? Let's remember Guru Nanak and hope for better things. Let's sleep."

CHAPTER EIGHT

THE FINAL LEAP

Morning began in the dead of the night. Robin carefully stepped over a sleeping Roni on the ground to feel the winter chill outside in an oversized woolen cap. It was early morning and he could see smoke issuing out of the tea stall in the distance with meager customers surrounding the centre of heat with outstretched hands. He flipped the stiffened papers for visa to be shown at the window and made sure they captured the complete identity and past history. The city had not woken up and the kettle and the steam broke the silent rhythm of the night and indicated the beginning of the crucial day when fates could be tossed either way. The hot tea wet dried lips and enveloped the body in a warm sensation including the aromatic leg that had healed effulgently. He had stood up to many sleepless nights in the past. This time he made sure he slept and not feels like a stranger in the dead of the night like on those sleepless nights. The birds were waiting for the right moment to jump out of their nests and were a harbinger of a new morning in their soft twittering. Roni gently pushed himself into Robin's gaze in a surprise, covered in wool from his head to toe.

"Good Morning Rob, I saw you leaving, did you sleep well? And if you are still thinking about our visa, I like to assure you that we are going to face no problem. They can't deny students after all and that we shall stay there only for the duration of the course. So don't worry, have one more cup of tea with me"

All the employees of Sofrek India Pvt. Ltd. arrived before the scheduled time, some on tipsy motorbikes, some on dilapidated auto rickshaws and very few with cars. Papers for a few were not in order, with a few essential ones missing and each one crowded up Reman for an assurance that they had the complete set. They compared their paper with the rest and even a fastidious Robin found a few discrepancies and the possibility of breaking a sweat in the early winter chill. Reman asked everyone to stay where they were and that each did possess the complete set of papers. The difference was mainly because each one had different case histories.

"Only make sure you have enough photocopies for all your documents, and the appointment letter. And why are you all getting so excited at the moment. I am the first one who is going in and I will let you know exactly what you need once I come out. Pray for me guys, and stop fussing over small things, get the fluids into your system and stay away from danger. In another fifteen minutes I shall step in. Relax everybody." Reman spoke like a true leader.

Reman was sucked in the next moment like a vacuum pump sucking up dirt. He was lost on the insides without a trace and hanging in there forever with no inkling of street wise hollers. It did take some time, however, to get in, standing in a slowly wafting queue and stepping forward in a trickle with his bulbous bag, swinging softly as a true friend. He gladly sank into a warm good bye at the precipice of the entrance when he was about to enter into the building and be lost in its working corners. The group stood under the warm sun, their thoughts like black clouds building up on a parched day, bent on creating a sudden havoc and hidden cravings of the unusual. Each one had emerged with smooth utterances of English language to raise a sudden eyebrow and perfectly fit a stipulated minute. Most of them were like those sales people wandering with their products door to door, swatting phrases in English. What the students didn't realize was that the Americans consider everyone their pals especially with the ones they converse in English. They could go the Roni way and try to divert the attention of those window officials to a road they knew. Yet the officials would probably be aware of all such tactics and dimensions, having dealt with a large number of people and countered their intentions for years.

The group could see hopeless faces, despairingly holding on to their papers, hardly walking, and not wanting to mince words with any soul on their way. There had been too many denials on the way and Robin wondered if he could leave all the worries behind and play a flute by the honest and quiet lake at sundown. Some were locked under a tree praying for some hope, some lay on the grass uprooting some tender roots while others were riding high on spicy food from the wayside hawker.

Two hours into the dome of heat of an emerging afternoon and there were no signs of Reman. They wondered if Reman had lost his way in his pleadings to carefully consider their application even after a stern rejection. They grouped together to eke out a decision in the trying circumstances. They all felt that it made sense to wait a little longer before someone among them could romp through the entrance. Rank and Roshan had a lot of catching up to do it seemed and they were onto each other like ladies at the end of the day. While others struggled to come out with words to match the occasion those two never needed a hint to break out into a conversation. Their faces seemed rather intimidating to Robin as he could recollect their warning to stay away from Roni for good. Rodney was nowhere to be seen. Perhaps he had found a quiet corner all to himself and was keeping a constant eye on the proceedings from a rare angle.

When three hours passed without any news from Reman, the crowd began to ponder. They formed an irregular circle and stood in silence for moments. Roni was the first among the volunteers to jump into the building and track Reman. He was evenly seconded by all and all his papers were securely handed over to him before he melted into the queue. He smiled at Robin and patted him on the back before pulling up his sleeve for a ride. The queue moved forward gradually in inches and centimeters until they reached the magnanimous black hole and subsequently sucked in for lost time. The heat was getting to the boys, their faces were shining with sweat and the liquids were not enough to keep them hydrated. One more hour and then somebody would faint to the hostile sun. It was a time of the year when winter was solely meant for the night and the afternoon would elicit minimal wear around the chest and sleeves. Roni was one with the crowd that sang a different tune and people readily buried into the working queue without a murmur. They were bound in seriousness and worked in perfect harmony hardly requiring any intervention, softly closing the gap between them and the entrance. The trees stood in silence with a canopy of shade with the dead leaves hanging in futility and forgetting the tune of the lost wind. They could hardly dance on their own without their playful mate from heaven. The brows of the boys were mingled with sweat and dust and their hair was still just like the state of minds. Some lay still on a stony bed and the estranged block of stone which was the obvious pillow that could hardly pretend knocking someone off to sleep. The air was totally dead and there was no excitement for the boys who borrowed niches and shades from the kind folk who had just descended to try their luck. Waiting period was the worst to tackle when people within forgot that their wasteful expressions and uncalled for movements was costing somebody waiting. It could drive the people waiting outside, insane. Water supply was scarce and each one swallowed a quart from a moderately cold bottle of water. Another moment of intensity and anything could happen. Roni was under the fan, glad to have made the move and stood clear of the steaming weather. Eyes were beginning to wilt under the oppressive heat, faces agape in the final lap. There was no noise except that of a heart pounding for a reason and ready to blow like a time bomb. Roni was about to enter into the dome when a holler pumped some life into the seething atmosphere. It was a rejuvenated and vivacious reman ready to move a rock with his dangling master by his side, emerging too late, one thought, from the office. He quickly gathered everyone around him including Roni, who appeared rather disgruntled and smiled as if Reman had been playing a practical joke on his colleagues.

"Sorry guys, that one took a long time, I know. They were happy to receive me as a representative of Sofrek India Pvt. Ltd. and from their gestures it seemed they were keen on giving us the visa. Yes, that's right they have called us together and not individually and I think we have sailed through the rough sea together this time. They have given us two hours to assemble at the window. So please guys, freshen up and cheer up. The battle is almost won. This time you don't have to wait in a queue, we'll go in together as a group. Have lunch guys, there is a restaurant nearby and drink lots of water. You have one hour and twenty minutes before we meet here again. Don't despair guys, we are almost through and we are sailing together to the land of the free. Come to me if you have any questions. See ya"

Eyes were forced open and crumpled limbs were straightened and energy sought from an impoverished reservoir. After hours of null and void of intense silence and heat, words of life echoed through the saviour. All of them renounced their canopies for a word with the sun. They joined their groups when it came down to culinary exploits and each one searched their pockets for some extra cash for that extra garnish and gravy. They all walked down scattered to the restaurant that was not far away and it would not take a long time to negotiate lunch in the hectic weather. The group had probably not known thirst this way before and they were bent on deserting their meager pockets on compassionate bottles of water. They once again amicably formed groups depending on their palates, sometimes being forced down more towards others taste, but all in good humour and bonhomie. The group looked relaxed and left all the planning and plotting for a later juncture. They had enough time to stretch the tearing of their breads or to dip them in sauce and gravy concoction for as a long as they wished to. Rank and Roshan saw this as a perfect opportunity to break into a conversation, devouring each other's company with rank sensibility. The seriousness of the mission didn't bother them and they broke off into their own wavelength finding peace and laughter in each other's company.

The crowd began to slowly part the restaurant for the incomplete mission. The wind had emerged from nowhere to lend them its hand and make the place cooler and bearable. The sun was fading in the distance and the bobbing leaves were signaling the onset of the cold winter night. Bare chests were overdone with sheaths of wool and the occasional muffler curved around the neck for protection from the unpredictable winter. The sun whipped its last for the day and lent its blessings for the day to the boys.

Reman was already standing at the entrance with his heavy overload and addressed the boys for one final occasion,

"Come nearer boys, stand together. Thank you for coming on time. We still have sometime before we go in. Remember, be relaxed and pray before you go in. They know all they wanted to know about us, our company, from me and I don't think they will ask too many questions. Listen to them carefully before you answer and be brief. They have allergy to long submissions and don't have the time to empathize with a million stories. Just hand them your papers and let them do the rest. I hope you guys had good lunch and have all the energy for this final and critical mission. One more careful step and we are there. And remember I want each one of us to get the visa. It's either going to be none of us or all of us. On that note, let's form a queue and we shall enter together. Rodney, you come first. That's right. Here we go."

The black hole was conquered in no time and all of them were in the dark lit up by incandescent white light and were asked to stand in a line at a particular window. This was the first opportunity for Robin to observe the working of the Consulate within. There were many windows with the interviewers, mostly Americans, calling out the candidates in order. They made their decisions within seconds on the fate of the pursuer even before papers were presented. Rodney moved to the window first with all his papers. Moments seemed tricky like a tight rope walk and they didn't want to hear too soon as it may spell prison for some and holiday under the soothing sun for others. He didn't take long to come out, cheerful and euphoric, running away from the gallows, like he had felt divinity and wanted to hold it in his heart lest the feeling escaped. He could hardly breathe when he appeared before his colleagues and in a panting laughter remembered to nod his head if nothing else.

"*We are home guys, run for your ticket. He's stamping them all, go get your share*" Rodney couldn't hold himself back.

All the employees went one by one and were granted visa. Robin was given the visa on the promise that he would not stay in the US for more than four months. He would take the first flight back after he received the certificate for the course. Robin couldn't agree more and thanked the official at the window several times until the official pushed him away in good spirit. Reman was the first on that dream ship and the gamble by Sofrek India Pvt. Ltd paid off, indeed.

They outrageously broke the decorum and the peace around the Consulate with hugs and cheer. Voices turned to noises that vehemently disturbed the proceedings of the Consulate. Someone sang a paean of the dusky landscape of the countryside of the Northern plains of the Punjab and Haryana. There was a jubilant pat on the thighs as recursive percussion and all joined in trying to fit into the rhythm. They hugged each other for miles and their song never seemed to end. They formed rings on the main road singing and dancing like never before. Their weakened bodies through the rut of the day had seen a sudden upsurge of energy from undisclosed reserves. They wondered how the cross questioning of the window officials had dwindled in the heat. Very soon the phones started ringing as they drifted to the corners of the streets, scattered and ring less. They pretended despair and then finally letting out their tears of joy and making everyone count in their triumph. The boys were on the move, getting early tickets booked, arranging for a selloff of their land for some cash.

"*Slap me, I can hardly hold my nerves. Do something, is it true, or is it Santa rubbing his silken moustache too hard for a tale that seems like a tale*" Roni had been struck by lightning. Laughter and gaiety echoed through the confluence of the heightened. They were hooked on the word that had puzzled them and their forefathers for centuries – America.

"That's right guys we're all going to the USA. My God even I don't believe it" Reman was still in a state of shock. Their mindless shrieks tangled in synchronicity and they thoroughly enjoyed the euphoric plunge. The common agenda and achievement melted away all the differences among the boys and they mingled in one colour of brotherhood and togetherness. They forgot their petty clashes that had chocked the horizon once and created narrow dividing paths that led to their own dominion. The feeling of oneness was there to be seen. They hollered invectives in the air, loud and clear, that somehow justified their state and place in the world in the cold. Robin was waiting for some peace to talk to 'R' man and when he found a quiet corner he connected to 'R' man,

"Pa, how are you? I got the visa. Very soon I can now go to America, Congratulations"

"Yippee- yoyo congratulations to you too. Ahhhhahaaaa... You've made it. Didn't I tell you so? This is the best news I have heard for ages. Say ol' chap there comes a time in everyone's life. But believe me you are destined for higher plains. I can't tell you how happy I am. This yellow oleander had been telling me something in the last few days. Seems like I totally misread it. You are a jolly good fellow; you've made my dreams come true. Make a wish, son! This is your day."

Back home people could see the smile in 'R' man's eyes. He stretched his lips to accommodate a rare smile and subsequent laughter when he disclosed the news to 'R' lady. The choppy breeze cut across the bells of yellow oleander swallowing even the newer green one. They formed glistening yellow patches on the ground. The whole tree shrieked with laughter like a fat man poked substantially all over his torso. The whole body trembled with fat waves that never seemed to subside. The music of laughter was replaced by the mighty rustle of the leaves, long and slender. They shook their heads in total surrender without a clue to the turnstile adventure. 'R' man called up his handful friends who were caught in their own web, singing in their own tunes, shriveled up in the melee of life, for a drink to celebrate the occasion. There were a few left in the group to whom 'R' man could deliberate and lighten up like young boys. Life had indeed a few pleasures and this was a rare one in 'R' man's basket and he thanked his jubilant stars for the grand victory. He could just look up into the dark night sky to see his two stars once they leave far away in the skies and bless them for their onward journey. Life always makes a full circle. There was a time when he had made his plans to go to the US too soon and now both his young ones made it to the cherished land without any help.

Each of the ten employees of Sofrek India Pvt. Ltd had booked their ticket to LA from New Delhi. They were to fly tonight and 'R' man was by Robin's side helping him with the last minute packing and rearranging important documents.

"How will I carry on without you Pa, I feel sad and lonely. Can't you come with us, Pa? We'll climb onto the candy store or the coffee shop for some cakes by the evening. How can I ever manage without you" Robin felt like missing eternity.

"Don't worry sugar. I am walking right behind you. I will come to visit you and don't forget Reuben will be there at the airport to receive you. So why worry? We are all set, do you have the tickets?" 'R' man made sure everything was in place.

'R' man wondered that this bird had left too soon. It was getting near evening and Roni and Robin booked a cab to the airport. Robin would soon disappear into the aisles with longing eyes losing grip over the colour of his shirt. Even the hollers and wave of the hand would turn ineffective and deemed perpetual waste. 'R' man soon turned into a waving silhouette disappearing in the distance and Robin turned his head to incumbent matters. Gone were the days when 'R' man carried little Robin on his shoulders and Robin all too shy for the perch and running his hands like little feathers over the huge face of 'R' man. The little boy with shorts and a constant finger in his mouth had grown up to travel Economy class all on his own to the dazzle of a dream. 'R' man was lost more than ever in the culmination of a dream and he wondered why he felt so forlorn. Like in the frequent train rides when he would perch and fix the children together on the upper berth, this time he had fixed them together to the same destination to support and ride smoothly on the road of life. Was it a vendetta against life or a stubborn plea that never seemed to accrue in his lifetime until he was too old and grey on his first ever visit to Reuben in the US to think of settling down on the easy lanes of the cherished land. He suddenly realized he had never been so lonely and the excesses of life could never replace the two reasons why he hung on to the game so long.

Two years into the breeze and soft chowder and Robin was not giving up. His friends had aptly deserted him to encumbered soft voices leaving behind tinge of pure and pristine woods and a culture they called bizarre. They were back in the thoroughfare of a job and life at home. They had seen and conquered like never before and garnered a glimpse of the other side. They stormed through those Robin nights on the threshold of convincing him that he should revert to niches of grace and the splendours of the little working space back home. They dragged him to strap his belongings, tipsy and overdone with the local brew, high on the smoky rings of freedom. They unearthed the promising future that awaited Robin back home deep into the night under the brightening sky until it irked the hotel staff driving away the boys to their rooms. But that was long ago when his friends urged Robin to hop onto the same flight they were on to take them home and not hold onto his rigid mind until it was too late. Robin listened to them carefully that night and was convinced that four months were not enough to blend with the place and discover the heart of America.

They had seen enough of dark blue skies, tangerine mornings, and freshness of a morning bath. Food so pure that it could induce rapid growth, those smooth bus rides carefully scripted and cleanliness that could remind one of heaven. They had lived together as a group rife with arguments and squabbles but had battled their way through to celebrate birthdays and special days with romp and gaiety.

Robin finally reached the gates of Stonewood University for a Masters program in Engineering. Two years of studies in various colleges, hopping on a plane frequently to meet Reuben who was not far away, Robin never realized how time slipped under the sole of his feet. He had been abiding Dr. Rishi getting abundant supplies of his wonder drug to keep him sane and mobile. He kept the small yellow pill by his bedside to remind him of the dosage and was like fresh oxygen pumped into his system. It however did occur to Robin to get checked up with the best psychiatrist in the area, and probably the world who could bring him out of religion of timely doses.

Robin wrote regular letters to 'R' man before the end of each day. He assiduously clicked on the 'send' button after compiling a dossier. It had a taste of the American weather and faintly revealed the reason why the world was hooked on this land.

'R' man shared glimpses of his own battle with torrid times in his life. 'R' man's uttering abruptly ended with the reminder of his doses and that he should not restrain from a second opinion of an American psychiatrist. Robin had moved in with Reuben and within a few weeks was to join the University for higher studies. It was the winter month and Robin could feel the chill in his toes. He went for a stroll early morning to latch on the fresh supplies of donuts and mild coffee that was warm and not too bitter. Back home 'R' man took his customary cold water shower to cut the winter chill. He had been very active this winter starting his day with a tinge of morning prayer and walking the city streets all day because of a faulty ignition of his scooter.

Besides he didn't have enough change each day for him to swing by the streets in an assertive auto rickshaw, a shade faster than a brisk walk. He lend his sumptuous and imaginative hand at helping ex-servicemen at his doorstep everyday blinded by the light of everyday hassles and yearnings. He was exerting himself beyond his body limits while Robin sank in this dream; he had with his father and mother by his side. There was a soft realization of 'R' man's dream of visiting places he had only read about in novels like Los Angeles and San Francisco. The office that stood miles away was like a joke to 'R' man who cut through the weeds and the dust. He was dodged incessantly by the venomous traffic, passing through in short decisive steps until he reached the destination. This routine was exercised each day making him quietly abandon his scooter. The world was aloof and swinging about in their worldly frivolous games as he walked by in a lost gaze, sweating and breathing heavily when collapsing seemed the obvious. He searched for a purpose to be alive. He somehow felt lonely without the boys and their grace and infinite possibilities back home that could give him a reason to persevere.

His ramblings didn't take him anywhere when one night he had chest pains. 'R' lady panicked and he was taken to the nearby hospital with the help of relatives. It had been bulging all this while until the harsh pounding of the body lead to an unbearable pain that perhaps knocks once in a lifetime. It was the dead of the night and he was given the oxygen mask for a normal breathing. The boys were informed and Reuben insisted on returning home immediately only to be urged against it by 'R' man.

"Say ol' chap this is just a small hiccup. I will be up and about in no time. I have never been admitted to the hospital in all so many years. I think this was due. You take care now, don't worry about me. I will call you when I need you. Bye for now." 'R' man consoled an upset Reuben.

Reuben was sad and never thought that life would turn out this way. 'R' man, he thought had crucified himself for the sake of his dreams and made his young boys strangers to their own land. Preparations were initiated in their childhood when they were swung heartily in their cradles to English lullabies. The 'American' often ricocheted off the walls and danced on the ceilings. So when Reuben was off to the best college in the country with his education directed towards getting a PhD abroad, 'R' man was glad to have directed the crashing waves to a place they call paradise.

The next day the boys kept their keen eye on the phone for it to ring and bring in the fresh news of 'R' man's health. 'R' man was the one that walked with bare chest to the heat and cold, meeting the day with strength and a body that never erred. It was evening and Reuben was reconsidering his decision to fly home to be by his father's side. The phone rang and 'R' lady was crying on the receiver trying to form complete words in her upsurge of grief.

"Please come Reuben, Pa is not well. Anything can happen anytime. Don't wait"

Reuben was in shock and contacted his travel agent in panic wanting the earliest flight back possible.

The phone rang once again and this time 'R' lady could hardly utter a word.

"Pa has p...assed awa...y."

The receiver dropped from Reuben's hand and he couldn't fathom the moment of grief, was dumb and speechless until he formed the words that meant an end of the 'R' family. He fell on the floor with Robin by his side and cried like he had lost all hope fully drenched in tears and sweat and felt somewhere that he should never have gone so far away from 'R' man. Robin was in a state of shock and could never understand what had happened. He never cried and instead appeased Reuben answering his childlike questions and trying to get fluids back into his system.

The proud flame that exuded warmth and evoked laughter on those tough tidings even though he carried a load of sadness and futility on his chest had entered sleep forever. Not many knew him, but those who did would always remember him as a man who bequeathed his life for selfless service of humankind. He lend a piece of his soul whenever he found someone in distress, regardless of the outcome and never holding a penny for his own winters or scorching summers. He felt always that he was on a fast moving plane that would take him away too soon and knew the time when the end came knocking on his doorstep. He was a man who was not only honest with his pennies at work and never carrying the chaff home that was not his but he was also honest with his emotions. Sometimes he thought he had treated the boys and 'R' lady rather harshly and he cried before Robin several times in apology and came forth as a very caring and honest man with a clear conscience. His life was a symbol of love and devotion. He never left the sight of his loved ones till the day he died even though he could never accept the civilian life far in the pockets of hoodlums. Yet he had created a spark in the boys, a thirst that could make them seek the highest in a constant pursuit.

'There walked a man,
In total surrender,
In a rhythm unknown,
Untouched and forlorn,
Someone heard an English sigh,
And when time drew nigh,
He walked on by,
Unheard and forgotten,
To One who is,
Heaven and desire.

A proud flame extinguished too soon before 'R' man could drift into old age. He exhorted plenty about his end when he was alive and thrived on times when he was young and the days were measured in milk and honey. Robin had last seen him at the airport watching him leave and as night fell he couldn't see his father and the sharp brightness of the lights within blinded him. All that was left were a few letters sprinkled with words of encouragement from 'R' man and reflections on the current state of affairs in the disorderly world. 'R' man had magically turned into a fairy that dwelled in the skies. Robin felt he was not going to be around for long whenever he saw 'R' man. Reuben went back home to perform the final rites and Robin stayed on, too shocked and loneliest he had ever been. The protector, the divinity, person who showed the right way to prosperity and happiness had suddenly become silent. He uttered no words of apologies or solace to his folk, or an evening resolve to start fresh and new and forget the past. Robin shifted to a dormitory and would spend the entire day lying down on his single bed and didn't want to light up the stove or satiate his appetite by those on-the-run sandwiches. He had been quiet and pensive for quite some time until finally one day he broke down, tearing his heart out with his cries in the corner and carrying on until dusk. He followed the ritual for days until finally one day there was nothing left to cry. He had wept alone in a cosmic strife when there were no kind shoulders or arm to bury his face into. He had been left accosting the pain and the tears that washed his face and elicited the purity of the soul amidst the helpless walls of his dormitory.

There were images of his father in his mind and he never knew where to bury himself in the deft claws of time. He felt 'R' man, with a bare chest and a stumbling *'pyjama'* (casual trousers), lean into the boys in their room neatly discussing the next step in their agenda. He felt 'R' man's calling in the distance in the far depths of his mind. He believed firmly that there were words left unspoken to 'R' man and vice versa and that they were destined to meet again, somewhere and somehow. He would holler out to his father on the other side of the river. He would softly walk through brooks totally burying his shoes in water and wetting the extreme fold of his trousers until they embraced and lived together forever. He would wait for that time with sinking eyes and somehow wade through the sea of life that lay before him speaking out his father's name wherever he went. Father was dust, he would never see him walk to him, yet the longing and the love would see them together in a real reincarnation. It was hard to bear the loss of someone so close, tirelessly honing on a line of thought and bringing the world to the doorstep in graceful steps and collapsing thereafter in looms of tiredness. 'R' man hurried at the hospital rather amazed at being there for his own treatment rather than attending somebody else like always. He trudged on the scythe turf, presuming he was totally out of pangs of breathlessness to pay bills that could hardly wait. He fell down hard on the ground with a major cardiac arrest. He was tight robed, in the essential business shoes and the shirt that could make a statement in one of those meetings at his house. He abandoned his wheel chair, assuming that it was a minor glitch and he would check out like after a bout of drinks at a party in the local mess. There he lay on the pyre, totally lifeless, listening to the wood and had entered a different world for one who went away too soon.

Robin was getting ready for college. The clangour, chatter and the noise on the streets, in stores, in halls, in the parking lot and everywhere were enough to pull him out of his moaning for the loss of a friend and guide in a harsh world. He would push his pocket for a cup of coffee at the local store surrounded by the normal heathen milieu. It was like all the world could exist without the brilliant scarf of the strong, amiable 'R' man who was like the wind that blew in its own course with no care of its beginning or end. He framed a picture of 'R' man and placed it in line to his bed to gaze and ponder when the daytime was too chaotic to even consider sitting beside him and reminisce. One day it was too late in the night to even consider a new line of thought. He was just about to shut down when his hands softly touched his waist that seemed rather round than straight and a stomach that was beginning to bulge. He remembered 'R' man's words when he stressed on burning the overload, being as light as the feather. He had advised eating to the extent to leaving some room for the stomach to ponder and consider being flat like the road under the road roller. He got up when a lightning of the new thought struck him like straight out of 'R' man's stuck posture. He decided to forgo sweet reclining on those catastrophic mornings and those lazy afternoons when he would bend his head out of his bed until it was upside down and the blood rejoiced in stumbling to a place they had hardly ever been. To undo the irritating feeling of holding folds around his body that only looked good in animals; he decided to deny the body the reason for menacing thick bulge. It was summer and he conveniently rummaged his wardrobe for a pair of shorts. He decided to go for a run each day starting with short laps that his body could initially bear and increasing the weights as he went along. It would be a perfect preparation for college when he would need all the strength and poise to battle the mysteries of logic with a healthy and diligent mind. It was time for a new drain but he ought not to extend it to outrageous limits. He ran the distance he could digest the next day. As a penultimate melody to his adventure he added a ritual of a tempestuous sprint that summarized his intensions of challenging the world. It ended before he realized that he was actually stretching his body early morning and he was into the coffee zone in a blink to carefully consider the next day.

College had started and the new students were greeted by the staff graciously mixed with an assault of cups of warm coffee and potato chips and invited questions in an open house. There was a stampede to get the right kind of books, stationery and other essentials and in the struggle Robin almost forgot what it was for.

He joined the University library for some extra income and he had to constantly cajole Mr. Rucker for a place until he finally agreed without harping on an interview.

Mr. Rucker was kind and amiable and there was plenty going on in the library. They were shifting books out of the library for its demolition and construction of a new one in its place. Hence they required an efficient workforce to transfer the huge number of books out of the library into room specifically designed for its storage.

Robin would earn enough to meet his daily expenses, extend it to buying some course books but could not pay his rent with the cushion money.

One month passed and Robin pursued his daily burn to the hilt, increasing his limits ever so softly until he could endure four to five miles at a stretch. His last leap had almost become legendary as he plonked his footsteps in air like a horse and breezed through the sprint in a blaze and a splash like a cheetah in hot pursuit and it never seemed to end. People would shut their eyes, trying to avoid the gibber and the mindless burn, show of strength and a hint of what the human spirit stands for but he persevered to military precision. Winter had changed to spring and he ran true when it poured and people escaped for some shade and ignored the maniacal strain of Robin and his pursuit. He had turned gaunt and his belly had shrivelled with little or no fat around his waist. There was a lot of catching up to do in his studies. Settling down in a new trade required previous intervention at the undergraduate level and his college studies earlier were starkly different from what the new trade demanded. He could start from scratch overworked with convoluted and byzantine arithmetic logic. It bamboozled the layman with his mundane and trivial grasp over aspiring models that required careful hours of consideration. Time was of the essence and he blankly nodded his head to astute postulations in agreement with the learned crowd of students gathered. To them the serpentine logic was another day with words and the way they refreshingly made sense. He was a step behind his fellow graduate friends and entered the world of the undergraduate like he willingly embraced his new set of friends when he had flunked once some time ago. He was worked up trying to dazzle in the frequent quizzes and test thrown at him and soon found out that his might couldn't outdo the average scores. Yet he graduated from that class with a mild stare from the smirking instructor and let it be. He was to handle classes later at the graduate level that required intuition and rare mathematical acumen.

He ran with greater vigour covering miles in a jiffy and stank of sweat and dust. His legs moved effortlessly in a mechanical precision. They would have covered the entire world if not directed elsewhere to farfetched obligations and tidings of suffocating day. He let them speak on frisky mornings when his senses were hardly alive to claustrophobic conquests and the real fun was under the blue and grey. His legs conveniently bore the load and there were no signs of weakening on account of a previous injury. They strengthened with every lunge and gave the impression that they were never incapacitated.

One fine morning when he had accomplished his father's death wish and the little band army of young students followed his footsteps and begun to run after him, he decided to have a word with the doctor (psychiatrist) on duty at the university hospital.

Dr. Roland Murphy, practicing psychiatry at the University hospital in addition to a private clinic he ran, was a sensible man. He had broken into the minds of his numerous patients through artifice and logic. He could pre-determine the programmed move of his patients and how they could probably react to a situation or a question thrown at them. The Bible of psychiatry religiously sat next to him. The Bible was the answer to all his patients' deviant questions and the panacea to the anomalous contortions of his patients' complicated behaviour that went over his bald head. His grey beard and little tufts of grey hair on the sides of his head leaving the centre portion completely bare was a testament to his long years of practice and achievement. He had the most sensible eyes and they kept coming to his patients given his years of hard work trying to break the usual code and discover a new facet of the human mind. He climbed on the Freudian bus by mistake when he was once trying to impress his girl friend, fresh out of high school. But the frivolous trampoline took a serious turn, rating human psychology as the most spectacular thing since the invention of the wheel. Before he could think of topping an art form, he was totally immersed and gone, playing around with his patients and milking the Bible. He was gaunt and tireless, little under nourished. He guzzled tonnes of coffee each morning to make his eyes penetrating and intimidating to the sound of irreprehensible questions, too simple for their own good. He decided to take his life seriously when he was once driving through a desert, totally broke and searching for a meaning to his life. He felt the desert was like the human mind where once can drive for miles and still get the impression that one stands at the same point from where the journey began. One cannot stop until once sees a mirage or an oasis and for most parts even that is hallucinatory. He tried his hands at pottery trying to shape the extraordinary to find out that his hands were too rough for the clay. He had gradually become stiff and a no-nonsense man with age and even suspected the street children poking at him as he climbed into his car each morning with his cuppa. His voice had gained clarity and penetration with age and everyone around was forced to lend a patient ear to his uttering each day, especially in the morning when his sessions began. Risk was an everyday event at his sessions and he always kept a documentary proof of his patient's words. He practically noted down every small detail of the sessions so that the patient's could not refute him later. He felt desperate when he lost his son. He grew twenty years older in one night with locks of grey posing difficult times and questions that buried in the dark lines below his eyes.

His scalp didn't hold much hair although it promised to crown the head for good and entertain even the direst of petitions without dropping off. He sat in his sad room all by himself for hours trying to find a reason to further a genuine effort to better understand human actions and the depth of human mind. He had let his child breathe easy and never let a shadow of bickering parents disrupt his humongous plans to spatter his own colours of freedom. But a freak accident silenced Dr. Roland's own voices in a way and he didn't want to be a revelation peeking in shifted minds in his box of tragedies. He shared the pain with his better half and groped for a strong reason to continue his practice. The upswing of time and weather and the ricochet to bees drowning themselves into a new season looking for unrivalled honey could not be stopped. Life moves on and we find new reasons to illuminate and dress the surroundings with our own voices and heal the constantly suffering human spirit. He became noisier, cramping up the subtle nuances of his patients with his ordained rules, getting irritated too soon. He searched for the apt word and phrase he wanted to hear from his patients. He cut through his patient's uttering with his voluble tread and not giving up too soon. He listened to the hush of the crowded leaves on trees and those dead ones strewn all over the ground with a slap of the fluctuating breeze. He planted a tree in his garden for his boy until it would toss leaves into the wide open skies and turn into a full grown tree with a thick bark. His questions were far more penetrative that dug into the true reason for his patients to be alive. His prognosis was final and he never went back on his decisions.

Robin, the perpetual stargazer decided to peek into Dr. Roland's room to hear the latest word regarding the state of his supple mind. He reached the counter desk for an appointment with the doctor early one morning with a cold cup of coffee in one hand. The doctor was not in yet and the kind counter desk official asked him to flip through the glossy in the interim in the waiting room. Robin heard the murmur at the front desk. A group of ladies, quite old and few young ones buried their gaze in tomes of paper tucked in files and managed the office to soft music that never ceased. They caressed the paper all day, hardly looking out of the window to watch the birds in the beautiful garden outside and branches of trees. The paper weights travelled the entire office keeping a constant eye over paper and amusing the engaged by being tossed low into the air.

Dr. Roland entered the office at ten to nine enquiring about his appointments at the front desk. He pressed his eyes open with a warm cup of coffee in his hands and headed for his room. His eyes barely wandered for his patients waiting in the adjoining waiting room. One could hear the usual noises of a morning medical centre. He cantered along ignoring the obvious music and called his first patient for the day, Robin.

Robin gingerly entered his room to make Dr. Roland look up once at him before submerging in piles of paper with a swift pen. He captured the depth of swing of Robin's arms and how he sung waveringly in high and low monotones.

"Welcome Mr. Robin, how have you been? I would like to hear a brief history of your suffering from the time you first felt alienated from the rest of the crowd. Go on..."

Robin took a deep breath and narrated the happenings and the environment that probably sparked off the fusillade of sorrows. He described the loss of appetite, lurking in shadows trying to avoid human trails, trying to self destruct and tiring the body to manic limits. Dr. Roland listened carefully ever so busy making notes and sipping coffee intermittently and sometimes shaking his head to fill up the blank that Robin expressed in his conversation. He seemed not totally in tune with the words trying to unearth certain tricky situations in the past. Robin tried to cover every small part of his past life and how he had shrivelled up in the heat, stung by an over worked mind until his brain cells caved in. An hour passed and there were moments of silence with the doctor tapping his pen gently on paper and softly running his hands over his soft beard.

"I have fully studied your case and have finally come to a conclusion. Your abnormality is marked by streaks of highs and lows. You were either too happy to get a hold over things, euphoric in the least or were too sad, breaking down into an acute depression. I think you are

suffering from bipolar disorder just like in the Bible and I do sniff some more questions coming my way. Please do ask, don't hesitate but my investigation is thorough and complete and my conclusion is accurate."

Robin was speechless. He was glad to have consulted a top psychiatrist and was convinced that he was indeed going through some changes in his mind. He thought and that he had been falsely implicated to those yellow pills that sounded and felt too meagre to usher any psychosomatic changes. He felt that Dr. Rishi had seen the wrong end of his psyche and moreover he never consulted any kind of Bible or an assistant to help him in the final diagnosis. Dr. Roland was precise and he had cured many with the disorder. Robin was chirpy, trying to open up to the doctor who probably jotted down the unspeakable, grinning plenty in return. Dr. Roland returned,

"There are some tests that need to be done before we are certain about our course of action and the final medicine that has to be taken for quite some time. Give your blood sample at the counter and meet me tomorrow when I shall disclose the name of the new medicine and the dosage and you shall never have any discrepancies."

Robin ran out of the unit trembling with happiness, wanting to climb onto the trees and hum together with the song birds. He wanted to run for miles for no good reason, a mere expression of excitement and elation of his limbs. He longed for yellow oleanders and wondered how they were fairing in the ferries of time standing in their garden. Yellow oleanders perhaps missed the persistent gaze of 'R' man in seasons as they touched its spiked leaves and tender flowers. They stood there in silence nonchalantly playing in the random wind with sparingly few flowers in the sad vibe of 'R' house.

But Robin was happy and he didn't want to delve on the chocolate croissant too long. He wanted to tear off the blanket of cloud in a greyish sky with the warmth of his breath and let the sun glow once again. Time had called for a change of line of thought and he wanted to extract all the information about the disorder that was perhaps hampering normal subsistence. He would probably hear the last of those minuscule yellow pills that had kept him intact for quite some time. He faced no problems ever since he met with an accident. He came to the US, stayed with friends in a hotel, studied for two years in various universities and worked in the library to eke out a survival mechanism that never failed. But this could fetch better results and he observed it was a common occurrence that the person who wore glasses with corrective lens had better view of things than one without the glasses. So in summary, it was a corrective measure with his behaviour better modulated. It would give a stronger grip over emotions of sadness and happiness, heat and grey, warm and cold, black and white. He had felt the light of silky drizzles falling in his sensitive eyes. His senses were sharper inviting even the faintest of disturbance in the skies. The leaves had suddenly turned brighter and he could gaze at roses for hours without getting enough.

Next day he ran lost in thought at the fresh new diagnosis and if it will hurt him in the future. He arrived at the medical unit way before the doctor's arrival. He was once again lost in the gloss and gossip that spun his senses to places that hardly existed for him. His blood test was in and it looked pretty normal with a slight deviation on some counts. The doctor arrived in time not allowing Robin to wander too much and headed for his corner room. Robin was the second patient that day and Dr. Roland had already finished a mug of coffee and tossed the glass away. His Bible lay open on his table to some indiscriminate page that only the doctor could assimilate. He read out the minutes of the last check up to himself and prepared the write up of the current proceedings. Robin once again pushed through the lanes of by gone days and would be asked to rummage certain occurrences on the insistence of the doctor. For a moment Robin felt at ease with the doctor as he inched towards laughter and mirth on the doctor's sense of humour. He doctor hardly ever broke into laughter except at times when he crafted one, on greeting somebody or bidding good bye. Moreover, the recent happenings in his life had dried down any kind of affirmative fondling of laughter or gaiety. He hardly reacted to anything off the normal track. He somehow started believing that the shadow of mirth and frivolous gaiety was essentially a waste of time and a bane of modern existence. He hardly sought the word or expression that could do some damage to his repertoire and poke him into spreading his lips and illustrate his scarce cheeks in disdain. For this purpose his eyes were constantly nailed to the partially bare record book and some random page of his beloved Bible. For any discrepancy uttered by Robin, he conveniently flipped the pages of the Bible for an answer until its read out lines made complete sense. It explained Robin's frequent derailment from normal pulses, relating completely to Robin's plight. It was the Bible that gave him the logical conclusion that his treatment be directed towards treating dipolar disorder and not schizophrenia. Robin's efforts to break into a normal conversation were thwarted as every effort bounced off invariably to the Bible. It acted as a balm to the senses and the point of discussion plummeted to zilch.

"Mr. Robin, I'm afraid that yellow one has to go and sit untouched in your closet. I am introducing a fresh new white tablet which is much thicker than the yellow one. It will hold you from flying off the handle on those cold mornings and elicit genteel behaviour especially towards the vulnerable. At the same time you won't have sadness peek at you at adverse angles. You have a lot of pent up energy, use it wisely with prudence. Keep coming to me as long as your studies last here at the University and we shall nail the inhospitable, discomforting and disconcerting. This medicine has been tried and tested for ages and has shown the way to the adequate treatment of this disorder. Respect it and it will do wonders to your life. Bless you. Until we meet again... Take care."

Robin walked off singing in praise of the doctor. There was a dramatic twist in his life living with a new member and how it could stoke his insides for a grain of civil behaviour. His eyes crashed on the people in the office as each one raised a warm smile like the world had been waiting for the results. The light of the sun looked new and over powering and the leaves stood in silence waiting for the final verdict. The grass in the small lawn was inclined to a soft corner required pruning to make it more amiable for a walk. Robin had a long day ahead, going for classes until midday and then pushing carts with books down secret aisles in the library. A quick lunch ensued to rejuvenate before lugging more books in the meekly built cart until sundown and longer when the sun never showed up. His day would sometimes end with the evening classes. His mind was one with the movement of the instructor's lips, refined body movements, darkness outside and ducking to avoid the speaker's gaze. His morning began with a celluloid run, breaking miles with his soft shoes with ever expanding boundaries. In the end until it was time for the kill, a hundred metre sprint with no inkling of the clocked time. He wished to run the rest of his life until time spotted grey on his head and it was near time to bid adieu to this life. In one of his runs it he was running faster than he could. He lost the balance and his feet caved in and his body was thrown into vicious somersaults. His spectacles colluded with the thick breeze and were smashed to pieces. His I-pod ran for miles from the place of disaster until it was spotted by keen eyes. Blood poured from a slit in the leg just below his left knee cap, and his wrist too bled profusely. He got up and walked back without allowing the blood and pain to ebb and exciting no shoulder to help him back. He felt the perfect rhythm of his body even after it was bailed out from the uncontrollable and the inimitable. His body had turned to steel. His trousers never fit him and he was reduced to size zero and there was a clump of loose cloth that dangled uneasily around his slight waist. His meagre food was reluctantly swallowed and he held onto caffeine for some impulsive heat.

One month elapsed with the new medicine and he still hung onto laps in auspicious mornings. His vision had suddenly brightened and the foliage appeared greener and tangier than they ever had been and he could pierce the distance with his eyes. He had suddenly become talkative and uttered too loud sometimes for consideration. His mind was swinging with illusions and delusions once again. He saw his favourite singers and musicians of a bygone era walk together arm in arm in a chain with a dazzle of evening sunlight on their shoulders. They talked of peace and getting it right this time round. This was a recurring image and it pushed him to spread their message of oneness and solidarity through his songs that he had to effortlessly construct. He got sick of being followed and being forced to fuddle his mind with promiscuity as a reward for near perfect body. He hugged the streets ranting like a lunatic in the summer sun. He invited the usurper on to the blazing streets to let it out in the open and not hold any unholy desires. He was mildly tipsy without wine and liquor and the security got in his way trying to avoid any kind of street display. His shouts rang in the corridors of the college premises and there were a few eyes soaking in the shocker and walked on without being perturbed.

"What has the world come to? What do these people want? Why do they hide their faces behind faceless expressions? They can have a piece of me if that will make them happy. Where do you think we are headed to? If anybody out there wants to do it, why don't we do it right here in the streets. We have nothing to hide. Come out people, let's do it out in the streets, I am waiting."

Robin was not his own. He was angry and blurted out things that weren't true and he felt the need to break the ominous silence that had surrounded him for months. He then came up with contorted facts that were best avoided,

"You know I have known a homosexual for good eight years. Yes I had him in my life for so many years. Does anybody care? Where are we headed to, officer?"

Robin was blowing it up just to fill up the air. He changed the facts to suit the weather and create enough panic to burden the lips of the security with a smirk as they lead him to his room. The dormitory building was locked up with the sign *'The Doctor's in'* hanging outside and had been evacuated for the new doctor, Robin, in town. He had redesigned his stethoscope to soft earplugs that played enthralling music to parched ears. Unusual happenings stipulated the day and he never expected the dramatic turn of events. The very next morning he saw a girl in her car waiting for him in the parking lot of the dormitory, the one he saw a couple of times at an Indian restaurant behind the counter. She was probably inviting him to come along and take her away into the deserted and peaceful for romance by the lake in the morning sun that was still in earth's womb. He somehow ignored her and disappeared into the wind where nobody could find him. Or he would get up very early in the morning only to find an officer in a suit and hat waiting at the bus stop to keep an eye over Robin and would chase him without making it too obvious. He felt they were chasing him when he chose to walk by the side of busy roads, in pickups and SUV's with light that screamed at the senses. He felt the world was conspiring against him, his moves restricted by the sound of conniving footsteps in the distance, giving into the morbid chase too soon. He confirmed from the folks at the coffee shop counter if they could sense a semblance of brutality at him being narrowed in by spies that never directly sought their prey. They confirmed of no such occurrence and the policemen were simply patrolling the area and didn't have anybody in mind, in particular. They suggested a warm glass of steaming hot black coffee for the nascent grey morning that spoke of chilly fingertips and cold faces. His fleet footed rush in the morning to break the minute barrier had been replaced by soft saunters through the woods. The empty streets that just had his taciturn footsteps to break its ominous silence. He let darkness fall and then gingerly stepped out of his dormitory for another journey in the quiet and the tranquil. He walked freely for miles until it was difficult to find his way back lest he make the wrong turn and end up in a new world. He had turned into an innocuous stranger once again. He walked the countryside as long as the darkness and the damp permitted and then fell lifeless on his bed under the effect of those big round white tablets. On off days he crossed his limits and tread even longer with no inkling of time and the obligations of a routine existence. Pretty soon he found the sidewalks of haunted roads that had tossed in silence for ages filled with old men, women and children. They were out on the streets to enjoy the simple pleasures of a walk in the fresh and the open swinging to the pulses of footsteps of little children. They were out with balloons and festoons filling the dead streets with laughter and gaiety. Robin had never envisaged this kind of a climactic adoration of a self proclaimed effort. Was it really his effort that saw people let it be for moments before they turn numb and lifeless? Was it one of those short lived coincidences that held its nerve and initiate the spectacular? He couldn't make up his mind and was reminded of the cheerleader that joined Robin in the run each morning. He had been to the fast food restaurant one day and as he was talking to Reuben. A sea of people emerged from nowhere with smiles and cheer. An announcer appeared with a microphone with lots of people, like they wanted to hear Robin, until he was forced to leave because of the stampede. A lady with a camera taking pictures of her little girl stepping out of a car with Robin in the background. Taking pictures was just an excuse; the drive was bent on putting Robin into the picture. The same lady pumped her fists in the air with her little girl jumping in the air. The girl clapped with her tiny hands at having been rewarded for a quest that made them rummage the countryside for ages. Or the library staff that secretly took Robin's picture pulling a cart full of books and printed it in the library's monthly magazine on the front cover. Robin just groaned when he was told about the library picture. He didn't care to look up the magazine with his picture and was deep down stranded in his work ignoring all pleadings to see the magazine. And the strange occurred with him everywhere he went.

Sometimes he stepped into the unknown with his supportive shoes. The circuitous route led him to novel manifestations of dwellings that he had hardly ever tasted. He looked up suddenly to find oblong patches of sun through shrubs and the reeds on the smooth and alien roads ready to carry him even further into oblivion. He had walked assiduously into the afternoon before the sudden realization that he didn't know where he was headed. He walked until he was totally lost.

He then despairingly called up Reuben to picture the street where he stood on his satellite map of his car and follow astute instructions to get there and carry him with his overworked legs.

This procedure was repeated umpteen times until Reuben no longer required satellite assistance. He suggested that Robin rather stay at his dormitory and try walking straight into the university campus or a friendly coffee shop if he had to, far away from abstract. He had become voluble, often ruminating over his past and the friends he made as a child. He wondered how they might have fared in the Ferris wheel of life. It was as if they had been locked in a tight can all this while and waited for their master to free them. The words spoken in the past and incidents that had not reached their climax needed to be addressed. The frozen figurines that had solidified with snow needed some warmth. Incidents that had not culminated had to be brought to completion.

He didn't have all their numbers. He could reach just a few and that too their family members and not them directly as they had drifted to the unknown with time.

He started calling everyone he knew back home, dwelling on the past and how each one had touched him as a child. He was indebted to them even though some had turned foes with passing time. He called his uncle to share the time when he brought gum in colourful wrappers and pampered him with a ride to the local market collecting goodies and lots of jangling pencils in decent boxes. The uncle had married since then, had grownup children and had clean forgotten about those gay moments in the past. He remembered his multifarious aunts and uncles that crowded his room one night inviting him into the nebula of college life. They prodded him and teased him with their full force until he ran way to hide behind the opaque and secure. He could never forget his first kiss by those painted lips on his cheeks that he wiped away too soon by his aunt with a sturdy hand holding his chin. He was a child running all over the earth for cover lest someone utter his name in a gathering in the drawing room. He was kissed several times by aunts who just loved to entangle their lips and press his cheeks with a ...Mmmmmmmm...uh. They held chocolates on their manicured glossy finger nails and he locked his eyes to the floor while receiving them with those eyes that wanted to peep and suggest. He was short and sweet before the final stretch into the blemished shadows of a man, ruing over hostile games played abundantly and the loneliness of the dark. He was at the precipice of those fleeting moments of childhood when the world serves a big cake on a round table and everyone claps and wishes and sweet kisses are the order of the day. And now everyone seemed to have forgotten that he was once a darling, adored, swung in air and embraced to everyone's heart's content. How did he ever turn into the forbidden dust?

His aunts succumbed to Hindu weddings and discovered new homes, husbands and fast growing up kids to forget their time with the grasshopper in their garden. Robin never saw them ever since and doubted their existence. Uncles too joined their own families far away leaving him in oblivion. Robin had outgrown in shorts, shot high to the size of a man with tussocks of uneven beard. He had transcended the aisles of free jumping and rolling in hoops, rushing to pillar and post for blushing in the wet of a recurring kiss.

They all negated his nostalgia and asked the bland question of a well wisher,

"All that is OK but tell me how are you doing? Are you keeping fit and tell where you are at the moment? Please don't hang up Robu, we are there for you."

He called up 'R' lady several time back home in India who was in grandpa's house to celebrate his ninetieth. Grandpa could hardly hear that too at an unearthly hour way past midnight when it was late afternoon in the US.

"You can use some hot oil Grandpa, in both of your ears. Insert the oil softly through one ear until it drips through the other ear. Your hearing problem will vanish and save some litchis for me this summer, for I will be there soon."

Grandpa could hardly make out a single word and persisted with his rhyme,

"Who's that, please?"

He sent emails to his professor of Reuben's college under whom he had worked for some time. Professor Ram was happy to receive his emails initially and had often wondered where life had taken Robin after he left at the completion of his projects.

Robin regretted on the deadlock of his projects and that their open ended inference had not been aptly discussed. He further admitted that he had left a note too many while paying the restaurant for the dinner that night in which his parents were also invited. He couldn't figure out the direction in which he had turned the tap of the hostel while leaving for home at the completion of his projects. Another faux pas that erupted from his negligence was that he had not handed over the bicycle that he had used for so many months. It was probably sinking in the dust with no hands to revive the machine. He apologized for arriving on time on that pouring evening when Dr. Ram was drenched to the bone. Dr. Ram promised to be careful while fixing appointments with Robin in the future. Moreover he had forgotten his pillow and a bed sheet in the hostel room. He pleaded that it be handed over to one of the workers of the canteen. He had forgotten to tip Rutthayya, the silent worker of the canteen, who had so deftly helped him decipher hostel norms. He helped him with ways to earn a fresh glass of milk with cream by getting up early enough in the morning. He further suggested that the phones of the hostel for receiving incoming calls from relatives and friends far off in different cities be replaced. The receivers were too bulky and ineffective. Holding them for hours sapped all the energy when even dodging them intermittently to the ears seemed futile. He could inform Sakia the Pan-wala that he was looking for a break from studies, job to finally think of starting his own venture but very soon he too would join the club. Prof. Ram was upset and didn't want to avoid his pleadings. He wished he had an answer to his anxious past that had buried itself under the new sheath of mud. The town had coloured itself many times since then and the people were no more there where they stood in the past and had graduated to a different state of mind.

Robin wanted to talk to Prof. Ram on several occasion only to find that he was not available. His persistent efforts however bore fruit one evening and Robin grabbed the opportunity,

"Sir, what is this, you don't even want to talk to me. I have been trying to reach you for the last so many days and somebody informs me that you are out for a walk or some other place. Have you become such a big professor who has no time to listen to his students? I hope you have done all that was required and brought peace to a lot of minds that may have been wondering what happened. I hope you have pardoned me for the last time when I really couldn't carry on in your last project because of home sickness and impingent shifts in my state of mind because of the recurring episodes of schizophrenia." Robin hardly allowed Prof. Ram to speak who was feeling smidge irritated and failed at balancing so many questions on his forehead. He was anxious and disappointed at the same time for Robin and wondered how he could graduate from the Master's program. Robin posed as a difficult proposition for Prof. Ram who didn't want to mingle with him too soon and at the same time couldn't avoid him. He closed his eyes and decided this as the last opportunity that he would ever talk to Robin letting the boy figure put things by himself in the comforts of his home. So he gulped for the last time, cleared his throat with a loud grunt at the receiver, pressed his eyes for a fresh vision and began trying to explain the nonsensical and matters dead long ago.

"Listen Rob, listen to me. I have completed all the work you asked me to do. I can understand your feelings but you got to take good care of yourself, now. I have a good friend of mine over here who is suffering with the same disorder as you are. He is my best friend and we have shared a lot amongst each other. He is a brave man and a big name contributing to the society in a big way. So I don't see how you can't do the same. Take your medicines in time, concentrate on your studies for a while and you will never have any more problems in the future. My friend recently received a lifetime achievement award from the President of India and we are his followers. We need people like you, so don't despair and please I may not be always with you. You may have to walk alone.

About that girl you left behind while you were here and wanted to have before the evening back then, she has left the campus. Your efforts to track her down later were in vain because she had left. She was not fit for you and probably might have gotten married and had children by now. Please find some other girl. My best wishes. Phew, that settles all matters! As an aside let's break off, don't try to call me again, I just had enough from one man. Live your life and it is true that I was once concerned for you. But now it doesn't matter, God really cares for his children. So goodbye Rob, I have closed the chapter and promise never to like a student this way too soon. Ciao."

Before Robin could breathe again, another door was closed forever. Earlier a school friend who had settled on this side of the ocean had invited Robin for an evening at his upstate bungalow. He sat with his newlywed wife and offered some juices to fit the warm season. He remembered how his friend had softly carried him to school one morning on the pillion of his motorbike when he couldn't find a seat on an auto rickshaw. They met when Robin went to the Reuben's college for his first ever income working under Prof. Ram where his friend was a student. His friend was kind and affectionate, carrying off from their last meeting in school. His friend presented certificates of conquests in black and white, perfectly laminated with a glimpse of a harmonic and persistent achievement. Robin stood muted in the silence and could never digest how a topper and high achiever could descend to the ground and speak to him let alone continuing his friendship. He invited Robin for the afternoon meal and talked of the idiosyncrasies of the teachers and the general crowd in school and how it all seemed too frivolous and humorous now. Robin once happened to walk by his room in the dead of the night and found him bouncing off his nose over a stiff book. He had perished this way too many times in the open spaces of his small room in different positions trying to tame the book with his mind. Robin could never settle in to a career whereas as his friend had handpicked his career following his passion and dreams and had been undoubtedly successful.

"I've been trying to reach you for some time now, but each time I am directed to your voicemail and I must have left at least ten messages and haven't received a single reply..."

"Rob, I was not in town, I had gone to Thailand and just checked my voice mail to find your messages. My apologies. Tell me what's happening?"

"I am thinking of returning home after my studies. Say, why you don't you do the same. It will come as a nice gift for the nation and you can't be near your loved ones."

"We'll think about that Rob, there is still ample time to come to that. I'll catch you later, bye."

Robin kept in touch by sending him long emails talking mostly of the time gone by. In one of his email Robin bleakly mentioned his relationship with Augustus and how he had begun to derive a meaning off his worthless life with a dose of the gifted and graceful hands. His friend was petrified to hear of his time with Augustus who was like a flowing river with not ebbs or boundaries and who didn't know for most where he was headed. So he sat down one day and wrote to Robin,

"My friend, I don't know how to say this. We have come a long way from our school days pursuing out dreams and our own sought out destinations. I am really your well wisher. Yet the facts from you past life that you have disclosed have disturbed me immensely.

I have respect for you but for our old friendship sake let's break off because I can't fit into your shoes or offer any help. I hope you understand my feelings and will never try wasting your time in trying to get my attention or patience. Goodbye for ever my friend, it was good to have you for as long as it lasted. Take care..."

The disorder had already done the damage for Robin uttered things that didn't matter in the present. He had spoken aloud about things that time had swept under the rug and didn't matter anymore. He had contorted the facts until his relationship with Augustus was tagged as deviant and far way from normal that was not true. He had lost another one to his disorder and knew that relationships were like glass that couldn't be mended once broken. He didn't know how many storms he had to conquer that lay hidden on the way and could he blame Dr. Ronald for the mistimed jeopardy. However he never gave up and continued writing to them hoping that they could discover the facts just the way he did. For once he realized that he had spoken too loud to Prof. Ram, treating him as a friend rather than a teacher, which he might not have tolerated. He had no control over the sea of emotions clouding his mind and never knew when it skirted off normal. He thought he was a singer, songwriter and composer who didn't press being famous intentionally lest it take him away from his near and dear ones. His cherished moments were far from the normal and he was fast drifting away on the obscure land baking under the most wondrous sun. He would rise at four in the morning in a dark and sleepy town in Reuben's house and walked along listening to songs of centuries as he softly made his way to his dorm. His eyes were filled with nostalgia and tears as he composed his own melody and melted his verse onto a CD. He sang softly lest it incite the hungry ogles of the other people of the dormitory. He was redundantly riding on the boat of suspicion where every movement in the background raised his eye brows of doubt.

He painted his glasses with scrounging dust that made his skewed view rather hazy and strenuous. He was preparing for the last dazzle on the streets that would throw away all the rumours aside that there was something perilous forming on his horizon.

It was another evening emerging out of light on his dorm window. There were the usual steps in the stifled light, busy with yearnings and obligations that kept the world turning. Very soon he would take to the streets and be even steven with those conspiring against him. He felt like a star performer waiting backstage with almost a million packed in the arena waiting for his appearance which was due at the end of the prologue. He would then pump his fist in air and take a deep breath before the walk up to the stage. They would be bouncing on their seats and in the aisles for a glimpse of the star.

There was darkness outside although the blue of the sky had not totally disappeared. The trees spoke of a hushed shiver in the night managing a bleak ray of wind in its warm bosom. They very nearly entered a silent posture to last till the dawn of a new day. The mud on the sidewalks lay still waiting for certain impressions to make it bounce off the turf and mingle with the soft air above. There were people in the distance hardly making any noise shifting to places near and far, carrying huge bags out of a nearby grocery store.

Robin ran the comb over his stiff hair preparing for the night ahead. The fragrance of perfume still lurked under his nose but had somewhat died down, lasting almost a complete day from the morning when he sprayed himself all over. The dorm looked deserted with a young girl at the counter, writing on a notebook, bent down low, with her left hand. She let the 'doctor' out without asking questions. He did exit the building but not before stirring up the corridor and the walkway with the infamous slamming of the doors that shook the windows in a mild tremor. The punching of the doors was reminiscent of 'R' man when he was not his own and the outer world pestered him. He made his statement and buried himself into an annoying sleep.

Robin could see a crumpled dead leaf wobbling in the sharp flickering yellow light.

Robin had to rise to the occasion and make a memorable and defining move for the ubiquitous cameras prying on him.

He was finally out in the open and for starters to his left he saw the television crew with their cab preparing their cameras for a wide coverage. They were checking the intensity of their glitzy and voluminous microphones. Their cameras probably started rolling the moment he stepped out into the open, and his soft tread was on air as the rising star, that had probably surpassed the minute mile. He decided to walk up to the store for a mild cup of coffee. He quickly paid for his coffee and fleet footed made his way out. The people at the store were probably conspiring against him for not clearing his dues. He ran away as fast as he could and kept wobbling his head around to notice the happenings around him. He saw a truck flashing its light on him. He surmised that they would grab him any moment and were keeping the distance just to construe the movements of their prey. He gave them the eye and rushed away from their sight. In a fizzled haste he gulped the entire cup of coffee and his feet started to move swiftly forming a scamper and a run. Suddenly he found himself in the folds of his trade; he picked up speed and ran for dear life. He ran on the fields onto the open streets where cars swung by in a rhythm without the need for horns. However one car did honk at him when he was running right at the centre of the main road. Rare honking gave way to claps and cheers from the passing crowd with some tossed their caps in air. He was the hero to Reuben and the rest of his family who probably had been watching his live video on some corner of the television among the flurry of channels dumped onto it. He ran with little strength left in him to the periphery until the dorm premises and then again turned around to run the same distance in the opposite direction. One of the viewers pointed to an unzipped trouser and instead of correcting it he bent down low and ran in a slumped posture. The glittering night ended with a final collapse on the lawn and he was never going to be up too soon.

He thought of stumbling onto the night train to meet his employer who wanted him to earn a Master's degree before thinking of being useful to his company. The night ended softly on his dorm bed when he could still see flashing lights on the window pane and his suspicion never ended until he drifted off into deep sleep.

The next day he jumped onto the library pretty soon and settled in a corner in a kind of a cave that the library had become with sparingly few books to hold. He was uptight and off course when that petite Russian lady kept peeping at him in class without a hint of her intentions. He never returned her glances to steal the lush off his lips and the lanky and attractive physique that had resulted over a change of seasons and persevering legs. He raced out the exit door the moment he heard the last of the lecture. She had probably fancied her chance with Robin and never looked straight when he looked into her eyes on many occasions. So he let it be and stayed away from her proximity.

The bright slowly faded away to cold slabs of winds and Robin was a relentless stream of words without any ebb. It bothered

Reuben who could sense a tinge of episodic malaise trapping the vulnerable under its claws. Robin accompanied Reuben in his car that jostled about the endless roads until a clear stream emerged and they were finally headed somewhere.

"That worthless women Da, she chases me the moment I enter class. I just don't have any clue to deal with her. I don't know what she wants from me. I don't appreciate people sneaking behind my back and perishing too soon when I give them my hand. It seems they would take me to a corner through inhibited signs and explode revealing a world hidden and licentious."

"Relax, these things are normal occurrence in any college, don't dig in too deep. I have a surprise for you, we are almost there. This is the psychiatric ward of the city and I have brought you here for a fifteen minute check up. Before you know it we'd be heading home and I will be waiting for you outside. Don't worry I am right here for you."

Robin had been talking too much. For someone who preferred being confined to his own thoughts, this was strange and out of place. He was trying to trace roads and glimpses that had been left far behind and lay dead in the billows of time. For one he was trying too hard, voluble like his aunts and all the ladies who loved to unearth the nitty gritty of life in a boisterous gabber.

The air was a bit nippy in overcast conditions. Robin adored the built of the black man stationed at the door for checking inmates into the ward. He felt the stone in his body when the black man ran his rugged hand over his body. Unequivocal and rigid in his perusal Robin was directed into the ward. There were a number of people lounging away on sofas, some hysterical over screened matters, while others nervously anxious imploring authorities to leave them alone. Some treated the ward like their home watching television honestly. There were apple pies and strudels with fresh juice for inmates with few takers who cherished a glimpse of the pavement outside. There was a woman on a stretcher being moved to a dingy room by a boisterous and huge black man.

He shuddered with a quick round of loud invectives hurled at the woman catching breath in bursts. Besides there were employees or workers streaming in and out of hidden rooms with the head honchos leading them. Robin was taken to a tight corner and interrogated. The black man never missed a chime of laughter and was amazed at Robin's qualification.

"Thus there is a PhD. They always find their way, don't they?" the gentle stranger wore mouthful of parroted laughter. Fifteen minutes were over way back as the disarrayed ward swept into the next hour. A black lady, sparse and skinny drew a line for Robin who sounded a little unstable. He was asked to rest on the sofa and not beat around the bush with a plea to be discharged that was hardly acceptable. Reuben might be waiting outside with a warm engine to take him away from these maniacal environs and rest in the warmth of his bed. Yet he grew even more aggressive before a worker quietly exclaimed into Robin's tortured ears,

"Lay back, we gonna have some fun" and smiled her way back to her desk. Friends close to him were probably having fun while Robin was down with a malaise as a model of psychiatry. The huge black man in the side room was still grooming his invectives and sometimes cried for help. The music died into the night and Robin jerked his neck in sleep at the stroke of two. It was his stride in keeping awake that his eyes fell on Susan. An old lady, she kept turning on faces for someone to hear her grief. Robin obliged and for no good reason she was plucked from her garden in the evening and dumped in the ward. She had a few heated exchanges with her daughter-in-law and they stole her in frenzy. Robin offered a taxi at the break of dawn lest they hold him for neurotic imbalance.

He sometimes scratched his forehead or his beard with cold fingers in anxious bursts. Sometimes he thought the entire milieu was a concocted drama with seasoned actors in their preferred role. How can a young lady brandish around a choked room repeatedly bringing the same file for perusal with a sudden lapse of thought and turn around for hours. Or the black man hurling invectives seemed to tire and sound peeved but was never flustered. Also there were scores of people on sofas or other places with food or television in a state of manufactured bliss off to a town of nowhere.

Only Susan had a normal air about her.

Come morning and there was no room for squinty eyes or perilously hanging about for redemption. He would rather restrict himself to a few words that mildly matched the occasion than roam about places he couldn't decipher. His heavy foot sank into the room with a lady, probably the chief working with some files. She was a blonde hair lady a little on the heavier side and did acknowledge Robin's presence and a prayer for acquittal for none of his fault. She was calm and ready to hear him out reciprocating with wet eyes at the pitiful plight. He was rewarded, exonerated from all intentions and pushed into a truck. An afterthought about Susan made him feel uneasy that he couldn't help her.

"This aint no paradise son, yet we'll show you some, hang on" the policeman on routine pick up retorted. The prickly policemen did seem to listen but Robin gradually gave up to the sound of the engine and screech of tough tyres. In silent polishes of soft dawn the heated engine came to an abrupt halt with the load jerking forward in recoil. Robin was directed to the main gate of the city mental centre. He recalled his pet dog Rover locked in a blind room in quarantine growing viciously insane when he was meant to roam the discoloured open streets. A new case was welcomed by the community of helpless yet perishable doctors and Robin was transferred to his allotted room. Shirley was the clerk always at her window whom Robin befriended with ease. The supervisor Carl introduced himself and offered his services even on blind calls. He would be sent by Robin out of his way to fetch some orange soda and chilly crackers. He was the soothsayer, the answer to paradoxical senses, a black man and a kind soul. The room was well furnished but inmates were not allowed to carry belongings except books. Night fell and Robin was swamped with darkness and Timothy Garox. Tim was to share the room with Robin, donned with heavy wrists, bulging chest and a clean shaven head. He lived in a cocoon of frustration and sadness with swinging hands that solved no matter, and made him even lonelier. Robin rose incessantly from his bed to ask for items from Shirley like paper,

pen and some phone numbers. Robin couldn't bear an absconding Shirley and she often retorted,

"What will you do sir if I cannot make it, whom will you consider?"

The authorities were suspicious of too much going on at the clerk window. So the next day Shirley refused to oblige Robin and would disappear from the window forcibly when Robin came looking for her. Shirley couldn't resist her footsteps defying authority and walked up to Robin one day to console him and they were good friends. She never recalled pushing him away from her sight. She wept quietly for Robin and asked him to talk to her when he wanted to. The day after eyes met Peggy, the fat old lady with blonde hair who adored Robin and stuck to him for no reason. She believed that the world was on the brink of a major change thanks to a charismatic Robin. One day his eyes followed a young girl Rubenna as he entered his classroom bulging with inmates. She was painstakingly filling in colours in a drawing of a flower vase with flowers. Robin jumped into an impromptu dialogue with Rubenna asking for her whereabouts just like in Western movies where the protagonist freely accosts an unnamed guest. She smiled back and hearts sank in a love with no boundaries. Carl informed Robin that she was from Russia and had recently joined the party. Robin often belched out in anger at the existing situation. He was loud and tossed around words to people he hardly knew, with confidence. He had softly entered into yet another episode. There was also the ugly Rinietta who hung around Robin's eyes and wanted a piece of him somewhere in a quiet corner. She envied Rubenna and Peggy and wanted to harm them with opinionated eyes. The inmates were given taken to the sprawling garden within the premises. Rubenna and Robin walked the green turf together. Robin expressed his undying love by giving her quiet yellow flowers growing wildly on grass. Days were spent in imaginings with Robin's bed swamped in sheets of paper where he penned his feelings of love for Rubenna. Every morning before breakfast in a room packed with inmates he surrendered his love in writing in bold letters. He engaged her brother Roger into a fiendish discussion at the breakfast table asking for Rubenna's hand in marriage. Roger did utter in smiles yet considered it a breach of conduct.

Robin was admired for a big heart, and for words that must be spoken. Peggy was the glowing example of his keen impression on people and considered him to be smart and tacky never leaving his sight. His kindness knew no bounds when he offered his warm black coat to a black inmate, reclusive and suffering. So to improve the plight of the inmates the authorities gave away a figment of freedom to all.

The abandoned games room was reopened with games of basketball and collages on colourful papers. They were given an elaborate luncheon at the restaurant on the ground floor.

Five days had passed and Robin was clueless on his date of discharge. He didn't want to leave for Rubenna but sometimes in his musings thought that he had to separate. Sometimes he desperately tried to call his relatives with the single phone stationed at the corridor but it was always busy.

Next day at the breakfast table with Peggy, he was in deep thought. Rubenna was seated across on another table while Robin didn't actually adore the taste of chowder on his plate. It was a fitting ensemble to his love story when her relatives, uncles and aunts came to have a glimpse of Robin. Rubenna stood softly beside Robin and smiled looking down. That was the last holler in space praying for a touch of Rubenna. They took her away.

His love story never fetched Rubenna, the gentle and subtle young lady.

So an uptight Robin accosted Dr. Rehana, the psychiatrist from Asia handling his case. By that time Rubenna had probably left, who knew. He presented himself before the doctor as a normal person that ought to be discharged. But the stern lady kept on asking questions and thought his condition was far from normal. She felt the yearnings of a solitary heart but her profession demanded her to be totally sure before making a decision. However she did acknowledge the subtle improvement over days since he descended to that place. His motions had been rather disorderly and his stifling efforts to be free struck a chord in her compassionate heart. She often rejected his plea and asked him to stay put in his room and let he treatment carry on with no intentional disruptions from his side. He decided to nail it on their third meeting and it was hard holding onto another day without Rubenna around. She finally folded her hands, in a long hard breath unearthed the suppressed desire to let Robin go free.

That was one day and for all the days spent in sick wards, Robin wondered what had gone amiss.

THE FINAL DUNGEON

The yellow magic was fleeting in all those moments of deep introspection, and surviving the moments in hypnotic wards. Dr. Rishi was probably right in his diagnosis and Dr. Ronald had wrongfully done away with those yellow tablets and introduced the one that was not required.

Robin was far away from Dr. Rishi and back to his country after his stay in the US.

He had left his job because they demanded too much from him. Robin had been reading a lot about Osho lately. He began meditating and wondered what could be the right effort in attaining 'Nirvana'. All souls were headed in that direction and would incarnate over and over again until all were set free. Until then the world would not end and no one knew how long it would survive given the countless living organisms in motion in this world. He wondered if he had attained 'Nirvana' one night when a spark of energy left his mouth and suddenly the world became a brighter place. However his friend reminded him that all good 'karma' was a step in the right direction and each spiritual encounter did count in the final analysis. Robin would get up at two in the mornings in that winter chill and wake up his mother too early with a warm cup of tea. He would wait until five for the tea shop to open and then go for a morning walk. All the folks of the night surrounded him as he sank into the warmth of the tea. He got annoyed too often and shouted at his mother to pull the neighbourhood and create panic. He was that street gypsy with loud music playing in his ears and stopping by at his usual places in the course of a day. The day would bring euphoria one with the coiling streets and sometimes sadness broke loose with a sudden loss of temper.

He knew something was wrong and tried to get in touch with Dr. Rishi.

Years later Robin found his way back home to his mother. He immediately contacted Dr. Rishi for the right kind of dosage. He joined a computer training institute as a faculty and was trained for a few weeks. Very soon he started taking classes. He was still unknowingly fighting battles against episodes. He had a hallucination meeting Lord Krishna and his imaginary friend Stella. He could talk to the Lord whenever he wanted to. The Lord was fair and had an eternal smile on his face. He met his father in heaven and he asked him all about that place and how he spent his time on that wondrous land. When Dr. Rishi asked him to write a short story of his experiences in the US he submitted a one liner that didn't mean anything. A girl of the institute liked him and he made excuses just to be beside her. There was a glass window separating them and they often avoided each other lest somehow found out that there was something going on. Robin was very loud in his classes and spoke of things irrelevant and sensitive.

Somebody passed a comment that he came to class just for frivolous banter. He lost his cool and shouted at the students. The students resented with a plea to end his classes. Robin was asked to go home and his classes were suspended. That was his last day of lecturing and he didn't even get to meet the girl he loved. Robin was convinced that heaven did exist where his forefathers lived by snow clad mountains happily including many that he had hardly met. Their good deeds and work had transported them onto an eternal life where there was no procreation. There were rivers of milk and honey and each one worked perfectly with their craft raising it higher to a new level of consummation. He had already earned a place in heaven and he just had to see off the rest of what mattered and bring good name to his clan.

He waited in expectation of the girl he had left behind. The good Lord informed him that true love was always rewarded, regardless, and he just had to wait patiently for an answer.

Seasons passed and there was no response from the girl. Dr. Rishi's yellow dose had started penetrating deep into his senses. He was left with Stella, the beautiful lady who would accompany him on walks around the countryside. She would arise in the dead of the night to comfort him and never parted ways. She smiled at what Robin uttered and encouraged him to live and sink in to the rest of what was left in his life.

There would be celebrations in heaven on the arrival of a fresh soul. Each artist and performer was given a world of time to evolve given the rush and paucity of time on earth. For one, 'R' man had hardly settled in his trade on earth and spent most of his time dealing with nonsense. The good Lord promised an eternal life and all his forefathers were locked in gaze after their torrid time on earth. They had time on their hands to work on a dream that they often confessed to while on earth.

"Oh! It's so nice out here son. You must come here and taste the fruits of you effort. I've never tasted this kind of food and the celebrations are humungous. I've reserved a place for you here right next to the abode of Lord Krishna. I meet him quite often and discuss the affairs of this world and throw in my piece of advice which is so graciously received and even executed. He strives hard to keep up the good spirit on earth and cranks the souls for newer creations of life on earth. All my forefathers are here, enjoying the sunshine and many that I hardly know. There are all here and know all about you. The songs you have sung are already popular over here and it would be nice to have the creator of those beautiful numbers over here. You can do a lot more over here, that's what I have learnt after coming here and not limit yourself to a few known crafts. Cheerio son, this orange concoction tastes really nice and everything around here is free. There is no currency over here. Until we meet again, bye!" Robin heard these words over and over

again. Robin talked to his guests for hours until it was time to swing to the daily bustle and eke out a living.

The doses seeped deeper into his bloodstream and suddenly one day he lost the hallucinations to the extent of losing Stella. He breathed normal and heaven seemed a farfetched dream, highly improbable. There was no trace of the good Lord and his dad could not be heard in the daylight. He was convinced with Osho's words that each one was pushed into this earth as a soul until that person attained 'Moksha'.

He got glued to the person he was and lived for his dream each day in an effort to make his life worthwhile.

About The Author

Neeshant Srivastava has a bachelor's degree in Mechanical Engineering. This is his first novel. His father, an unrivalled inspiration, was a poet and a writer and his works came out in several Indian dailies. Neeshant has written several short stories and articles, some technical based on his past experience. Some articles were carried by the blog page of the company he worked in. His short

Enter Caption

story 'Karma Yogi' was a winner of 'The MAG 2011 short story writing competition'. Another short story 'Divine Pigeon' featured in the annual magazine 'Touching the Sky Part-II' brought out by the Air Force Association. He lives in Patna, India.